GW01087097

The Collected
Supernatural and Weird
Fiction of
Edith Wharton
Volume 1

The Collected Supernatural and Weird Fiction of Edith Wharton Volume 1

Seventeen Short Tales of the Strange and Unusual

Edith Wharton

LEONAUR

The Collected
Supernatural and Weird
Fiction of
Edith Wharton
Volume 1
Seventeen Short Tales
of the Strange and Unusual
by Edith Wharton

FIRST EDITION

Leonaur is an imprint of Oakpast Ltd

Copyright in this form © 2016 Oakpast Ltd

ISBN: 978-1-78282-545-6 (hardcover)
ISBN: 978-1-78282-546-3 (softcover)

http://www.leonaur.com

Contents

The Looking Glass
(*A.k.a.* The Mirror)

1

Mrs Attlee had never been able to understand why there was any harm in giving people a little encouragement when they needed it. Sitting back in her comfortable armchair by the fire, her working days over, and her muscular masseuse's hands lying swollen and powerless on her knee, she was at leisure to turn the problem over, and ponder it as there had never been time to do before.

Mrs Attlee was so infirm now that, when her widowed daughter-in-law was away for the day, her granddaughter Moyra Attlee had to stay with her until the kitchen girl had prepared the cold supper, and could come in and sit in the parlour.

'You'd be surprised, you know, my dear, to find how discouraged the grand people get, in those big houses with all the help, and the silver dinner plates, and a bell always handy if the fire wants poking, or the pet dog asks for a drink . . . And what'd a masseuse be good for, if she didn't jolly up their minds a little along with their muscles? as Dr Welbridge used to say to me many a time, when he'd given me a difficult patient. And he always gave me the most difficult,' she added proudly.

She paused, aware (for even now little escaped her) that Moyra had ceased to listen, but accepting the fact resignedly, as she did most things in the slow decline of her days.

'It's a fine afternoon,' she reflected, 'and likely she's fidgety because there's a new movie on; or that young fellow's fixed it up to get back earlier from New York . . . '

She relapsed into silence, following her thoughts; but presently, as happens with old people, they came to the surface again.

'And I hope I'm a good Catholic, as I said to Father Divott the other day, and at peace with heaven, if ever I was took suddenly—but

7

no matter what happens I've got to risk my punishment for the wrong I did to Mrs Clingsland, because as long as I've never repented it there's no use telling Father Divott about it. Is there?'

Mrs Attlee heaved an introspective sigh. Like many humble persons of her kind and creed, she had a vague idea that a sin unrevealed was, as far as the consequences went, a sin uncommitted; and this conviction had often helped her in the difficult task of reconciling doctrine and practice.

2

Moyra Attlee interrupted her listless stare down the empty Sunday street of the New Jersey suburb, and turned an astonished glance on her grandmother.

'Mrs Clingsland? A wrong you did to Mrs Clingsland?' Hitherto she had lent an inattentive ear to her grandmother's ramblings; the talk of old people seemed to be a language hardly worth learning. But it was not always so with Mrs Attlee's. Her activities among the rich had ceased before the first symptoms of the financial depression; but her tenacious memory was stored with pictures of the luxurious days of which her granddaughter's generation, even in a wider world, knew only by hearsay.

Mrs Attlee had a gift for evoking in a few words scenes of half-understood opulence and leisure, like a guide leading a stranger through the gallery of a palace in the twilight, and now and then lifting a lamp to a shimmering Rembrandt *or* a jewelled Rubens; and it was particularly when she mentioned Mrs Clingsland that Moyra caught these dazzling glimpses. Mrs Clingsland had always been something more than a name to the Attlee family. They knew (though they did not know why) that it was through her help that Grandmother Attlee had been able, years ago, to buy the little house at Montclair, with a patch of garden behind it, where, all through the depression, she had held out, thanks to fortunate investments made on the advice of Mrs Clingsland's great friend, the banker.

'She had so many friends, and they were all high-up people, you understand. Many's the time she'd say to me: "Cora" (think of the loveliness of her calling me Cora), "Cora, I'm going to buy some Golden Flyer shares on Mr Stoner's advice; Mr Stoner of the National Union Bank, you know. He's getting me in on the ground floor, as they say, and if you want to step in with me, why come along. There's nothing too good for you, in my opinion," she used to say. And, as it turned out, those shares have kept their head above water all through the bad years, and now I think they'll see me through, and be there when I'm gone, to help out you children.'

Today Moyra Attlee heard the revered name with a new interest. The phrase: 'the wrong I did to Mrs Clingsland', had struck through her listlessness, rousing her to sudden curiosity. What could her grand-mother mean by saying she had done a wrong to the benefactress whose bounties she was never tired of recording? Moyra believed her grandmother to be a very good woman—certainly she had been wonderfully generous in all her dealings with her children and grand-children; and it seemed incredible that, if there had been one grave lapse in her life, it should have taken the form of an injury to Mrs Clingsland. True, whatever the lapse was, she seemed to have made peace with herself about it; yet it was clear that its being unconfessed lurked disquietingly in the back of her mind.

'How can you say you ever did harm to a friend like Mrs Clings-land, Gran?'

Mrs Attllee's eyes grew sharp behind her spectacles, and she fixed them half distrustfully on the girl's face. But in a moment she seemed to recover herself. 'Not harm, I don't say; I'll never think I harmed her. Bless you, it wasn't to harm her I'd ever have lifted a finger. All I wanted was to help. But when you try to help too many people at once, the devil sometimes takes note of it. You see, there's quotas nowadays for everything, doing good included, my darling.'

Moyra made an impatient movement. She did not care to hear her grandmother philosophise. 'Well—but you said you did a wrong to Mrs Clingsland.'

Mrs Attlee's sharp eyes seemed to draw back behind a mist of age. She sat silent, her hands lying heavily over one another in their tragic uselessness.

'What would *you* have done, I wonder,' she began suddenly, 'if you'd ha' come in on her that morning, and seen her laying in her lovely great bed, with the lace a yard deep on the sheets, and her face buried in the pillows, so I knew she was crying? Would you have opened your bag same as usual, and got out your coconut cream and talcum powder, and the nail polishers, and all the rest of it, and waited there like a statue till she turned over to you; or'd you have gone up to her, and turned her softly round, like you would a baby, and said to her: "Now, my dear, I guess you can tell Cora Attlee what's the trouble?" Well, that's what I did, anyhow; and there she was, with her

9

face streaming with tears, and looking like a martyred saint on an altar, and when I said to her: "Come, now, you tell me, and it'll help you", she just sobbed out: "Nothing can ever help me, now I've lost it."'

"'Lost what?" I said, thinking first of her boy, the Lord help me, though I'd heard him whistling on the stairs as I went up; but she said: "My beauty, Cora—I saw it suddenly slipping out of the door from me this morning"...Well, at that I had to laugh, and half angrily too. "Your beauty," I said to her, "and is that all? And me that thought it was your husband, or your son—or your fortune even. If it's only your beauty, can't I give it back to you with these hands of mine? But what are you saying to me about beauty, with that seraph's face looking up at me this minute?" I said to her, for she angered me as if she'd been blaspheming.'

'Well, was it true?' Moyra broke in, impatient and yet curious. 'True that she'd lost her beauty?' Mrs Attlee paused to consider. 'Do you know how it is, sometimes when you're doing a bit of fine darning, sitting by the window in the afternoon; and one minute it's full daylight, and your needle seems to find the way of itself; and the next minute you say: "Is it my eyes?" because the work seems blurred; and presently you see it's the daylight going, stealing away, softlike, from your corner, though there's plenty left overhead. Well—it was that way with her ...'

But Moyra had never done fine darning, or strained her eyes in fading light, and she intervened again, more impatiently: 'Well, what did she do?'

Mrs Attlee once more reflected. 'Why, she made me tell her every morning that it wasn't true; and every morning she believed me a little less. And she asked everybody in the house, beginning with her husband, poor man—him so bewildered when you asked him anything outside of his business, or his club or his horses, and never noticing any difference in her looks since the day he'd led her home as his bride, twenty years before, maybe ...

'But there—nothing he could have said, if he'd had the wit to say it, would have made any difference. From the day she saw the first little line around her eyes she thought of herself as an old woman, and the thought never left her for more than a few minutes at a time. Oh, when she was dressed up, and laughing, and receiving company, then I don't say the faith in her beauty wouldn't come back to her, and go to her head like champagne; but it wore off quicker than champagne, and I've seen her run upstairs with the foot of a girl, and then, before she'd tossed off her finery, sit down in a heap in front of one of her big looking glasses—it was looking glasses everywhere in her room—and stare and stare till the tears ran down over her powder.'

'Oh, well, I suppose it's always hateful growing old,' said Moyra, her indifference returning.

Mrs Attlee smiled retrospectively. 'How can I say that, when my own old age has been made so peaceful by all her goodness to me?'

Moyra stood up with a shrug. 'And yet you tell me you acted wrong to her. How am I to know what you mean?'

Her grandmother made no answer. She closed her eyes, and leaned her head against the little cushion behind her neck. Her lips seemed to murmur, but no words came. Moyra reflected that she was probably falling asleep, and that when she woke she would not remember what she had been about to reveal.

'It's not much fun sitting here all this time, if you can't even keep awake long enough to tell me what you mean about Mrs Clingsland,' she grumbled.

Mrs Attlee roused herself with a start.

3

Well (she began) you know what happened in the war—I mean, the way all the fine ladies, and the poor shabby ones too, took to running to the mediums and the clairvoyants, or whatever the stylish folk call 'em. The women had to have news of their men; and they were made to pay high enough for it... Oh, the stories I used to hear—and the price paid wasn't only money, either! There was a fair lot of swindlers and blackmailers in the business, there was. I'd sooner have trusted a gypsy at a fair . . . but the women just *had to* go to them.

Well, my dear, I'd always had a way of seeing things; from the cradle, even. I don't mean reading the tea leaves, or dealing the cards; that's for the kitchen. No, no; I mean, feeling there's things about you, behind you, whispering over your shoulder . . . Once my mother, on the Connemara hills, saw the leprechauns at dusk; and she said they smelt fine and high, too . . . Well, when I used to go from one grand house to another, to give my massage and face treatment, I got more and more sorry for those poor wretches that the soothsaying swindlers were dragging the money out of for a pack of lies; and one day I couldn't stand it any longer, and though I knew the Church against it, when I saw one lady nearly crazy, because for months she'd had no news of her boy at the front, I said to her: 'If you'll come over to my place tomorrow, I might have a word for you.' And the wonder of it was that I *had!* For that night I dreamt a message came saying there was good news for her, and the next day, sure enough, she had a cable, telling her her son had escaped from a German camp . . .

After that the ladies came in flocks—in flocks fairly . . . you're too young to remember, child; but your mother could tell you. Only she wouldn't, because after a bit the priest got wind of it, and then it had to stop . . . so she won't even talk of it any more. But I always said: how could I help it? For I *did* see things, and hear things, at that time . . . And of course the ladies were supposed to come just for the face treatment. . . . and was I to blame if I kept hearing those messages for them, poor souls, or seeing things they wanted me to see?

It's no matter now, for I made it all straight with Father Divott years ago; and now nobody comes after me anymore, as you can see for yourself. And all I ask is to be left alone in my chair . . .

But with Mrs Clingsland—well, that was different. To begin with, she was the patient I liked best. There was nothing she wouldn't do for you, if ever for a minute you could get her to stop thinking of herself. . . and that's saying a good deal, for a rich lady. Money's an armour, you see; and there's few cracks in it. But Mrs Clingsland was a loving nature, if only anybody'd shown her how to love . . . Oh, dear, and wouldn't she have been surprised if you'd told her that! Her that thought she was living up to her chin in love and love-making. But as soon as the lines began to come about her eyes, she didn't believe in it any more. And she had to be always hunting for new people to tell her she was as beautiful as ever; because she wore the others out, forever asking them: 'Don't you think I'm beginning to go off a little?'—till finally fewer and fewer came to the house, and as far as a poor masseuse like me can judge, I didn't much fancy the looks of those that did; and I saw Mr Clingsland didn't either.

But there was the children, you'll say. I know, I know! And she did love her children in a way; only it wasn't their way. The girl, who was a good bit the eldest, took after her father: a plain face and plain words. Dogs and horses and athletics. With her mother she was cold and scared; so her mother was cold and scared with her. The boy was delicate when he was little, so she could curl him up, and put him into black velvet pants, like that boy in the book—little Lord Something. But when his long legs grew out of the pants, and they sent him to school, she said he wasn't her own little cuddly baby anymore; and it riles a growing boy to hear himself talked about like that.

She had good friends left, of course; mostly elderly ladies they were, of her own age (for she *was* elderly now; the change had come), who used to drop in often for a gossip; but, bless your heart, they weren't much help, for what she wanted, and couldn't do without, was the gaze of men struck dumb by her beauty. And that was what she couldn't get any longer, except she paid for it. And even so—!

For, you see, she was too quick and clever to be humbugged long by the kind that tried to get things out of her. How she used to laugh at the old double-chinners trotting round to the nightclubs with their boyfriends! She laughed at old ladies in love; and yet she couldn't bear to be out of love, though she knew she was getting to be an old lady herself.

Well, I remember one day another patient of mine, who'd never had much looks beyond what you can buy in Fifth Avenue, laughing at me about Mrs Clingsland, about her dread of old age, and her crave for admiration—and as I listened, I suddenly thought: 'Why, we don't either of us know anything about what a beautiful woman suffers when she loses her beauty. For you and me, and thousands like us, beginning to grow old is like going from a bright warm room to one a little less warm and bright; but to a beauty like Mrs Clingsland it's like being pushed out of an illuminated ballroom, all flowers and chandeliers, into the winter night and the snow.' And I had to bite the words back, not to say them to my patient . . .

4

Mrs Clingsland brightened up a little when her own son grew up and went to college. She used to go over and see him now and again; or he'd come home for the holidays. And he used to take her out for lunch, or to dance at those cabaret places; and when the head waiters took her for his sweetheart she'd talk about it for a week. But one day a hall porter said: 'Better hurry up, mister. There's your mother waiting for you over there, looking clean fagged out'; and after that she didn't go round with him so much.

For a time, she used to get some comfort out of telling me about her early triumphs; and I used to listen patiently, because I knew it was safer for her to talk to me than to the flatterers who were beginning to get round her.

You mustn't think of her, though, as an unkind woman. She was friendly to her husband, and friendly to her children; but they meant less and less to her. What she wanted was a looking glass to stare into;

13

and when her own people took enough notice of her to serve as looking glasses, which wasn't often, she didn't much fancy what she saw there. I think this was about the worst time of her life. She lost a tooth; she began to dye her hair; she went into retirement to have her face lifted, and then got frightened, and came out again looking like a ghost, with a pouch under one eye, where they'd begun the treatment . . .

I began to be really worried about her then. She got sour and bitter toward everybody, and I seemed to be the only person she could talk out to. She used to keep me by for hours, always paying for the appointments she made me miss, and going over the same thing again and again; how when she was young and came into a ballroom, or a restaurant or a theatre, everybody stopped what they were doing to turn and look at her—even the actors on the stage did, she said; and it was the truth, I dare say. But that was over . . .

Well, what could I say to her? She'd heard it all often enough. But there were people prowling about in the background that I didn't like the look of; people, you understand, who live on weak women that can't grow old. One day she showed me a love letter. She said she didn't know the man who'd sent it; but she knew about him. He was a Count Somebody; a foreigner. He'd had adventures. Trouble in his own country, I guess . . . She laughed and tore the letter up. Another came from him, and I saw that too—but I didn't see her tear it up.

'Oh, I know what he's after,' she said. 'Those kind of men are always looking out for silly old women with money . . . Ah,' says she, 'it was different in old times. I remember one day I'd gone into a florist's to buy some violets, and I saw a young fellow there; well, maybe he was a little younger than me—but I looked like a girl still. And when he saw me he just stopped short with what he was saying to the florist, and his face turned so white I thought he was going to faint. I bought my violets; and as I went out a violet dropped from the bunch, and I saw him stoop and pick it up, and hide it away as if it had been money he'd stolen . . .

'Well,' she says, 'a few days after that I met him at a dinner, and it turned out he was the son of a friend of mine, a woman older than myself, who'd married abroad. He'd been brought up in England, and had just come to New York to take up a job there . . . '

She lay back with her eyes closed, and a quiet smile on her poor tormented face. 'I didn't *know* it then, but I suppose that was the only time I've ever been in love . . . ' For a while she didn't say anything more, and I noticed the tears beginning to roll down her cheeks. 'Tell me about it, now do, you poor soul,' I says; for I thought, this is better for her than fandangoing with that oily count whose letter she hasn't torn up.

'There's so little to tell,' she said. 'We met only four or five times —and then Harry went down on *Titanic.*'

'Mercy,' says I, 'and was it all those years ago?'

'The years don't make any difference, Cora,' she says. 'The way he looked at me I know no one ever worshipped me as he did.'

'And did he tell you so?' I went on, humouring her; though I felt kind of guilty toward her husband.

'Some things don't have to be told,' says she, with the smile of a bride. 'If only he hadn't died, Cora . . . It's the sorrowing for him that's made me old before my time.' (Before her time! And her well over fifty.)

Well, a day or two after that I got a shock. Coming out of Mrs Clingsland's front door as I was going into it I met a woman I'd know among a million if I was to meet her again in hell—where I will, I know, if I don't mind my steps . . . You see, Moyra, though I broke years ago with all that crystal-reading, and table-rapping, and what the Church forbids, I was mixed up in it for a time (till Father Divott ordered me to stop), and I knew, by sight at any rate, most of the big mediums and their touts. And this woman on the doorstep was a tout, one of the worst and most notorious in New York; I knew cases where she'd sucked people dry selling them the news they wanted, like she was selling them a forbidden drug. And all of a sudden it came to me that I'd heard it said that she kept a foreign count, who was sucking *her* dry—and I gave one jump home to my own place, and sat down there to think it over.

I saw well enough what was going to happen. Either she'd per-suade my poor lady that the count was mad over her beauty, and get a hold over her that way; or else—and this was worse—she'd make Mrs Clingsland talk, and get at the story of the poor young man called Harry, who was drowned, and bring her messages from him; and that might go on forever, and bring in more money than the count. . . .

Well, Moyra, could I help it? I was so sorry for her, you see. I could see she was sick and fading away, and her will weaker than it used to be; and if I was to save her from those gangsters I had to do it right away, and make it straight with my conscience afterward—if I could . . .

5

I don't believe I ever did such hard thinking as I did that night. For what was I after doing? Something that was against my Church and against my own principles; and if ever I got found out, it was all up with me—me, with my thirty years' name of being the best masseuse in New York, and none honester, nor more respectable!

Well, then, I says to myself, what'll happen if that woman gets hold of Mrs Clingsland? Why, one way or another, she'll bleed her white, and then leave her without help or comfort. I'd seen households where that had happened, and I wasn't going to let it happen to my poor lady. What I was after was to make her believe in herself again, so that she'd be in a kindlier mind toward others . . . and by the next day I'd thought my plan out, and set it going.

It wasn't so easy, neither; and I sometimes wonder at my nerve. I'd figured it out that the other woman would have to work the stunt of the young man who was drowned, because I was pretty sure Mrs Clingsland, at the last minute, would shy away from the count. Well, then, thinks I, I'll work the same stunt myself—but how?

You see, dearie, those big people, when they talk and write to each other, they use lovely words we ain't used to; and I was afraid if I began to bring messages to her, I'd word them wrong, and she'd suspect something. I knew I could work it the first day or the second; but after that I wasn't so sure. But there was no time to lose, and when I went back to her next morning I said: 'A queer thing happened to me last night. I guess it was the way you spoke to me about that gentleman—the one on the *Titanic*. Making me see him as clear as if he was in the room with us—' and at that I had her sitting up in bed with her great eyes burning into me like gimlets. 'Oh, Cora, perhaps he *is!* Oh, tell me quickly what happened!'

'Well, when I was laying in my bed last night something came to me from him. I knew at once it was from him; it was a word he was telling me to bring you . . .'

I had to wait then, she was crying so hard, before she could listen to me again; and when I went on she hung on to me, saving the word, as if I'd been her Saviour. The poor woman!

The message I'd hit on for that first day was easy enough. I said he'd told me to tell her he'd always loved her. It went down her throat like honey, and she just lay there and tasted it. But after a while she lifted up her head. 'Then why didn't he tell me so?' says she.

'Ah,' says I, 'I'll have to try to reach him again, and ask him that.'

And that day she fairly drove me off on my other jobs, for fear I'd be late getting home, and too tired to hear him if he came again. 'And he *will come,* Cora; I know he will! And you must be ready for him, and write down everything. I want every word written down the minute he says it, for fear you'll forget a single one.'

Well, that was a new difficulty. Writing wasn't ever my strong point; and when it came to finding the words for a young gentleman in love who'd gone down on the *Titanic,* you might as well have asked me to write a Chinese dictionary. Not that I couldn't imagine how he'd have felt; but I didn't for Mary's grace know how to say it for him.

But it's wonderful, as Father Divott says, how Providence sometimes seems to be listening behind the door. That night when I got home I found a message from a patient, asking me to go to see a poor young fellow she'd befriended when she was better off—he'd been her children's tutor, I believe—who was down and out, and dying in a miserable rooming house down here at Montclair. Well, I went; and 1 saw at once why he hadn't kept this job, or any other job. Poor fellow, it was the drink; and now he was dying of it. It was a pretty bad story, but there's only a bit of it belongs to what I'm telling you.

He was a highly educated gentleman, and as quick as a flash; and before I'd half explained, he told me what to say, and wrote out the message for me. I remember it now.

'He was so blinded by your beauty that he couldn't speak—and when he saw you the next time, at that dinner, in your bare shoulders and your pearls, he felt farther away from you than ever. And he walked the streets till morning, and then went home, and wrote you a letter; but he didn't dare to send it after all.'

This time Mrs Clingsland swallowed it down like champagne. Blinded by her beauty; struck dumb by love of her! Oh, but that's what she'd been thirsting and hungering for all these years. Only, once it had begun, she had to have more of it, and always more . . . and my job didn't get any easier.

Luckily, though, I had that young fellow to help me; and after a while, when I'd given him a hint of what it was all about, he got as much interested as I was, and began to fret for me the days I didn't come.

But, my, what questions she asked. 'Tell him, if it's true that I took his breath away that first evening at dinner, to describe to you how I was dressed. They must remember things like that even in the other world, don't you think so? And you say he noticed my pearls?'

17

Luckily she'd described that dress to me so often that I had no difficulty about telling the young man what to say—and so it went on, and it went on, and one way or another I managed each time to have an answer that satisfied her. But one day, after Harry'd sent her a particularly lovely message from the Over There (as those people call it) she burst into tears and cried out: 'Oh, why did he never say things like that to me when we were together?'

That was a poser, as they say; I couldn't imagine why he hadn't. Of course I knew it was all wrong and immoral, anyway; hut, poor thing, I don't see who it can hurt to help the love-making between a sick woman and a ghost. And I'd taken care to say a *Novena* against Father Divott finding me out.

Well, I told the poor young man what she wanted to know, and he said: 'Oh, you can tell her an evil influence came between them. Someone who was jealous, and worked against him—here, give me a pencil, and I'll write it out. . . .' and he pushed out his hot twitching hand for the paper.

That message fairly made her face burn with joy. 'I knew it—I always knew it!' She flung her thin arms about me, and kissed me. 'Tell me again, Cora, how he said *I* looked the first day he saw me. . . .'

'Why, you must have looked as you look now,' says I to her, 'for there's twenty years fallen from your face.' And so there was.

What helped me to keep on was that she'd grown so much gentler and quieter. Less impatient with the people who waited on her, more understanding with the daughter and Mr Clingsland. There was a different atmosphere in the house. And sometimes she'd say: 'Cora, there must be poor souls in trouble, with nobody to hold out a hand to them; and I want you to come to me when you run across anybody like that.' So I used to keep that poor young fellow well looked after, and cheered up with little dainties. And you'll never make me believe there was anything wrong in that—or in letting Mrs Clingsland help me out with the new roof on this house, either.

But there was a day when I found her sitting up in bed when I came in, with two red spots on her thin cheeks. And all the peace had gone out of her poor face. 'Why, Mrs Clingsland, my dear, what's the matter?' But I could see well enough what it was. Somebody'd been undermining her belief in spirit communications, or whatever they call them, and she'd been crying herself into a fever, thinking I'd made up all I'd told her. 'How do I know you're a medium, anyhow,' she flung out at me with pitiful furious eyes, 'and not taking advantage of me with all this stuff every morning?'

Well, the queer thing was that I took offence at that, not because I was afraid of being found out, but because—heaven help us!—I'd somehow come to believe in that young man Harry and his love-making, and it made me angry to be treated as a fraud. But I kept my temper and my tongue, and went on with the message as if I hadn't heard her; and she was ashamed to say any more to me. The quarrel between us lasted a week; and then one day, poor soul, she said, whimpering like a drug taker: 'Cora, I can't get on without the messages you bring me. The ones I get through other people don't sound like Harry—and yours do.'

I was so sorry for her then that I had hard work not to cry with her; but I kept my head, and answered quietly: 'Mrs Clingsland, I've been going against my Church, and risking my immortal soul, to get those messages through to you; and if you've found others that can help you, so much the better for me, and I'll go and make my peace with Heaven this very evening,' I said.

'But the other messages don't help me, and I don't want to disbelieve in you,' she sobbed out. 'Only lying awake all night and turning things over, I get so miserable. I shall die if you can't prove to me that it's really Harry speaking to you.'

I began to pack up my things. 'I can't prove that, I'm afraid,' I says in a cold voice, turning away my head so she wouldn't see the tears running down my cheeks.

'Oh, but you must, Cora, or I shall die!' she entreated me; and she-looked as if she would, the poor soul.

'How can I prove it to you?' I answered. For all my pity for her, I still resented the way she'd spoken; and I thought how glad I'd be to get the whole business off my soul that very night in the confessional.

She opened her great eyes and looked up at me; and I seemed to see the wraith of her young beauty looking out of them. 'There's only one way,' she whispered.

'Well,' I said, still offended, 'what's the way?'

'You must ask him to repeat to you that letter he wrote, and didn't dare send to me. I'll know instantly then if you're in communication with him, and if you are I'll never doubt you anymore.'

Well, I sat down and gave a laugh. 'You think it's as easy as that to talk with the dead, do you?'

'I think he'll know I'm dying too, and have pity on me, and do as I ask.' I said nothing more, but packed up my things and went away.

That letter seemed to me a mountain in my path; and the poor young man, when I told him, thought so too. 'Ah, that's too difficult,' he said. But he told me he'd think it over, and do his best—and I was to come back the next day if I could. 'If only I knew more about her—or about *him*. It's damn difficult, making love for a dead man to a woman you've never seen,' says he with his little cracked laugh. I couldn't deny that it was; but I knew he'd do what he could, and I could see that the difficulty of it somehow spurred him on, while me it only cast down.

So I went back to his room the next evening; and as I climbed the stairs I felt one of those sudden warnings that sometimes used to take me by the throat.

'It's as cold as ice on these stairs,' I thought, 'and I'll wager there's no one made up the fire in his room since morning.' But it wasn't really the cold I was afraid of; I could tell there was worse than that waiting for me.

I pushed open the door and went in. 'Well,' says I, as cheerful as I could, 'I've got a pint of champagne and a thermos of hot soup for you; but before you get them you've got to tell me—'

He laid there in his bed as if he didn't see me, though his eyes were open; and when I spoke to him he didn't answer. I tried to laugh. 'Mercy!' I says, 'are you so sleepy you can't even look round to see the champagne? Hasn't that slut of a woman been in to 'tend to the stove for you? The room's as cold as death—' I says, and at the word I stopped short. He neither moved nor spoke; and I felt that the cold came from him, and not from the empty stove. I took hold of his hand, and held the cracked looking glass to his lips; and I knew he was gone to his Maker. I drew his lids down, and fell on my knees beside the bed. 'You shan't go without a prayer, you poor fellow,' I whispered to him, pulling out my beads.

But though my heart was full of mourning I dursn't pray for long, for I knew I ought to call the people of the house. So I just muttered a prayer for the dead, and then got to my feet again. But before calling in anybody I took a quick look around; for I said to myself it would be better not to leave about any of those bits he'd written down for me. In the shock of finding the poor young man gone I'd clean forgotten all about the letter; but I looked among his few books and papers for anything about the spirit messages, and found nothing. After that I turned back for a last look at him, and a last blessing; and then it was, fallen on the floor and half under the bed, I saw a sheet of paper scribbled over in pencil in his weak writing. I picked it up, and, holy Mother, it was the letter! I hid it away quick in my bag, and I stooped down and kissed him. And then I called the people in.

Well, I mourned the poor young man like a son, and I had a busy day arranging things, and settling about the funeral with the lady that used to befriend him. And with all there was to do I never went near Mrs Clingsland nor so much as thought of her, that day or the next; and the day after that there was a frantic message, asking what had happened, and saying she was very ill, and I was to come quick, no matter how much else I had to do.

I didn't more than half believe in the illness; I've been about too long among the rich not to be pretty well used to their scares and fusses. But I knew Mrs Clingsland was just pining to find out if I'd got the letter, and that my only chance of keeping my hold over her was to have it ready in my bag when 1 went back. And if I didn't keep my hold over her, I knew what slimy hands were waiting in the dark to pull her down.

Well, the labour I had copying out that letter was so great that I didn't hardly notice what was in it; and if I thought about it at all, it was only to wonder if it wasn't worded too plain-like, and if there oughtn't to have been more long words in it, coming from a gentleman to his lady. So with one thing and another I wasn't any too easy in my mind when I appeared again at Mrs Clingsland's; and if ever I wished myself out of a dangerous job, my dear, I can tell you that was the day . . .

I went up to her room, the poor lady, and found her in bed, and tossing about, her eyes blazing, and her face full of all the wrinkles I'd worked so hard to rub out of it; and the sight of her softened my heart. After all, I thought, these people don't know what real trouble is; but they've manufactured something so like it that it's about as bad as the genuine thing.

'Well,' she said in a fever, 'well, Cora—the letter? Have you brought me the letter?'

I pulled it out of my bag, and handed it to her; and then I sat down and waited, my heart in my boots. I waited a long time, looking away from her; you couldn't stare at a lady who was reading a message from her sweetheart, could you?

I waited a long time; she must have read the letter very slowly, and then reread it. Once she sighed, ever so softly; and once she said:

'Oh, Harry, no, no—how foolish' . . . and laughed a little under her breath. Then she was still again for so long that at last I turned my head and took a stealthy look at her. And there she lay on her pillows, the hair waving over them, the letter clasped tight in her hands, and her face smoothed out the way it was years before, when I first knew her. Yes—those few words had done more for her than all my labour.

'Well—?' said I, smiling a little at her.

'Oh, Cora—now at last he's spoken to me, really spoken.' And the tears were running down her young cheeks.

I couldn't hardly keep back my own, the heart was so light in me. 'And now you'll believe in me, I hope, ma'am, won't you?'

'I was mad ever to doubt you, Cora . . . ' She lifted the letter to her breast, and slipped it in among her laces. 'How did you manage to get it, you darling, you?'

Dear me, thinks I, and what if she asks me to get her another one like it, and then another? I waited a moment, and then I spoke very gravely. 'It's not an easy thing, ma'am, coaxing a letter like that from the dead.' And suddenly, with a start, I saw that I'd spoken the truth. It was from the dead that I'd got it.

'No, Cora; I can well believe it. But this is a treasure I can live on for years. Only you must tell me how I can repay you ... In a hundred years I could never do enough for you,' she says.

Well, that word went to my heart; but for a minute I didn't know how to answer. For it was true I'd risked my soul, and that was something she couldn't pay me for; but then maybe I'd saved hers, in getting her away from those foul people, so the whole business was more of a puzzle to me than ever. But then I had a thought that made me easier.

'Well, ma'am, the day before yesterday I was with a young man about the age of—of your Harry; a poor young man, without health or hope, lying sick in a mean rooming house. I used to go there and see him sometimes—'

Mrs Clingsland sat up in bed in a flutter of pity. 'Oh, Cora, how dreadful! Why did you never tell me? You must hire a better room for him at once. Has he a doctor? Has he a nurse? Quick—give me my chequebook!'

'Thank you, ma'am. But he don't need no nurse nor no doctor; and he's in a room underground by now. All I wanted to ask you for,' said I at length, though I knew I might have got a king's ransom from her, 'is money enough to have a few masses said for his soul—because maybe there's no one else to do it.'

I had hard work making her believe there was no end to the masses you could say for a hundred dollars; but somehow it's comforted me ever since that I took no more from her that day. I saw to it that Father Divott said the masses and got a good bit of the money; so he was a sort of accomplice too, though he never knew it.

A Bottle of Perrier

1.

A two day's struggle over the treacherous trails in a well-intentioned but short-winded "flivver", and a ride of two more on a hired mount of unamiable temper, had disposed young Medford, of the American School of Archaeology at Athens, to wonder why his queer English friend, Henry Almodham, had chosen to live in the desert.

Now he understood.

He was leaning against the roof parapet of the old building, half Christian fortress, half Arab palace, which had been Almodham's pretext; or one of them. Below, in an inner court, a little wind, rising as the sun sank, sent through a knot of palms the rain-like rattle so cooling to the pilgrims of the desert. An ancient fig tree, enormous, exuberant, writhed over a whitewashed well-head, sucking life from what appeared to be the only source of moisture within the walls. Beyond these, on every side, stretched away the mystery of the sands, all golden with promise, all livid with menace, as the sun alternately touched or abandoned them.

Young Medford, somewhat weary after his journey from the coast, and awed by his first intimate sense of the omnipresence of the desert, shivered and drew back. Undoubtedly, for a scholar and a misogynist, it was a wonderful refuge; but one would have to be, incurably, both.

"Let's take a look at the house," Medford said to himself, as if speedy contact with man's handiwork were necessary to his reassurance.

The house, he already knew, was empty save for the quick cosmopolitan man-servant, who spoke a sort of palimpsest Cockney lined with Mediterranean tongues and desert dialects—English, Italian or Greek, which was he?—and two or three *burnoused* underlings who, having carried Medford's bags to his room, had relieved the palace of their gliding presences. Mr. Almodham, the servant told him, was away; suddenly summoned by a friendly chief to visit some unexplored ruins to the south, he had ridden off at dawn, too hurriedly to write, but leaving messages of excuse and regret. That evening late he might be back, or next morning. Meanwhile Mr. Medford was to make himself at home.

Almodham, as young Medford knew, was always making these archaeological explorations; they had been his ostensible reason for settling in that remote place, and his desultory search had already resulted in the discovery of several early Christian ruins of great interest.

Medford was glad that his host had not stood on ceremony, and rather relieved, on the whole, to have the next few hours to himself. He had had a malarial fever the previous summer, and in spite of his cork helmet he had probably caught a touch of the sun; he felt curiously, helplessly tired, yet deeply content.

And what a place it was to rest in! The silence, the remoteness, the illimitable air! And in the heart of the wilderness green leafage, water, comfort—he had already caught a glimpse of wide wicker chairs under the palms—a humane and welcoming habitation. Yes, he began to understand Almodham. To anyone sick of the Western fret and fever the very walls of this desert fortress exuded peace.

As his foot was on the ladder-like stair leading down from the roof, Medford saw the man-servant's head rising toward him. It rose slowly and Medford had time to remark that it was sallow, bald on the top, diagonally dented with a long white scar, and ringed with thick ash-blond hair. Hitherto Medford had noticed only the man's face—youngish, but sallow also—and been chiefly struck by its wearing an odd expression which could best be defined as surprise.

The servant, moving aside, looked up, and Medford perceived that his air of surprise was produced by the fact that his intensely blue eyes were rather wider open than most eyes, and fringed with thick ash-blond lashes; otherwise there was nothing noticeable about him.

"Just to ask—what wine for dinner, sir? Champagne, or—"

"No wine, thanks."

The man's disciplined lips were played over by a faint flicker of deprecation or irony, or both.

"Not any at all, sir?"

Medford smiled back. "It's not out of respect for Prohibition." He was sure that the man, of whatever nationality, would understand that; and he did.

25

"Oh, I didn't suppose, sir—"

"Well, no; but I've been rather seedy, and wine's forbidden."

The servant remained incredulous. "Just a little light Moselle, though, to colour the water, sir?"

"No wine at all," said Medford, growing bored. He was still in the stage of convalescence when it is irritating to be argued with about one's dietary.

"Oh—what's your name, by the way?" he added, to soften the curtness of his refusal.

"Gosling," said the other unexpectedly, though Medford didn't in the least know what he had expected him to be called.

"You're English, then?"

"Oh, yes, sir."

"You've been in these parts a good many years, though?"

Yes, he had, Gosling said; rather too long for his own liking; and added that he had been born at Malta. "But I know England well too." His deprecating look returned. "I will confess, sir, I'd like to have 'ad a look at Wembley. (The famous exhibition at Wembley, near London, took place in 1924.) Mr. Almodham 'ad promised me—but there—" As if to minimize the abandon of this confidence, he followed it up by a ceremonious request for Medford's keys, and an enquiry as to when he would like to dine. Having received a reply, he still lingered, looking more surprised than ever.

"Just a mineral water, then, sir?"

"Oh, yes—anything."

"Shall we say a bottle of Perrier?"

Perrier in the desert! Medford smiled assentingly, surrendered his keys and strolled away.

The house turned out to be smaller than he had imagined, or at least the habitable part of it; for above this towered mighty dilapidated walls of yellow stone, and in their crevices clung plaster chambers, one above the other, cedar-beamed, crimson-shuttered but crumbling. Out of this jumble of masonry and stucco, Christian and Moslem, the latest tenant of the fortress had chosen a cluster of rooms tucked into an angle of the ancient keep. These apartments opened on the uppermost court, where the palms chattered and the fig tree coiled above the well. On the broken marble pavement, chairs and a low table were grouped, and a few geraniums and blue morning-glories had been coaxed to grow between the slabs.

A white-skirted boy with watchful eyes was watering the plants;

but at Medford's approach he vanished like a wisp of vapour.

There was something vaporous and insubstantial about the whole scene; even the long arcaded room opening on the court, furnished with saddlebag cushions, divans with gazelle skins and rough indigenous rugs; even the table piled with the old *Timeses* and ultra-modern French and English reviews—all seemed, in that clear mocking air, born of the delusion of some desert wayfarer.

A seat under the fig tree invited Medford to doze, and when he woke the hard blue dome above him was gemmed with stars and the night breeze gossiped with the palms.

Rest—beauty—peace. Wise Almodham!

2.

Wise Almodham! Having carried out—with somewhat disappointing results—the excavation with which an archaeological society had charged him twenty-five years ago, he had lingered on, taken possession of the Crusader's stronghold, and turned his attention from ancient to mediaeval remains. But even these investigations, Medford suspected, he prosecuted only at intervals, when the enchantment of his leisure did not lie on him too heavily.

The young American had met Henry Almodham at Luxor the previous winter; had dined with him at old Colonel Swordsley's, on that perfumed starlit terrace above the Nile; and, having somehow awakened the archaeologist's interest, had been invited to look him up in the desert the following year.

They had spent only that one evening together, with old Swordsley blinking at them under memory-laden lids, and two or three charming women from the Winter Palace chattering and exclaiming; but the two men had ridden back to Luxor together in the moonlight, and during that ride Medford fancied he had puzzled out the essential lines of Henry Almodham's character. A nature saturnine yet sentimental; chronic indolence alternating with spurts of highly intelligent activity; gnawing self-distrust soothed by intimate self-appreciation; a craving for complete solitude coupled with the inability to tolerate it for long.

There was more, too, Medford suspected; a dash of Victorian romance, gratified by the setting, the remoteness, the inaccessibility of his retreat, and by being known as *The* Henry Almodham—"the one who lives in a Crusaders' castle, you know"—the gradual imprisonment in a pose assumed in youth, and into which middle age had

27

slowly stiffened; and something deeper, darker, too, perhaps, though the young man doubted that; probably just the fact that living in that particular way had brought healing to an old wound, an old mortification, something which years ago had touched a vital part and left him writhing. Above all, in Almodham's hesitating movements and the dreaming look of his long well-featured brown face with its shock of grey hair, Medford detected an inertia, mental and moral, which life in this castle of romance must have fostered and excused.

"Once here, how easy not to leave!" he mused, sinking deeper into his deep chair.

"Dinner, sir," Gosling announced.

The table stood in an open arch of the living-room; shaded candles made a rosy pool in the dusk. Each time he emerged into their light the servant, white-jacketed, velvet-footed, looked more competent and more surprised than ever. Such dishes, too—the cook also a Maltese? Ah, they were geniuses, these Maltese! Gosling bridled, smiled his acknowledgment, and started to fill the guest's glass with Chablis.

"No wine," said Medford patiently.

"Sorry, sir. But the fact is—"

"You said there was Perrier?"

"Yes, sir; but I find there's none left. It's been awfully hot, and Mr. Almodham has been and drank it all up. The new supply isn't due till next week. We 'ave to depend on the caravans going south."

"No matter. Water, then. I really prefer it."

Gosling's surprise widened to amazement. "Not water, sir? Water—in these parts?"

Medford's irritability stirred again. "Something wrong with your water? Boil it then, can't you? I won't—" He pushed away the half-filled wineglass.

"Oh—boiled? Certainly, sir." The man's voice dropped almost to a whisper. He placed on the table a succulent mess of rice and mutton, and vanished.

Medford leaned back, surrendering himself to the night, the coolness, the ripple of wind in the palms.

One agreeable dish succeeded another. As the last appeared, the diner began to feel the pangs of thirst, and at the same moment a beaker of water was placed at his elbow. "Boiled, sir, and I squeezed a lemon into it."

"Right. I suppose at the end of the summer your water gets a bit muddy?"

"That's it, sir. But you'll find this all right, sir."

Medford tasted. "Better than Perrier." He emptied the glass, leaned back and groped in his pocket. A tray was instantly at his hand with cigars and cigarettes.

"You don't—smoke sir?"

Medford, for answer, held up his cigar to the man's light. "What do you call this?"

"Oh, just so. I meant the other style." Gosling glanced discreetly at the opium pipes of jade and amber laid out on a low table.

Medford shrugged away the invitation—and wondered. Was that perhaps Almodham's other secret—or one of them? For he began to think there might be many; and all, he was sure, safely stored away behind Gosling's vigilant brow.

"No news yet of Mr. Almodham?"

Gosling was gathering up the dishes with dexterous gestures. For a moment he seemed not to hear. Then—from beyond the candle gleam—"News, sir? There couldn't 'ardly be, could there? There's no wireless in the desert, sir; not like London." His respectful tone tempered the slight irony. "But tomorrow evening ought to see him riding in." Gosling paused, drew nearer, swept one of his swift hands across the table in pursuit of the last crumbs, and added tentatively: "You'll surely be able, sir, to stay till then?"

Medford laughed. The night was too rich in healing; it sank on his spirit like wings. Time vanished, fret and trouble were no more. "Stay, I'll stay a year if I have to!"

"Oh—a year?" Gosling echoed it playfully, gathered up the dessert dishes and was gone.

3.

Medford had said that he would wait for Almodham a year; but the next morning he found that such arbitrary terms had lost their meaning. There were no time measures in a place like this. The silly face of his watch told its daily tale to emptiness. The wheeling of the constellations over those ruined walls marked only the revolutions of the earth; the spasmodic motions of man meant nothing.

The very fact of being hungry, that stroke of the inward clock, was minimized by the slightness of the sensation—just the ghost of a pang, that might have been quieted by dried fruit and honey. Life had the light monotonous smoothness of eternity.

Toward sunset Medford shook off this queer sense of otherwhereness and climbed to the roof. Across the desert he spied for Almodham. Southward the Mountains of Alabaster hung like a blue veil lined with light. In the west a great column of fire shot up, spraying into plumy cloudlets which turned the sky to a fountain of rose-leaves, the sands beneath to gold.

No riders specked them. Medford watched in vain for his absent host till night fell, and the punctual Gosling invited him once more to table.

In the evening Medford absently fingered the ultra-modern reviews—three months old, and already so stale to the touch—then tossed them aside, flung himself on a divan and dreamed. Almodham must spend a lot of time dreaming; that was it. Then, just as he felt himself sinking down into torpor, he would be off on one of these dashes across the desert in quest of unknown ruins. Not such a bad life.

Gosling appeared with Turkish coffee in a cup cased in *filigree*.

"Are there any horses in the stable?" Medford suddenly asked.

"Horses? Only what you might call pack-horses, sir. Mr. Almodham has the two best saddle-horses with him."

"I was thinking I might ride out to meet him."

Gosling considered. "So you might, sir."

"Do you know which way he went?"

"Not rightly sir. The *caid's* man was to guide them."

"Them? Who went with him?"

"Just one of our men, sir. They've got the two thoroughbreds. There's a third, but he's lame."

Gosling paused. "Do you know the trails, sir? Excuse me, but I don't think I ever saw you here before."

"No," Medford acquiesced, "I've never been here before."

"Oh, then"—Gosling's gesture added: "In that case, even the best thoroughbred wouldn't help you."

"I suppose he may still turn up tonight?"

"Oh, easily, sir. I expect to see you both breakfasting here tomorrow morning," said Gosling cheerfully.

Medford sipped his coffee. "You said you'd never seen me here before. How long have you been here yourself?"

Gosling answered instantly, as though the figures were never long out of his memory: "Eleven years and seven months altogether, sir,"

"Nearly twelve years! That's a longish time."

"Yes, it is."

"And I don't suppose you often get away?"

Gosling was moving off with the tray. He halted, turned back, and said with sudden emphasis: "I've never once been away. Not since Mr. Almodham first brought me here."

"Good Lord! Not a single holiday?"

"Not one, sir."

"But Mr. Almodham goes off occasionally. I met him at Luxor last year."

"Just so, sir. But when he's here he needs me for himself; and when he's away he needs me to watch over the others. So you see—"

"Yes, I see. But it must seem to you devilish long."

"It seems long, sir."

"But the others? You mean they're not—wholly trustworthy?"

"Well, sir, they're just Arabs," said Gosling with careless contempt.

"I see. And not a single old reliable among them?"

"The term isn't in their language, sir."

Medford was busy lighting his cigar. When he looked up he found that Gosling still stood a few feet off.

"It wasn't as if it 'adn't been a promise, you know, sir," he said, almost passionately.

"A promise?"

"To let me 'ave my holiday, sir. A promise—agine and agine."

"And the time never came?"

"No, sir, the days just drifted by—"

"Ah. They would, here. Don't sit up for me," Medford added. "I think I shall wait up—wait for Mr. Almodham."

Gosling's stare widened. "Here, sir? Here in the court?"

The young man nodded, and the servant stood still regarding him, turned by the moonlight to a white spectral figure, the unquiet ghost of a patient butler who might have died without his holiday.

"Down here in the court all night, sir? It's a lonely spot. I couldn't 'ear you if you was to call. You're best in bed, sir. The air's bad. You might bring your fever on again."

Medford laughed and stretched himself in his long chair. "Decidedly," he thought, "the fellow needs a change." Aloud he remarked: "Oh, I'm all right. It's you who are nervous Gosling. When Mr. Almodham comes back I mean to put in a word for you. You shall have your holiday."

Gosling still stood motionless. For a minute he did not speak. "You would, sir, you would?" He gasped it out on a high cracked note, and the last word ran into a laugh—a brief shrill cackle, the laugh of one long unused to such indulgences.

"Thank you, sir. Goodnight, sir." He was gone.

4.

"You do boil my drinking-water, always?" Medford questioned, his hand clasping the glass without lifting it.

The tone was amicable, almost confidential; Medford felt that since his rash promise to secure a holiday for Gosling he and Gosling were on terms of real friendship.

"Boil it? Always, sir. Naturally." Gosling spoke with a slight note of reproach, as though Medford's question implied a slur—unconscious, he hoped—on their newly established relation. He scrutinized Medford with his astonished eyes, in which a genuine concern showed itself through the glaze of professional indifference.

"Because, you know, my bath this morning—"

Gosling was in the act of receiving from the hands of a gliding Arab a fragrant dish of *kuskus*. Under his breath he hissed to the native: "You damned aboriginy, you, can't even 'old a dish steady? Ugh!"

The Arab vanished before the imprecation, and Gosling, with a calm deliberate hand, set the dish before Medford. "All alike, they are." Fastidiously he wiped a trail of grease from his linen sleeve.

"Because, you know, my bath this morning simply stank," said Medford, plunging fork and spoon into the dish.

"Your bath, sir?" Gosling stressed the word. Astonishment, to the exclusion of all other emotion, again filled his eyes as he rested them on Medford. "Now, I wouldn't 'ave 'ad that 'appen for the world," he said self-reproachfully.

"There's only the one well here, eh? The one in the court?"

Gosling aroused himself from absorbed consideration of the visitor's complaint. "Yes, sir; only the one."

"What sort of a well is it? Where does the water come from?"

"Oh, it's just a cistern, sir. Rain-water. There's never been any other here. Not that I ever knew it to fail; but at this season sometimes it does turn queer. Ask any o' them Arabs, sir; they'll tell you. Liars as they are, they won't trouble to lie about that."

Medford was cautiously tasting the water in his glass. "This seems all right," he pronounced.

Sincere satisfaction was depicted on Gosling's countenance. "I seen to its being boiled myself, sir. I always do. I 'ope that Perrier'll turn up tomorrow, sir."

"Oh, tomorrow"—Medford shrugged, taking a second helping. "Tomorrow I may not be here to drink it."

"What—going away, sir?" cried Gosling.

Medford, wheeling round abruptly, caught a new and incomprehensible look in Gosling's eyes. The man had seemed to feel a sort of dog-like affection for him; had wanted, Medford could have sworn, to keep him on, persuade him to patience and delay; yet now, Medford could equally have sworn, there was relief in his look, satisfaction, almost, in his voice.

"So soon, sir?"

"Well, this is the fifth day since my arrival. And as there's no news yet of Mr. Almodham, and you say he may very well have forgotten all about my coming—"

"Oh, I don't say that, sir; not forgotten! Only, when one of those old piles of stones takes 'old of him, he does forget about the time, sir. That's what I meant. The days drift by—'e's in a dream. Very likely he thinks you're just due now, sir." A small thin smile sharpened the lustreless gravity of Gosling's features. It was the first time that Medford had seen him smile.

"Oh, I understand. But still—" Medford paused. Through the spell of inertia laid on him by the drowsy place and its easeful comforts his instinct of alertness was struggling back. "It's odd—"

"What's odd?" Gosling echoed unexpectedly, setting the dried dates and figs on the table.

"Everything," said Medford.

He leaned back in his chair and glanced up through the arch at the lofty sky from which noon was pouring down in cataracts of blue and gold. Almodham was out there somewhere under that canopy of fire, perhaps, as the servant said, absorbed in his dream. The land was full of spells.

"Coffee, sir?" Gosling reminded him. Medford took it.

"It's odd that you say you don't trust any of these fellows—these Arabs—and yet that you don't seem to feel worried at Mr. Almodham's being off God knows where, all alone with them."

Gosling received this attentively, impartially; he saw the point. "Well, sir, no—you wouldn't understand. It's the very thing that can't be taught, when to trust 'em and when not. It's 'ow their interests lie, of course, sir; and their religion, as they call it." His contempt was unlimited. "But even to begin to understand why I'm not worried about

33

Mr. Almodham, you'd 'ave to 'ave lived among them, sir, and you'd 'ave to speak their language."

"But I—" Medford began. He pulled himself up short and bent above his coffee.

"Yes, sir."

"But I've travelled among them more or less."

"Oh, travelled!" Even Gosling's intonation could hardly conciliate respect with derision in his reception of this boast.

"This makes the fifth day, though," Medford continued argumentatively. The midday heat lay heavy even on the shaded side of the court, and the sinews of his will were weakening.

"I can understand, sir, a gentleman like you 'aving other engagements—being pressed for time, as it were," Gosling reasonably conceded.

He cleared the table, committed its freight to a pair of Arab arms that just showed and vanished, and finally took himself off while Medford sank into the divan. A land of dreams. . . .

The afternoon hung over the place like a great velarium of cloth-of-gold stretched across the battlements and drooping down in ever slacker folds upon the heavy-headed palms. When at length the gold turned to violet, and the west to a bow of crystal clasping the desert sands, Medford shook off his sleep and wandered out. But this time, instead of mounting to the roof, he took another direction.

He was surprised to find how little he knew of the place after five days of loitering and waiting. Perhaps this was to be his last evening alone in it. He passed out of the court by a vaulted stone passage which led to another walled enclosure. At his approach two or three Arabs who had been squatting there rose and melted out of sight. It was as if the solid masonry had received them.

Beyond, Medford heard a stamping of hoofs, the stir of a stable at night-fall. He went under another archway and found himself among horses and mules. In the fading light an Arab was rubbing down one of the horses, a powerful young chestnut. He too seemed about to vanish; but Medford caught him by the sleeve.

"Go on with your work," he said in Arabic.

The man, who was young and muscular, with a lean Bedouin face, stopped and looked at him.

"I didn't know your Excellency spoke our language."

"Oh, yes," said Medford.

The man was silent, one hand on the horse's restless neck, the other thrust into his woollen girdle. He and Medford examined each other in the faint light.

"Is that the horse that's lame?" Medford asked.

"Lame?" The Arab's eyes ran down the animal's legs. "Oh, yes; lame," he answered vaguely.

Medford stooped and felt the horses knees and fetlocks. "He seems pretty fit. Couldn't he carry me for a canter this evening if I felt like it?"

The Arab considered; he was evidently perplexed by the weight of responsibility which the question placed on him.

"Your Excellency would like to go for a ride this evening?"

"Oh, just a fancy. I might or I might not." Medford lit a cigarette and offered one to the groom, whose white teeth flashed his gratification. Over the shared match they drew nearer and the Arab's diffidence seemed to lessen.

"Is this one of Mr. Almodham's own mounts?" Medford asked.

"Yes, sir; it's his favourite," said the groom, his hand passing proudly down the horse's bright shoulder.

"His favourite? Yet he didn't take him on this long expedition?"

The Arab fell silent and stared at the ground.

"Weren't you surprised at that?" Medford queried.

The man's gesture declared that it was not his business to be surprised.

The two remained without speaking while the quick blue night descended.

At length Medford said carelessly: "Where do you suppose your master is at this moment?"

The moon, unperceived in the radiant fall of day, had now suddenly possessed the world, and a broad white beam lay full on the Arab's white smock, his brown face and the turban of camel's hair knotted above it. His agitated eyeballs glistened like jewels.

"If *Allah* would vouchsafe to let us know!"

"But you suppose he's safe enough, don't you? You don't think it's necessary yet for a party to go out in search of him?"

The Arab appeared to ponder this deeply. The question must have taken him by surprise. He flung a brown arm about the horse's neck and continued to scrutinize the stones of the court.

"When the master is away Mr. Gosling is our master."

"And he doesn't think it necessary?"

The Arab signed: "Not yet."

35

"But if Mr. Almodham were away much longer—"

The man was again silent, and Medford continued: "You're the head groom, I suppose?"

"Yes, Excellency."

There was another pause. Medford half turned away; then over his shoulder: "I suppose you know the direction Mr. Almodham took? The place he's gone to?"

"Oh, assuredly, Excellency."

"Then you and I are going to ride after him. Be ready an hour before daylight. Say nothing to anyone—Mr. Gosling or anybody else. We two ought to be able to find him without other help."

The Arab's face was all a responsive flash of eyes and teeth. "Oh, sir, I undertake that you and my master shall meet before tomorrow night. And none shall know of it."

"He's as anxious about Almodham as I am," Medford thought; and a faint shiver ran down his back. "All right. Be ready," he repeated.

He strolled back and found the court empty of life, but fantastically peopled by palms of beaten silver and a white marble fig tree.

"After all," he thought irrelevantly, "I'm glad I didn't tell Gosling that I speak Arabic."

He sat down and waited till Gosling, approaching from the living-room, ceremoniously announced for the fifth time that dinner was served.

5.

Medford sat up in bed with the jerk which resembles no other. Someone was in his room. The fact reached him not by sight or sound—for the moon had set, and the silence of the night was complete—but by a peculiar faint disturbance of the invisible currents that enclose us.

He was awake in an instant, caught up his electric hand-lamp and flashed it into two astonished eyes. Gosling stood above the bed.

"Mr. Almodham—he's back?" Medford exclaimed.

"No, sir; he's not back." Gosling spoke in low controlled tones. His extreme self-possession gave Medford a sense of danger—he couldn't say why, or of what nature. He sat upright, looking hard at the man.

"Then what's the matter?"

"Well, sir, you might have told me you talk Arabic"—Gosling's tone was now wistfully reproachful—"before you got 'obnobbing with that Selim. Making randy-voos with 'im by night in the desert."

36

Medford reached for his matches and lit the candle by the bed. He did not know whether to kick Gosling out of the room or to listen to what the man had to say; but a quick movement of curiosity made him determine on the latter course.

"Such folly! First I thought I'd lock you in. I might 'ave." Gosling drew a key from his pocket and held it up. "Or again I might 'ave let you go. Easier than not. But there was Wembley."

"Wembley?" Medford echoed. He began to think that the man was going mad. One might, so conceivably, in that place of postponements and enchantments! He wondered whether Almodham himself were not a little mad—if, indeed, Almodham were still in a world where such a fate is possible.

"Wembley. You promised to get Mr. Almodham to give me an 'oliday—to let me go back to England in time for a look at Wembley. Every man 'as 'is fancies, 'asn't he sir? And that's mine. I've told Mr. Almodham so, agine and agine. He'd never listen, or only make believe to; say: 'We'll see, now, Gosling, we'll see'; and no more 'eard of it. But you was different, sir. You said it, and I knew you meant it—about my 'oliday. So I'm going to lock you in." Gosling spoke composedly, but with an under-thrill of emotion in his queer Mediterranean-Cockney voice.

"Lock me in?"

"Prevent you somehow from going off with that murderer. You don't suppose you'd ever 'ave come back alive from that ride, do you?"

A shiver ran over Medford, as it had the evening before when he had said to himself that the Arab was as anxious as he was about Almodham. He gave a slight laugh.

"I don't know what you're talking about. But you're not going to lock me in."

The effect of this was unexpected. Gosling's face was drawn up into a convulsive grimace and two tears rose to his pale eyelashes and ran down his cheeks.

"You don't trust me, after all," he said plaintively.

Medford leaned on his pillow and considered. Nothing as queer had ever before happened to him. The fellow looked almost ridiculous enough to laugh at; yet his tears were certainly not simulated. Was he weeping for Almodham, already dead, or for Medford, about to be committed to the same grave?

"I should trust you at once," said Medford, "if you'd tell me where your master is."

37

Gosling's face resumed its usual guarded expression, though the trace of the tears still glittered on it.

"I can't do that, sir."

"Ah, I thought so!"

"Because—'ow do I know?"

Medford thrust a leg out of bed. One hand, under the blanket, lay on his revolver.

"Well, you may go now. Put that key down on the table first. And don't try to do anything to interfere with my plans. If you do I'll shoot you," he added concisely.

"Oh, no, you wouldn't shoot a British subject; it makes such a fuss. Not that I'd care—I've often thought of doing it myself. Sometimes in the *sirocco* season. That don't scare me. And you shan't go."

Medford was on his feet now, the revolver visible. Gosling eyed it with indifference.

"Then you do know where Mr. Almodham is? And you're determined that I shan't find out?" Medford challenged him.

"Selim's determined," said Gosling, "and all the others are. They all want you out of the way. That's why I've kept 'em to their quarters—done all the waiting on you myself. Now will you stay here? For God's sake, sir! The return caravan is going through to the coast the day after tomorrow. Join it, sir—it's the only safe way! I darsn't let you go with one of our men, not even if you was to swear you'd ride straight for the coast and let this business be."

"This business? What business?"

"This worrying about where Mr. Almodham is, sir. Not that there's anything to worry about. The men all know that. But the plain fact is they've stolen some money from his box, since he's been gone, and if I hadn't winked at it they'd 'ave killed me; and all they want is to get you to ride out after 'im, and put you safe away under a 'eap of sand somewhere off the caravan trails. Easy job. There; that's all, sir. My word it is."

There was a long silence. In the weak candle-light the two men stood considering each other.

Medford's wits began to clear as the sense of peril closed in on him. His mind reached out on all sides into the enfolding mystery, but it was everywhere impenetrable. The odd thing was that, though he did not believe half of what Gosling had told him, the man yet inspired him with a queer sense of confidence as far as their mutual relation was concerned. "He may be lying about Almodham, to hide God knows what; but I don't believe he's lying about Selim."

Medford laid his revolver on the table. "Very well," he said. "I won't ride out to look for Mr. Almodham, since you advise me not to. But I won't leave by the caravan; I'll wait here till he comes back."

He saw Gosling whiten under his sallowness. "Oh, don't do that, sir; I couldn't answer for them if you was to wait. The caravan'll take you to the coast the day after tomorrow as easy as if you was riding in Rotten Row."

"Ah, then you know that Mr. Almodham won't be back by the day after tomorrow?" Medford caught him up.

"I don't know anything, sir."

"Not even where he is now?"

Gosling reflected. "He's been gone too long, sir, for me to know that," he said from the threshold.

The door closed on him.

Medford found sleep unrecoverable. He leaned in his window and watched the stars fade and the dawn break in all its holiness. As the stir of life rose among the ancient walls he marvelled at the contrast between that fountain of purity welling up into the heavens and the evil secrets clinging bat-like to the nest of masonry below.

He no longer knew what to believe or whom. Had some enemy of Almodham's lured him into the desert and bought the connivance of his people? Or had the servants had some reason of their own for spiriting him away, and was Gosling possibly telling the truth when he said that the same fate would befall Medford if he refused to leave?

Medford, as the light brightened, felt his energy return. The very impenetrableness of the mystery stimulated him. He would stay, and he would find out the truth.

6.

It was always Gosling himself who brought up the water for Medford's bath; but this morning he failed to appear with it, and when he came it was to bring the breakfast tray. Medford noticed that his face was of a pasty pallor, and that his lids were reddened as if with weeping. The contrast was unpleasant, and a dislike for Gosling began to shape itself in the young man's breast.

"My bath?" he queried.

"Well, sir, you complained yesterday of the water—"

"Can't you boil it?"

"I 'ave, sir."

"Well, then—"

Gosling went out sullenly and presently returned with a brass jug. "It's the time of year—we're dying for rain," he grumbled, pouring a scant measure of water into the tub.

Yes, the well must be pretty low, Medford thought. Even boiled, the water had the disagreeable smell that he had noticed the day before, though of course, in a slighter degree. But a bath was a necessity in that climate. He splashed the few cupfuls over himself as best as he could.

He spent the day in rather fruitlessly considering his situation. He had hoped the morning would bring counsel, but it brought only courage and resolution, and these were of small use without enlightenment. Suddenly he remembered that the caravan going south from the coast would pass near the castle that afternoon. Gosling had dwelt on the date often enough, for it was the caravan which was to bring the box of Perrier water.

"Well, I'm not sorry for that," Medford reflected, with a slight shrinking of the flesh. Something sick and viscous, half smell, half substance, seemed to have clung to his skin since his morning bath, and the idea of having to drink that water again was nauseating.

But his chief reason for welcoming the caravan was the hope of finding in it some European, or at any rate some native official from the coast, to whom he might confide his anxiety. He hung about, listening and waiting, and then mounted to the roof to gaze northward along the trail. But in the afternoon glow he saw only three Bedouins guiding laden pack mules toward the castle.

As they mounted the steep path he recognized some of Almodham's men, and guessed at once that the southward caravan trail did not actually pass under the walls and that the men had been out to meet it, probably at a small oasis behind some fold of the sand-hills. Vexed at his own thoughtlessness in not foreseeing such a possibility, Medford dashed down to the court, hoping the men might have brought back some news of Almodham, though, as the latter had ridden south, he could at best only have crossed the trail by which the caravan had come. Still, even so, someone might know something, some report might have been heard—since everything was always known in the desert.

As Medford reached the court, angry vociferations, and retorts as vehement, rose from the stable-yard. He leaned over the wall and listened. Hitherto nothing had surprised him more than the silence of the place. Gosling must have had a strong arm to subdue the shrill voices of his underlings. Now they had all broken loose, and it was Gosling's own voice—usually so discreet and measured—which dominated them.

Gosling, master of all the desert dialects, was cursing his subordinates in a half-dozen.

"And you didn't bring it—and you tell me it wasn't there, and I tell you it was, and that you know it, and that you either left it on a sand-heap while you were jawing with some of those slimy fellows from the coast, or else fastened it on to the horse so carelessly that it fell off on the way—and all of you too sleepy to notice. Oh, you sons of females I wouldn't soil my lips by naming! Well, back you go to hunt it up, that's all."

"By *Allah* and the tomb of his Prophet, you wrong us unpardonably. There was nothing left at the oasis, nor yet dropped off on the way back. It was not there, and that is the truth in its purity."

"Truth! Purity! You miserable lot of shirks and liars, you—and the gentleman here not touching a drop of anything but water—as you profess to do, you liquor-swilling humbugs!"

Medford drew back from the parapet with a smile of relief. It was nothing but a case of Perrier—the missing case—which had raised the passions of these grown men to the pitch of frenzy! The anti-climax lifted a load from his breast. If Gosling, the calm and self-controlled, could waste his wrath on so slight a hitch in the working of the commissariat, he at least must have a free mind. How absurd this homely incident made Medford's speculations seem!

He was at once touched by Gosling's solicitude, and annoyed that he should have been so duped by the hallucinating fancies of the East.

Almodham was off on his own business; very likely the men knew where and what the business was; and even if they had robbed him in his absence, and quarrelled over the spoils, Medford did not see what he could do. It might even be that his eccentric host—with whom, after all, he had had but one evening's acquaintance—repenting an invitation too rashly given, had ridden away to escape the boredom of entertaining him. As this alternative occurred to Medford it seemed so plausible that he began to wonder if Almodham had not simply withdrawn to some secret suite of that intricate dwelling, and were waiting there for his guest's departure.

So well would this explain Gosling's solicitude to see the visitor off—so completely account for the man's nervous and contradictory behaviour—that Medford, smiling at his own obtuseness, hastily resolved to leave on the morrow. Tranquillized by this decision, he lingered about the court till dusk fell, and then, as usual, went up to the roof. But today his eyes, instead of raking the horizon, fastened on the clustering edifice of which, after six days' residence, he knew so little. Aerial chambers, jutting out at capricious angles, baffled him with closely shuttered windows, or here and there with the enigma of painted panes. Behind which window was his host concealed, spying, it might be, at this very moment on the movements of his lingering guest?

The idea that that strange moody man, with his long brown face and shock of white hair, his half-guessed selfishness and tyranny, and his morbid self-absorption, might be actually within a stone's throw, gave Medford, for the first time, a sharp sense of isolation. He felt himself shut out, unwanted—the place, now that he imagined someone might be living in it unknown to him, became lonely, inhospitable, dangerous.

"Fool that I am—he probably expected me to pack up and go as soon as I found he was away!" the young man reflected. Yes; decidedly he would leave the next morning.

Gosling had not shown himself all the afternoon. When at length, belatedly, he came to set the table, he wore a look of sullen, almost surly, reserve which Medford had not yet seen on his face. He hardly returned the young man's friendly "Hallo—dinner?" and when Medford was seated handed him the first dish in silence. Medford's glass remained unfilled till he touched its brim.

"Oh, there's nothing to drink, sir. The men lost the case of Perrier—or dropped it and smashed the bottles. They say it never came. 'Ow do I know, when they never open their 'eathen lips but to lie?" Gosling burst out with sudden violence.

He set down the dish he was handing, and Medford saw that he had been obliged to do so because his whole body was shaking as if with fever.

"My dear man, what does it matter? You're going to be ill," Medford exclaimed, laying his hand on the servant's arm. But the latter, muttering: "Oh, God, if I'd only 'a' gone for it myself," jerked away and vanished from the room.

Medford sat pondering; it certainly looked as if poor Gosling were on the edge of a break-down. No wonder, when Medford himself was so oppressed by the uncanniness of the place. Gosling reappeared after an interval, correct, close-lipped, with the desert and a bottle of white wine. "Sorry, sir."

To pacify him, Medford sipped the wine and then pushed his chair away and returned to the court. He was making for the fig tree by the well when Gosling, slipping ahead, transferred his chair and wicker table to the other end of the court.

"You'll be better here—there'll be a breeze presently," he said. "I'll fetch your coffee."

He disappeared again, and Medford sat gazing up at the pile of masonry and plaster, and wondering whether he had not been moved away from his favourite corner to get him out of—or into?—the angle of vision of the invisible watcher. Gosling, having brought the coffee, went away and Medford sat on.

At length he rose and began to pace up and down as he smoked. The moon was not up yet, and darkness fell solemnly on the ancient walls. Presently the breeze arose and began its secret commerce with the palms.

Medford went back to his seat; but as soon as he had resumed it he fancied that the gaze of his hidden watcher was jealously fixed on the red spark of his cigar. The sensation became increasingly distasteful; he could almost feel Almodham reaching out long ghostly arms from somewhere above him in the darkness. He moved back into the living-room, where a shaded light hung from the ceiling; but the room was airless, and finally he went out again and dragged his seat to its old place under the fig tree. From there the windows which he suspected could not command him, and he felt easier, though the corner was out of the breeze and the heavy air seemed tainted with the exhalation of the adjoining well.

"The water must be very low," Medford mused. The smell, though faint, was unpleasant; it smirched the purity of the night. But he felt safer there, somehow, farther from those unseen eyes which seemed mysteriously to have become his enemies.

"If one of the men had knifed me in the desert, I shouldn't wonder if it would have been at Almodham's orders," Medford thought. He drowsed.

When he woke the moon was pushing up its ponderous orange disk above the walls, and the darkness in the court was less dense. He must have slept for an hour or more. The night was delicious, or would have been anywhere but there. Medford felt a shiver of his old fever and remembered that Gosling had warned him that the court was unhealthy at night.

"On account of the well, I suppose. I've been sitting too close to it," he reflected. His head ached, and he fancied that the sweetish foulish smell clung to his face as it had after his bath. He stood up and approached the well to see how much water was left in it. But the moon was not yet high enough to light those depths, and he peered down into blackness.

Suddenly he felt both shoulders gripped from behind and forcibly pressed forward, as if by someone seeking to push him over the edge. An instant later, almost coinciding with his own swift resistance, the push became a strong tug backward, and he swung round to confront Gosling, whose hands immediately dropped from his shoulders.

"I thought you had the fever, sir—I seemed to see you pitching over," the man stammered.

Medford's wits returned. "We must both have it, for I fancied you were pitching me," he said with a laugh.

"Me, sir?" Gosling gasped. "I pulled you back as 'ard as ever—"

"Of course. I know."

"Whatever are you doing here, anyhow, sir? I warned you it was un'ealthy at night," Gosling continued irritably.

Medford leaned against the well-head and contemplated him. "I believe the whole place is unhealthy."

Gosling was silent. At length he asked: "Aren't you going up to bed, sir?"

"No," said Medford, "I prefer to stay here."

Gosling's face took on an expression of dogged anger. "Well, then, I prefer that you shouldn't."

Medford laughed again. "Why? Because it's the hour when Mr. Almodham comes out to take the air?"

The effect of this question was unexpected. Gosling dropped back a step or two and flung up his hands, pressing them to his lips as if to stifle a low outcry.

"What's the matter?" Medford queried. The man's antics were beginning to get on his nerves.

"Matter?" Gosling still stood away from him, out of the rising slant of moonlight.

"Come! Own up that he's here and have done with it!" cried Medford impatiently.

"Here? What do you mean by 'here'? You 'aven't seen 'im, 'ave you?" Before the words were out of the man's lips he flung up his arms

44

again, stumbled forward and fell in a heap at Medford's feet.

Medford, still leaning against the well-head, smiled down contemptuously at the stricken wretch. His conjecture had been the right one, then; he had not been Gosling's dupe after all.

"Get up, man. Don't be a fool! It's not your fault if I guessed that Mr. Almodham walks here at night—"

"Walks here!" wailed the other, still cowering.

"Well, doesn't he? He won't kill you for owning up will he?"

"Kill me? Kill me? I wish I'd killed *You!*" Gosling half got to his feet, his head thrown back in ashen terror. "And I might' 'ave, too, so easy! You felt me pushing of you over, didn't you? Coming 'ere spying and sniffing—" His anguish seemed to choke him.

Medford had not changed his position. The very abjectness of the creature at his feet gave him an easy sense of power. But Gosling's last cry had suddenly deflected the course of his speculations. Almodham was here, then; that was certain; but just where was he, and in what shape? A new fear scuttled down Medford's spine.

"So you did want to push me over?" he said. "Why? As the quickest way of joining your master?"

The effect was more immediate than he had foreseen.

Gosling, getting to his feet, stood there bowed and shrunken in the accusing moonlight.

"Oh, God—and I 'ad you 'arf over! You know I did! And then—it was what you said about Wembley. So help me, sir, I felt you meant it, and it 'eld me back." The man's face was again wet with tears, but this time Medford recoiled from them as if they had been drops splashed up by a falling body from the foul waters below.

Medford was silent. He did not know if Gosling were armed or not, but he was no longer afraid; only aghast, and yet shudderingly lucid.

Gosling continued to ramble on half deliriously: "And if only that Perrier 'ad of come. I don't believe it'd ever 'ave crossed your mind, if only you'd 'ave had your Perrier regular, now would it? But you say 'e walks—and I knew he would! Only—what was I to do with him, with you turning up like that the very day?"

Still Medford did not move.

"And 'im driving me to madness, sir, sheer madness, that same morning. Will you believe it? The very week before you come, I was to sail for England and 'ave my 'oliday, a 'ole month, sir—and I was entitled to six, if there was any justice—a 'ole month in 'Ammersmith,

45

sir, in a cousin's 'ouse, and the chance to see Wembley thoroughly; and then 'e 'eard you was coming, sir, and 'e was bored and lonely 'ere, you understand—'e 'ad to have new excitements provided for 'im or 'e'd go off 'is bat—and when 'e 'eard you was coming, 'e come out of his black mood in a flash and was 'arf crazy with pleasure, and said 'I'll keep 'im 'ere all winter—a remarkable young man, Gosling—just my kind.' And when I says to him: 'And 'ow about my 'oliday?' he stares at me with those stony eyes of 'is and says: "Oliday? Oh, to be sure; why next year—we'll see what can be done about it next year.' Next year, sir, as if 'e was doing me a favour! And that's the way it 'ad been for nigh on twelve years.

"But this time, if you 'adn't 'ave come I do believe I'd 'ave got away, for he was getting used to 'aving Selim about 'im and his 'ealth was never better—and, well, I told 'im as much, and 'ow a man 'ad his rights after all, and my youth was going, and me that 'ad served him so well chained up 'ere like 'is watchdog, and always next year and next year—and, well, sir, 'e just laughed, sneering-like, and lit 'is cigarette. 'Oh, Gosling, cut it out,' 'e says.

"He was standing on the very spot where you are now, sir; and he turned to walk into the 'ouse. And it was then I 'it 'im. He was a heavy man, and he fell against the well kerb. And just when you were expected any minute—oh, my God!"

Gosling's voice died out in a strangled murmur.

Medford, at his last words, had involuntarily shrunk back a few feet. The two men stood in the middle of the court and stared at each other without speaking. The moon, swinging high above the battlements, sent a searching spear of light down into the guilty darkness of the well.

The Seed of the Faith

1

The blinding June sky of Africa hung over the town. In the doorway of an Arab coffee-house a young man stood listening to the remarks exchanged by the patrons of the establishment, who lay in torpid heaps on the low shelf bordering the room.

The young man's *caftan* was faded to a dingy brown, but the muslin garment covering it was clean, and so was the turban wound about his shabby *fez*.

Cleanliness was not the most marked characteristic of the conversation to which he lent a listless ear. It was no prurient curiosity that fixed his attention on this placid exchange of obscenities: he had lived too long in Morocco for obscenities not to have lost their savour. But he had never quite overcome the fascinated disgust with which he listened, nor the hope that one among the talkers would suddenly reveal some sense of a higher ideal, of what, at home, the earnest women he knew used solemnly to call a Purpose. He was sure that, some day, such a sign would come, and then—

Meanwhile, at that hour, there was nothing on earth to do in Eloued but to stand and listen—

The bazaar was beginning to fill up. Looking down the vaulted tunnel which led to the coffee-house the young man watched the thickening throng of shoppers and idlers. The fat merchant whose shop faced the end of the tunnel had just ridden up and rolled off his mule, while his black boy unbarred the door of the niche hung with embroidered slippers where the master throned. The young man in the faded *caftan*, watching the merchant scramble up and sink into his cushions, wondered for the thousandth time what he thought about all day in his dim stifling kennel, and what he did when he was away from it. . . . for no length of residence in that dark land seemed to bring one nearer to finding out what the heathen thought and did when the eye of the Christian was off him.

Suddenly a wave of excitement ran through the crowd. Every head turned in the same direction, and even the camels bent their frowning faces and stretched their necks all one way, as animals do before a storm. A wild hoot had penetrated the bazaar, howling through the long white tunnels and under the reed-woven roofs like a *Djinn* among dishonoured graves. The heart of the young man began to beat.

"It sounds," he thought, "like a motor. . . ."

But a motor at Eloued! There was one, everyone knew, in the *sultan's* palace. It had been brought there years ago by a foreign ambassador, as a gift from his sovereign, and was variously reported to be made entirely of aluminium, platinum or silver. But the parts had never been put together, the body had long been used for breeding silkworms in—a not wholly successful experiment—and the acetylene lamps adorned the *pasha's* gardens on state occasions. As for the horn, it had been sent as a gift, with a choice panoply of arms, to the *caïd* of the Red Mountain; but as the india-rubber bulb had accidentally been left behind, it was certainly not the *caïd's* visit which the present discordant cries announced. . . .

"Hullo, you old dromedary! How's the folks up state?" cried a ringing voice. The awestruck populace gave way, and a young man in linen duster and motor cap, slipping under the interwoven necks of the astonished camels, strode down the tunnel with an air of authority and clapped a hand on the dreamer in the doorway.

"Harry Spink!" the latter gasped in a startled whisper, and with an intonation as un-African as his friend's. At the same instant he glanced over his shoulder, and his mild lips formed a cautious: "sh."

"Who'd you take me for—Gabby Deslys?" asked the newcomer gaily; then, seeing that this topical allusion hung fire: "And what the dickens are you 'hushing' for, anyhow? You don't suppose, do you, that anybody in the bazaar thinks you're a *native?* D'y' ever look at your chin? Or that Adam's apple running up and down you like a bead on a billiard marker's wire? See here, Willard Bent. . . ."

The young man in the *caftan* blushed distressfully, not so much at the graphic reference to his looks as at the doubt cast on his disguise.

"I do assure you, Harry, I pick up a great deal of. . . . of useful information. . . . in this way. . . ."

"Oh, get out," said Harry Spink cheerfully. "You believe all that still, do you? What's the good of it all, anyway?"

Willard Bent passed a hand under the other's arm and led him through the coffeehouse into an empty room at the back. They sat down on a shelf covered with matting and looked at each other earnestly.

"Don't *you* believe any longer, Harry Spink?" asked Willard Bent.

"Don't have to. I'm travelling for rubber now."

"Oh, merciful heaven! Was that your automobile?"

"Sure."

There was a long silence, during which Bent sat with bowed head gazing on the earthen floor, while the bead in his throat performed its most active gymnastics. At last he lifted his eyes and fixed them on the tight red face of his companion.

"When did your faith fail you?" he asked.

The other considered him humorously. "Why—when I got onto this job, I guess."

Willard Bent rose and held out his hand.

"Goodbye. . . . I must go. . . . If I can be of any use. . . . you know where to find me. . . ."

"Any use? Say, old man, what's wrong? Are you trying to shake me?" Bent was silent, and Harry Spink continued insidiously: "Ain't you a mite hard on me? I thought the heathen was just what you was laying for."

Bent smiled mournfully. "There's no use trying to convert a renegade."

"That what I am? Well—all right. But how about the others? Say—let's order a lap of tea and have it out right here."

Bent seemed to hesitate; but at length he rose, put back the matting that screened the inner room, and said a word to the proprietor. Presently a scrofulous boy with gazelle eyes brought a brass tray bearing glasses and pipes of *kif*, gazed earnestly at the stranger in the linen duster, and slid back behind the matting.

"Of course," Bent began, "a good many people know I am a Baptist missionary"—("*No?*" from Spink, incredulously)—"but in the crowd of the bazaar they don't notice me, and I hear things. . . ."

"Golly! I should suppose you did."

"I mean, things that may be useful. You know Mr. Blandhorn's idea. . . ."

A tinge of respectful commiseration veiled the easy impudence of the drummer's look. "The old man still here, is he?"

"Oh, yes; of course. He will never leave Eloued."

"And the missus—?"

Bent again lowered his naturally low voice. "She died—a year ago—of the climate. The doctor had warned her; but Mr. Blandhorn felt a call to remain here."

"And she wouldn't leave without him?"

"Oh, *she* felt a call too. . . . among the women. . . ."

Spink pondered. "How many years you been here, Willard?"

"Ten next July," the other responded, as if he had added up the weeks and months so often that the reply was always on his lips.

"And the old man?"

"Twenty-five last April. We had planned a celebration. . . . before Mrs. Blandhorn died. There was to have been a testimonial offered. . . . but, owing to her death, Mr. Blandhorn preferred to devote the sum to our dispensary."

"I see. How much?" said Spink sharply.

"It wouldn't seem much to you. I believe about fifty *pesetas*. . . . ."

"Two *pesetas* a year? Lucky the Society looks after you, ain't it?"

Willard Bent met his ironic glance steadily. "We're not here to trade," he said with dignity.

"No—that's right too—" Spink reddened slightly. "Well, all I meant was—look at here, Willard, we're old friends, even if I did go wrong, as I suppose you'd call it. I was in this thing near on a year myself, and what always tormented me was this: *What does it all amount to?*"

"Amount to?"

"Yes. I mean, what's the results? Supposing you was a fisherman. Well, if you fished a bit of river year after year, and never had a nibble, you'd do one of two things, wouldn't you? Move away—or lie about it. See?"

Bent nodded without speaking. Spink set down his glass and busied himself with the lighting of his long slender pipe. "Say, this mint-julep feels like old times," he remarked.

Bent continued to gaze frowningly into his untouched glass. At length he swallowed the sweet decoction at a gulp, and turned to his companion.

"I'd never lie. . . ." he murmured. "Well—"

"I'm—I'm still—waiting. . . ."

"Waiting—?"

"Yes. The wind bloweth where it listeth. If St. Paul had stopped to count...in Corinth, say. As I take it—" he looked long and passionately at the drummer—"as I take it, the thing is to *be* St. Paul."

Harry Spink remained unimpressed. "That's all talk—I heard all that when I was here before. What I want to know is: What's your bag? How many?"

"It's difficult—"

"I see: like the pigs. They run around so!"

Both the young men were silent, Spink pulling at his pipe, the other sitting with bent head, his eyes obstinately fixed on the beaten floor. At length Spink rose and tapped the missionary on the shoulder.

"Say—s'posin' we take a look around Corinth? I got to get onto my job tomorrow, but I'd like to take a turn round the old place first."

Willard Bent rose also. He felt singularly old and tired, and his mind was full of doubt as to what he ought to do. If he refused to accompany Harry Spink, a former friend and fellow-worker, it might look like running away from his questions...

They went out together.

2

The bazaar was seething. It seemed impossible that two more people should penetrate the throng of beggars, pilgrims, traders, slave-women, water-sellers, hawkers of dates and sweetmeats, leather-gaitered country-people carrying bunches of hens head-downward, jugglers' touts from the market-place, Jews in black *caftans* and greasy turbans, and scrofulous children reaching up to the high counters to fill their jars and baskets. But every now and then the Arab "Look out!" made the crowd divide and flatten itself against the stalls, and a long line of donkeys loaded with water-barrels or bundles of reeds, a string of musk-scented camels swaying their necks like horizontal question marks, or a great man perched on a pink-saddled mule and followed by slaves and clients, swept through the narrow passage without other peril to the pedestrians than that of a fresh exchange of vermin.

As the two young men drew back to make way for one of these processions, Willard Bent lifted his head and looked at his friend with a smile. "That's what Mr. Blandhorn says we ought to remember—it's one of his favourite images."

"What is?" asked Harry Spink, following with attentive gaze the movements of a young Jewess whose uncovered face and bright head-dress stood out against a group of muffled Arab women.

Instinctively Willard's voice took on a hortatory roll.

"Why, the way this dense mass of people, so heedless, so preoccupied, is imperceptibly penetrated—"

"By a handful of asses? That's so. But the asses have got some kick in 'em, remember!"

The missionary flushed to the edge of his *fez*, and his mild eyes grew dim. It was the old story: Harry Spink invariably got the better of him in bandying words—and the interpretation of allegories had never been his strong point. Mr. Blandhorn always managed to make them sound unanswerable, whereas on his disciple's lips they fell to pieces at a touch. What *was* it that Willard always left out?

A mournful sense of his unworthiness overcame him, and with it the discouraged vision of all the long months and years spent in the struggle with heat and dust and flies and filth and wickedness, the long lonely years of his youth that would never come back to him. It was the vision he most dreaded, and turning from it he tried to forget himself in watching his friend.

"Golly! The vacuum-cleaner ain't been round since my last visit," Mr. Spink observed, as they slipped in a mass of offal beneath a butcher's stall. "Let's get into another *soukh*—the flies here beat me."

They turned into another long lane chequered with a criss-cross of black reed-shadows. It was the saddlers' quarter, and here an even thicker crowd wriggled and swayed between the cramped stalls hung with bright leather and spangled ornaments.

"Say! It might be a good idea to import some of this stuff for Fourth of July processions—Knights of Pythias and Secret Societies' kinder thing," Spink mused, pausing before the brilliant spectacle. At the same moment a lad in an almond-green *caftan* sidled up and touched his arm.

Willard's face brightened. "Ah, that's little Ahmed—you don't remember him? Surely—the water-carrier's boy. Mrs. Blandhorn saved his mother's life when he was born, and he still comes to prayers. Yes, Ahmed, this is your old friend Mr. Spink."

Ahmed raised prodigious lashes from seraphic eyes and reverently surveyed the face of his old friend. "Me 'member."

"Hullo, old chap. . . . why, of course. . . . so do I," the drummer beamed. The missionary laid a brotherly hand on the boy's shoulder. It was really providential that Ahmed—whom they hadn't seen at the Mission for more weeks than Willard cared to count—should have "happened by" at that moment: Willard took it as a rebuke to his own doubts.

"You'll be in this evening for prayers, won't you, Ahmed?" he said, as if Ahmed never failed them. "Mr. Spink will be with us."

"Yessir," said Ahmed with unction. He slipped from under Willard's hand, and outflanking the drummer approached him from the farther side.

"Show you Souss boys dance? Down to old Jewess's, Bab-el-Soukh," he breathed angelically.

Willard saw his companion turn from red to a wrathful purple.

"Get out, you young swine, you—do you hear me?"

Ahmed grinned, wavered and vanished, engulfed in the careless crowd. The young men walked on without speaking.

3

In the market-place they parted. Willard Bent, after some hesitation, had asked Harry Spink to come to the Mission that evening. "You'd better come to supper—then we can talk quietly afterward. Mr. Blandhorn will want to see you," he suggested; and Mr. Spink had affably acquiesced.

The prayer-meeting was before supper, and Willard would have liked to propose that his friend should come to that also; but he did not dare. He said to himself that Harry Spink, who had been merely a lay assistant, might have lost the habit of reverence, and that it would be too painful to risk his scandalising Mr. Blandhorn. But that was only a sham reason; and Willard, with his incorrigible habit of self-exploration, fished up the real one from a lower depth. What he had most feared was that there would be no one at the meeting.

During Mrs. Blandhorn's lifetime there had been no reason for such apprehension: they could always count on a few people. Mrs. Blandhorn, who had studied medicine at Ann Arbor, Michigan, had early gained renown in Eloued by her miraculous healing powers. The dispensary, in those days, had been beset by anxious-eyed women who unwound skinny fig-coloured children from their dirty draperies; and there had even been a time when Mr. Blandhorn had appealed to the Society for a young lady missionary to assist his wife. But, for reasons not quite clear to Willard Bent, Mrs. Blandhorn, a thin-lipped determined little woman, had energetically opposed the coming of this youthful "Sister," and had declared that their Jewish maid-servant, old Myriem, could give her all the aid she needed.

Mr. Blandhorn yielded, as he usually did—as he had yielded, for instance, when one day, in a white inarticulate fury, his wife had banished her godson, little Ahmed (whose life she had saved), and issued orders that he should never show himself again except at prayer-meeting, and accompanied by his father. Mrs. Blandhorn, small, silent and passionate, had always—as Bent made out in his long retrospective musings—ended by having her way in the conflicts that occasionally shook the monotony of life at the Mission. After her death the young man had even suspected, beneath his superior's sincere and vehement sorrow, a lurking sense of relief. Mr. Blandhorn had snuffed the air of freedom, and had been, for the moment, slightly intoxicated by it. But not for long. Very soon his wife's loss made itself felt as a lasting void.

She had been (as Spink would have put it) "the whole show"; had led, inspired, organised her husband's work, held it together, and given it the brave front it presented to the unheeding heathen. Now the heathen had almost entirely fallen away, and the too evident inference was that they had come rather for Mrs. Blandhorn's pills than for her husband's preaching. Neither of the missionaries had avowed this discovery to the other, but to Willard at least it was implied in all the circumlocutions and evasions of their endless talks.

The young man's situation had been greatly changed by Mrs. Blandhorn's death. His superior had grown touchingly dependent on him. Their conversation, formerly confined to parochial matters, now ranged from abstruse doctrinal problems to the question of how to induce Myriem, who had deplorably "relapsed," to keep the kitchen cleaner and spend less time on the roofs. Bent felt that Mr. Blandhorn needed him at every moment, and that, during any prolonged absence, something vaguely "unfortunate" might happen at the Mission.

"I'm glad Spink has come; it will do him good to see somebody from outside," Willard thought, nervously hoping that Spink (a good fellow at bottom) would not trouble Mr. Blandhorn by any of his "unsettling" questions.

At the end of a labyrinth of lanes, on the farther side of the Jewish quarter, a wall of heat-cracked clay bore the inscription: "American Evangelical Mission." Underneath it a door opened into a court where an old woman in a bright head-dress sat under a fig-tree pounding something in a mortar.

She looked up, and, rising, touched Bent's draperies with her lips. Her small face, withered as a dry *medlar*, was full of an ancient wisdom: Mrs. Blandhorn had certainly been right in trusting Myriem.

A narrow house-front looked upon the court. Bent climbed the stairs to Mr. Blandhorn's study. It was a small room with a few dog-eared books on a set of rough shelves, the table at which Mr. Blandhorn wrote his reports for the Society, and a mattress covered with a bit of faded carpet, on which he slept. Near the window stood Mrs. Blandhorn's sewing-machine; it had never been moved since her death.

The missionary was sitting in the middle of the room, in the rocking chair which had also been his wife's. His large veined hands were clasped about its arms and his head rested against a patch-work cushion tied to the back by a shoe-lace. His mouth was slightly open, and a deep breath, occasionally rising to a whistle, proceeded with rhythmic regularity from his delicately-cut nostrils. Even surprised in sleep he was a fine man to look upon; and when, at the sound of Bent's approach, he opened his eyes and pulled himself out of his chair, he became magnificent.

He had taken off his turban, and thrown a handkerchief over his head, which was shaved like an Arab's for coolness. His long beard was white, with the smoker's yellow tinge about the lips; but his eyebrows were jet-black, arched and restless. The grey eyes beneath them shed a mild benedictory beam, confirmed by the smile of a mouth which might have seemed weak if the beard had not so nearly concealed it. But the forehead menaced, fulminated or awed with the ever-varying play of the eyebrows. Willard Bent never beheld that forehead without thinking of Sinai.

Mr. Blandhorn brushed some shreds of tobacco from his white *djellabah* and looked impressively at his assistant.

"The heat is really overwhelming," he said, as if excusing himself. He readjusted his turban, and then asked: "Is everything ready downstairs?"

Bent assented, and they went down to the long bare room where the prayer-meetings were held. In Mrs. Blandhorn's day it had also served as the dispensary, and a cupboard containing drugs and bandages stood against the wall under the text: "*Come unto me, all ye that labour and are heavy laden.*"

Myriem, abandoning her mortar, was vaguely tidying the Arab tracts and leaflets that lay on the divan against the wall. At one end of the room stood a table covered with a white cloth, with a Bible lying on it; and to the left a sort of pulpit-lectern, from which Mr. Blandhorn addressed his flock. In the doorway squatted Ayoub, a silent grey-headed negro; Bent, on his own arrival at Eloued, ten years earlier, had found him there in the same place and the same attitude. Ayoub was supposed to be a rescued slave from the Soudan, and was shown to visitors as "our first convert." He manifested no interest at the approach of the missionaries, but continued to gaze out into the sun-baked court cut in half by the shadow of the fig-tree.

Mr. Blandhorn, after looking about the empty room as if he were surveying the upturned faces of an attentive congregation, placed himself at the lectern, put on his spectacles, and turned over the pages of his prayer-book. Then he knelt and bowed his head in prayer. His devotions ended, he rose and seated himself in the cane arm-chair that faced the lectern. Willard Bent sat opposite in another armchair. Mr. Blandhorn leaned back, breathing heavily, and passing his hand-kerchief over his face and brow. Now and then he drew out his watch, now and then he said: "The heat is really overwhelming."

Myriem had drifted back to her fig-tree, and the sound of the pestle mingled with the drone of flies on the window-pane. Occasionally the curses of a muleteer or the rhythmic chant of a water-carrier broke the silence; once there came from a neighbouring roof the noise of a short cat-like squabble ending in female howls; then the afternoon heat laid its leaden hush on all things.

Mr. Blandhorn opened his mouth and slept.

Willard Bent, watching him, thought with wonder and admiration of his past. What had he not seen, what secrets were not hidden in his bosom? By dint of sheer "sticking it out" he had acquired to the younger man a sort of visible sanctity. Twenty-five years of Eloued! He had known the old mad torturing *sultan*, he had seen, after the defeat of the rebels, the long line of prisoners staggering in under a torrid sky, chained wrist to wrist, and dragging between them the putrefying bodies of those who had died on the march.

He had seen the Great Massacre, when the rivers were red with French blood, and the Blandhorns had hidden an officer's wife and children in the rat-haunted drain under the court; he had known robbery and murder and intrigue, and all the dark maleficence of Africa; and he remained as serene, as confident and guileless, as on the day when he had first set foot on that evil soil, saying to himself (as he had told Willard): "*I will tread upon the lion and the adder, the young lion and the dragon will I tread under foot.*"

Willard Bent hated Africa; but it awed and fascinated him. And as he contemplated the splendid old man sleeping opposite him, so mysterious, so childlike and so weak (Mrs. Blandhorn had left him no doubts on that point), the disciple marvelled at the power of the faith which had armed his master with a sort of infantile strength against such dark and manifold perils.

Suddenly a shadow fell in the doorway, and Bent, roused from his dream, saw Harry Spink tiptoeing past the unmoved Ayoub. The drummer paused and looked with astonishment from one of the missionaries to the other. "Say," he asked, "is prayer-meeting over? I thought I'd be round in time."

He spoke seriously, even respectfully; it was plain that he felt flippancy to be out of place. But Bent suspected a lurking malice under his astonishment: he was sure Harry Spink had come to "count heads."

Mr. Blandhorn, wakened by the voice, stood up heavily.

"Harry Spink! Is it possible you are amongst us?"

"Why, yes, sir—I'm amongst. Didn't Willard tell you? I guess Willard Bent's ashamed of me."

Spink, with a laugh, shook Mr. Blandhorn's hand, and glanced about the empty room.

"I'm only here for a day or so—on business. Willard'll explain. But I wanted to come round to meeting—like old times. Sorry it's over."

The missionary looked at him with a grave candour. "It's not over—it has not begun. The overwhelming heat has probably kept away our little flock."

"I see," interpolated Spink.

"But now," continued Mr. Blandhorn with majesty, "that two or three are gathered together in His name, there is no reason why we should wait.—Myriem! Ayoub!"

He took his place behind the lectern and began: "Almighty and merciful Father—"

4

The night was exceedingly close. Willard Bent, after Spink's departure, had undressed and stretched himself on his camp bed; but the mosquitoes roared like lions, and lying down made him more wakeful.

"In any Christian country," he mused, "this would mean a thunderstorm and a cool-off. Here it just means months and months more of the same thing." And he thought enviously of Spink, who, in two or three days, his "deal" concluded, would be at sea again, heading for the north.

Bent was honestly distressed at his own state of mind: he had feared that Harry Spink would "unsettle" Mr. Blandhorn, and, instead, it was he himself who had been unsettled. Old slumbering distrusts and doubts, bursting through his surface-apathy, had shot up under the drummer's ironic eye. It was not so much Spink, individually, who had loosened the crust of Bent's indifference; it was the fact of feeling his whole problem suddenly viewed and judged from the outside. At Eloued, he was aware, nobody, for a long time, had thought much about the missionaries. The French authorities were friendly, the *pacha* was tolerant, the American Consul at Mogador had always stood by them in any small difficulties. But beyond that they were virtually non-existent. Nobody's view of life was really affected by their presence in the great swarming mysterious city: if they should pack up and leave that night, the story-tellers of the market would not interrupt their tales, or one less bargain be struck in the bazaar. Ayoub would still doze in the door, and old Myriem continue her secret life on the roofs. . . .

The roofs were of course forbidden to the missionaries, as they are to men in all Moslem cities. But the Mission-house stood close to the walls, and Mr. Blandhorn's room, across the passage, gave on a small terrace overhanging the court of a *caravansary* upon which it was no sin to look. Willard wondered if it were any cooler on the terrace.

Someone tapped on his open door, and Mr. Blandhorn, in turban and *caftan*, entered the room, shading a small lamp.

"My dear Willard—can you sleep?"

"No, sir." The young man stumbled to his feet.

"Nor I. The heat is really. . . . Shall we seek relief on the terrace?"

Bent followed him, and having extinguished the lamp Mr. Blandhorn led the way out. He dragged a strip of matting to the edge of the parapet, and the two men sat down on it side by side.

There was no moon, but a sky so full of stars that the city was outlined beneath it in great blue-grey masses. The air was motionless, but every now and then a wandering tremor stirred it and died out. Close under the parapet lay the bales and saddle-packs of the caravansary, between vaguer heaps, presumably of sleeping camels. In one corner, the star-glitter picked out the shape of a trough brimming with water, and stabbed it with long silver beams. Beyond the court rose the crenulations of the city walls, and above them one palm stood up like a tree of bronze.

"Africa—" sighed Mr. Blandhorn.

Willard Bent started at the secret echo of his own thoughts.

"Yes. Never anything else, sir—"

"Ah—" said the old man.

A tang-tang of stringed instruments, accompanied by the lowing of an earthenware drum, rose exasperatingly through the night. It was the kind of noise that, one knew, had been going on for hours before one began to notice it, and would go on, unchecked and unchanging, for endless hours more: like the heat, like the drought—like Africa.

Willard slapped at a mosquito.

"It's a party at the wool-merchant's, Myriem tells me," Mr. Blandhorn remarked. It really seemed as if, that night, the thoughts of the two men met without the need of words. Willard Bent was aware that, for both, the casual phrase had called up all the details of the scene: fat merchants in white bunches on their cushions, negresses coming and going with trays of sweets, champagne clandestinely poured, ugly singing-girls yowling, slim boys in petticoats dancing—perhaps little Ahmed among them.

"I went down to the court just now. Ayoub has disappeared," Mr. Blandhorn continued. "Of course. When I heard in the bazaar that a black caravan was in from the south I knew he'd be off..."

Mr. Blandhorn lowered his voice. "Willard—have you reason to think...that Ayoub joins in their rites?"

"Myriem has always said he was a Hamatcha, sir. Look at those queer cuts and scars on him. . . . It's a much bloodier sect than the Aissaouas."

Through the nagging throb of the instruments came a sound of human wailing, cadenced, terrible, relentless, carried from a long way off on a lift of the air. Then the air died, and the wailing with it.

"From somewhere near the Potter's Field. . . .there's where the caravan is camping," Willard murmured.

The old man made no answer. He sat with his head bowed, his veined hands grasping his knees; he seemed to his disciple to be whispering fragments of Scripture.

"Willard, my son, this is our fault," he said at length.

"What—? Ayoub?"

"Ayoub is a poor ignorant creature, hardly more than an animal. Even when he witnessed for Jesus I was not very sure the Word reached him. I refer to—to what Harry Spink said this evening...It has kept me from sleeping, Willard Bent."

"Yes—I know, sir."

"Harry Spink is a worldly-minded man. But he is not a bad man. He did a manly thing when he left us, since he did not feel the call. But we have felt the call, Willard, you and I—and when a man like Spink puts us a question such as he put this evening we ought to be able to answer it. And we ought not to want to avoid answering it."

"You mean when he said: '*What is there in it for Jesus?*'"

"The phrase was irreverent, but the meaning reached me. He meant, I take it: 'What have your long years here profited to Christ?' You understood it so—?"

"Yes. He said to me in the bazaar: 'What's your bag?'"

Mr. Blandhorn sighed heavily. For a few minutes Willard fancied he had fallen asleep; but he lifted his head and, stretching his hand out, laid it on his disciple's arm.

"The Lord chooses His messengers as it pleaseth Him: I have been awaiting this for a long time." The young man felt his arm strongly grasped. "Willard, you have been much to me all these years; but that is nothing. All that matters is what you are to Christ...and the test of that, at this moment, is your willingness to tell me the exact truth, as you see it."

Willard Bent felt as if he were a very tall building, and his heart a lift suddenly dropping down from the roof to the cellar. He stirred nervously, releasing his arm, and cleared his throat; but he made no answer. Mr. Blandhorn went on.

"Willard, this is the day of our accounting—of *my* accounting. What have I done with my twenty-five years in Africa? I might deceive myself as long as my wife lived—I cannot now." He added, after a pause: "Thank heaven *she* never doubted. . . ."

The younger man, with an inward shiver, remembered some of Mrs. Blandhorn's confidences. "I suppose that's what marriage is," he mused—"just a fog, like everything else."

Aloud he asked: "Then why should you doubt, sir?"

"Because my eyes have been opened—"

"By Harry Spink?" the disciple sneered.

The old man raised his hand. "'*Out of the mouths of babes*—' But it is not Harry Spink who first set me thinking. He has merely loosened my tongue. He has been the humble instrument compelling me to exact the truth of you."

Again Bent felt his heart dropping down a long dark shaft. He found no words at the bottom of it, and Mr. Blandhorn continued: "The truth and the whole truth, Willard Bent. We have failed—*I* have failed. We have not reached the souls of these people. Those who still come to us do so from interested motives—or, even if I do some few of them an injustice, if there is in some a blind yearning for the light, is there one among them whose eyes we have really opened?"

Willard Bent sat silent, looking up and down the long years, as if to summon from the depths of memory some single incident that should permit him to say there was.

"You don't answer, my poor young friend. Perhaps you have been clearer-sighted; perhaps you saw long ago that we were not worthy of our hire."

"I never thought that of you, sir!"

"Nor of yourself? For we have been one—or so I have believed—in all our hopes and efforts. Have you been satisfied with *your* results?"

Willard saw the dialectical trap, but some roused force in him refused to evade it. "No, sir—God knows."

"Then I am answered. We have failed: Africa has beaten us. It has always been my way, as you know, Willard, to face the truth squarely," added the old man who had lived so long in dreams; "and now that *this* truth has been borne in on me, painful as it is, I must act on it... act in accordance with its discovery."

He drew a long breath, as if oppressed by the weight of his resolution, and sat silent for a moment, fanning his face with a corner of his white draperies.

"And here too—here too I must have your help, Willard," he began presently, his hand again weighing on the young man's arm. "I will tell you the conclusions I have reached; and you must answer me—as you would answer your Maker."

"Yes, sir."

The old man lowered his voice. "It is our lukewarmness, Willard—it is nothing else. We have not witnessed for Christ as His saints and martyrs witnessed for Him. What have we done to fix the attention of these people, to convince them of our zeal, to overwhelm them with the irresistibleness of the Truth? Answer me on your word—what have we done?"

Willard pondered. "But the saints and martyrs. . . . were persecuted, sir."

"*Persecuted!* You have spoken the word I wanted."

"But the people here," Willard argued, "don't *want* to persecute anybody. They're not fanatical unless you insult their religion."

Mr. Blandhorn's grasp grew tighter. "Insult their religion! That's it.. . . .tonight you find just the words. . . ."

Willard felt his arm shake with the tremor that passed through the other's body. "The saints and martyrs insulted the religion of the heathen—they spat on it, Willard—they rushed into the temples and knocked down the idols. They said to the heathen: '*Turn away your faces from all your abominations*'; and after the manner of men they fought with beasts at Ephesus. What is the Church on earth called? The Church Militant! You and I are soldiers of the Cross."

The missionary had risen and stood leaning against the parapet, his right arm lifted as if he spoke from a pulpit. The music at the wool-merchant's had ceased, but now and then, through the midnight silence, there came an echo of ritual howls from the Potters' Field.

Willard was still seated, his head thrown back against the parapet, his eyes raised to Mr. Blandhorn. Following the gesture of the missionary's lifted hand, from which the muslin fell back like the sleeve of a surplice, the young man's gaze was led upward to another white figure, hovering small and remote above their heads. It was a *muezzin* leaning from his airy balcony to drop on the blue-grey masses of the starlit city the cry: "Only *Allah* is great."

Mr. Blandhorn saw the white figure too, and stood facing it with motionless raised arm.

"Only Christ is great, only Christ crucified!" he suddenly shouted in Arabic with all the strength of his broad lungs.

The figure paused, and seemed to Willard to bend over, as if peering down in their direction; but a moment later it had moved to the other corner of the balcony, and the cry fell again on the sleeping roofs:

"*Allah—Allah—only Allah!*"

"Christ—Christ—only Christ crucified!" roared Mr. Blandhorn, exalted with wrath and shaking his fist at the aerial puppet.

The puppet once more paused and peered; then it moved on and vanished behind the flank of the minaret.

The missionary, still towering with lifted arm, dusky-faced in the starlight, seemed to Willard to have grown in majesty and stature. But presently his arm fell and his head sank into his hands. The young man knelt down, hiding his face also, and they prayed in silence, side by side, while from the farther corners of the minaret, less audibly, fell the *infidel* call.

Willard, his prayer ended, looked up, and saw that the old man's garments were stirred as if by a ripple of air. But the air was quite still, and the disciple perceived that the tremor of the muslin was communicated to it by Mr. Blandhorn's body.

"He's trembling—trembling all over. He's afraid of something. What's he afraid of?" And in the same breath Willard had answered his own question: "He's afraid of what he's made up his mind to do."

5

Two days later Willard Bent sat in the shade of a ruined tomb outside the Gate of the Graves, and watched the people streaming in to Eloued. It was the eve of the feast of the local saint, Sidi Oman, who slept in a corner of the Great Mosque, under a segment of green-tiled cupola, and was held in deep reverence by the country people, many of whom belonged to the powerful fraternity founded in his name.

The ruin stood on a hillock beyond the outer wall. From where the missionary sat he overlooked the fortified gate and the irregular expanse of the Potters' Field, with its primitive furnaces built into hollows of the ground, between ridges shaded by stunted olive-trees. On the farther side of the trail which the pilgrims followed on entering the gate lay a sun-blistered expanse dotted with crooked grave-stones, where hucksters traded, and the humblest caravans camped in a waste of refuse, offal and stripped date-branches. A cloud of dust, perpetually subsiding and gathering again, hid these sordid details from Bent's eyes, but not from his imagination.

"Nowhere in Eloued," he thought with a shudder, "are the flies as fat and blue as they are inside that gate."

But this was a fugitive reflection: his mind was wholly absorbed in what had happened in the last forty-eight hours, and what was likely to happen in the next.

"To think," he mused, "that after ten years I don't really know him. . . .A labourer in the Lord's vineyard—shows how much good I am!"

His thoughts were moody and oppressed with fear. Never, since his first meeting with Mr. Blandhorn, had he pondered so deeply the problem of his superior's character. He tried to deduce from the past some inference as to what Mr. Blandhorn was likely to do next; but, as far as he knew, there was nothing in the old man's previous history resembling the midnight scene on the Mission terrace.

That scene had already had its repercussion.

On the following morning, Willard, drifting as usual about the bazaar, had met a friendly French official, who, taking him aside, had told him there were strange reports abroad—which he hoped Mr. Bent would be able to deny. . . .In short, as it had never been Mr. Blandhorn's policy to offend the native population, or insult their religion, the Administration was confident that. . . .

Surprised by Willard's silence, and visibly annoyed at being obliged to pursue the subject, the friendly official, growing graver, had then asked what had really occurred; and, on Willard's replying, had charged him with an earnest recommendation to his superior—a warning, if necessary—that the government would not, under any circumstances, tolerate a repetition. . . . "But I daresay it was the heat?" he concluded; and Willard weakly acquiesced.

He was ashamed now of having done so; yet, after all, how did he know it was not the heat? A heavy sanguine man like Mr. Blandhorn would probably never quite accustom himself to the long strain of the African summer. "Or his wife's death—" he had murmured to the sympathetic official, who smiled with relief at the suggestion.

And now he sat overlooking the enigmatic city, and asking himself again what he really knew of his superior. Mr. Blandhorn had come to Eloued as a young man, extremely poor, and dependent on the pittance which the Missionary Society at that time gave to its representatives. To ingratiate himself among the people (the expression was his own), and also to earn a few *pesetas*, he had worked as a carpenter in the bazaar, first in the *soukh* of the ploughshares and then in that of the cabinet-makers.

His skill in carpentry had not been great, for his large eloquent hands were meant to wave from a pulpit, and not to use the adze or the chisel; but he had picked up a little Arabic (Willard always marvelled that it remained so little), and had made many acquaintances— and, as he thought, some converts. At any rate, no one, either then or later, appeared to wish him ill, and during the massacre his house had been respected, and the insurgents had even winked at the aid he had courageously given to the French.

Yes—he had certainly been courageous. There was in him, in spite of his weaknesses and his vacillations, a streak of moral heroism that perhaps only waited its hour. . . But hitherto his principle had always been that the missionary must win converts by kindness, by tolerance, and by the example of a blameless life.

Could it really be Harry Spink's question that had shaken him in this belief? Or was it the long-accumulated sense of inefficiency that so often weighed on his disciple? Or was it simply the call—did it just mean that their hour had come?

Shivering a little in spite of the heat, Willard pulled himself together and descended into the city. He had been seized with a sudden desire to know what Mr. Blandhorn was about, and avoiding the crowd he hurried back by circuitous lanes to the Mission. On the way he paused at a certain corner and looked into a court full of the murmur of water. Beyond it was an arcade detached against depths of shadow, in which a few lights glimmered. White figures, all facing one way, crouched and touched their foreheads to the tiles, the soles of their bare feet, wet with recent ablutions, turning up as their bodies swayed forward. Willard caught the scowl of a beggar on the threshold, and hurried past the forbidden scene.

He found Mr. Blandhorn in the meeting-room, tying up Ayoub's head.

"I do it awkwardly," the missionary mumbled, a safety-pin between his teeth. "Alas, my hands are not *hers*."

"What's he done to himself?" Willard growled; and above the bandaged head Mr. Blandhorn's expressive eyebrows answered.

There was a dark stain on the back of Ayoub's faded shirt, and another on the blue scarf he wore about his head.

"Ugh—it's like cats slinking back after a gutter-fight," the young man muttered.

Ayoub wound his scarf over the bandages, shambled back to the doorway, and squatted down to watch the fig-tree.

The missionaries looked at each other across the empty room.

"What's the use, sir?" was on Willard's lips; but instead of speaking he threw himself down on the divan. There was to be no prayer-meeting that afternoon, and the two men sat silent, gazing at the back of Ayoub's head. A smell of disinfectants hung in the heavy air. . . .

"Where's Myriem?" Willard asked, to say something.

"I believe she had a ceremony of some sort. . . . a family affair. . . ."

"A circumcision, I suppose?"

Mr. Blandhorn did not answer, and Willard was sorry he had made the suggestion. It would simply serve as another reminder of their failure. . . .

He stole a furtive glance at Mr. Blandhorn, nervously wondering if the time had come to speak of the French official's warning. He had put off doing so, half-hoping it would not be necessary. The old man seemed so calm, so like his usual self, that it might be wiser to let the matter drop. Perhaps he had already forgotten the scene on the terrace; or perhaps he thought he had sufficiently witnessed for the Lord in shouting his insult to the *muezzin*. But Willard did not really believe this: he remembered the tremor which had shaken Mr. Blandhorn after the challenge, and he felt sure it was not a retrospective fear.

"Our friend Spink has been with me," said Mr. Blandhorn suddenly. "He came in soon after you left."

"Ah? I'm sorry I missed him. I thought he'd gone, from his not coming in yesterday."

"No; he leaves tomorrow morning for Mogador." Mr Blandhorn paused, still absently staring at the back of Ayoub's neck; then he added: "I have asked him to take you with him."

"To take me—Harry Spink? In his automobile?" Willard gasped. His heart began to beat excitedly.

"Yes. You'll enjoy the ride. It's a long time since you've been away, and you're looking a little pulled down."

"You're very kind, sir: so is Harry." He paused. "But I'd rather not."

Mr. Blandhorn, turning slightly, examined him between half-dropped lids.

"I have business for you—with the Consul," he said with a certain sternness. "I don't suppose you will object—"

"Oh, of course not." There was another pause. "Could you tell me—give me an idea—of what the business is, sir?"

It was Mr. Blandhorn's turn to appear perturbed. He coughed, passed his hand once or twice over his beard, and again fixed his gaze on Ayoub's inscrutable nape.

"I wish to send a letter to the Consul."

"A letter? If it's only a letter, couldn't Spink take it?"

"Undoubtedly. I might also send it by post—if I cared to transmit it in that manner. I presumed," added Mr. Blandhorn with threatening brows, "that you would understand I had my reasons—"

"Oh, in that case, of course, sir—" Willard hesitated, and then spoke with a rush. "I saw Lieutenant Lourdenay in the bazaar yesterday—" he began.

When he had finished his tale Mr. Bland-horn meditated for a long time in silence. At length he spoke in a calm voice. "And what did you answer, Willard?"

"I—I said I'd tell you—"

"Nothing more?"

"No. Nothing."

"Very well. We'll talk of all this more fully. . . . when you get back from Mogador. Remember that Mr. Spink will be here before sunrise. I advised him to get away as early as possible on account of the Feast of Sidi Oman. It's always a poor day for foreigners to be seen about the streets."

66

At a quarter before four on the morning of the Feast of Sidi Oman, Willard Bent stood waiting at the door of the Mission.

He had taken leave of Mr. Blandhorn the previous night, and stumbled down the dark stairs on bare feet, his bundle under his arm, just as the sky began to whiten around the morning star.

The air was full of a mocking coolness which the first ray of the sun would burn up; and a hush as deceptive lay on the city that was so soon to blaze with religious frenzy. Ayoub lay curled up on his doorstep like a dog, and old Myriem, presumably, was still stretched on her mattress on the roof.

What a day for a flight across the desert in Harry's tough little car! And after the hours of heat and dust and glare, how good, at twilight, to see the cool welter of the Atlantic, a spent sun dropping into it, and the rush of the stars. . . . Dizzy with the vision, Willard leaned against the door-post with closed eyes.

A subdued hoot aroused him, and he hurried out to the car, which was quivering and growling at the nearest corner. The drummer nodded a welcome, and they began to wind cautiously between sleeping animals and huddled heaps of humanity till they reached the nearest gate.

On the waste land beyond the walls the people of the caravans were already stirring, and pilgrims from the hills streaming across the palmetto scrub under emblazoned banners. As the sun rose the air took on a bright transparency in which distant objects became unnaturally near and vivid, like pebbles seen through clear water: a little turban-shaped tomb far off in the waste looked as lustrous as ivory, and a tiled minaret in an angle of the walls seemed to be carved out of turquoise. How Eloued lied to eyes looking back on it at sunrise!

"Something wrong," said Harry Spink, putting on the brake and stopping in the thin shade of a cork-tree. They got out and Willard leaned against the tree and gazed at the red walls of Eloued. They were already about two miles from the town, and all around them was the wilderness. Spink shoved his head into the bonnet, screwed and greased and hammered, and finally wiped his hands on a black rag and called out: "I thought so—. Jump in!"

Willard did not move.

"Hurry up, old man. She's all right, I tell you. It was just the carburettor."

The missionary fumbled under his draperies and pulled out Mr.

Blandhorn's letter.

"Will you see that the Consul gets this tomorrow?"

"Will I—what the hell's the matter, Willard?" Spink dropped his rag and stared.

"I'm not coming. I never meant to."

The young men exchanged a long look.

"It's no time to leave Mr. Blandhorn—a day like this," Willard continued, moistening his dry lips.

Spink shrugged, and sounded a faint whistle. "Queer—!"

"What's queer?"

"He said just the same thing to me about *you*—wanted to get you out of Eloued on account of the goings on today. He said you'd been rather worked up lately about religious matters, and might do something rash that would get you both into trouble."

"Ah—" Willard murmured.

"And I believe you might, you know—you look sorter funny."

Willard laughed.

"Oh, come along," his friend urged, disappointed.

"I'm sorry—I can't. I had to come this far so that he wouldn't know. But now I've got to go back. Of course what he told you was just a joke—but I must be there today to see that nobody bothers him."

Spink scanned his companion's face with friendly flippant eyes. "Well, I give up—. What's the *use*, when he don't want you?—Say," he broke off, "what's the truth of that story about the old man's having insulted a *marabout* in a mosque night before last? It was all over the bazaar—"

Willard felt himself turn pale. "Not a *marabout*. It was—where did you hear it?" he stammered.

"All over—the way you hear stories in these places."

"Well—it's not true." Willard lifted his bundle from the motor and tucked it under his arm. "I'm sorry, Harry—I've got to go back," he repeated.

"What? The Call, eh?" The sneer died on Spink's lips, and he held out his hand. "Well, I'm sorry too. So long." He turned the crank, scrambled into his seat, and cried back over his shoulder: "What's the *use*, when he don't want you?"

Willard was already labouring home across the plain.

★★★★★★

After struggling along for half an hour in the sand he crawled under the shade of an abandoned well and sat down to ponder. Two courses were open to him, and he had not yet been able to decide between them. His first impulse was to go straight to the Mission, and present himself to Mr. Blandhorn. He felt sure, from what Spink had told him, that the old missionary had sent him away purposely, and the fact seemed to confirm his apprehensions. If Mr. Blandhorn wanted him away, it was not through any fear of his imprudence, but to be free from his restraining influence. But what act did the old man contemplate, in which he feared to involve his disciple? And if he were really resolved on some rash measure, might not Willard's unauthorized return merely serve to exasperate this resolve, and hasten whatever action he had planned?

The other step the young man had in mind was to go secretly to the French Administration, and there drop a hint of what he feared. It was the course his sober judgment commended. The echo of Spink's "What's the use?" was in his ears: it was the expression of his own secret doubt. What *was* the use? If dying could bring any of these darkened souls to the light. . . .well, that would have been different. But what least sign was there that it would do anything but rouse their sleeping blood-lust?

Willard was oppressed by the thought that had always lurked beneath his other doubts. They talked, he and Mr. Blandhorn, of the poor ignorant heathen—but were not they themselves equally ignorant in everything that concerned the heathen? What did they know of these people, of their antecedents, the origin of their beliefs and superstitions, the meaning of their habits and passions and precautions? Mr. Blandhorn seemed never to have been troubled by this question, but it had weighed on Willard ever since he had come across a quiet French ethnologist who was studying the tribes of the Middle Atlas. Two or three talks with this traveller—or listenings to him—had shown Willard the extent of his own ignorance.

He would have liked to borrow books, to read, to study; but he knew little French and no German, and he felt confusedly that there was in him no soil sufficiently prepared for facts so overwhelmingly new to root in it. . . .And the heat lay on him, and the little semblance of his missionary duties deluded him. . . . and he drifted. . . .

As for Mr. Blandhorn, he never read anything but the Scriptures, a volume of his own sermons (printed by subscription, to commemorate his departure for Morocco), and—occasionally—a back number of the missionary journal that arrived at Eloued at long intervals, in thick mouldy batches, consequently no doubts disturbed him, and Willard felt the hopelessness of grappling with an ignorance so much deeper and denser than his own. Whichever way his mind turned, it seemed to bring up against the blank wall of Harry Spink's; "What's the use?"

★★★★★★

He slipped through the crowds in the congested gateway, and made straight for the Mission. He had decided to go to the French Administration, but he wanted first to find out from the servants what Mr. Blandhorn was doing, and what his state of mind appeared to be.

The Mission door was locked, but Willard was not surprised; he knew the precaution was sometimes taken on feast days, though seldom so early. He rang, and waited impatiently for Myriem's old face in the crack; but no one came, and below his breath he cursed her with expurgated curses.

"Ayoub—*Ayoub!*" he cried, rattling at the door; but still no answer. Ayoub, apparently, was off too. Willard rang the bell again, giving the three long pulls of the "emergency call"; it was the summons which always roused Mr. Blandhorn. But no one came.

Willard shook and pounded, and hung on the bell till it tinkled its life out in a squeak. . . .but all in vain. The house was empty: Mr. Blandhorn was evidently out with the others.

Disconcerted, the young man turned, and plunged into the red clay purlieus behind the Mission. He entered a mud-hut where an emaciated dog, dozing on the threshold, lifted a recognizing lid, and let him by. It was the house of Ahmed's father, the water-carrier, and Willard knew it would be empty at that hour.

A few minutes later there emerged into the crowded streets a young American dressed in a black coat of vaguely clerical cut, with a soft felt hat shading his flushed cheek-bones, and a bead running up and down his nervous throat.

The bazaar was already full of a deep holiday rumour, like the rattle of wind in the palm-tops. The young man in the clerical coat, sharply examined as he passed by hundreds of long Arab eyes, slipped into the lanes behind the *soukhs*, and by circuitous passages gained the neighbourhood of the Great Mosque. His heart was hammering against his black coat, and under the buzz in his brain there boomed out insistently the old question: "What's the use?"

Suddenly, near the fountain that faced one of the doors of the Great Mosque, he saw the figure of a man dressed like himself. The

70

eyes of the two men met across the crowd, and Willard pushed his way to Mr. Blandhorn's side.

"Sir, why did you—why are you—? I'm back—I couldn't help it," he gasped out disconnectedly.

He had expected a vehement rebuke; but the old missionary only smiled on him sadly. "It was noble of you, Willard. . . . I understand. . ." He looked at the young man's coat. "We had the same thought—again—at the same hour." He paused, and drew Willard into the empty passage of a ruined building behind the fountain. "But what's the use,—what's the use?" he exclaimed.

The blood rushed to the young man's forehead. "Ah—then you feel it too?"

Mr. Blandhorn continued, grasping his arm: "I've been out—in this dress—ever since you left; I've hung about the doors of the Medersas, I've walked up to the very threshold of the Mosque, I've leaned against the wall of Sidi Oman's shrine; once the police warned me, and I pretended to go away. . . . but I came back. . . . I pushed up closer. . . . I stood in the doorway of the Mosque, and they saw me. . . . the people inside saw me. . . . and no one touched me. . . . I'm too harmless. . . . *they don't believe in me!*"

He broke off, and under his struggling eyebrows Willard saw the tears on his old lids.

The young man gathered courage. "But don't you see, sir, that that's the reason it's no use? We don't understand them any more than they do us; they know it, and all our witnessing for Christ will make no difference."

Mr. Blandhorn looked at him sternly. "Young man, no Christian has the right to say that."

Willard ignored the rebuke. "Come home, sir, come home. . . . it's no use. . . .."

"It was because I foresaw you would take this view that I sent you to Mogador. Since I was right," exclaimed Mr. Blandhorn, facing round on him fiercely, "how is it you have disobeyed me and come back?"

Willard was looking at him with new eyes. All his majesty seemed to have fallen from him with his Arab draperies. How short and heavy and weak he looked in his scant European clothes! The coat, tightly strained across the stomach, hung above it in loose wrinkles, and the ill-fitting trousers revealed their wearer's impressive legs as slightly bowed at the knees. This diminution in his physical prestige was strangely moving to his disciple. What was there left, with that gone—?

"Oh, do come home, sir," the young man groaned. "Of course they don't care what we do—of course—"

"Ah—" cried Mr. Blandhorn, suddenly dashing past him into the open.

The rumour of the crowd had become a sort of roaring chant. Over the thousands of bobbing heads that packed every cranny of the streets leading to the space before the Mosque there ran the mysterious sense of something new, invisible, but already imminent. Then, with the strange Oriental elasticity, the immense throng divided, and a new throng poured through it, headed by riders ritually draped, and overhung with banners which seemed to be lifted and floated aloft on the shouts of innumerable throats. It was the Pasha of Eloued coming to pray at the tomb of Sidi Oman.

Into this mass Mr. Blandhorn plunged and disappeared, while Willard Bent, for an endless minute, hung back in the shelter of the passage, the old "What's the use?" in his ears.

A hand touched his sleeve, and a cracked voice echoed the words. "What's the use, master?" It was old Myriem, clutching him with scared face and pulling out a limp *djellabah* from under her holiday shawl.

"I saw you. . . . Ahmed's father told me. . . ." (How everything was known in the bazaars!) "Here, put this on quick, and slip away. They won't trouble you. . . ."

"Oh, but they will—they *shall!*" roared Willard, in a voice unknown to his own ears, as he flung off the old woman's hand and, trampling on the *djellabah* in his flight, dashed into the crowd at the spot where it had swallowed up his master.

They would—they *should!* No more doubting and weighing and conjecturing! The sight of the weak unwieldy old man, so ignorant, so defenceless and so convinced, disappearing alone into that red furnace of fanaticism, swept from the disciple's mind every thought but the single passion of devotion.

That he lay down his life for his friend—If he couldn't bring himself to believe in any other reason for what he was doing, that one seemed suddenly to be enough. . . .

The crowd let him through, still apparently indifferent to his advance. Closer, closer he pushed to the doors of the Mosque, struggling and elbowing through a mass of people so densely jammed that the heat of their breathing was in his face, the rank taste of their bodies on his parched lips—closer, closer, till a last effort of his own thin body, which seemed a mere cage of ribs with a wild heart dashing against it, brought him to the doorway of the Mosque, where Mr. Blandhorn, his head thrown back, his arms crossed on his chest, stood steadily facing the heathen multitude.

As Willard reached his side their glances met, and the old man, glaring out under prophetic brows, whispered without moving his lips: "Now—*now!*"

Willard took it as a signal to follow, he knew not where or why: at that moment he had no wish to know.

Mr. Blandhorn, without waiting for an answer, had turned, and, doubling on himself, sprung into the great court of the Mosque. Willard breathlessly followed, the glitter of tiles and the blinding sparkle of fountains in his dazzled eyes...

The court was almost empty, the few who had been praying having shortened their devotions and joined the *pasha's* train, which was skirting the outer walls of the Mosque to reach the shrine of Sidi Oman. Willard was conscious of a moment of detached reconnoitring: once or twice, from the roof of a deserted college to which the government architect had taken him, he had looked down furtively on the forbidden scene, and his sense of direction told him that the black figure speeding across the blazing mirror of wet tiles was making for the hall where the *Koran* was expounded to students.

Even now, as he followed, through the impending sense of something dangerous and tremendous he had the feeling that after all perhaps no one would bother them, that all the effort of will pumped up by his storming heart to his lucid brain might conceivably end in some pitiful anti-climax in the French Administration offices.

"They'll treat us like whipped puppies—"

But Mr. Blandhorn had reached the school, had disappeared under its shadowy arcade, and emerged again into the blaze of sunlight, clutching a great parchment *Koran*.

"Ah," thought Willard, "*now—!*"

He found himself standing at the missionary's side, so close that they must have made one black blot against the white-hot quiver of tiles. Mr. Blandhorn lifted up the book and spoke.

"The God whom ye ignorantly worship, Him declare I unto you," he cried in halting Arabic.

A deep murmur came from the turbaned figures gathered under

the arcade of the Mosque. Swarthy faces lowered, eyes gleamed like agate, teeth blazed under snarling lips; but the group stood motionless, holding back, visibly restrained by the menace of the long arm of the Administration.

"Him declare I unto you—Christ crucified!" cried Mr. Blandhorn.

An old man, detaching himself from the group, advanced across the tiles and laid his hand on the missionary's arm. Willard recognised the *cadi* of the Mosque.

"You must restore the book," the *cadi* said gravely to Mr. Blandhorn, "and leave this court immediately; if not—"

He held out his hand to take the *Koran*. Mr. Blandhorn, in a flash, dodged the restraining arm, and, with a strange new elasticity of his cumbrous body, rolling and bouncing across the court between the dazed spectators, gained the gateway opening on the market-place behind the Mosque. The centre of the great dusty space was at the moment almost deserted. Mr. Blandhorn sprang forward, the *Koran* clutched to him, Willard panting at his heels, and the turbaned crowd after them, menacing but still visibly restrained.

In the middle of the square Mr. Blandhorn halted, faced about and lifted the *Koran* high above his head. Willard, rigid at his side, was obliquely conscious of the gesture, and at the same time aware that the free space about them was rapidly diminishing under the mounting tide of people swarming in from every quarter. The faces closest were no longer the gravely wrathful countenances of the Mosque, but lean fanatical masks of pilgrims, beggars, wandering "saints" and miracle-makers, and dark tribesmen of the hills careless of their creed but hot to join in the halloo against the hated stranger. Far off in the throng, bobbing like a float on the fierce sea of turbans, Willard saw the round brown face of a native officer frantically fighting his way through. Now and then the face bobbed nearer, and now and then a tug of the tide rolled it back.

Willard felt Mr. Blandhorn's touch on his arm.

"You're with me—?"

"Yes—"

The old man's voice sank and broke. "Say a word to. . . . strengthen me. . . . .I can't find any. . . . Willard," he whispered.

Willard's brain was a blank. But against the blank a phrase suddenly flashed out in letters of fire, and he turned and spoke it to his master. "*Say among the heathen that the Lord reigneth.*"

"Ah—." Mr. Blandhorn, with a gasp, drew himself to his full height and hurled the *Koran* down at his feet in the dung-strewn dust.

"Him, Him declare I unto you—Christ crucified!" he thundered: and to Willard, in a fierce aside: "Now spit!"

Dazed a moment, the young man stood uncertain; then he saw the old missionary draw back a step, bend forward, and deliberately spit upon the sacred pages.

"This. . . . is abominable. . . ." the disciple thought; and, sucking up the last drop of saliva from his dry throat, he also bent and spat.

"Now trample—*trample!*" commanded Mr. Blandhorn, his arms stretched out, towering black and immense, as if crucified against the flaming sky; and his foot came down on the polluted Book.

Willard, seized with the communicative frenzy, fell on his knees, tearing at the pages, and scattering them about him, smirched and defiled in the dust.

"Spit—spit! Trample—trample! . . . Christ! I see the heavens opened!" shrieked the old missionary, covering his eyes with his hands. But what he said next was lost to his disciple in the rising roar of the mob which had closed in on them. Far off, Willard caught a glimpse of the native officer's bobbing head, and then of Lieutenant Lourdenay's scared face. But a moment later he had veiled his own face from the sight of the struggle at his side. Mr. Blandhorn had fallen on his knees, and Willard heard him cry out once: "Sadie—*Sadie!*" It was Mrs. Blandhorn's name.

Then the young man was himself borne down, and darkness descended on him. Through it he felt the sting of separate pangs indescribable, melting at last into a general mist of pain. He remembered Stephen, and thought: "Now they're stoning me—" and tried to struggle up and reach out to Mr. Blandhorn...

But the market-place seemed suddenly empty, as though the throng of their assailants had been demons of the desert, the thin spirits of evil that dance on the noonday heat. Now the dusk seemed to have dispersed them, and Willard looked up and saw a quiet star above a wall, and heard the cry of the *muezzin* dropping down from a nearby minaret: "*Allah—Allah—*only *Allah* is great!"

Willard closed his eyes, and in his great weakness felt the tears run down between his lids. A hand wiped them away, and he looked again, and saw the face of Harry Spink stooping over him.

He supposed it was a dream-Spink, and smiled a little, and the dream smiled back.

"Where am I?" Willard wondered to himself; and the dream-Spink answered: "In the hospital, you infernal fool. I got back too late—"

"You came back—?"

"Of course. Lucky I did—I saw this morning you were off your base."

Willard, for a long time, lay still. Impressions reached him slowly, and he had to deal with them one by one, like a puzzled child.

At length he said: "Mr. Blandhorn—?" Spink bent his head, and his voice was grave in the twilight.

"They did for him in no time; I guess his heart was weak. I don't think he suffered. Anyhow, if he did he wasn't sorry; I know, because I saw his face before they buried him. . . . Now you lie still, and I'll get you out of this tomorrow," he commanded, waving a fly-cloth above Willard's sunken head.

Bewitched

1

The snow was still falling thickly when Orrin Bosworth, who farmed the land south of Lone-top, drove up in his cutter to Saul Rutledge's gate. He was surprised to see two other cutters ahead of him. From them descended two muffled figures. Bosworth, with increasing surprise, recognised Deacon Hibben, from North Ashmore, and Sylvester Brand, the widower, from the old Bearcliff farm on the way to Lonetop.

It was not often that anybody in Hemlock County entered Saul Rutledge's gate; least of all in the dead of winter, and summoned (as Bosworth, at any rate, had been) by Mrs. Rutledge, who passed, even in that unsocial region, for a woman of cold manners and solitary character. The situation was enough to excite the curiosity of a less imaginative man than Orrin Bosworth.

As he drove in between the broken-down white gate-posts topped by fluted urns the two men ahead of him were leading their horses to the adjoining shed. Bosworth followed, and hitched his horse to a post. Then the three tossed off the snow from their shoulders, clapped their numb hands together, and greeted each other.

"Hallo, Deacon."

"Well, well, Orrin—." They shook hands.

"'Day, Bosworth," said Sylvester Brand, with a brief nod. He seldom put any cordiality into his manner, and on this occasion he was still busy about his horse's bridle and blanket.

Orrin Bosworth, the youngest and most communicative of the three, turned back to Deacon Hibben, whose long face, queerly blotched and mouldy-looking, with blinking peering eyes, was yet less forbidding than Brand's heavily-hewn countenance.

"Queer, our all meeting here this way. Mrs. Rutledge sent me a message to come," Bosworth volunteered.

The deacon nodded. "I got a word from her too—Andy Pond come with it yesterday noon. I hope there's no trouble here—"

He glanced through the thickening fall of snow at the desolate front of the Rutledge house, the more melancholy in its present neglected state because, like the gate-posts, it kept traces of former elegance. Bosworth had often wondered how such a house had come to be built in that lonely stretch between North Ashmore and Cold Corners. People said there had once been other houses like it, forming a little township called Ashmore, a sort of mountain colony created by the caprice of an English Royalist officer, one Colonel Ashmore, who had been murdered by the Indians, with all his family, long before the Revolution.

This tale was confirmed by the fact that the ruined cellars of several smaller houses were still to be discovered under the wild growth of the adjoining slopes, and that the Communion plate of the moribund Episcopal church of Cold Corners was engraved with the name of Colonel Ashmore, who had given it to the church of Ashmore in the year 1723. Of the church itself no traces remained. Doubtless it had been a modest wooden edifice, built on piles, and the conflagration which had burnt the other houses to the ground's edge had reduced it utterly to ashes. The whole place, even in summer, wore a mournful solitary air, and people wondered why Saul Rutledge's father had gone there to settle.

"I never knew a place," Deacon Hibben said, "as seemed as far away from humanity. And yet it ain't so in miles."

"Miles ain't the only distance," Orrin Bosworth answered; and the two men, followed by Sylvester Brand, walked across the drive to the front door. People in Hemlock County did not usually come and go by their front doors, but all three men seemed to feel that, on an occasion which appeared to be so exceptional, the usual and more familiar approach by the kitchen would not be suitable.

They had judged rightly; the deacon had hardly lifted the knocker when the door opened and Mrs. Rutledge stood before them.

"Walk right in," she said in her usual dead-level tone; and Bosworth, as he followed the others, thought to himself, "Whatever's happened, she's not going to let it show in her face."

It was doubtful, indeed, if anything unwonted could be made to show in Prudence Rutledge's face, so limited was its scope, so fixed were its features. She was dressed for the occasion in a black calico with white spots, a collar of crochet-lace fastened by a gold brooch, and a grey woollen shawl crossed under her arms and tied at the back. In her small narrow head the only marked prominence was that of the brow projecting roundly over pale spectacled eyes. Her dark hair, parted above this prominence, passed tight and flat over the tips of her ears into a small braided coil at the nape; and her contracted head looked still narrower from being perched on a long hollow neck with cord-like throat-muscles. Her eyes were of a pale cold grey, her complexion was an even white. Her age might have been anywhere from thirty-five to sixty.

The room into which she led the three men had probably been the dining-room of the Ashmore house. It was now used as a front parlour, and a black stove planted on a sheet of zinc stuck out from the delicately fluted panels of an old wooden mantel. A newly-lit fire smouldered reluctantly, and the room was at once close and bitterly cold.

"Andy Pond," Mrs. Rutledge cried to someone at the back of the house, "step out and call Mr. Rutledge. You'll likely find him in the wood-shed, or round the barn somewheres." She rejoined her visitors. "Please suit yourselves to seats," she said.

The three men, with an increasing air of constraint, took the chairs she pointed out, and Mrs. Rutledge sat stiffly down upon a fourth, behind a rickety bead-work table. She glanced from one to the other of her visitors.

"I presume you folks are wondering what it is I asked you to come here for," she said in her dead-level voice. Orrin Bosworth and Deacon Hibben murmured an assent; Sylvester Brand sat silent, his eyes, under their great thicket of eyebrows, fixed on the huge boot-tip swinging before him.

"Well, I allow you didn't expect it was for a party," continued Mrs. Rutledge.

No one ventured to respond to this chill pleasantry, and she continued: "We're in trouble here, and that's the fact. And we need advice—Mr. Rutledge and myself do." She cleared her throat, and added in a lower tone, her pitilessly clear eyes looking straight before her: "There's a spell been cast over Mr. Rutledge."

The deacon looked up sharply, an incredulous smile pinching his thin lips. "A spell?"

"That's what I said: he's bewitched."

Again the three visitors were silent; then Bosworth, more at ease or less tongue-tied than the others, asked with an attempt at humour:

"Do you use the word in the strict Scripture sense, Mrs. Rutledge?"

She glanced at him before replying: "That's how *he* uses it."

The deacon coughed and cleared his long rattling throat. "Do you care to give us more particulars before your husband joins us?"

Mrs. Rutledge looked down at her clasped hands, as if considering the question. Bosworth noticed that the inner fold of her lids was of the same uniform white as the rest of her skin, so that when she dropped them her rather prominent eyes looked like the sightless orbs of a marble statue. The impression was unpleasing, and he glanced away at the text over the mantelpiece, which read:

The Soul That Sinneth It Shall Die.

"No," she said at length, "I'll wait."

At this moment Sylvester Brand suddenly stood up and pushed back his chair. "I don't know," he said, in his rough bass voice, "as I've got any particular lights on Bible mysteries; and this happens to be the day I was to go down to Starkfield to close a deal with a man."

Mrs. Rutledge lifted one of her long thin hands. Withered and wrinkled by hard work and cold, it was nevertheless of the same leaden white as her face. "You won't be kept long," she said. "Won't you be seated?"

Farmer Brand stood irresolute, his purplish underlip twitching. "The deacon here—-such things is more in his line. . . . ."

"I want you should stay," said Mrs. Rutledge quietly; and Brand sat down again.

A silence fell, during which the four persons present seemed all to be listening for the sound of a step; but none was heard, and after a minute or two Mrs. Rutledge began to speak again.

"It's down by that old shack on Lamer's pond; that's where they meet," she said suddenly.

Bosworth, whose eyes were on Sylvester Brand's face, fancied he saw a sort of inner flush darken the farmer's heavy leathern skin. Deacon Hibben leaned forward, a glitter of curiosity in his eyes.

"They—*who*, Mrs. Rutledge?"

"My husband, Saul Rutledge. . . . .and her. . . ."

Sylvester Brand again stirred in his seat. "Who do you mean by *her?*" he asked abruptly, as if roused out of some far-off musing.

Mrs. Rutledge's body did not move; she simply revolved her head on her long neck and looked at him.

"Your daughter, Sylvester Brand."

The man staggered to his feet with an explosion of inarticulate sounds. "My—my daughter? What the hell are you talking about? My daughter? It's a damned lie. . . . it's. . . . it's. . . ."

"Your daughter *Ora*, Mr. Brand," said Mrs. Rutledge slowly.

Bosworth felt an icy chill down his spine. Instinctively he turned his eyes away from Brand, and, they rested on the mildewed countenance of Deacon Hibben. Between the blotches it had become as white as Mrs. Rutledge's, and the deacon's eyes burned in the whiteness like live embers among ashes.

Brand gave a laugh: the rusty creaking laugh of one whose springs of mirth are never moved by gaiety. "My daughter *Ora?*" he repeated.

"Yes."

"My *dead* daughter?"

"That's what he says."

"Your husband?"

"That's what Mr. Rutledge says."

Orrin Bosworth listened with a sense of suffocation; he felt as if he were wrestling with long-armed horrors in a dream. He could no longer resist letting his eyes return to Sylvester Brand's face. To his surprise it had resumed a natural imperturbable expression. Brand rose to his feet. "Is that all?" he queried contemptuously.

"All? Ain't it enough? How long is it since you folks seen Saul Rutledge, any of you?" Mrs. Rutledge flew out at them.

Bosworth, it appeared, had not seen him for nearly a year; the deacon had only run across him once, for a minute, at the North Ashmore post office, the previous autumn, and acknowledged that he wasn't looking any too good then. Brand said nothing, but stood irresolute.

"Well, if you wait a minute you'll see with your own eyes; and he'll tell you with his own words. That's what I've got you here for—to see for yourselves what's come over him. Then you'll talk different," she added, twisting her head abruptly toward Sylvester Brand.

The deacon raised a lean hand of interrogation.

"Does your husband know we've been sent for on this business, Mrs. Rutledge?" Mrs. Rutledge signed assent.

"It was with his consent, then—?"

She looked coldly at her questioner. "I guess it had to be," she said. Again Bosworth felt the chill down his spine. He tried to dissipate the sensation by speaking with an affectation of energy.

"Can you tell us, Mrs. Rutledge, how this trouble you speak of shows itself. . . . .what makes you think. . . . .?"

She looked at him for a moment; then she leaned forward across the rickety bead-work table. A thin smile of disdain narrowed her colourless lips. "I don't think—I know."

"Well—but how?"

She leaned closer, both elbows on the table, her voice dropping. "I seen 'em."

In the ashen light from the veiling of snow beyond the windows the deacon's little screwed-up eyes seemed to give out red sparks. "Him and the dead?"

"Him and the dead."

"Saul Rutledge and—and Ora Brand?"

"That's so."

Sylvester Brand's chair fell backward with a crash. He was on his feet again, crimson and cursing. "It's a God-damned fiend-begotten lie. . . . ."

"Friend Brand. . . . .friend Brand. . . . ." the deacon protested.

"Here, let me get out of this. I want to see Saul Rutledge himself, and tell him—"

"Well, here he is," said Mrs. Rutledge.

The outer door had opened; they heard the familiar stamping and shaking of a man who rids his garments of their last snowflakes before penetrating to the sacred precincts of the best parlour. Then Saul Rutledge entered.

2

As he came in he faced the light from the north window, and Bosworth's first thought was that he looked like a drowned man fished out from under the ice—"self-drowned," he added. But the snow-light plays cruel tricks with a man's colour, and even with the shape of his features; it must have been partly that, Bosworth reflected, which transformed Saul Rutledge from the straight muscular fellow he had been a year before into the haggard wretch now before them.

The deacon sought for a word to ease the horror. "Well, now, Saul—you look's if you'd ought to set right up to the stove. Had a touch of ague, maybe?"

The feeble attempt was unavailing. Rutledge neither moved nor answered. He stood among them silent, incommunicable, like one risen from the dead.

Brand grasped him roughly by the shoulder. "See here, Saul Rutledge, what's this dirty lie your wife tells us you've been putting about?"

Still Rutledge did not move. "It's no lie," he said.

Brand's hand dropped from his shoulder. In spite of the man's rough bullying power he seemed to be undefinably awed by Rutledge's look and tone.

"No lie? You've gone plumb crazy, then, have you?"

Mrs. Rutledge spoke. "My husband's not lying, nor he ain't gone crazy. Don't I tell you I seen 'em?"

Brand laughed again. "Him and the dead?"

"Yes."

"Down by the Lamer pond, you say?"

"Yes."

"And when was that, if I might ask?"

"Day before yesterday."

A silence fell on the strangely assembled group. The deacon at length broke it to say to Mr. Brand: "Brand, in my opinion we've got to see this thing through."

Brand stood for a moment in speechless contemplation: there was something animal and primitive about him, Bosworth thought, as he hung thus, lowering and dumb, a little foam beading the corners of that heavy purplish underlip. He let himself slowly down into his chair. "I'll see it through."

The two other men and Mrs. Rutledge had remained seated. Saul Rutledge stood before them, like a prisoner at the bar, or rather like a sick man before the physicians who were to heal him. As Bosworth scrutinized that hollow face, so wan under the dark sunburn, so sucked inward and consumed by some hidden fever, there stole over the sound healthy man the thought that perhaps, after all, husband and wife spoke the truth, and that they were all at that moment really standing on the edge of some forbidden mystery. Things that the rational mind would reject without a thought seemed no longer so easy to dispose of as one looked at the actual Saul Rutledge and remembered the man he had been a year before. Yes; as the deacon said, they would have to see it through...

"Sit down then, Saul; draw up to us, won't you?" the deacon suggested, trying again for a natural tone.

Mrs. Rutledge pushed a chair forward, and her husband sat down on it. He stretched out his arms and grasped his knees in his brown bony fingers; in that attitude he remained, turning neither his head nor his eyes.

"Well, Saul," the deacon continued, "your wife says you thought mebbe we could do something to help you through this trouble, whatever it is."

Rutledge's grey eyes widened a little. "No; I didn't think that. It was her idea to try what could be done."

"I presume, though, since you've agreed to our coming, that you don't object to our putting a few questions?"

Rutledge was silent for a moment; then he said with a visible effort: "No; I don't object."

"Well—you've heard what your wife says?"

Rutledge made a slight motion of assent. "And—what have you got to answer? How do you explain. . . . .?"

Mrs. Rutledge intervened. "How can he explain? I seen 'em."

There was a silence; then Bosworth, trying to speak in an easy reassuring tone, queried: "That so, Saul?"

"That's so."

Brand lifted up his brooding head. "You mean to say you. . . . .you sit here before us all and say..."

The deacon's hand again checked him. "Hold on, friend Brand. We're all of us trying for the facts, ain't we?" He turned to Rutledge. "We've heard what Mrs. Rutledge says. What's your answer?"

"I don't know as there's any answer. She found us."

"And you mean to tell me the person with you was...was what you took to be. . . . . " the deacon's thin voice grew thinner: "Ora Brand?"

Saul Rutledge nodded.

"You knew.. . . . or thought you knew. . . . you were meeting with the dead?"

Rutledge bent his head again. The snow continued to fall in a steady unwavering sheet against the window, and Bosworth felt as if a winding-sheet were descending from the sky to envelop them all in a common grave.

"Think what you're saying! It's against our religion! Ora. . . . .poor child! . . . . .died over a year ago. I saw you at her funeral, Saul. How can you make such a statement?"

"What else can he do?" thrust in Mrs. Rutledge.

There was another pause. Bosworth's resources had failed him, and Brand once more sat plunged in dark meditation. The deacon laid his quivering finger-tips together, and moistened his lips.

"Was the day before yesterday the first time?" he asked.

The movement of Rutledge's head was negative.

"Not the first? Then when. . . . ."

"Nigh on a year ago, I reckon."

"God! And you mean to tell us that ever since—?"

"Well. . . . . look at him," said his wife. The three men lowered their eyes.

After a moment Bosworth, trying to collect himself, glanced at the deacon. "Why not ask Saul to make his own statement, if that's what we're here for?"

"That's so," the deacon assented. He turned to Rutledge. "Will you try and give us your idea . . . .of . . . .of how it began?"

There was another silence. Then Rutledge tightened his grasp on his gaunt knees, and still looking straight ahead, with his curiously clear unseeing gaze: "Well," he said, "I guess it begun away back, afore even I was married to Mrs. Rutledge. . . . ." He spoke in a low automatic tone, as if some invisible agent were dictating his words, or even uttering them for him. "You know," he added, "Ora and me was to have been married."

Sylvester Brand lifted his, head. "Straighten that statement out first, please," he interjected.

"What I mean is, we kept company. But Ora she was very young. Mr. Brand here he sent her away. She was gone nigh to three years, I guess. When she come back I was married."

"That's right," Brand said, relapsing once more into his sunken attitude.

"And after she came back did you meet her again?" the deacon continued.

"Alive?" Rutledge questioned.

A perceptible shudder ran through the room.

"Well—of course," said the deacon nervously.

Rutledge seemed to consider. "Once I did—only once. There was a lot of other people round. At Cold Corners fair it was."

"Did you talk with her then?"

"Only a minute."

"What did she say?"

His voice dropped. "She said she was sick and knew she was going to die, and when she was dead she'd come back to me."

"And what did you answer?"

"Nothing."

"Did you think anything of it at the time?"

"Well, no. Not till I heard she was dead I didn't. After that I thought of it—and I guess she drew me." He moistened his lips.

"Drew you down to that abandoned house by the pond?"

Rutledge made a faint motion of assent, and the deacon added: "How did you know it was there she wanted you to come?"

"She. . . . just drew me. . . . ."

There was a long pause. Bosworth felt, on himself and the other two men, the oppressive weight of the next question to be asked. Mrs. Rutledge opened and closed her narrow lips once or twice, like some beached shell-fish gasping for the tide. Rutledge waited.

"Well, now, Saul, won't you go on with what you was telling us?" the deacon at length suggested.

"That's all. There's nothing else."

The deacon lowered his voice. "She just draws you?"

"Yes."

"Often?"

"That's as it happens. . . . ."

"But if it's always there she draws you, man, haven't you the strength to keep away from the place?"

For the first time, Rutledge wearily turned his head toward his questioner. A spectral smile narrowed his colourless lips. "Ain't any use. She follers after me . . . ."

There was another silence. What more could they ask, then and there? Mrs. Rutledge's presence checked the next question. The deacon seemed hopelessly to revolve the matter. At length he spoke in a more authoritative tone. "These are forbidden things. You know that, Saul. Have you tried prayer?"

Rutledge shook his head.

"Will you pray with us now?"

Rutledge cast a glance of freezing indifference on his spiritual adviser. "If you folks want to pray, I'm agreeable," he said. But Mrs. Rutledge intervened.

"Prayer ain't any good. In this kind of thing it ain't no manner of use; you know it ain't. I called you here, deacon, because you remember the last case in this parish. Thirty years ago it was, I guess; but you remember. Lefferts Nash—did praying help him? I was a little girl then, but I used to hear my folks talk of it winter nights. Lefferts Nash and Hannah Cory. They drove a stake through her breast. That's what cured him."

"Oh—" Orrin Bosworth exclaimed.

Sylvester Brand raised his head. "You're speaking of that old story as if this was the same sort of thing?"

"Ain't it? Ain't my husband pining away the same as Lefferts Nash did? The deacon here knows—"

The deacon stirred anxiously in his chair. "These are forbidden things," he repeated. "Supposing your husband is quite sincere in thinking himself haunted, as you might say. Well, even then, what proof have we that the . . . . .the dead woman. . . . .is the spectre of that poor girl?"

"Proof? Don't he say so? Didn't she tell him? Ain't I seen 'em?" Mrs. Rutledge almost screamed.

The three men sat silent, and suddenly the wife burst out: "A stake through the breast That's the old way; and it's the only way. The deacon knows it!"

"It's against our religion to disturb the dead."

"Ain't it against your religion to let the living perish as my husband is perishing?" She sprang up with one of her abrupt movements and took the family Bible from the what-not in a corner of the parlour. Putting the book on the table, and moistening a livid finger-tip, she turned the pages rapidly, till she came to one on which she laid her hand like a stony paper-weight. "See here," she said, and read out in her level chanting voice:

"'*Thou shalt not suffer a witch to live.*'

"That's in Exodus, that's where it is," she added, leaving the book open as if to confirm the statement.

Bosworth continued to glance anxiously from one to the other of the four people about the table. He was younger than any of them, and had had more contact with the modern world; down in Starkfield, in the bar of the Fielding House, he could hear himself laughing with the rest of the men at such old wives' tales. But it was not for nothing that he had been born under the icy shadow of Lonetop, and had shivered and hungered as a lad through the bitter Hemlock County winters. After his parents died, and he had taken hold of the farm himself, he had got more out of it by using improved methods, and by supplying the increasing throng of summer-boarders over Stotesbury way with milk and vegetables.

He had been made a selectman of North Ashmore; for so young a man he had a standing in the county. But the roots of the old life were still in him. He could remember, as a little boy, going twice a year with his mother to that bleak hill-farm out beyond Sylvester Brand's, where Mrs. Bosworth's aunt, Cressidora Cheney, had been shut up for years in a cold clean room with iron bars in the windows.

When little Orrin first saw Aunt Cressidora she was a small white old woman, whom her sisters used to "make decent" for visitors the day that Orrin and his mother were expected. The child wondered why there were bars to the window. "Like a canary-bird," he said to his mother. The phrase made Mrs. Bosworth reflect. "I do believe they keep Aunt Cressidora too lonesome," she said; and the next time she went up the mountain with the little boy he carried to his great-aunt a canary in a little wooden cage. It was a great excitement; he knew it would make her happy.

The old woman's motionless face lit up when she saw the bird, and her eyes began to glitter. "It belongs to me," she said instantly, stretching her soft bony hand over the cage.

"Of course it does, Aunt Cressy," said Mrs. Bosworth, her eyes filling.

But the bird, startled by the shadow of the old woman's hand, began to flutter and beat its wings distractedly. At the sight, Aunt Cressidora's calm face suddenly became a coil of twitching features. "You she-devil, you!" she cried in a high squealing voice; and thrusting her hand into the cage she dragged out the terrified bird and wrung its neck. She was plucking the hot body, and squealing "she-devil, she-devil!" as they drew little Orrin from the room. On the way down the mountain his mother wept a great deal, and said: "You must never tell anybody that poor Auntie's crazy, or the men would come and take her down to the asylum at Starkfield, and the shame of it would kill us all. Now promise." The child promised.

He remembered the scene now, with its deep fringe of mystery, secrecy and rumour. It seemed related to a great many other things below the surface of his thoughts, things which stole up anew, making him feel that all the old people he had known, and who "believed in these things," might after all be right. Hadn't a witch been burned at North Ashmore? Didn't the summer folk still drive over in jolly buckboard loads to see the meeting-house where the trial had been held, the pond where they had ducked her and she had floated? . . . . . Deacon Hibben believed; Bosworth was sure of it. If he didn't, why did people from all over the place come to him when their animals had queer sicknesses, or when there was a child in the family that had to be kept shut up because it fell down flat and foamed? Yes, in spite of his religion, Deacon Hibben *knew*. . .

And Brand? Well, it came to Bosworth in a flash: that North Ashmore woman who was burned had the name of Brand. The same stock, no doubt; there had been Brands in Hemlock County ever since the white men had come there. And Orrin, when he was a child, remembered hearing his parents say that Sylvester Brand hadn't ever oughter married his own cousin, because of the blood. Yet the couple had had two healthy girls, and when Mrs. Brand pined away and died nobody suggested that anything had been wrong with her mind. And Vanessa and Ora were the handsomest girls anywhere round.

Brand knew it, and scrimped and saved all he could to send Ora, the eldest, down to Starkfield to learn book-keeping. "When she's married I'll send you," he used to say to little Venny, who was his favourite.

But Ora never married. She was away three years, during which Venny ran wild on the slopes of Lonetop; and when Ora came back she sickened and died—poor girl! Since then Brand had grown more savage and morose. He was a hard-working farmer, but there wasn't much to be got out of those barren Bearcliff acres. He was said to have taken to drink since his wife's death; now and then men ran across him in the "dives" of Stotesbury. But not often.

And between times he laboured hard on his stony acres and did his best for his daughters. In the neglected graveyard of Cold Corners there was a slanting headstone marked with his wife's name; near it, a year since, he had laid his eldest daughter. And sometimes, at dusk, in the autumn, the village people saw him walk slowly by, turn in between the graves, and stand looking down on the two stones. But he never brought a flower there, or planted a bush; nor Venny either. She was too wild and ignorant. . . . .

Mrs. Rutledge repeated: "That's in Exodus."

The three visitors remained silent, turning about their hats in reluctant hands. Rutledge faced them, still with that empty pellucid gaze which frightened Bosworth. What was he seeing?

"Ain't any of you folks got the grit—?" his wife burst out again, half hysterically.

Deacon Hibben held up his hand. "That's no way, Mrs. Rutledge. This ain't a question of having grit. What we want first of all is. . . . .proof. . . . ."

"That's so," said Bosworth, with an explosion of relief, as if the words had lifted something black and crouching from his breast. Involuntarily the eyes of both men had turned to Brand. He stood there smiling grimly, but did not speak.

"Ain't it so, Brand?" the deacon prompted him.

"Proof that spooks walk?" the other sneered.

"Well—I presume you want this business settled too?"

The old farmer squared his shoulders. "Yes—I do. But I ain't a sperritualist. How the hell are you going to settle it?"

Deacon Hibben hesitated; then he said, in a low incisive tone: "I don't see but one way—Mrs. Rutledge's."

There was a silence.

"What?" Brand sneered again. "Spying?"

The deacon's voice sank lower. "If the poor girl *does* walk.....her that's your child.....wouldn't you be the first to want her laid quiet? We all know there've been such cases.....mysterious visitations.... Can any one of us here deny it?"

"I seen 'em," Mrs. Rutledge interjected.

There was another heavy pause. Suddenly Brand fixed his gaze on Rutledge. "See here, Saul Rutledge, you've got to clear up this damned calumny, or I'll know why. You say my dead girl comes to you." He laboured with his breath, and then jerked out: "When? You tell me that, and I'll be there."

Rutledge's head drooped a little, and his eyes wandered to the window. "Round about sunset, mostly."

"You know beforehand?"

Rutledge made a sign of assent.

"Well, then—tomorrow, will it be?" Rutledge made the same sign.

Brand turned to the door. "I'll be there." That was all he said. He strode out between them without another glance or word. Deacon Hibben looked at Mrs. Rutledge. "We'll be there too," he said, as if she had asked him; but she had not spoken, and Bosworth saw that her thin body was trembling all over. He was glad when he and Hibben were out again in the snow.

3

They thought that Brand wanted to be left to himself, and to give him time to unhitch his horse they made a pretence of hanging about in the doorway while Bosworth searched his pockets for a pipe he had no mind to light.

But Brand turned back to them as they lingered. "You'll meet me down by Lamer's pond tomorrow?" he suggested. "I want witnesses. Round about sunset."

They nodded their acquiescence, and he got into his sleigh, gave the horse a cut across the flanks, and drove off under the snow-smothered hemlocks. The other two men went to the shed.

"What do you make of this business, deacon?" Bosworth asked, to break the silence.

The deacon shook his head. "The man's a sick man—that's sure. Something's sucking the life clean out of him."

But already, in the biting outer air, Bosworth was getting himself under better control. "Looks to me like a bad case of the ague, as you said."

"Well—ague of the mind, then. It's his brain that's sick."

Bosworth shrugged. "He ain't the first in Hemlock County."

"That's so," the deacon agreed. "It's a worm in the brain, solitude is."

"Well, we'll know this time tomorrow, maybe," said Bosworth. He scrambled into his sleigh, and was driving off in his turn when he heard his companion calling after him. The deacon explained that his horse had cast a shoe; would Bosworth drive him down to the forge near North Ashmore, if it wasn't too much out of his way? He didn't want the mare slipping about on the freezing snow, and he could probably get the blacksmith to drive him back and shoe her in Rutledge's shed. Bosworth made room for him under the bearskin, and the two men drove off, pursued by a puzzled whinny from the deacon's old mare.

The road they took was not the one that Bosworth would have followed to reach his own home. But he did not mind that. The shortest way to the forge passed close by Lamer's pond, and Bosworth, since he was in for the business, was not sorry to look the ground over. They drove on in silence.

The snow had ceased, and a green sunset was spreading upward into the crystal sky. A stinging wind barbed with ice-flakes caught them in the face on the open ridges, but when they dropped down into the hollow by Lamer's pond the air was as soundless and empty as an unswung bell. They jogged along slowly, each thinking his own thoughts.

"That's the house. . . . .that tumble-down shack over there, I suppose?" the deacon said, as the road drew near the edge of the frozen pond.

"Yes: that's the house. A queer hermit-fellow built it years ago, my father used to tell me. Since then I don't believe it's ever been used but by the gipsies."

Bosworth had reined in his horse, and sat looking through pine-trunks purpled by the sunset at the crumbling structure. Twilight already lay under the trees, though day lingered in the open. Between two sharply-patterned pine-boughs he saw the evening star, like a white boat in a sea of green.

His gaze dropped from that fathomless sky and followed the blue-white undulations of the snow. It gave him a curious agitated feeling to think that here, in this icy solitude, in the tumble-down house he had so often passed without heeding it, a dark mystery, too deep for thought, was being enacted. Down that very slope, coming from the graveyard at Cold Corners, the being they called "Ora" must pass toward the pond. His heart began to beat stiflingly. Suddenly he gave an exclamation: "Look!"

He had jumped out of the cutter and was stumbling up the bank toward the slope of snow. On it, turned in the direction of the house by the pond, he had detected a woman's foot-prints; two; then three; then more. The deacon scrambled out after him, and they stood and stared.

"God—barefoot!" Hibben gasped. "Then it *is*. . . . .the dead. . . . ."

Bosworth said nothing. But he knew that no live woman would travel with naked feet across that freezing wilderness. Here, then, was the proof the deacon had asked for—they held it. What should they do with it?

"Supposing we was to drive up nearer—round the turn of the pond, till we get close to the house," the deacon proposed in a colourless voice. "Mebbe then. . . . ."

Postponement was a relief. They got into the sleigh and drove on. Two or three hundred yards farther the road, a mere lane under steep bushy banks, turned sharply to the right, following the bend of the pond. As they rounded the turn they saw Brand's cutter ahead of them. It was empty, the horse tied to a tree-trunk. The two men looked at each other again. This was not Brand's nearest way home.

Evidently he had been actuated by the same impulse which had made them rein in their horse by the pond-side, and then hasten on to the deserted hovel. Had he too discovered those spectral foot-prints? Perhaps it was for that very reason that he had left his cutter and vanished in the direction of the house. Bosworth found himself shivering all over under his bearskin. "I wish to God the dark wasn't coming on," he muttered. He tethered his own horse near Brand's, and without a word he and the deacon ploughed through the snow, in the track of Brand's huge feet. They had only a few yards to walk to overtake him. He did not hear them following him, and when Bosworth spoke his name, and he stopped short and turned, his heavy face was dim and confused, like a darker blot on the dusk. He looked at them dully, but without surprise.

"I wanted to see the place," he merely said.

The deacon cleared his throat. "Just take a look. . . . .yes. . . . .We thought so...But I guess there won't be anything to *see*. . . . ." He attempted a chuckle.

The other did not seem to hear him, but laboured on ahead through the pines. The three men came out together in the cleared space before the house. As they emerged from beneath the trees they seemed to have left night behind. The evening star shed a lustre on the speckless snow, and Brand, in that lucid circle, stopped with a jerk, and pointed to the same light foot-prints turned toward the house—the track of a woman in the snow. He stood still, his face working. "Bare feet. . . . ." he said.

The deacon piped up in a quavering voice: "The feet of the dead."

Brand remained motionless. "The feet of the dead," he echoed.

Deacon Hibben laid a frightened hand on his arm. "Come away now, Brand; for the love of God come away."

The father hung there, gazing down at those light tracks on the snow—light as fox or squirrel trails they seemed, on the white immensity. Bosworth thought to himself "The living couldn't walk so light—not even Ora Brand couldn't have, when she lived. . . . ." The cold seemed to have entered into his very marrow. His teeth were chattering.

Brand swung about on them abruptly. "*Now!*" he said, moving as if to an assault, his head bowed forward on his bull neck.

"Now—now? Not in there?" gasped the deacon. "What's the use? It was tomorrow he said—." He shook like a leaf.

"It's now," said Brand. He went up to the door of the crazy house, pushed it inward, and meeting with an unexpected resistance, thrust his heavy shoulder against the panel. The door collapsed like a playing-card, and Brand stumbled after it into the darkness of the hut. The others, after a moment's hesitation, followed.

Bosworth was never quite sure in what order the events that succeeded took place. Coming in out of the snow-dazzle, he seemed to be plunging into total blackness. He groped his way across the threshold, caught a sharp splinter of the fallen door in his palm, seemed to see something white and wraithlike surge up out of the darkest corner of the hut, and then heard a revolver shot at his elbow, and a cry—

Brand had turned back, and was staggering past him out into the lingering daylight. The sunset, suddenly flushing through the trees, crimsoned his face like blood. He held a revolver in his hand and looked about him in his stupid way.

"They *do* walk, then," he said and began to laugh. He bent his head to examine his weapon. "Better here than in the churchyard. They shan't dig her up *now*," he shouted out. The two men caught him by the arms, and Bosworth got the revolver away from him.

4

The next day Bosworth's sister Loretta, who kept house for him, asked him, when he came in for his midday dinner, if he had heard the news.

Bosworth had been sawing wood all the morning, and in spite of the cold and the driving snow, which had begun again in the night, he was covered with an icy sweat, like a man getting over a fever.

"What news?"

"Venny Brand's down sick with pneumonia. The deacon's been there. I guess she's dying."

Bosworth looked at her with listless eyes. She seemed far off from him, miles away. "Venny Brand?" he echoed.

"You never liked her, Orrin."

"She's a child. I never knew much about her."

"Well," repeated his sister, with the guileless relish of the unimaginative for bad news, "I guess she's dying." After a pause she added: "It'll kill Sylvester Brand, all alone up there."

Bosworth got up and said: "I've got to see to poulticing the grey's fetlock." He walked out into the steadily falling snow.

Venny Brand was buried three days later. The deacon read the service; Bosworth was one of the pall-bearers. The whole countryside turned out, for the snow had stopped falling, and at any season a funeral offered an opportunity for an outing that was not to be missed. Besides, Venny Brand was young and handsome—at least some people thought her handsome, though she was so swarthy—and her dying like that, so suddenly, had the fascination of tragedy.

"They say her lungs filled right up.....Seems she'd had bronchial troubles before.....I always said both them girls was frail.....Look at Ora, how she took and wasted away! And it's colder'n all outdoors up there to Brand's.....Their mother, too, *she* pined away just the same. They don't ever make old bones on the mother's side of the family..."

. . There's that young Bedlow over there; they say Venny was engaged to him . . . . Oh, Mrs. Rutledge, excuse *me*. . . . . Step right into the pew; there's a seat for you alongside of grandma. . . . ."

Mrs. Rutledge was advancing with deliberate step down the narrow aisle of the bleak wooden church. She had on her best bonnet, a monumental structure which no one had seen out of her trunk since old Mrs. Silsee's funeral, three years before. All the women remembered it. Under its perpendicular pile her narrow face, swaying on the long thin neck, seemed whiter than ever; but her air of fretfulness had been composed into a suitable expression of mournful immobility.

"Looks as if the stone-mason had carved her to put atop of Venny's grave," Bosworth thought as she glided past him; and then shivered at his own sepulchral fancy. When she bent over her hymn book her lowered lids reminded him again of marble eye-balls; the bony hands clasping the book were bloodless. Bosworth had never seen such hands since he had seen old Aunt Cressidora Cheney strangle the canary-bird because it fluttered.

The service was over, the coffin of Venny Brand had been lowered into her sister's grave, and the neighbours were slowly dispersing. Bosworth, as pall-bearer, felt obliged to linger and say a word to the stricken father. He waited till Brand had turned from the grave with the deacon at his side. The three men stood together for a moment; but not one of them spoke. Brand's face was the closed door of a vault, barred with wrinkles like bands of iron.

Finally, the deacon took his hand and said: "The Lord gave—"

Brand nodded and turned away toward the shed where the horses were hitched. Bosworth followed him. "Let me drive along home with you," he suggested.

Brand did not so much as turn his head. "Home? What home?" he said; and the other fell back.

Loretta Bosworth was talking with the other women while the men unblanketed their horses and backed the cutters out into the heavy snow. As Bosworth waited for her, a few feet off, he saw Mrs. Rutledge's tall bonnet lording it above the group. Andy Pond, the Rutledge farm-hand, was backing out the sleigh.

"Saul ain't here today, Mrs. Rutledge, is he?" one of the village elders piped, turning a benevolent old tortoise-head about on a loose neck, and blinking up into Mrs. Rutledge's marble face.

Bosworth heard her measure out her answer in slow incisive words. "No. Mr. Rutledge he ain't here. He would 'a' come for certain, but his aunt Minorca Cummins is being buried down to Stotesbury this very day and he had to go down there. Don't it sometimes seem zif we was all walking right in the Shadow of Death?"

As she walked toward the cutter, in which Andy Pond was already seated, the deacon went up to her with visible hesitation. Involuntarily Bosworth also moved nearer. He heard the deacon say: "I'm glad to hear that Saul is able to be up and around."

She turned her small head on her rigid neck, and lifted the lids of marble.

"Yes, I guess he'll sleep quieter now.—And her too, maybe, now she don't lay there alone any longer," she added in a low voice, with a sudden twist of her chin toward the fresh black stain in the grave-yard snow. She got into the cutter, and said in a clear tone to Andy Pond: "'S long as we're down here I don't know but what I'll just call round and get a box of soap at Hiram Pringle's."

Miss Mary Pask

1

It was not till the following spring that I plucked up courage to tell Mrs. Bridgeworth what had happened to me that night at Morgat.

In the first place, Mrs. Bridgeworth was in America; and after the night in question I lingered on abroad for several months—not for pleasure, God knows, but because of a nervous collapse supposed to be the result of having taken up my work again too soon after my touch of fever in Egypt. But, in any case, if I had been door to door with Grace Bridgeworth I could not have spoken of the affair before, to her or to any one else; not till I had been rest-cured and built up again at one of those wonderful Swiss sanatoria where they clean the cobwebs out of you. I could not even have written to her—not to save my life. The happenings of that night had to be overlaid with layer upon layer of time and forgetfulness before I could tolerate any return to them.

The beginning was idiotically simple; just the sudden reflex of a New England conscience acting on an enfeebled constitution. I had been painting in Brittany, in lovely but uncertain autumn weather, one day all blue and silver, the next shrieking gales or driving fog. There is a rough little white-washed inn out on the Pointe du Raz, swarmed over by tourists in summer but a sea-washed solitude in autumn; and there I was staying and trying to do waves, when someone said: "You ought to go over to Cape something else, beyond Morgat."

I went, and had a silver-and-blue day there; and on the way back the name of Morgat set up an unexpected association of ideas: Morgat—Grace Bridgeworth—Grace's sister, Mary Pask—"You know my darling Mary has a little place now near Morgat; if you ever go to Brittany do go to see her. She lives such a lonely life—it makes me so unhappy."

That was the way it came about. I had known Mrs. Bridgeworth well for years, but had only a hazy intermittent acquaintance with Mary Pask, her older and unmarried sister. Grace and she were greatly attached to each other, I knew; it had been Grace's chief sorrow, when she married my old friend Horace Bridgeworth, and went to live in New York, that Mary, from whom she had never before been separated, obstinately lingered on in Europe, where the two sisters had been travelling since their mother's death.

I never quite understood why Mary Pask refused to join Grace in America. Grace said it was because she was "too artistic"—but, knowing the elder Miss Pask, and the extremely elementary nature of her interest in art, I wondered whether it were not rather because she disliked Horace Bridgeworth. There was a third alternative—more conceivable if one knew Horace—and that was that she may have liked him too much. But that again became untenable (at least I supposed it did) when one knew Miss Pask: Miss Pask with her round flushed face, her innocent bulging eyes, her old-maidish flat decorated with art-tidies, and her vague and timid philanthropy. Aspire to Horace—!

Well, it was all rather puzzling, or would have been if it had been interesting enough to be worth puzzling over. But it was not. Mary Pask was like hundreds of other dowdy old maids, cheerful derelicts content with their innumerable little substitutes for living. Even Grace would not have interested me particularly if she hadn't happened to marry one of my oldest friends, and to be kind to his friends. She was a handsome capable and rather dull woman, absorbed in her husband and children, and without an ounce of imagination; and between her attachment to her sister and Mary Pask's worship of her there lay the inevitable gulf between the feelings of the sentimentally unemployed and those whose affections are satisfied.

But a close intimacy had linked the two sisters before Grace's marriage, and Grace was one of the sweet conscientious women who go on using the language of devotion about people whom they live happily without seeing; so that when she said: "You know it's years since Mary and I have been together—not since little Molly was born. If only she'd come to America! Just think. . . . Molly is six, and has never seen her darling auntie. . . ." when she said this, and added: "If you go to Brittany promise me you'll look up my Mary," I was moved in that dim depth of one where unnecessary obligations are contracted.

And so it came about that, on that silver-and-blue afternoon, the idea "Morgat—Mary Pask—to please Grace" suddenly unlocked the sense of duty in me. Very well: I would chuck a few things into my bag, do my day's painting, go to see Miss Pask when the light faded, and spend the night at the inn at Morgat. To this end I ordered a rickety one-horse vehicle to await me at the inn when I got back from my painting, and in it I started out toward sunset to hunt for Mary Pask. . . .

As suddenly as a pair of hands clapped over one's eyes, the sea-fog shut down on us. A minute before we had been driving over a wide bare upland, our backs turned to a sunset that crimsoned the road ahead; now the densest night enveloped us. No one had been able to tell me exactly where Miss Pask lived; but I thought it likely that I should find out at the fishers' hamlet toward which we were trying to make our way. And I was right. . . .an old man in a doorway said: Yes—over the next rise, and then down a lane to the left that led to the sea; the American lady who always used to dress in white. Oh, *he,* knew. . . near the *Baie des Trépassés.*

"Yes; but how can we see to find it? I don't know the place," grumbled the reluctant boy who was driving me.

"You will when we get there," I remarked.

"Yes—and the horse foundered meantime! I can't risk it, sir; I'll get into trouble with the *patron.*"

Finally, an opportune argument induced him to get out and lead the stumbling horse, and we continued on our way. We seemed to crawl on for a long time through a wet blackness impenetrable to the glimmer of our only lamp. But now and then the pall lifted or its folds divided; and then our feeble light would drag out of the night some perfectly commonplace object—a white gate, a cow's staring face, a heap of roadside stones—made portentous and incredible by being thus detached from its setting, capriciously thrust at us, and as suddenly withdrawn. After each of these projections the darkness grew three times as thick; and the sense I had had for some time of descending a gradual slope now became that of scrambling down a precipice. I jumped out hurriedly and joined my young driver at the horse's head.

"I can't go on—I won't, sir!" he whimpered.

"Why, see, there's a light over there—just ahead!"

The veil swayed aside, and we beheld two faintly illuminated squares in a low mass that was surely the front of a house.

"Get me as far as that—then you can go back if you like."

The veil dropped again; but the boy had seen the lights and took heart. Certainly there was a house ahead of us; and certainly it must be Miss Pask's, since there could hardly be two in such a desert. Besides, the old man in the hamlet had said: "Near the sea"; and those endless modulations of the ocean's voice, so familiar in every corner of the Breton land that one gets to measure distances by them rather than by visual means, had told me for some time past that we must be making for the shore. The boy continued to lead the horse on without making any answer. The fog had shut in more closely than ever, and our lamp merely showed us the big round drops of wet on the horse's shaggy quarters.

The boy stopped with a jerk. "There's no house—we're going straight down to the sea."

"But you saw those lights, didn't you?"

"I thought I did. But where are they now? The fog's thinner again. Look—I can make out trees ahead. But there are no lights anymore."

"Perhaps the people have gone to bed," I suggested jocosely.

"Then hadn't we better turn back, sir?"

"What—two yards from the gate?"

The boy was silent: certainly there was a gate ahead, and presumably, behind the dripping trees, some sort of dwelling. Unless there was just a field and the sea. . . .the sea whose hungry voice I heard asking and asking, close below us. No wonder the place was called the Bay of the Dead! But what could have induced the rosy benevolent Mary Pask to come and bury herself there? Of course the boy wouldn't wait for me. . . .I knew that. . . .the *Baie des Trépassés* indeed! The sea whined down there as if it were feeding-time, and the Furies, its keepers, had forgotten it. . . .

There *was* the gate! My hand had struck against it. I felt along to the latch, undid it, and brushed between wet bushes to the house-front. Not a candle-glint anywhere. If the house were indeed Miss Pask's, she certainly kept early hours. . . . .

2

Night and fog were now one, and the darkness as thick as a blanket. I felt vainly about for a bell. At last my hand came in contact with a knocker and I lifted it. The clatter with which it fell sent a prolonged echo through the silence; but for a minute or two nothing else happened.

"There's no one there, I tell you!" the boy called impatiently from the gate.

But there was. I had heard no steps inside, but presently a bolt shot back, and an old woman in a peasant's cap pushed her head out. She had set her candle down on a table behind her, so that her face, aureoled with lacy wings, was in obscurity; but I knew she was old by the stoop of her shoulders and her fumbling movements. The candlelight, which made her invisible, fell full on my face, and she looked at me.

"This is Miss Mary Pask's house?"

"Yes, sir." Her voice—a very old voice—was pleasant enough, unsurprised and even friendly.

"I'll tell her," she added, shuffling off.

"Do you think she'll see me?" I threw after her.

"Oh, why not? The idea!" she almost chuckled. As she retreated I saw that she was wrapped in a shawl and had a cotton umbrella under her arm. Obviously she was going out—perhaps going home for the night. I wondered if Mary Pask lived all alone in her hermitage.

The old woman disappeared with the candle and I was left in total darkness. After an interval I heard a door shut at the back of the house and then a slow clumping of aged *sabots* along the flags outside. The old woman had evidently picked up her *sabots* in the kitchen and left the house. I wondered if she had told Miss Pask of my presence before going, or whether she had just left me there, the butt of some grim practical joke of her own. Certainly there was no sound within doors. The footsteps died out, I heard a gate click—then complete silence closed in again like the fog.

"I wonder—" I began within myself; and at that moment a smothered memory struggled abruptly to the surface of my languid mind.

"But she's *dead*—Mary Pask is *dead*!"

I almost screamed it aloud in my amazement. It was incredible, the tricks my memory had played on me since my fever! I had known for nearly a year that Mary Pask was dead—had died suddenly the previous autumn—and though I had been thinking of her almost continuously for the last two or three days it was only now that the forgotten fact of her death suddenly burst up again to consciousness.

Dead! But hadn't I found Grace Bridgeworth in tears and crape the very day I had gone to bid her goodbye before sailing for Egypt? Hadn't she laid the cable before my eyes, her own streaming with tears while I read: "Sister died suddenly this morning requested burial in garden of house particulars by letter"—with the signature of the American Consul at Brest, a friend of Bridgeworth's I seemed to recall? I could see the very words of the message printed on the darkness before me.

As I stood there I was a good deal more disturbed by the discovery of the gap in my memory than by the fact of being alone in a pitch-dark house, either empty or else inhabited by strangers. Once before of late I had noted this queer temporary blotting-out of some well-known fact; and here was a second instance of it. Decidedly, I wasn't as well over my illness as the doctors had told me. . . . Well, I would get back to Morgat and lie up there for a day or two, doing nothing, just eating and sleeping. . . .

In my self-absorption I had lost my bearings, and no longer remembered where the door was. I felt in every pocket in turn for a match—but since the doctors had made me give up smoking, why should I have found one?

The failure to find a match increased my sense of irritated helplessness, and I was groping clumsily about the hall among the angles of unseen furniture when a light slanted along the rough-cast wall of the stairs. I followed its direction, and on the landing above me I saw a figure in white shading a candle with one hand and looking down. A chill ran along my spine, for the figure bore a strange resemblance to that of Mary Pask as I used to know her.

"Oh, it's *you!*" she exclaimed in the cracked twittering voice which was at one moment like an old woman's quaver, at another like a boy's *falsetto*. She came shuffling down in her baggy white garments, with her usual clumsy swaying movements; but I noticed that her steps on the wooden stairs were soundless. Well—they would be, naturally!

I stood without a word, gazing up at the strange vision above me, and saying to myself: "There's nothing there, nothing whatever. It's your digestion, or your eyes, or some damned thing wrong with you somewhere—"

But there was the candle, at any rate; and as it drew nearer, and lit up the place about me, I turned and caught hold of the door-latch. For, remember, I had seen the cable, and Grace in crape. . . .

"Why, what's the matter? I assure you, you don't disturb me!" the white figure twittered; adding, with a faint laugh: "I don't have so many visitors nowadays—"

She had reached the hall, and stood before me, lifting her candle shakily and peering up into my face. "You haven't changed—not as much as I should have thought. But I have, haven't I?" she appealed to me with another laugh; and abruptly she laid her hand on my arm. I looked down at the hand, and thought to myself: "*That* can't deceive me."

I have always been a noticer of hands. The key to character that other people seek in the eyes, the mouth, the modelling of the skull, I find in the curve of the nails, the cut of the finger-tips, the way the palm, rosy or sallow, smooth or seamed, swells up from its base. I remembered Mary Pask's hand vividly because it was so like a caricature of herself; round, puffy, pink, yet prematurely old and useless. And there, unmistakably, it lay on my sleeve: but changed and shrivelled—somehow like one of those pale freckled toadstools that the least touch resolves to dust. . . . Well—to dust? Of course. . . .

I looked at the soft wrinkled fingers, with their foolish little oval finger-tips that used to be so innocently and naturally pink, and now were blue under the yellowing nails—and my flesh rose in ridges of fear.

"Come in, come in," she fluted, cocking her white untidy head on one side and rolling her bulging blue eyes at me. The horrible thing was that she still practised the same arts, all the childish wiles of a clumsy capering *coquetry*. I felt her pull on my sleeve and it drew me in her wake like a steel cable.

The room she led me into was—well, "unchanged" is the term generally used in such cases. For as a rule, after people die, things are tidied up, furniture is sold, remembrances are despatched to the family. But some morbid piety (or Grace's instructions, perhaps) had kept this room looking exactly as I supposed it had in Miss Pask's lifetime. I wasn't in the mood for noting details; but in the faint dabble of moving candle-light I was half aware of bedraggled cushions, odds and ends of copper pots, and a jar holding a faded branch of some late-flowering shrub. A real Mary Pask "interior"!

The white figure flitted spectrally to the chimney-piece, lit two more candles, and set down the third on a table. I hadn't supposed I was superstitious—but those three candles! Hardly knowing what I did, I hurriedly bent and blew one out. Her laugh sounded behind me.

"Three candles—you still mind that sort of thing? I've got beyond all that, you know," she chuckled. "Such a comfort. . . .such a sense of freedom. . . ." A fresh shiver joined the others already coursing over me.

"Come and sit down by me," she entreated, sinking to a sofa. "It's such an age since I've seen a living being!"

Her choice of terms was certainly strange, and as she leaned back on the white slippery sofa and beckoned me with one of those unburied hands my impulse was to turn and run. But her old face, hovering there in the candle-light, with the unnaturally red cheeks like varnished apples and the blue eyes swimming in vague kindliness, seemed to appeal to me against my cowardice, to remind me that, dead or alive, Mary Pask would never harm a fly.

"Do sit down!" she repeated, and I took the other corner of the sofa.

"It's so wonderfully good of you—I suppose Grace asked you to come?" She laughed again—her conversation had always been punctuated by rambling laughter. "It's an event—quite an event! I've had so few visitors since my death, you see."

Another bucketful of cold water ran over me; but I looked at her resolutely, and again the innocence of her face disarmed me.

I cleared my throat and spoke—with a huge panting effort, as if I had been heaving up a grave-stone. "You live here alone?" I brought out.

"Ah, I'm glad to hear your voice—I still remember voices, though I hear so few," she murmured dreamily. "Yes—I live here alone. The old woman you saw goes away at night. She won't stay after dark. . . she says she can't. Isn't it funny? But it doesn't matter; I like the darkness." She leaned to me with one of her irrelevant smiles. "The dead," she said, "naturally get used to it."

Once more I cleared my throat; but nothing followed.

She continued to gaze at me with confidential blinks. "And Grace? Tell me all about my darling. I wish I could have seen her again...just once." Her laugh came out grotesquely. "When she got the news of my death—were you with her? Was she terribly upset?"

I stumbled to my feet with a meaningless stammer. I couldn't answer—I couldn't go on looking at her.

"Ah, I see. . . .it's too painful," she acquiesced, her eyes brimming, and she turned her shaking head away.

"But after all. . . .I'm glad she was so sorry. . . .It's what I've been longing to be told, and hardly hoped for. Grace forgets. . . ." She stood up too and flitted across the room, wavering nearer and nearer to the door.

"Thank God," I thought, "she's going."

"Do you know this place by daylight?" she asked abruptly.

I shook my head.

"It's very beautiful. But you wouldn't have seen *me* then. You'd have had to take your choice between me and the landscape. I hate the light—it makes my head ache. And so I sleep all day. I was just waking up when you came." She smiled at me with an increasing air of confidence. "Do you know where I usually sleep? Down below there—in the garden!" Her laugh shrilled out again. "There's a shady corner down at the bottom where the sun never bothers one. Sometimes I sleep there till the stars come out."

The phrase about the garden, in the consul's cable, came back to me and I thought: "After all, it's not such an unhappy state. I wonder if she isn't better off than when she was alive?"

Perhaps she was—but I was sure I wasn't, in her company. And her way of sidling nearer to the door made me distinctly want to reach it before she did. In a rush of cowardice I strode ahead of her—but a second later she had the latch in her hand and was leaning against the panels, her long white raiment hanging about her like grave-clothes. She drooped her head a little sideways and peered at me under her lashless lids.

"You're not going?" she reproached me.

I dived down in vain for my missing voice, and silently signed that I was.

"Going going away? Altogether?" Her eyes were still fixed on me, and I saw two tears gather in their corners and run down over the red glistening circles on her cheeks. "Oh, but you mustn't," she said gently. "I'm too lonely..."

I stammered something inarticulate, my eyes on the blue-nailed hand that grasped the latch. Suddenly the window behind us crashed open, and a gust of wind, surging in out of the blackness, extinguished the candle on the nearest chimney-corner. I glanced back nervously to see if the other candle were going out too.

"You don't like the noise of the wind? I do. It's all I have to talk to. . . .People don't like me much since I've been dead. Queer, isn't it? The peasants are so superstitious. At times I'm really lonely. . . ." Her voice cracked in a last effort at laughter, and she swayed toward me, one hand still on the latch.

"Lonely, lonely! If you knew how *lonely*! It was a lie when I told you I wasn't! And now you come, and your face looks friendly. . . and you say you're going to leave me! No—no—no—you shan't! Or else, why did you come? It's cruel. . . .I used to think I knew what loneliness was. . . .after Grace married, you know. Grace thought she was always thinking of me, but she wasn't. She called me 'darling,' but she was thinking of her husband and children. I said to myself then: 'You couldn't be lonelier if you were dead.' But I know better now. . . .There's been no loneliness like this last year's. . . .none! And sometimes I sit here and think: 'If a man came along some day and took a fancy to you?'"

She gave another wavering cackle. "Well, such things *have* happened, you know, even after youth's gone. . . .a man who'd had his troubles too. But no one came till tonight. . . .and now you say you're going!" Suddenly she flung herself toward me. "Oh, stay with me, stay with me. . . .just tonight. . . .It's so sweet and quiet here. . . .No one need know. . . .no one will ever come and trouble us."

I ought to have shut the window when the first gust came. I might have known there would soon be another, fiercer one. It came now, slamming back the loose-hinged lattice, filling the room with the noise of the sea and with wet swirls of fog, and dashing the other candle to the floor. The light went out, and I stood there—we stood there—lost to each other in the roaring coiling darkness. My heart seemed to stop beating; I had to fetch up my breath with great heaves that covered me with sweat. The door—the door—well, I knew I had been facing it when the candle went.

Something white and wraithlike seemed to melt and crumple up before me in the night, and avoiding the spot where it had sunk away I stumbled around it in a wide circle, got the latch in my hand, caught my foot in a scarf or sleeve, trailing loose and invisible, and freed myself with a jerk from this last obstacle. I had the door open now. As I got into the hall I heard a whimper from the blackness behind me; but I scrambled on to the hall door, dragged it open and bolted out into the night. I slammed the door on that pitiful low whimper, and the fog and wind enveloped me in healing arms.

3

When I was well enough to trust myself to think about it all again I found that a very little thinking got my temperature up, and my heart hammering in my throat. No use. . . .I simply couldn't stand it...for I'd seen Grace Bridgeworth in crape, weeping over the cable, and yet I'd sat and talked with her sister, on the same sofa—her sister who'd been dead a year!

The circle was a vicious one; I couldn't break through it. The fact that I was down with fever the next morning might have explained it; yet I couldn't get away from the clinging reality of the vision. Supposing it *was* a ghost I had been talking to, and not a mere projection of my fever? Supposing something survived of Mary Pask—enough to cry out to me the unuttered loneliness of a lifetime, to express at last what the living woman had always had to keep dumb and hidden? The thought moved me curiously—in my weakness I lay and wept over it. No end of women were like that, I supposed, and perhaps, after death, if they got their chance they tried to use it. . . .Old tales and legends floated through my mind; the bride of Corinth, the mediaeval vampire—but what names to attach to the plaintive image of Mary Pask!

My weak mind wandered in and out among these visions and conjectures, and the longer I lived with them the more convinced I became that something *which had been Mary Pask* had talked with me that night. . . .I made up my mind, when I was up again, to drive back to the place (in broad daylight, this time), to hunt out the grave in the garden—that "shady corner where the sun never bothers one"—and appease the poor ghost with a few flowers.

But the doctors decided otherwise; and perhaps my weak will unknowingly abetted them. At any rate, I yielded to their insistence that I should be driven straight from my hotel to the train for Paris, and thence transhipped, like a piece of luggage, to the Swiss sanatorium they had in view for me.

Of course I meant to come back when I was patched up again. . . and meanwhile, more and more tenderly, but more intermittently, my thoughts went back from my snow-mountain to that wailing autumn night above the *Baie des Trépassés*, and the revelation of the dead Mary Pask who was so much more real to me than ever the living one had been.

4

After all, why should I tell Grace Bridgeworth—ever? I had had a glimpse of things that were really no business of hers. If the revelation had been vouchsafed to me, ought I not to bury it in those deepest depths where the inexplicable and the unforgettable sleep together? And besides, what interest could there be to a woman like Grace in a tale she could neither understand nor believe in? She would just set me down as "queer"—and enough people had done that already. My first object, when I finally did get back to New York, was to convince everybody of my complete return to mental and physical soundness; and into this scheme of evidence my experience with Mary Pask did not seem to fit. All things considered, I would hold my tongue.

But after a while the thought of the grave began to trouble me. I wondered if Grace had ever had a proper grave-stone put on it. The queer neglected look of the house gave me the idea that perhaps she had done nothing—had brushed the whole matter aside, to be attended to when she next went abroad. "Grace forgets," I heard the poor ghost quaver. . . . .No, decidedly, there could be no harm in putting (tactfully) just that one question about the care of the grave; the more so as I was beginning to reproach myself for not having gone back to see with my own eyes how it was kept. . . .

Grace and Horace welcomed me with all their old friendliness, and I soon slipped into the habit of dropping in on them for a meal when I thought they were likely to be alone. Nevertheless, my opportunity didn't come at once—I had to wait for some weeks. And then one evening, when Horace was dining out and I sat alone with Grace, my glance lit on a photograph of her sister—an old faded photograph which seemed to meet my eyes reproachfully.

"By the way, Grace," I began with a jerk, "I don't believe I ever told you: I went down to that little place of. . . .of your sister's the day before I had that bad relapse."

At once her face lit up emotionally. "No, you never told me. How sweet of you to go!" The ready tears over-brimmed her eyes. "I'm so glad you did." She lowered her voice and added softly: "And did you see her?"

The question sent one of my old shudders over me. I looked with amazement at Mrs. Bridgeworth's plump face, smiling at me through a veil of painless tears. "I do reproach myself more and more about darling Mary," she added tremulously. "But tell me—tell me everything."

There was a knot in my throat; I felt almost as uncomfortable as I had in Mary Pask's own presence. Yet I had never before noticed anything uncanny about Grace Bridgeworth. I forced my voice up to my lips.

"Everything? Oh, I can't—." I tried to smile.

"But you did see her?"

I managed to nod, still smiling.

Her face grew suddenly haggard—yes, haggard! "And the change was so dreadful that you can't speak of it? Tell me—was that it?"

I shook my head. After all, what had shocked me was that the change was so slight—that between being dead and alive there seemed after all to be so little difference, except that of a mysterious increase in reality. But Grace's eyes were still searching me insistently. "You must tell me," she reiterated. "I know I ought to have gone there long ago—"

"Yes; perhaps you ought." I hesitated. "To see about the grave, at least. . . ."

She sat silent, her eyes still on my face. Her tears had stopped, but her look of solicitude slowly grew into a stare of something like terror. Hesitatingly, almost reluctantly, she stretched out her hand and laid it on mine for an instant. "Dear old friend—" she began.

"Unfortunately," I interrupted, "I couldn't get back myself to see the grave. . . .because I was taken ill the next day. . . ."

"Yes, yes; of course. I know." She paused. "Are you *sure* you went there at all?" she asked abruptly.

"Sure? Good Lord—" It was my turn to stare. "Do you suspect me of not being quite right yet?" I suggested with an uneasy laugh.

"No—no. . . .of course not. . . .but I don't understand."

"Understand what? I went into the house. . . .I saw everything, in fact, but her grave. . . ."

"Her grave?" Grace jumped up, clasping her hands on her breast and darting away from me. At the other end of the room she stood and gazed, and then moved slowly back.

"Then, after all—I wonder?" She held her eyes on me, half fearful and half reassured. "Could it be simply that you never heard?"

"Never heard?"

"But it was in all the papers! Don't you ever read them? I meant to write. . . . .I thought I *had* written. . . .but I said: 'At any rate he'll see it in the papers'. . . . You know I'm always lazy about letters. . . ."

"See what in the papers?"

"Why, that she *didn't* die. . . .She isn't dead! There isn't any grave, my dear man! It was only a cataleptic trance. . . .An extraordinary case, the doctors say. . . .But didn't she tell you all about it—if you say you saw her?" She burst into half-hysterical laughter: "Surely she must have told you that she wasn't dead?"

"No," I said slowly, "she didn't tell me that."

We talked about it together for a long time after that—talked on till Horace came back from his men's dinner, after midnight. Grace insisted on going in and out of the whole subject, over and over again. As she kept repeating, it was certainly the only time that poor Mary had ever been in the papers. But though I sat and listened patiently I couldn't get up any real interest in what she said. I felt I should never again be interested in Mary Pask, or in anything concerning her.

A Venetian Night's Entertainment

This is the story that, in the dining-room of the old Beacon Street house (now the Aldebaran Club), Judge Anthony Bracknell, of the famous East India firm of Bracknell & Saulsbee, when the ladies had withdrawn to the oval parlour (and Maria's harp was throwing its gauzy web of sound across the Common), used to relate to his grandsons, about the year that Buonaparte marched upon Moscow.

★★★★★★

1

"Him Venice!" said the *lascar* with the big earrings; and Tony Bracknell, leaning on the high gunwale of his father's East Indiaman, the Hepzibah B., saw far off, across the morning sea, a faint vision of towers and domes dissolved in golden air.

It was a rare February day of the year 1760, and a young Tony, newly of age, and bound on the grand tour aboard the crack merchantman of old Bracknell's fleet, felt his heart leap up as the distant city trembled into shape. *Venice!* The name, since childhood, had been a magician's wand to him. In the hall of the old Bracknell house at Salem there hung a series of yellowing prints which Uncle Richard Saulsbee had brought home from one of his long voyages: views of heathen mosques and palaces, of the Grand Turk's *Seraglio*, of St. Peter's Church in Rome; and, in a corner—the corner nearest the rack where the old flintlocks hung—a busy merry populous scene, entitled: *St. Mark's Square in Venice*. This picture, from the first, had singularly taken little Tony's fancy.

His unformulated criticism on the others was that they lacked action. True, in the view of St. Peter's an experienced-looking gentleman in a full-bottomed wig was pointing out the fairly obvious monument to a bashful companion, who had presumably not ventured to raise his eyes to it; while, at the doors of the Seraglio, a group of turbaned *infidels* observed with less hesitancy the approach of a veiled lady on a camel. But in Venice so many things were happening at once—more, Tony was sure, than had ever happened in Boston in a twelve-month or in Salem in a long lifetime. For here, by their garb, were people of every nation on earth, Chinamen, Turks, Spaniards, and many more, mixed with a parti-coloured throng of gentry, lacqueys, chapmen, hucksters, and tall personages in parsons' gowns who stalked through the crowd with an air of mastery, a string of parasites at their heels.

And all these people seemed to be diverting themselves hugely, chaffering with the hucksters, watching the antics of trained dogs and monkeys, distributing doles to maimed beggars or having their pockets picked by slippery-looking fellows in black—the whole with such an air of ease and good-humour that one felt the cut-purses to be as much a part of the show as the tumbling acrobats and animals.

As Tony advanced in years and experience this childish mumming lost its magic; but not so the early imaginings it had excited. For the old picture had been but the spring-board of fancy, the first step of a cloud-ladder leading to a land of dreams. With these dreams the name of Venice remained associated; and all that observation or report subsequently brought him concerning the place seemed, on a sober warranty of fact, to confirm its claim to stand midway between reality and illusion. There was, for instance, a slender Venice glass, gold-powdered as with lily-pollen or the dust of sunbeams, that, standing in the corner cabinet betwixt two Lowestoft caddies, seemed, among its lifeless neighbours, to palpitate like an impaled butterfly. There was, farther, a gold chain of his mother's, spun of that same sun-pollen, so thread-like, impalpable, that it slipped through the fingers like light, yet so strong that it carried a heavy pendant which seemed held in air as if by magic.

Magic! That was the word which the thought of Venice evoked. It was the kind of place, Tony felt, in which things elsewhere impossible might naturally happen, in which two and two might make five, a paradox elope with a syllogism, and a conclusion give the lie to its own premiss. Was there ever a young heart that did not, once and again, long to get away into such a world as that? Tony, at least, had felt the longing from the first hour when the axioms in his horn-book had brought home to him his heavy responsibilities as a Christian and a sinner. And now here was his wish taking shape before him, as the distant haze of gold shaped itself into towers and domes across the morning sea!

The Reverend Ozias Mounce, Tony's governor and bear-leader, was just putting a hand to the third clause of the fourth part of a sermon on Free-Will and Predestination as the *Hepzibah B.'s* anchor rattled overboard. Tony, in his haste to be ashore, would have made one plunge with the anchor; but the Reverend Ozias, on being roused from his lucubrations, earnestly protested against leaving his argument in suspense. What was the trifle of an arrival at some Papistical foreign city, where the very churches wore turbans like so many Moslem idolators, to the important fact of Mr. Mounce's summing up his conclusions before the Muse of Theology took flight? He should be happy, he said, if the tide served, to visit Venice with Mr. Bracknell the next morning.

The next morning, ha!—Tony murmured a submissive "Yes, sir," winked at the subjugated captain, buckled on his sword, pressed his hat down with a flourish, and before the Reverend Ozias had arrived at his next deduction, was skimming merrily shoreward in the Hepzibah's gig.

A moment more and he was in the thick of it! Here was the very world of the old print, only suffused with sunlight and colour, and bubbling with merry noises. What a scene it was! A square enclosed in fantastic painted buildings, and peopled with a throng as fantastic: a bawling, laughing, jostling, sweating mob, parti-coloured, parti-speeched, crackling and sputtering under the hot sun like a dish of fritters over a kitchen fire. Tony, agape, shouldered his way through the press, aware at once that, spite of the tumult, the shrillness, the gesticulation, there was no undercurrent of clownishness, no tendency to horse-play, as in such crowds on market-day at home, but a kind of facetious suavity which seemed to include everybody in the circumference of one huge joke. In such an air the sense of strangeness soon wore off, and Tony was beginning to feel himself vastly at home, when a lift of the tide bore him against a droll-looking bell-ringing fellow who carried above his head a tall metal tree hung with sherbet-glasses.

The encounter set the glasses spinning and three or four spun off and clattered to the stones. The sherbet-seller called on all the saints, and Tony, clapping a lordly hand to his pocket, tossed him a *ducat* by mistake for a *sequin*. The fellow's eyes shot out of their orbits, and just then a personable-looking young man who had observed the transaction stepped up to Tony and said pleasantly, in English:

"I perceive, sir, that you are not familiar with our currency."

"Does he want more?" says Tony, very lordly; whereat the other laughed and replied: "You have given him enough to retire from his business and open a gaming-house over the arcade."

Tony joined in the laugh, and this incident bridging the preliminaries, the two young men were presently hobnobbing over a glass of Canary in front of one of the coffee-houses about the square. Tony counted himself lucky to have run across an English-speaking companion who was good-natured enough to give him a clue to the labyrinth; and when he had paid for the Canary (in the coin his friend selected) they set out again to view the town. The Italian gentleman, who called himself Count Rialto, appeared to have a very numerous acquaintance, and was able to point out to Tony all the chief dignitaries of the state, the men of ton and ladies of fashion, as well as a number of other characters of a kind not openly mentioned in taking a census of Salem.

Tony, who was not averse from reading when nothing better offered, had perused the *Merchant of Venice* and Mr. Otway's fine tragedy; but though these pieces had given him a notion that the social usages of Venice differed from those at home, he was unprepared for the surprising appearance and manners of the great people his friend named to him. The gravest senators of the Republic went in prodigious striped trousers, short cloaks and feathered hats. One nobleman wore a ruff and doctor's gown, another a black velvet tunic slashed with rose-colour; while the President of the dreaded Council of Ten was a terrible strutting fellow with a rapier-like nose, a buff leather jerkin and a trailing scarlet cloak that the crowd was careful not to step on.

It was all vastly diverting, and Tony would gladly have gone on forever; but he had given his word to the captain to be at the landing-place at sunset, and here was dusk already creeping over the skies! Tony was a man of honour; and having pressed on the count a handsome damascened dagger selected from one of the goldsmiths' shops in a narrow street lined with such wares, he insisted on turning his face toward the *Hepzibah's* gig. The count yielded reluctantly; but as they came out again on the square they were caught in a great throng pouring toward the doors of the cathedral.

"They go to Benediction," said the count. "A beautiful sight, with many lights and flowers. It is a pity you cannot take a peep at it."

Tony thought so too, and in another minute a legless beggar had pulled back the leathern flap of the cathedral door, and they stood in a haze of gold and perfume that seemed to rise and fall on the mighty undulations of the organ. Here the press was as thick as without; and as Tony flattened himself against a pillar, he heard a pretty voice at his elbow:—"Oh, sir, oh, sir, your sword!"

He turned at sound of the broken English, and saw a girl who matched the voice trying to disengage her dress from the tip of his scabbard. She wore one of the voluminous black hoods which the Venetian ladies affected, and under its projecting eaves her face spied out at him as sweet as a nesting bird.

In the dusk their hands met over the scabbard, and as she freed herself a shred of her lace flounce clung to Tony's enchanted fingers. Looking after her, he saw she was on the arm of a pompous-looking greybeard in a long black gown and scarlet stockings, who, on perceiving the exchange of glances between the young people, drew the lady away with a threatening look.

The count met Tony's eye with a smile. "One of our Venetian beauties," said he; "the lovely Polixena Cador. She is thought to have the finest eyes in Venice."

"She spoke English," stammered Tony.

"Oh—ah—precisely: she learned the language at the Court of Saint James's, where her father, the senator, was formerly accredited as ambassador. She played as an infant with the royal princes of England."

"And that was her father?"

"Assuredly: young ladies of Donna Polixena's rank do not go abroad save with their parents or a *duenna*."

Just then a soft hand slid into Tony's. His heart gave a foolish bound, and he turned about half-expecting to meet again the merry eyes under the hood; but saw instead a slender brown boy, in some kind of fanciful page's dress, who thrust a folded paper between his fingers and vanished in the throng. Tony, in a tingle, glanced surreptitiously at the count, who appeared absorbed in his prayers. The crowd, at the ringing of a bell, had in fact been overswept by a sudden wave of devotion; and Tony seized the moment to step beneath a lighted shrine with his letter.

"I am in dreadful trouble and implore your help. Polixena"—he read; but hardly had he seized the sense of the words when a hand fell on his shoulder, and a stern-looking man in a cocked hat, and bearing a kind of rod or mace, pronounced a few words in Venetian.

Tony, with a start, thrust the letter in his breast, and tried to jerk himself free; but the harder he jerked the tighter grew the other's grip, and the count, presently perceiving what had happened, pushed his way through the crowd, and whispered hastily to his companion: "For God's sake, make no struggle. This is serious. Keep quiet and do as I tell you."

Tony was no chicken-heart. He had something of a name for pugnacity among the lads of his own age at home, and was not the man to stand in Venice what he would have resented in Salem; but the devil of it was that this black fellow seemed to be pointing to the letter in his breast; and this suspicion was confirmed by the count's agitated whisper.

"This is one of the agents of the Ten.—For God's sake, no outcry." He exchanged a word or two with the mace-bearer and again turned to Tony. "You have been seen concealing a letter about your person—"

"And what of that?" says Tony furiously.

"Gently, gently, my master. A letter handed to you by the page of Donna Polixena Cador.—A black business! Oh, a very black business! This Cador is one of the most powerful nobles in Venice—I beseech you, not a word, sir! Let me think—deliberate—"

His hand on Tony's shoulder, he carried on a rapid dialogue with the potentate in the cocked hat.

"I am sorry, sir—but our young ladies of rank are as jealously guarded as the Grand Turk's wives, and you must be answerable for this scandal. The best I can do is to have you taken privately to the Palazzo Cador, instead of being brought before the Council. I have pleaded your youth and inexperience"—Tony winced at this—"and I think the business may still be arranged."

Meanwhile the agent of the Ten had yielded his place to a sharp-featured shabby-looking fellow in black, dressed somewhat like a lawyer's clerk, who laid a grimy hand on Tony's arm, and with many apologetic gestures steered him through the crowd to the doors of the church. The count held him by the other arm, and in this fashion they emerged on the square, which now lay in darkness save for the many lights twinkling under the arcade and in the windows of the gaming-rooms above it.

Tony by this time had regained voice enough to declare that he would go where they pleased, but that he must first say a word to the mate of the Hepzibah, who had now been awaiting him some two hours or more at the landing-place.

The count repeated this to Tony's custodian, but the latter shook his head and rattled off a sharp denial.

"Impossible, sir," said the count. "I entreat you not to insist. Any resistance will tell against you in the end."

Tony fell silent. With a rapid eye he was measuring his chances of escape. In wind and limb he was more than a mate for his captors, and boyhood's ruses were not so far behind him but he felt himself equal to outwitting a dozen grown men; but he had the sense to see that at a cry the crowd would close in on him. Space was what he wanted: a clear ten yards, and he would have laughed at *Doge* and Council. But the throng was thick as glue, and he walked on submissively, keeping his eye alert for an opening. Suddenly the mob swerved aside after some new show. Tony's fist shot out at the black fellow's chest, and before the latter could right himself the young New Englander was showing a clean pair of heels to his escort.

On he sped, cleaving the crowd like a flood-tide in Gloucester bay, diving under the first arch that caught his eye, dashing down a lane to an unlit water-way, and plunging across a narrow hump-back bridge which landed him in a black pocket between walls. But now his pursuers were at his back, reinforced by the yelping mob. The walls were too high to scale, and for all his courage Tony's breath came short as he paced the masonry cage in which ill-luck had landed him. Suddenly a gate opened in one of the walls, and a slip of a servant wench looked out and beckoned him. There was no time to weigh chances. Tony dashed through the gate, his rescuer slammed and bolted it, and the two stood in a narrow paved well between high houses.

2

The servant picked up a lantern and signed to Tony to follow her. They climbed a squalid stairway of stone, felt their way along a corridor, and entered a tall vaulted room feebly lit by an oil-lamp hung from the painted ceiling. Tony discerned traces of former splendour in his surroundings, but he had no time to examine them, for a figure started up at his approach and in the dim light he recognized the girl who was the cause of all his troubles.

She sprang toward him with outstretched hands, but as he advanced her face changed and she shrank back abashed.

"This is a misunderstanding—a dreadful misunderstanding," she cried out in her pretty broken English. "Oh, how does it happen that you are here?"

"Through no choice of my own, madam, I assure you!" retorted Tony, not over-pleased by his reception.

"But why—how—how did you make this unfortunate mistake?"

"Why, madam, if you'll excuse my candour, I think the mistake was yours—"

"Mine?"—"in sending me a letter—"

"*You*—a letter?"—"by a simpleton of a lad, who must needs hand it to me under your father's very nose—"

The girl broke in on him with a cry. "What! It was *you* who received my letter?" She swept round on the little maid-servant and submerged her under a flood of Venetian. The latter volleyed back in the same jargon, and as she did so, Tony's astonished eye detected in her the doubleted page who had handed him the letter in Saint Mark's.

"What!" he cried, "the lad was this girl in disguise?"

Polixena broke off with an irrepressible smile; but her face clouded instantly and she returned to the charge.

"This wicked, careless girl—she has ruined me, she will be my undoing! Oh, sir, how can I make you understand? The letter was not intended for you—it was meant for the English Ambassador, an old friend of my mother's, from whom I hoped to obtain assistance—oh, how can I ever excuse myself to you?"

"No excuses are needed, madam," said Tony, bowing; "though I am surprised, I own, that any one should mistake me for an ambassador."

Here a wave of mirth again overran Polixena's face. "Oh, sir, you must pardon my poor girl's mistake. She heard you speaking English, and—and—I had told her to hand the letter to the handsomest foreigner in the church." Tony bowed again, more profoundly. "The English Ambassador," Polixena added simply, "is a very handsome man."

"I wish, madam, I were a better proxy!"

She echoed his laugh, and then clapped her hands together with a look of anguish. "Fool that I am! How can I jest at such a moment? I am in dreadful trouble, and now perhaps I have brought trouble on you also—Oh, my father! I hear my father coming!" She turned pale and leaned tremblingly upon the little servant.

Footsteps and loud voices were in fact heard outside, and a moment later the red-stockinged senator stalked into the room attended by half-a-dozen of the *magnificoes* whom Tony had seen abroad in the square. At sight of him, all clapped hands to their swords and burst into furious outcries; and though their jargon was unintelligible to the young man, their tones and gestures made their meaning unpleasantly plain. The senator, with a start of anger, first flung himself on the intruder; then, snatched back by his companions, turned wrathfully on his daughter, who, at his feet, with outstretched arms and streaming face, pleaded her cause with all the eloquence of young distress.

Meanwhile the other nobles gesticulated vehemently among themselves, and one, a truculent-looking personage in ruff and Spanish cape, stalked apart, keeping a jealous eye on Tony. The latter was at his wit's end how to comport himself, for the lovely Polixena's tears had quite drowned her few words of English, and beyond guessing that the *magnificoes* meant him a mischief he had no notion what they would be at.

At this point, luckily, his friend Count Rialto suddenly broke in on the scene, and was at once assailed by all the tongues in the room. He pulled a long face at sight of Tony, but signed to the young man to be silent, and addressed himself earnestly to the senator. The latter, at first, would not draw breath to hear him; but presently, sobering, he walked apart with the count, and the two conversed together out of earshot.

"My dear sir," said the count, at length turning to Tony with a perturbed countenance, "it is as I feared, and you are fallen into a great misfortune."

"A great misfortune! A great trap, I call it!" shouted Tony, whose blood, by this time, was boiling; but as he uttered the word the beautiful Polixena cast such a stricken look on him that he blushed up to the forehead.

"Be careful," said the count, in a low tone. "Though his Illustriousness does not speak your language, he understands a few words of it, and—"

"So much the better!" broke in Tony; "I hope he will understand me if I ask him in plain English what is his grievance against me."

The senator, at this, would have burst forth again; but the count, stepping between, answered quickly: "His grievance against you is that you have been detected in secret correspondence with his daughter, the most noble Polixena Cador, the betrothed bride of this gentleman, the most illustrious Marquess Zanipolo—" and he waved a deferential hand at the frowning hidalgo of the cape and ruff.

"Sir," said Tony, "if that is the extent of my offence, it lies with the young lady to set me free, since by her own avowal—" but here he stopped short, for, to his surprise, Polixena shot a terrified glance at him.

"Sir," interposed the count, "we are not accustomed in Venice to take shelter behind a lady's reputation."

"No more are we in Salem," retorted Tony in a white heat. "I was merely about to remark that, by the young lady's avowal, she has never seen me before."

Polixena's eyes signalled her gratitude, and he felt he would have died to defend her.

The count translated his statement, and presently pursued: "His Illustriousness observes that, in that case, his daughter's misconduct has been all the more reprehensible."

"Her misconduct? Of what does he accuse her?"

"Of sending you, just now, in the church of Saint Mark's, a letter which you were seen to read openly and thrust in your bosom. The incident was witnessed by his Illustriousness the Marquess Zanipolo, who, in consequence, has already repudiated his unhappy bride."

Tony stared contemptuously at the black *marquess*. "If his Illustriousness is so lacking in gallantry as to repudiate a lady on so trivial a pretext, it is he and not I who should be the object of her father's resentment."

"That, my dear young gentleman, is hardly for you to decide. Your only excuse being your ignorance of our customs, it is scarcely for you to advise us how to behave in matters of *punctilio*."

It seemed to Tony as though the count were going over to his enemies, and the thought sharpened his retort.

"I had supposed," said he, "that men of sense had much the same behaviour in all countries, and that, here as elsewhere, a gentleman would be taken at his word. I solemnly affirm that the letter I was seen to read reflects in no way on the honour of this young lady, and has in fact nothing to do with what you suppose."

As he had himself no notion what the letter was about, this was as far as he dared commit himself.

There was another brief consultation in the opposing camp, and the count then said:—"We all know, sir, that a gentleman is obliged to meet certain enquiries by a denial; but you have at your command the means of immediately clearing the lady. Will you show the letter to her father?"

There was a perceptible pause, during which Tony, while appearing to look straight before him, managed to deflect an interrogatory glance toward Polixena. Her reply was a faint negative motion, accompanied by unmistakable signs of apprehension.

"Poor girl!" he thought, "she is in a worse case than I imagined, and whatever happens I must keep her secret."

He turned to the senator with a deep bow. "I am not," said he, "in the habit of showing my private correspondence to strangers."

The count interpreted these words, and Donna Polixena's father, dashing his hand on his hilt, broke into furious invective, while the *marquess* continued to nurse his outraged feelings aloof.

The count shook his head funereally. "Alas, sir, it is as I feared. This is not the first time that youth and propinquity have led to fatal imprudence. But I need hardly, I suppose, point out the obligation incumbent upon you as a man of honour."

Tony stared at him haughtily, with a look which was meant for the *marquess*. "And what obligation is that?"

"To repair the wrong you have done—in other words, to marry the lady."

Polixena at this burst into tears, and Tony said to himself: "Why in heaven does she not bid me show the letter?" Then he remembered that it had no superscription, and that the words it contained, supposing them to have been addressed to himself, were hardly of a nature to disarm suspicion. The sense of the girl's grave plight effaced all thought of his own risk, but the count's last words struck him as so preposterous that he could not repress a smile.

"I cannot flatter myself," said he, "that the lady would welcome this solution."

The count's manner became increasingly ceremonious. "Such modesty," he said, "becomes your youth and inexperience; but even if it were justified it would scarcely alter the case, as it is always assumed in this country that a young lady wishes to marry the man whom her father has selected."

"But I understood just now," Tony interposed, "that the gentleman yonder was in that enviable position."

"So he was, till circumstances obliged him to waive the privilege in your favour."

"He does me too much honour; but if a deep sense of my unworthiness obliges me to decline—"

"You are still," interrupted the count, "labouring under a misapprehension. Your choice in the matter is no more to be consulted than the lady's. Not to put too fine a point on it, it is necessary that you should marry her within the hour."

Tony, at this, for all his spirit, felt the blood run thin in his veins. He looked in silence at the threatening visages between himself and the door, stole a side-glance at the high barred windows of the apartment, and then turned to Polixena, who had fallen sobbing at her father's feet.

"And if I refuse?" said he.

The count made a significant gesture. "I am not so foolish as to threaten a man of your mettle. But perhaps you are unaware what the consequences would be to the lady."

Polixena, at this, struggling to her feet, addressed a few impassioned words to the count and her father; but the latter put her aside with an obdurate gesture.

The count turned to Tony. "The lady herself pleads for you—at what cost you do not guess—but as you see it is vain. In an hour his Illustriousness's chaplain will be here. Meanwhile his Illustriousness consents to leave you in the custody of your betrothed."

He stepped back, and the other gentlemen, bowing with deep ceremony to Tony, stalked out one by one from the room. Tony heard the key turn in the lock, and found himself alone with Polixena.

3

The girl had sunk into a chair, her face hidden, a picture of shame and agony. So moving was the sight that Tony once again forgot his own extremity in the view of her distress. He went and kneeled beside her, drawing her hands from her face.

"Oh, don't make me look at you!" she sobbed; but it was on his bosom that she hid from his gaze. He held her there a breathing-space, as he might have clasped a weeping child; then she drew back and put him gently from her.

"What humiliation!" she lamented.

"Do you think I blame you for what has happened?"

"Alas, was it not my foolish letter that brought you to this plight? And how nobly you defended me! How generous it was of you not to show the letter! If my father knew I had written to the ambassador to save me from this dreadful marriage his anger against me would be even greater."

"Ah—it was that you wrote for?" cried Tony with unaccountable relief.

"Of course—what else did you think?"

"But is it too late for the ambassador to save you?"

"From *you?*" A smile flashed through her tears. "Alas, yes." She drew back and hid her face again, as though overcome by a fresh wave of shame.

Tony glanced about him. "If I could wrench a bar out of that win-

121

dow—" he muttered.

"Impossible! The court is guarded. You are a prisoner, alas.—Oh, I must speak!" She sprang up and paced the room. "But indeed you can scarce think worse of me than you do already—"

"I think ill of you?"

"Alas, you must! To be unwilling to marry the man my father has chosen for me—"

"Such a beetle-browed lout! It would be a burning shame if you married him."

"Ah, you come from a free country. Here a girl is allowed no choice."

"It is infamous, I say—infamous!"

"No, no—I ought to have resigned myself, like so many others."

"Resigned yourself to that brute! Impossible!"

"He has a dreadful name for violence—his *gondolier* has told my little maid such tales of him! But why do I talk of myself, when it is of you I should be thinking?"

"Of me, poor child?" cried Tony, losing his head.

"Yes, and how to save you—for I *can* save you! But every moment counts—and yet what I have to say is so dreadful."

"Nothing from your lips could seem dreadful."

"Ah, if he had had your way of speaking!"

"Well, now at least you are free of him," said Tony, a little wildly; but at this she stood up and bent a grave look on him.

"No, I am not free," she said; "but you are, if you will do as I tell you."

Tony, at this, felt a sudden dizziness; as though, from a mad flight through clouds and darkness, he had dropped to safety again, and the fall had stunned him.

"What am I to do?" he said.

"Look away from me, or I can never tell you."

He thought at first that this was a jest, but her eyes commanded him, and reluctantly he walked away and leaned in the embrasure of the window. She stood in the middle of the room, and as soon as his back was turned she began to speak in a quick monotonous voice, as though she were reciting a lesson.

"You must know that the Marquess Zanipolo, though a great noble, is not a rich man. True, he has large estates, but he is a desperate spendthrift and gambler, and would sell his soul for a round sum of ready money.—If you turn round I shall not go on!—He wrangled

122

horribly with my father over my dowry—he wanted me to have more than either of my sisters, though one married a *procurator* and the other a *grandee* of Spain. But my father is a gambler too—oh, such fortunes as are squandered over the arcade yonder! And so—and so—don't turn, I implore you—oh, do you begin to see my meaning?"

She broke off sobbing, and it took all his strength to keep his eyes from her.

"Go on," he said.

"Will you not understand? Oh, I would say anything to save you! You don't know us Venetians—we're all to be bought for a price. It is not only the brides who are marketable—sometimes the husbands sell themselves too. And they think you rich—my father does, and the others—I don't know why, unless you have shown your money too freely—and the English are all rich, are they not? And—oh, oh—do you understand? Oh, I can't bear your eyes!"

She dropped into a chair, her head on her arms, and Tony in a flash was at her side.

"My poor child, my poor Polixena!" he cried, and wept and clasped her.

"You *are* rich, are you not? You would promise them a ransom?" she persisted.

"To enable you to marry the *marquess*?"

"To enable you to escape from this place. Oh, I hope I may never see your face again." She fell to weeping once more, and he drew away and paced the floor in a fever.

Presently she sprang up with a fresh air of resolution, and pointed to a clock against the wall. "The hour is nearly over. It is quite true that my father is gone to fetch his chaplain. Oh, I implore you, be warned by me! There is no other way of escape."

"And if I do as you say—?"

"You are safe! You are free! I stake my life on it."

"And you—you are married to that villain?"

"But I shall have saved you. Tell me your name, that I may say it to myself when I am alone."

"My name is Anthony. But you must not marry that fellow."

"You forgive me, Anthony? You don't think too badly of me?"

"I say you must not marry that fellow."

She laid a trembling hand on his arm. "Time presses," she adjured him, "and I warn you there is no other way."

For a moment he had a vision of his mother, sitting very upright, on a Sunday evening, reading Dr. Tillotson's sermons in the best parlour at Salem; then he swung round on the girl and caught both her hands in his. "Yes, there is," he cried, "if you are willing. Polixena, let the priest come!"

She shrank back from him, white and radiant. "Oh, hush, be silent!" she said.

"I am no noble *marquess*, and have no great estates," he cried. "My father is a plain India merchant in the colony of Massachusetts—but if you—"

"Oh, hush, I say! I don't know what your long words mean. But I bless you, bless you, bless you on my knees!" And she knelt before him, and fell to kissing his hands.

He drew her up to his breast and held her there.

"You are willing, Polixena?" he said.

"No, no!" She broke from him with outstretched hands. "I am not willing. You mistake me. I must marry the *marquess*, I tell you!"

"On my money?" he taunted her; and her burning blush rebuked him.

"Yes, on your money," she said sadly.

"Why? Because, much as you hate him, you hate me still more?" She was silent.

"If you hate me, why do you sacrifice yourself for me?" he persisted.

"You torture me! And I tell you the hour is past."

"Let it pass. I'll not accept your sacrifice. I will not lift a finger to help another man to marry you."

"Oh, madman, madman!" she murmured.

Tony, with crossed arms, faced her squarely, and she leaned against the wall a few feet off from him. Her breast throbbed under its lace and *falbalas*, and her eyes swam with terror and entreaty.

"Polixena, I love you!" he cried.

A blush swept over her throat and bosom, bathing her in light to the verge of her troubled brows.

"I love you! I love you!" he repeated.

And now she was on his breast again, and all their youth was in their lips. But her embrace was as fleeting as a bird's poise and before he knew it he clasped empty air, and half the room was between them.

She was holding up a little coral charm and laughing. "I took it from your fob," she said. "It is of no value, is it? And I shall not get any of the money, you know."

She continued to laugh strangely, and the rouge burned like fire in her ashen face.

"What are you talking of?" he said.

"They never give me anything but the clothes I wear. And I shall never see you again, Anthony!" She gave him a dreadful look. "Oh, my poor boy, my poor love—'*I love you, I love you, Polixena!*'"

He thought she had turned light-headed, and advanced to her with soothing words; but she held him quietly at arm's length, and as he gazed he read the truth in her face.

He fell back from her, and a sob broke from him as he bowed his head on his hands.

"Only, for God's sake, have the money ready, or there may be foul play here," she said.

As she spoke there was a great tramping of steps outside and a burst of voices on the threshold.

"It is all a lie," she gasped out, "about my marriage, and the *marquess*, and the ambassador, and the senator—but not, oh, not about your danger in this place—or about my love," she breathed to him. And as the key rattled in the door she laid her lips on his brow.

The key rattled, and the door swung open—but the black-cassocked gentleman who stepped in, though a priest indeed, was no votary of idolatrous rites, but that sound orthodox divine, the Reverend Ozias Mounce, looking very much perturbed at his surroundings, and very much on the alert for the Scarlet Woman. He was supported, to his evident relief, by the captain of the *Hepzibah B.,* and the procession was closed by an escort of stern-looking fellows in cocked hats and small-swords, who led between them Tony's late friends the *magnificoes*, now as sorry a looking company as the law ever landed in her net.

The captain strode briskly into the room, uttering a grunt of satisfaction as he clapped eyes on Tony.

"So, Mr. Bracknell," said he, "you have been seeing the carnival with this pack of mummers, have you? And this is where your pleasuring has landed you? H'm—a pretty establishment, and a pretty lady at the head of it." He glanced about the apartment and doffed his hat with mock ceremony to Polixena, who faced him like a princess.

"Why, my girl," said he, amicably, "I think I saw you this morning in the square, on the arm of the pantaloon yonder; and as for that Captain Spavent—" and he pointed a derisive finger at the *marquess*— "I've watched him drive his bully's trade under the arcade ever since

125

I first dropped anchor in these waters. Well, well," he continued, his indignation subsiding, "all's fair in carnival, I suppose, but this gentleman here is under sailing orders, and I fear we must break up your little party."

At this Tony saw Count Rialto step forward, looking very small and explanatory, and uncovering obsequiously to the captain.

"I can assure you, sir," said the count in his best English, "that this incident is the result of an unfortunate misunderstanding, and if you will oblige us by dismissing these myrmidons, any of my friends here will be happy to offer satisfaction to Mr. Bracknell and his companions."

Mr. Mounce shrank visibly at this, and the captain burst into a loud guffaw.

"Satisfaction?" says he. "Why, my cock, that's very handsome of you, considering the rope's at your throats. But we'll not take advantage of your generosity, for I fear Mr. Bracknell has already trespassed on it too long. You pack of galley-slaves, you!" he spluttered suddenly, "decoying young innocents with that devil's bait of yours—" His eye fell on Polixena, and his voice softened unaccountably. "Ah, well, we must all see the carnival once, I suppose," he said. "All's well that ends well, as the fellow says in the play; and now, if you please, Mr. Bracknell, if you'll take the reverend gentleman's arm there, we'll bid *adieu* to our hospitable entertainers, and right about face for the *Hepzibah*."

The Triumph of Night

It was clear that the sleigh from Weymore had not come; and the shivering young traveller from Boston, who had counted on jumping into it when he left the train at Northridge Junction, found himself standing alone on the open platform, exposed to the full assault of night-fall and winter.

The blast that swept him came off New Hampshire snow-fields and ice-hung forests. It seemed to have traversed interminable leagues of frozen silence, filling them with the same cold roar and sharpening its edge against the same bitter black-and-white landscape. Dark, searching and sword-like, it alternately muffled and harried its victim, like a bull-fighter now whirling his cloak and now planting his darts. This analogy brought home to the young man the fact that he himself had no cloak, and that the overcoat in which he had faced the relatively temperate air of Boston seemed no thicker than a sheet of paper on the bleak heights of Northridge.

George Faxon said to himself that the place was uncommonly well-named. It clung to an exposed ledge over the valley from which the train had lifted him, and the wind combed it with teeth of steel that he seemed actually to hear scraping against the wooden sides of the station. Other building there was none: the village lay far down the road, and thither—since the Weymore sleigh had not come—Faxon saw himself under the necessity of plodding through several feet of snow.

He understood well enough what had happened: his hostess had forgotten that he was coming. Young as Faxon was, this sad lucidity of soul had been acquired as the result of long experience, and he knew that the visitors who can least afford to hire a carriage are almost always those whom their hosts forget to send for. Yet to say that Mrs.

Culme had forgotten him was too crude a way of putting it Similar incidents led him to think that she had probably told her maid to tell the butler to telephone the coachman to tell one of the grooms (if no one else needed him) to drive over to Northridge to fetch the new secretary; but on a night like this, what groom who respected his rights would fail to forget the order?

Faxon's obvious course was to struggle through the drifts to the village, and there rout out a sleigh to convey him to Weymore; but what if, on his arrival at Mrs. Culme's, no one remembered to ask him what this devotion to duty had cost? That, again, was one of the contingencies he had expensively learned to look out for, and the perspicacity so acquired told him it would be cheaper to spend the night at the Northridge inn, and advise Mrs. Culme of his presence there by telephone. He had reached this decision, and was about to entrust his luggage to a vague man with a lantern, when his hopes were raised by the sound of bells.

Two sleighs were just dashing up to the station, and from the foremost there sprang a young man muffled in furs.

"Weymore?—No, these are not the Weymore sleighs."

The voice was that of the youth who had jumped to the platform—a voice so agreeable that, in spite of the words, it fell consolingly on Faxon's ears. At the same moment the wandering station-lantern, casting a transient light on the speaker, showed his features to be in the pleasantest harmony with his voice. He was very fair and very young—hardly in the twenties, Faxon thought—but his face, though full of a morning freshness, was a trifle too thin and fine-drawn, as though a vivid spirit contended in him with a strain of physical weakness. Faxon was perhaps the quicker to notice such delicacies of balance because his own temperament hung on lightly quivering nerves, which yet, as he believed, would never quite swing him beyond a normal sensibility.

"You expected a sleigh from Weymore?" the newcomer continued, standing beside Faxon like a slender column of fur.

Mrs. Culme's secretary explained his difficulty, and the other brushed it aside with a contemptuous "Oh, Mrs. Culme!" that carried both speakers a long way toward reciprocal understanding.

"But then you must be—" The youth broke off with a smile of interrogation.

"The new secretary? Yes. But apparently there are no notes to be answered this evening." Faxon's laugh deepened the sense of solidarity

128

which had so promptly established itself between the two.

His friend laughed also. "Mrs. Culme," he explained, "was lunching at my uncle's today, and she said you were due this evening. But seven hours is a long time for Mrs. Culme to remember anything."

"Well," said Faxon philosophically, "I suppose that's one of the reasons why she needs a secretary. And I've always the inn at Northridge," he concluded.

"Oh, but you haven't, though! It burned down last week."

"The deuce it did!" said Faxon; but the humour of the situation struck him before its inconvenience. His life, for years past, had been mainly a succession of resigned adaptations, and he had learned, before dealing practically with his embarrassments, to extract from most of them a small tribute of amusement.

"Oh, well, there's sure to be somebody in the place who can put me up."

"No one you could put up with. Besides, Northridge is three miles off, and our place—in the opposite direction—is a little nearer." Through the darkness, Faxon saw his friend sketch a gesture of self-introduction. "My name's Frank Rainer, and I'm staying with my uncle at Overdale. I've driven over to meet two friends of his, who are due in a few minutes from New York. If you don't mind waiting till they arrive I'm sure Overdale can do you better than Northridge. We're only down from town for a few days, but the house is always ready for a lot of people."

"But your uncle—?" Faxon could only object, with the odd sense, through his embarrassment, that it would be magically dispelled by his invisible friend's next words.

"Oh, my uncle—you'll see! I answer for him! I daresay you've heard of him—John Lavington?"

John Lavington! There was a certain irony in asking if one had heard of John Lavington! Even from a post of observation as obscure as that of Mrs. Culme's secretary the rumour of John Lavington's money, of his pictures, his politics, his charities and his hospitality, was as difficult to escape as the roar of a cataract in a mountain solitude. It might almost have been said that the one place in which one would not have expected to come upon him was in just such a solitude as now surrounded the speakers—at least in this deepest hour of its desertedness. But it was just like Lavington's brilliant ubiquity to put one in the wrong even there.

"Oh, yes, I've heard of your uncle."

"Then you will come, won't you? We've only five minutes to wait." young Rainer urged, in the tone that dispels scruples by ignoring them; and Faxon found himself accepting the invitation as simply as it was offered.

A delay in the arrival of the New York train lengthened their five minutes to fifteen; and as they paced the icy platform Faxon began to see why it had seemed the most natural thing in the world to accede to his new acquaintance's suggestion. It was because Frank Rainer was one of the privileged beings who simplify human intercourse by the atmosphere of confidence and good humour they diffuse. He produced this effect, Faxon noted, by the exercise of no gift but his youth, and of no art but his sincerity; and these qualities were revealed in a smile of such sweetness that Faxon felt, as never before, what Nature can achieve when she deigns to match the face with the mind.

He learned that the young man was the ward, and the only nephew, of John Lavington, with whom he had made his home since the death of his mother, the great man's sister. Mr. Lavington, Rainer said, had been "a regular brick" to him—"But then he is to everyone, you know"—and the young fellow's situation seemed in fact to be perfectly in keeping with his person. Apparently the only shade that had ever rested on him was cast by the physical weakness which Faxon had already detected.

Young Rainer had been threatened with tuberculosis, and the disease was so far advanced that, according to the highest authorities, banishment to Arizona or New Mexico was inevitable. "But luckily my uncle didn't pack me off, as most people would have done, without getting another opinion. Whose? Oh, an awfully clever chap, a young doctor with a lot of new ideas, who simply laughed at my being sent away, and said I'd do perfectly well in New York if I didn't dine out too much, and if I dashed off occasionally to Northridge for a little fresh air. So it's really my uncle's doing that I'm not in exile— and I feel no end better since the new chap told me I needn't bother." Young Rainer went on to confess that he was extremely fond of dining out, dancing and similar distractions; and Faxon, listening to him, was inclined to think that the physician who had refused to cut him off altogether from these pleasures was probably a better psychologist than his seniors.

"All the same you ought to be careful, you know." The sense of elder-brotherly concern that forced the words from Faxon made him, as he spoke, slip his arm through Frank Rainer's.

The latter met the movement with a responsive pressure. "Oh, I am: awfully, awfully. And then my uncle has such an eye on me!"

"But if your uncle has such an eye on you, what does he say to your swallowing knives out here in this Siberian wild?"

Rainer raised his fur collar with a careless gesture. "It's not that that does it—the cold's good for me."

"And it's not the dinners and dances? What is it, then?" Faxon good-humouredly insisted; to which his companion answered with a laugh: "Well, my uncle says it's being bored; and I rather think he's right!"

His laugh ended in a spasm of coughing and a struggle for breath that made Faxon, still holding his arm, guide him hastily into the shelter of the fireless waiting-room.

Young Rainer had dropped down on the bench against the wall and pulled off one of his fur gloves to grope for a handkerchief. He tossed aside his cap and drew the handkerchief across his forehead, which was intensely white, and beaded with moisture, though his face retained a healthy glow. But Faxon's gaze remained fastened to the hand he had uncovered: it was so long, so colourless, so wasted, so much older than the brow he passed it over.

"It's queer—a healthy face but dying hands," the secretary mused: he somehow wished young Rainer had kept on his glove.

The whistle of the express drew the young men to their feet, and the next moment two heavily-furred gentlemen had descended to the platform and were breasting the rigour of the night. Frank Rainer introduced them as Mr. Grisben and Mr. Balch, and Faxon, while their luggage was being lifted into the second sleigh, discerned them, by the roving lantern-gleam, to be an elderly grey-headed pair, of the average prosperous business cut.

They saluted their host's nephew with friendly familiarity, and Mr. Grisben, who seemed the spokesman of the two, ended his greeting with a genial—"and many many more of them, dear boy!" which suggested to Faxon that their arrival coincided with an anniversary. But he could not press the enquiry, for the seat allotted him was at the coachman's side, while Frank Rainer joined his uncle's guests inside the sleigh.

A swift flight (behind such horses as one could be sure of John Lavington's having) brought them to tall gateposts, an illuminated lodge, and an avenue on which the snow had been levelled to the smoothness of marble. At the end of the avenue the long house loomed up, its principal bulk dark, but one wing sending out a ray of welcome; and the next moment Faxon was receiving a violent impression of warmth and light, of hot-house plants, hurrying servants, a vast spectacular oak hall like a stage-setting, and, in its unreal middle distance, a small figure, correctly dressed, conventionally featured, and utterly unlike his rather florid conception of the great John Lavington.

The surprise of the contrast remained with him through his hurried dressing in the large luxurious bedroom to which he had been shown. "I don't see where he comes in," was the only way he could put it, so difficult was it to fit the exuberance of Lavington's public personality into his host's contracted frame and manner. Mr. Lavington, to whom Faxon's case had been rapidly explained by young Rainer, had welcomed him with a sort of dry and stilted cordiality that exactly matched his narrow face, his stiff hand, and the whiff of scent on his evening handkerchief. "Make yourself at home—at home!" he had repeated, in a tone that suggested, on his own part, a complete inability to perform the feat he urged on his visitor. "Any friend of Frank's....delighted.... make yourself thoroughly at home!"

2

In spite of the balmy temperature and complicated conveniences of Faxon's bedroom, the injunction was not easy to obey. It was wonderful luck to have found a night's shelter under the opulent roof of Overdale, and he tasted the physical satisfaction to the full. But the place, for all its ingenuities of comfort, was oddly cold and unwelcoming. He couldn't have said why, and could only suppose that Mr. Lavington's intense personality—intensely negative, but intense all the same—must, in some occult way, have penetrated every corner of his dwelling. Perhaps, though, it was merely that Faxon himself was tired and hungry, more deeply chilled than he had known till he came in from the cold, and unutterably sick of all strange houses, and of the prospect of perpetually treading other people's stairs.

"I hope you're not famished?" Rainer's slim figure was in the doorway. "My uncle has a little business to attend to with Mr. Grisben, and we don't dine for half an hour. Shall I fetch you, or can you find your way down? Come straight to the dining-room—the second door on the left of the long gallery."

He disappeared, leaving a ray of warmth behind him, and Faxon, relieved, lit a cigarette and sat down by the fire.

Looking about with less haste, he was struck by a detail that had escaped him. The room was full of flowers—a mere "bachelor's room," in the wing of a house opened only for a few days, in the dead middle of a New Hampshire winter! Flowers were everywhere, not in senseless profusion, but placed with the same conscious art that he had remarked in the grouping of the blossoming shrubs in the hall. A vase of arums stood on the writing-table, a cluster of strange-hued carnations on the stand at his elbow, and from bowls of glass and porcelain clumps of freesia-bulbs diffused their melting fragrance. The fact implied acres of glass—but that was the least interesting part of it. The flowers themselves, their quality, selection and arrangement, attested on some one's part—and on whose but John Lavington's?—a solicitous and sensitive passion for that particular form of beauty. Well, it simply made the man, as he had appeared to Faxon, all the harder to understand!

The half-hour elapsed, and Faxon, rejoicing at the prospect of food, set out to make his way to the dining-room. He had not noticed the direction he had followed in going to his room, and was puzzled, when he left it, to find that two staircases, of apparently equal importance, invited him. He chose the one to his right, and reached, at its foot, a long gallery such as Rainer had described. The gallery was empty, the doors down its length were closed; but Rainer had said: "The second to the left," and Faxon, after pausing for some chance enlightenment which did not come, laid his hand on the second knob to the left.

The room he entered was square, with dusky picture-hung walls. In its centre, about a table lit by veiled lamps, he fancied Mr. Lavington and his guests to be already seated at dinner; then he perceived that the table was covered not with viands but with papers, and that he had blundered into what seemed to be his host's study. As he paused Frank Rainer looked up.

"Oh, here's Mr. Faxon. Why not ask him—?"

Mr. Lavington, from the end of the table, reflected his nephew's smile in a glance of impartial benevolence.

"Certainly. Come in, Mr. Faxon. If you won't think it a liberty—"

Mr. Grisben, who sat opposite his host, turned his head toward the door. "Of course Mr. Faxon's an American citizen?"

Frank Rainer laughed. "That's all right. . . . Oh, no, not one of your pin-pointed pens, Uncle Jack! Haven't you got a quill somewhere?"

Mr. Balch, who spoke slowly and as if reluctantly, in a muffled voice of which there seemed to be very little left, raised his hand to say: "One moment: you acknowledge this to be—?"

"My last will and testament?" Rainer's laugh redoubled. "Well, I won't answer for the 'last.' It's the first, anyway."

"It's a mere formula," Mr. Balch explained.

"Well, here goes." Rainer dipped his quill in the inkstand his uncle had pushed in his direction, and dashed a gallant signature across the document.

Faxon, understanding what was expected of him, and conjecturing that the young man was signing his will on the attainment of his majority, had placed himself behind Mr. Grisben, and stood awaiting his turn to affix his name to the instrument. Rainer, having signed, was about to push the paper across the table to Mr. Balch; but the latter, again raising his hand, said in his sad imprisoned voice: "The seal—?"

"Oh, does there have to be a seal?"

Faxon, looking over Mr. Grisben at John Lavington, saw a faint frown between his impassive eyes. "Really, Frank!" He seemed, Faxon thought, slightly irritated by his nephew's frivolity.

"Who's got a seal?" Frank Rainer continued, glancing about the table. "There doesn't seem to be one here."

Mr. Grisben interposed. "A wafer will do. Lavington, you have a wafer?"

Mr. Lavington had recovered his serenity. "There must be some in one of the drawers. But I'm ashamed to say I don't know where my secretary keeps these things. He ought to have seen to it that a wafer was sent with the document."

"Oh, hang it—" Frank Rainer pushed the paper aside: "It's the hand of God—and I'm as hungry as a wolf. Let's dine first, Uncle Jack."

"I think I've a seal upstairs," said Faxon.

Mr. Lavington sent him a barely perceptible smile. "So sorry to give you the trouble—"

"Oh, I say, don't send him after it now. Let's wait till after dinner!"

Mr. Lavington continued to smile on his guest, and the latter, as if under the faint coercion of the smile, turned from the room and ran upstairs. Having taken the seal from his writing-case he came down again, and once more opened the door of the study. No one was speaking when he entered—they were evidently awaiting his return with the mute impatience of hunger, and he put the seal in Rainer's reach, and stood watching while Mr. Grisben struck a match and held it to one of the candles flanking the inkstand. As the wax descended on the paper Faxon remarked again the strange emaciation, the pre-mature physical weariness, of the hand that held it: he wondered if Mr. Lavington had ever noticed his nephew's hand, and if it were not poignantly visible to him now.

With this thought in his mind, Faxon raised his eyes to look at Mr. Lavington. The great man's gaze rested on Frank Rainer with an expression of untroubled benevolence; and at the same instant Faxon's attention was attracted by the presence in the room of another person, who must have joined the group while he was upstairs searching for the seal. The new-comer was a man of about Mr. Lavington's age and figure, who stood just behind his chair, and who, at the moment when Faxon first saw him, was gazing at young Rainer with an equal intensity of attention.

The likeness between the two men—perhaps increased by the fact that the hooded lamps on the table left the figure behind the chair in shadow—struck Faxon the more because of the contrast in their expression. John Lavington, during his nephew's clumsy attempt to drop the wax and apply the seal, continued to fasten on him a look of half-amused affection; while the man behind the chair, so oddly reduplicating the lines of his features and figure, turned on the boy a face of pale hostility.

The impression was so startling that Faxon forgot what was going on about him. He was just dimly aware of young Reiner's exclaiming; "Your turn, Mr. Grisben!" of Mr. Grisben's protesting: "No—no; Mr. Faxon first," and of the pen's being thereupon transferred to his own hand. He received it with a deadly sense of being unable to move, or even to understand what was expected of him, till he became conscious of Mr. Grisben's paternally pointing out the precise spot on which he was to leave his autograph. The effort to fix his attention and steady his hand prolonged the process of signing, and when he stood up—a strange weight of fatigue on all his limbs—the figure behind Mr. Lavington's chair was gone.

Faxon felt an immediate sense of relief. It was puzzling that the man's exit should have been so rapid and noiseless, but the door behind Mr. Lavington was screened by a tapestry hanging, and Faxon concluded that the unknown looker-on had merely had to raise it to pass out. At any rate he was gone, and with his withdrawal the strange weight was lifted. Young Rainer was lighting a cigarette, Mr. Balch inscribing his name at the foot of the document, Mr. Lavington—his eyes no longer on his nephew—examining a strange white-winged orchid in the vase at his elbow. Everything suddenly seemed to have grown natural and simple again, and Faxon found himself responding with a smile to the affable gesture with which his host declared: "And now, Mr. Faxon, we'll dine."

3

"I wonder how I blundered into the wrong room just now; I thought you told me to take the second door to the left," Faxon said to Frank Rainer as they followed the older men down the gallery.

"So I did; but I probably forgot to tell you which staircase to take. Coming from your bedroom, I ought to have said the fourth door to the right. It's a puzzling house, because my uncle keeps adding to it from year to year. He built this room last summer for his modern pictures."

Young Rainer, pausing to open another door, touched an electric button which sent a circle of light about the walls of a long room hung with canvases of the French impressionist school.

Faxon advanced, attracted by a shimmering Monet, but Rainer laid a hand on his arm.

"He bought that last week. But come along—I'll show you all this after dinner. Or he will, rather—he loves it."

"Does he really love things?"

Rainer stared, clearly perplexed at the question. "Rather! Flowers and pictures especially! Haven't you noticed the flowers? I suppose you think his manner's cold; it seems so at first; but he's really awfully keen about things."

Faxon looked quickly at the speaker. "Has your uncle a brother?"

"Brother? No—never had. He and my mother were the only ones."

"Or any relation who—who looks like him? Who might be mistaken for him?"

"Not that I ever heard of. Does he remind you of someone?"

"Yes."

"That's queer. We'll ask him if he's got a double. Come on!"

But another picture had arrested Faxon, and some minutes elapsed before he and his young host reached the dining-room. It was a large room, with the same conventionally handsome furniture and delicately grouped flowers; and Faxon's first glance showed him that only three men were seated about the dining-table. The man who had stood behind Mr. Lavington's chair was not present, and no seat awaited him.

When the young men entered, Mr. Grisben was speaking, and his host, who faced the door, sat looking down at his untouched soup-plate and turning the spoon about in his small dry hand.

"It's pretty late to call them rumours—they were devilish close to facts when we left town this morning," Mr. Grisben was saying, with an unexpected incisiveness of tone.

Mr. Lavington laid down his spoon and smiled interrogatively. "Oh, facts—what are facts? Just the way a thing happens to look at a given minute. . . ."

"You haven't heard anything from town?" Mr. Grisben persisted.

"Not a syllable. So you see. . . . . Balch, a little more of that petite marmite. Mr. Faxon. . . . . between Frank and Mr. Grisben, please."

The dinner progressed through a series of complicated courses, ceremoniously dispensed by a prelatical butler attended by three tall footmen, and it was evident that Mr. Lavington took a certain satisfaction in the pageant. That, Faxon reflected, was probably the joint in his armour—that and the flowers. He had changed the subject—not abruptly but firmly—when the young men entered, but Faxon perceived that it still possessed the thoughts of the two elderly visitors, and Mr. Balch presently observed, in a voice that seemed to come from the last survivor down a mine-shaft: "If it does come, it will be the biggest crash since '93."

Mr. Lavington looked bored but polite. "Wall Street can stand crashes better than it could then. It's got a robuster constitution."

"Yes; but—"

"Speaking of constitutions," Mr. Grisben intervened: "Frank, are you taking care of yourself?"

A flush rose to young Rainer's cheeks.

"Why, of course! Isn't that what I'm here for?"

"You're here about three days in the month, aren't you? And the rest of the time it's crowded restaurants and hot ballrooms in town. I thought you were to be shipped off to New Mexico?"

"Oh, I've got a new man who says that's rot."

"Well, you don't look as if your new man were right," said Mr. Grisben bluntly.

Faxon saw the lad's colour fade, and the rings of shadow deepen under his gay eyes. At the same moment his uncle turned to him with a renewed intensity of attention. There was such solicitude in Mr. Lavington's gaze that it seemed almost to fling a shield between his nephew and Mr. Grisben's tactless scrutiny.

"We think Frank's a good deal better," he began; "this new doctor—"

The butler, coming up, bent to whisper a word in his ear, and the communication caused a sudden change in Mr. Lavington's expression. His face was naturally so colourless that it seemed not so much to pale as to fade, to dwindle and recede into something blurred and blotted-out. He half rose, sat down again and sent a rigid smile about the table.

"Will you excuse me? The telephone. Peters, go on with the dinner." With small precise steps he walked out of the door which one of the footmen had thrown open.

A momentary silence fell on the group; then Mr. Grisben once more addressed himself to Rainer. "You ought to have gone, my boy; you ought to have gone."

The anxious look returned to the youth's eyes. "My uncle doesn't think so, really."

"You're not a baby, to be always governed by your uncle's opinion. You came of age today, didn't you? Your uncle spoils you. . . . .that's what's the matter . . ."

The thrust evidently went home, for Rainer laughed and looked down with a slight accession of colour.

"But the doctor—"

"Use your common sense, Frank! You had to try twenty doctors to find one to tell you what you wanted to be told."

A look of apprehension overshadowed Rainer', gaiety. "Oh, come—I say!. . . .What would you do?" he stammered.

"Pack up and jump on the first train." Mr. Grisben leaned forward and laid his hand kindly on the young man's arm. "Look here: my nephew Jim Grisben is out there ranching on a big scale. He'll take you in and be glad to have you. You say your new doctor thinks it won't do you any good; but he doesn't pretend to say it will do you harm, does he? Well, then—give it a trial. It'll take you out of hot theatres and night restaurants, anyhow. . . . And all the rest of it. . . . . Eh, Balch?"

"Go!" said Mr. Balch hollowly. "Go at once," he added, as if a closer look at the youth's face had impressed on him the need of backing up his friend.

Young Rainer had turned ashy-pale. He tried to stiffen his mouth into a smile. "Do I look as bad as all that?"

Mr. Grisben was helping himself to terrapin. "You look like the day after an earthquake," he said.

The terrapin had encircled the table, and been deliberately enjoyed by Mr. Lavington's three visitors (Rainer, Faxon noticed, left his plate untouched) before the door was thrown open to re-admit their host. Mr. Lavington advanced with an air of recovered composure. He seated himself, picked up his napkin and consulted the gold-monogrammed menu. "No, don't bring back the filet.... Some terrapin; yes...." He looked affably about the table. "Sorry to have deserted you, but the storm has played the deuce with the wires, and I had to wait a long time before I could get a good connection. It must be blowing up for a blizzard."

"Uncle Jack," young Rainer broke out, "Mr. Grisben's been lecturing me."

Mr. Lavington was helping himself to terrapin. "Ah—what about?"

"He thinks I ought to have given New Mexico a show."

"I want him to go straight out to my nephew at Santa Paz and stay there till his next birthday." Mr. Lavington signed to the butler to hand the terrapin to Mr. Grisben, who, as he took a second helping, addressed himself again to Rainer. "Jim's in New York now, and going back the day after tomorrow in Olyphant's private car. I'll ask Olyphant to squeeze you in if you'll go. And when you've been out there a week or two, in the saddle all day and sleeping nine hours a night, I suspect you won't think much of the doctor who prescribed New York."

Faxon spoke up, he knew not why. "I was out there once: it's a splendid life. I saw a fellow—oh, a really bad case—who'd been simply made over by it."

"It does sound jolly," Rainer laughed, a sudden eagerness in his tone.

His uncle looked at him gently. "Perhaps Grisben's right. It's an opportunity—"

Faxon glanced up with a start: the figure dimly perceived in the study was now more visibly and tangibly planted behind Mr. Lavington's chair.

"That's right, Frank: you see your uncle approves. And the trip out there with Olyphant isn't a thing to be missed. So drop a few dozen dinners and be at the Grand Central the day after tomorrow at five."

Mr. Grisben's pleasant grey eye sought corroboration of his host, and Faxon, in a cold anguish of suspense, continued to watch him as he turned his glance on Mr. Lavington. One could not look at Lavington without seeing the presence at his back, and it was clear that, the next minute, some change in Mr. Grisben's expression must give his watcher a clue.

But Mr. Grisben's expression did not change: the gaze he fixed on his host remained unperturbed, and the clue he gave was the startling one of not seeming to see the other figure.

Faxon's first impulse was to look away, to look anywhere else, to resort again to the champagne glass the watchful butler had already brimmed; but some fatal attraction, at war in him with an overwhelming physical resistance, held his eyes upon the spot they feared.

The figure was still standing, more distinctly, and therefore more resemblingly, at Mr. Lavington's back; and while the latter continued to gaze affectionately at his nephew, his counterpart, as before, fixed young Rainer with eyes of deadly menace.

Faxon, with what felt like an actual wrench of the muscles, dragged his own eyes from the sight to scan the other countenances about the table; but not one revealed the least consciousness of what he saw, and a sense of mortal isolation sank upon him.

"It's worth considering, certainly—" he heard Mr. Lavington continue; and as Rainer's face lit up, the face behind his uncle's chair seemed to gather into its look all the fierce weariness of old unsatisfied hates. That was the thing that, as the minutes laboured by, Faxon was becoming most conscious of. The watcher behind the chair was no longer merely malevolent: he had grown suddenly, unutterably tired. His hatred seemed to well up out of the very depths of balked effort and thwarted hopes, and the fact made him more pitiable, and yet more dire.

Faxon's look reverted to Mr. Lavington, as if to surprise in him a corresponding change. At first none was visible: his pinched smile was screwed to his blank face like a gas-light to a white-washed wall. Then the fixity of the smile became ominous: Faxon saw that its wearer was afraid to let it go. It was evident that Mr. Lavington was unutterably tired too, and the discovery sent a colder current through Faxon's veins. Looking down at his untouched plate, he caught the soliciting twinkle of the champagne glass; but the sight of the wine turned him sick.

"Well, we'll go into the details presently," he heard Mr. Lavington say, still on the question of his nephew's future. "Let's have a cigar first. No—not here, Peters." He turned his smile on Faxon. "When we've had coffee I want to show you my pictures."

"Oh, by the way, Uncle Jack—Mr. Faxon wants to know if you've got a double?"

"A double?" Mr. Lavington, still smiling, continued to address himself to his guest. "Not that I know of. Have you seen one, Mr. Faxon?"

Faxon thought: "My God, if I look up now they'll both be looking at me!" To avoid raising his eyes he made as though to lift the glass to his lips; but his hand sank inert, and he looked up. Mr. Lavington's glance was politely bent on him, but with a loosening of the strain about his heart he saw that the figure behind the chair still kept its gaze on Rainer.

"Do you think you've seen my double, Mr. Faxon?"

Would the other face turn if he said yes? Faxon felt a dryness in his throat. "No," he answered.

"Ah? It's possible I've a dozen. I believe I'm extremely usual-looking," Mr. Lavington went on conversationally; and still the other face watched Rainer.

"It was.....a mistake....a confusion of memory...." Faxon heard himself stammer. Mr. Lavington pushed back his chair, and as he did so Mr. Grisben suddenly leaned forward.

"Lavington! What have, we been thinking of? We haven't drunk Frank's health!"

Mr. Lavington reseated himself. "My dear boy! .....Peters, another bottle....." He turned to his nephew. "After such a sin of omission I don't presume to propose the toast myself... but Frank knows.....Go ahead, Grisben!"

The boy shone on his uncle. "No, no, Uncle Jack! Mr. Grisben won't mind. Nobody but you—today!"

The butler was replenishing the glasses. He filled Mr. Lavington's last, and Mr. Lavington put out his small hand to raise it.....As he did so, Faxon looked away.

"Well, then—All the good I've wished you in all the past years. . ... I put it into the prayer that the coming ones may be healthy and happy and many..... and many, dear boy!"

Faxon saw the hands about him reach out for their glasses. Automatically, he reached for his. His eyes were still on the table, and he repeated to himself with a trembling vehemence: "I won't look up! I won't..... I won't....."

His fingers clasped the glass and raised it to the level of his lips. He saw the other hands making the same motion. He heard Mr. Grisben's genial "Hear! Hear!" and Mr. Batch's hollow echo. He said to himself, as the rim of the glass touched his lips: "I won't look up! I swear I won't!—" and he looked.

The glass was so full that it required an extraordinary effort to hold it there, brimming and suspended, during the awful interval before he could trust his hand to lower it again, untouched, to the table. It was this merciful preoccupation which saved him, kept him from crying out, from losing his hold, from slipping down into the bottomless blackness that gaped for him. As long as the problem of the glass engaged him he felt able to keep his seat, manage his muscles, fit unnoticeably into the group; but as the glass touched the table his last link with safety snapped. He stood up and dashed out of the room.

4

In the gallery, the instinct of self-preservation helped him to turn back and sign to young Rainer not to follow. He stammered out something about a touch of dizziness, and joining them presently; and the boy nodded sympathetically and drew back.

At the foot of the stairs Faxon ran against a servant. "I should like to telephone to Weymore," he said with dry lips.

"Sorry, sir; wires all down. We've been trying the last hour to get New York again for Mr. Lavington."

Faxon shot on to his room, burst into it, and bolted the door. The lamplight lay on furniture, flowers, books; in the ashes a log still glimmered. He dropped down on the sofa and hid his face. The room was profoundly silent, the whole house was still: nothing about him gave a hint of what was going on, darkly and dumbly, in the room he had flown from, and with the covering of his eyes oblivion and reassurance seemed to fall on him. But they fell for a moment only; then his lids opened again to the monstrous vision. There it was, stamped on his pupils, a part of him forever, an indelible horror burnt into his body and brain.

But why into his—just his? Why had he alone been chosen to see what he had seen? What business was it of his, in God's name? Any one of the others, thus enlightened, might have exposed the horror and defeated it; but he, the one weaponless and defenceless spectator, the one whom none of the others would believe or understand if he attempted to reveal what he knew—he alone had been singled out as the victim of this dreadful initiation!

Suddenly he sat up, listening: he had heard a step on the stairs. Someone, no doubt, was coming to see how he was—to urge him, if he felt better, to go down and join the smokers. Cautiously he opened his door; yes, it was young Rainer's step. Faxon looked down the passage, remembered the other stairway and darted to it. All he wanted was to get out of the house. Not another instant would he breathe its abominable air! What business was it of his, in God's name?

He reached the opposite end of the lower gallery, and beyond it saw the hall by which he had entered. It was empty, and on a long table he recognised his coat and cap. He got into his coat, unbolted the door, and plunged into the purifying night.

The darkness was deep, and the cold so intense that for an instant it stopped his breathing. Then he perceived that only a thin snow was falling, and resolutely he set his face for flight. The trees along the avenue marked his way as he hastened with long strides over the beaten snow. Gradually, while he walked, the tumult in his brain subsided. The impulse to fly still drove him forward, but he began feel that he was flying from a terror of his own creating, and that the most urgent reason for escape was the need of hiding his state, of shunning other eyes till he should regain his balance.

He had spent the long hours in the train in fruitless broodings on a discouraging situation, and he remembered how his bitterness had turned to exasperation when he found that the Weymore sleigh was not awaiting him. It was absurd, of course; but, though he had joked with Rainer over Mrs. Culme's forgetfulness, to confess it had cost a pang. That was what his rootless life had brought him to: for lack of a personal stake in things his sensibility was at the mercy of such trifles. . . . . Yes; that, and the cold and fatigue, the absence of hope and the haunting sense of starved aptitudes, all these had brought him to the perilous verge over which, once or twice before, his terrified brain had hung.

Why else, in the name of any imaginable logic, human or devilish, should he, a stranger, be singled out for this experience? What could it mean to him, how was he related to it, what bearing had it on his case? . . . . Unless, indeed, it was just because he was a stranger—a stranger everywhere—because he had no personal life, no warm screen of private egotisms to shield him from exposure, that he had developed this abnormal sensitiveness to the vicissitudes of others. The thought pulled him up with a shudder. No! Such a fate was too abominable; all that was strong and sound in him rejected it. A thousand times better regard himself as ill, disorganized, deluded, than as the predestined victim of such warnings!

He reached the gates and paused before the darkened lodge. The wind had risen and was sweeping the snow into his race. The cold had him in its grasp again, and he stood uncertain. Should he put his sanity to the test and go back? He turned and looked down the dark drive to the house. A single ray shone through the trees, evoking a picture of the lights, the flowers, the faces grouped about that fatal room. He turned and plunged out into the road. . . . .

He remembered that, about a mile from Overdale, the coachman had pointed out the road to Northridge; and he began to walk in that direction. Once in the road he had the gale in his face, and the wet snow on his moustache and eye-lashes instantly hardened to ice. The same ice seemed to be driving a million blades into his throat and lungs, but he pushed on, the vision of the warm room pursuing him.

The snow in the road was deep and uneven. He stumbled across ruts and sank into drifts, and the wind drove against him like a granite cliff. Now and then he stopped, gasping, as if an invisible hand had tightened an iron band about his body; then he started again, stiffening himself against the stealthy penetration of the cold. The snow continued to descend out of a pall of inscrutable darkness, and once or twice he paused, fearing he had missed the road to Northridge; but, seeing no sign of a turn, he ploughed on.

At last, feeling sure that he had walked for more than a mile, he halted and looked back. The act of turning brought immediate relief, first because it put his back to the wind, and then because, far down the road, it showed him the gleam of a lantern. A sleigh was coming—a sleigh that might perhaps give him a lift to the village! Fortified by the hope, he began to walk back toward the light. It came forward very slowly, with unaccountable zigzags and waverings; and even when he was within a few yards of it he could catch no sound of sleigh-bells. Then it paused and became stationary by the roadside, as though carried by a pedestrian who had stopped, exhausted by the cold. The thought made Faxon hasten on, and a moment later he was stooping over a motionless figure huddled against the snow-bank. The lantern had dropped from its bearer's hand, and Faxon, fearfully raising it, threw its light into the face of Frank Rainer.

"Rainer! What on earth are you doing here?"

The boy smiled back through his pallor. "What are you, I'd like to know?" he retorted; and, scrambling to his feet with a clutch oh Faxon's arm, he added gaily: "Well, I've run you down!"

Faxon stood confounded, his heart sinking. The lad's face was grey.

"What madness—" he began.

"Yes, it is. What on earth did you do it for?"

"I? Do what? . . . . . Why I . . . . . I was just taking a walk. . . . . I often walk at night. . . . ."

Frank Rainer burst into a laugh. "On such nights? Then you hadn't bolted?"

"Bolted?"

"Because I'd done something to offend you? My uncle thought you had."

Faxon grasped his arm. "Did your uncle send you after me?"

"Well, he gave me an awful rowing for not going up to your room with you when you said you were ill. And when we found you'd gone we were frightened—and he was awfully upset—so I said I'd catch you....You're not ill, are you?"

"Ill? No. Never better." Faxon picked up the lantern. "Come; let's go back. It was awfully hot in that dining-room."

"Yes; I hoped it was only that."

They trudged on in silence for a few minutes; then Faxon questioned: "You're not too done up?"

"Oh, no. It's a lot easier with the wind behind us."

"All right Don't talk anymore."

They pushed ahead, walking, in spite of the light that guided them, more slowly than Faxon had walked alone into the gale. The fact of his companion's stumbling against a drift gave Faxon a pretext for saying: "Take hold of my arm," and Rainer obeying, gasped out: "I'm blown!"

"So am I. Who wouldn't be?"

"What a dance you led me! If it hadn't been for one of the servants happening to see you—"

"Yes; all right. And now, won't you kindly shut up?"

Rainer laughed and hung on him. "Oh, the cold doesn't hurt me. . . . ."

For the first few minutes after Rainer had overtaken him, anxiety for the lad had been Faxon's only thought. But as each labouring step carried them nearer to the spot he had been fleeing, the reasons for his flight grew more ominous and more insistent. No, he was not ill, he was not distraught and deluded—he was the instrument singled out to warn and save; and here he was, irresistibly driven, dragging the victim back to his doom!

The intensity of the conviction had almost checked his steps. But what could he do or say? At all costs he must get Rainer out of the cold, into the house and into his bed. After that he would act.

The snow-fall was thickening, and as they reached a stretch of the road between open fields the wind took them at an angle, lashing their faces with barbed thongs. Rainer stopped to take breath, and Faxon felt the heavier pressure of his arm.

"When we get to the lodge, can't we telephone to the stable for a sleigh?"

"If they're not all asleep at the lodge."

"Oh, I'll manage. Don't talk!" Faxon ordered; and they plodded on. . . . .

At length the lantern ray showed ruts that curved away from the road under tree-darkness.

Faxon's spirits rose. "There's the gate! We'll be there in five minutes."

As he spoke he caught, above the boundary hedge, the gleam of a light at the farther end of the dark avenue. It was the same light that had shone on the scene of which every detail was burnt into his brain; and he felt again its overpowering reality. No—he couldn't let the boy go back!

They were at the lodge at last, and Faxon was hammering on the door. He said to himself: "I'll get him inside first, and make them give him a hot drink. Then I'll see—I'll find an argument. . . . ."

There was no answer to his knocking, and after an interval Rainer said: "Look here—we'd better go on."

"No!"

"I can, perfectly—"

"You sha'n't go to the house, I say!" Faxon redoubled his blows, and at length steps sounded on the stairs. Rainer was leaning against the lintel, and as the door opened the light from the hall flashed on his pale face and fixed eyes. Faxon caught him by the arm and drew him in.

"It was cold out there." he sighed; and then, abruptly, as if invisible shears at a single stroke had cut every muscle in his body, he swerved, drooped on Faxon's arm, and seemed to sink into nothing at his feet.

The lodge-keeper and Faxon bent over him, and somehow, between them, lifted him into the kitchen and laid him on a sofa by the stove.

The lodge-keeper, stammering: "I'll ring up the house," dashed out of the room. But Faxon heard the words without heeding them: omens mattered nothing now, beside this woe fulfilled. He knelt down to undo the fur collar about Rainer's throat, and as he did so he felt a warm moisture on his hands. He held them up, and they were red....

5

The palms threaded their endless line along the yellow river. The little steamer lay at the wharf, and George Faxon, sitting in the verandah of the wooden hotel, idly watched the coolies carrying the freight across the gang-plank.

He had been looking at such scenes for two months. Nearly five had elapsed since he had descended from the train at Northridge and strained his eyes for the sleigh that was to take him to Weymore: Weymore, which he was never to behold! . . . . . Part of the interval—the first part—was still a great grey blur. Even now he could not be quite sure how he had got back to Boston, reached the house of a cousin, and been thence transferred to a quiet room looking out on snow under bare trees. He looked out a long time at the same scene, and finally one day a man he had known at Harvard came to see him and invited him to go out on a business trip to the Malay Peninsula.

"You've had a bad shake-up, and it'll do you no end of good to get away from things."

When the doctor came the next day it turned out that he knew of the plan and approved it. "You ought to be quiet for a year. Just loaf and look at the landscape," he advised.

Faxon felt the first faint stirrings of curiosity.

"What's been the matter with me, anyway?"

"Well, overwork, I suppose. You must have been bottling up for a bad breakdown before you started for New Hampshire last December. And the shock of that poor boy's death did the rest."

Ah, yes—Rainer had died. He remembered. . . . .

He started for the East, and gradually, by imperceptible degrees, life crept back into his weary bones and leaden brain. His friend was patient and considerate, and they travelled slowly and talked little. At first Faxon had felt a great shrinking from whatever touched on familiar things. He seldom looked at a newspaper and he never opened a letter without a contraction of the heart. It was not that he had any special cause for apprehension, but merely that a great trail of darkness lay on everything. He had looked too deep down into the abyss.... But little by little health and energy returned to him, and with them the common promptings of curiosity. He was beginning to wonder how the world was going, and when, presently, the hotel-keeper told him there were no letters for him in the steamer's mail-bag, he felt a distinct sense of disappointment. His friend had gone into the jungle on a long excursion, and he was lonely, unoccupied and wholesomely bored. He got up and strolled into the stuffy reading-room.

There he found a game of dominoes, a mutilated picture-puzzle, some copies of *Zion's Herald* and a pile of New York and London newspapers.

He began to glance through the papers, and was disappointed to find that they were less recent than he had hoped. Evidently the last numbers had been carried off by luckier travellers. He continued to turn them over, picking out the American ones first. These, as it happened, were the oldest: they dated back to December and January. To Faxon, however, they had all the flavour of novelty, since they covered the precise period during which he had virtually ceased to exist. It had never before occurred to him to wonder what had happened in the world during that interval of obliteration; but now he felt a sudden desire to know.

To prolong the pleasure, he began by sorting the papers chronologically, and as he found and spread out the earliest number, the date at the top of the page entered into his consciousness like a key slipping into a lock. It was the seventeenth of December: the date of the day after his arrival at Northridge. He glanced at the first page and read in blazing characters: "Reported Failure of Opal Cement Company. Lavington's name involved. Gigantic Exposure of Corruption Shakes Wall Street to Its Foundations."

He read on, and when he had finished the first paper he turned to the next. There was a gap of three days, but the Opal Cement "Investigation" still held the centre of the stage. From its complex revelations of greed and ruin his eye wandered to the death notices, and he read: "Rainer. Suddenly, at Northridge, New Hampshire, Francis John, only son of the late...."

His eyes clouded, and he dropped the newspaper and sat for a long time with his face in his hands. When he looked up again he noticed that his gesture had pushed the other papers from the table and scattered them at his feet. The uppermost lay spread out before him, and heavily his eyes began their search again. "John Lavington comes forward with plan for reconstructing Company. Offers to put in ten millions of his own—The proposal under consideration by the District Attorney."

Ten millions. . . . . ten millions of his own. But if John Lavington was ruined? . . . . . Faxon stood up with a cry. That was it, then—that was what the warning meant! And if he had not fled from it, dashed wildly away from it into the night, he might have broken the spell of iniquity, the powers of darkness might not have prevailed! He caught up the pile of newspapers and began to glance through each in turn for the head-line: "Wills Admitted to Probate." In the last of all he found the paragraph he sought, and it stared up at him as if with Rainer's dying eyes.

That—that was what he had done! The powers of pity had singled him out to warn and save, and he had closed his ears to their call, and washed his hands of it, and fled. Washed his hands of it! That was the word. It caught him back to the dreadful moment in the lodge when, raising himself up from Rainer's side, he had looked at his hands and seen that they were red. . . .

Kerfol

1

"You ought to buy it," said my host; "it's just the place for a sol-itary-minded devil like you. And it would be rather worthwhile to own the most romantic house in Brittany. The present people are dead broke, and it's going for a song—you ought to buy it."

It was not with the least idea of living up to the character my friend Lanrivain ascribed to me (as a matter of fact, under my unso-ciable exterior I have always had secret yearnings for domesticity) that I took his hint one autumn afternoon and went to Kerfol. My friend was motoring over to Quimper on business: he dropped me on the way, at a cross-road on a heath, and said: "First turn to the right and second to the left. Then straight ahead till you see an avenue. If you meet any peasants, don't ask your way. They don't understand French, and they would pretend they did and mix you up. I'll be back for you here by sunset—and don't forget the tombs in the chapel."

I followed Lanrivain's directions with the hesitation occasioned by the usual difficulty of remembering whether he had said the first turn to the right and second to the left, or the contrary. If I had met a peas-ant I should certainly have asked, and probably been sent astray; but I had the desert landscape to myself, and so stumbled on the right turn and walked on across the heath till I came to an avenue. It was so un-like any other avenue I have ever seen that I instantly knew it must be *the* avenue. The grey-trunked trees sprang up straight to a great height and then interwove their pale-grey branches in a long tunnel through which the autumn light fell faintly.

I know most trees by name, but I haven't to this day been able to decide what those trees were. They had the tall curve of elms, the tenuity of poplars, the ashen colour of olives under a rainy sky; and they stretched ahead of me for half a mile or more without a break in their arch. If ever I saw an avenue that unmistakeably led to something, it was the avenue at Kerfol. My heart beat a little as I began to walk down it.

Presently the trees ended and I came to a fortified gate in a long wall. Between me and the wall was an open space of grass, with other grey avenues radiating from it. Behind the wall were tall slate roofs mossed with silver, a chapel belfry, the top of a keep. A moat filled with wild shrubs and brambles surrounded the place; the drawbridge had been replaced by a stone arch, and the portcullis by an iron gate. I stood for a long time on the hither side of the moat, gazing about me, and letting the influence of the place sink in. I said to myself: "If I wait long enough, the guardian will turn up and show me the tombs—" and I rather hoped he wouldn't turn up too soon.

I sat down on a stone and lit a cigarette. As soon as I had done it, it struck me as a puerile and portentous thing to do, with that great blind house looking down at me, and all the empty avenues converging on me. It may have been the depth of the silence that made me so conscious of my gesture. The squeak of my match sounded as loud as the scraping of a brake, and I almost fancied I heard it fall when I tossed it onto the grass. But there was more than that: a sense of irrelevance, of littleness, of childish bravado, in sitting there puffing my cigarette-smoke into the face of such a past.

I knew nothing of the history of Kerfol—I was new to Brittany, and Lanrivain had never mentioned the name to me till the day before—but one couldn't as much as glance at that pile without feeling in it a long accumulation of history. What kind of history I was not prepared to guess: perhaps only the sheer weight of many associated lives and deaths which gives a kind of majesty to all old houses. But the aspect of Kerfol suggested something more—a perspective of stern and cruel memories stretching away, like its own grey avenues, into a blur of darkness.

Certainly no house had ever more completely and finally broken with the present. As it stood there, lifting its proud roofs and gables to the sky, it might have been its own funeral monument. "Tombs in the chapel? The whole place is a tomb!" I reflected. I hoped more and more that the guardian would not come. The details of the place, however striking, would seem trivial compared with its collective impressiveness; and I wanted only to sit there and be penetrated by the weight of its silence.

"It's the very place for you!" Lanrivain had said; and I was overcome by the almost blasphemous frivolity of suggesting to any living being that Kerfol was the place for him. "Is it possible that anyone could *not* see—?" I wondered. I did not finish the thought: what I meant was undefinable. I stood up and wandered toward the gate. I was beginning to want to know more; not to *see* more—I was by now so sure it was not a question of seeing—but to feel more: feel all the place had to communicate. "But to get in one will have to rout out the keeper," I thought reluctantly, and hesitated.

Finally, I crossed the bridge and tried the iron gate. It yielded, and I walked under the tunnel formed by the thickness of the *chemin de ronde*. At the farther end, a wooden barricade had been laid across the entrance, and beyond it I saw a court enclosed in noble architecture. The main building faced me; and I now discovered that one half was a mere ruined front, with gaping windows through which the wild growths of the moat and the trees of the park were visible. The rest of the house was still in its robust beauty. One end abutted on the round tower, the other on the small traceried chapel, and in an angle of the building stood a graceful well-head adorned with mossy urns. A few roses grew against the walls, and on an upper window-sill I remember noticing a pot of fuchsias.

My sense of the pressure of the invisible began to yield to my architectural interest. The building was so fine that I felt a desire to explore it for its own sake. I looked about the court, wondering in which corner the guardian lodged. Then I pushed open the barrier and went in. As I did so, a little dog barred my way. He was such a remarkably beautiful little dog that for a moment he made me forget the splendid place he was defending. I was not sure of his breed at the time, but have since learned that it was Chinese, and that he was of a rare variety called the "Sleeve-dog." He was very small and golden brown, with large brown eyes and a ruffled throat: he looked rather like a large tawny chrysanthemum. I said to myself: "These little beasts always snap and scream, and somebody will be out in a minute."

The little animal stood before me, forbidding, almost menacing: there was anger in his large brown eyes. But he made no sound, he came no nearer. Instead, as I advanced, he gradually fell back, and I noticed that another dog, a vague rough brindled thing, had limped up. "There'll be a hubbub now," I thought; for at the same moment a third dog, a long-haired white mongrel, slipped out of a doorway and joined the others. All three stood looking at me with grave eyes; but not a sound came from them. As I advanced they continued to fall back on muffled paws, still watching me.

"At a given point, they'll all charge at my ankles: it's one of the dodges that dogs who live together put up on one," I thought. I was not much alarmed, for they were neither large nor formidable. But they let me wander about the court as I pleased, following me at a little distance—always the same distance—and always keeping their eyes on me. Presently I looked across at the ruined facade, and saw that in one of its window-frames another dog stood: a large white pointer with one brown ear. He was an old grave dog, much more experienced than the others; and he seemed to be observing me with a deeper intentness.

"I'll hear from *him*," I said to myself; but he stood in the empty window-frame, against the trees of the park, and continued to watch me without moving. I looked back at him for a time, to see if the sense that he was being watched would not rouse him. Half the width of the court lay between us, and we stared at each other silently across it. But he did not stir, and at last I turned away. Behind me I found the rest of the pack, with a newcomer added: a small black greyhound with pale agate-coloured eyes. He was shivering a little, and his expression was more timid than that of the others. I noticed that he kept a little behind them. And still there was not a sound.

I stood there for fully five minutes, the circle about me—waiting, as they seemed to be waiting. At last I went up to the little golden-brown dog and stooped to pat him. As I did so, I heard myself laugh. The little dog did not start, or growl, or take his eyes from me—he simply slipped back about a yard, and then paused and continued to look at me. "Oh, hang it!" I exclaimed aloud, and walked across the court toward the well.

As I advanced, the dogs separated and slid away into different corners of the court. I examined the urns on the well, tried a locked door or two, and up and down the dumb facade; then I faced about toward the chapel. When I turned I perceived that all the dogs had disappeared except the old pointer, who still watched me from the empty window-frame. It was rather a relief to be rid of that cloud of witnesses; and I began to look about me for a way to the back of the house. "Perhaps there'll be somebody in the garden," I thought. I found a way across the moat, scrambled over a wall smothered in brambles, and got into the garden. A few lean hydrangeas and geraniums pined in the flower-beds, and the ancient house looked down on them indifferently. Its garden side was plainer and severer than the

153

other: the long granite front, with its few windows and steep roof, looked like a fortress-prison.

I walked around the farther wing, went up some disjointed steps, and entered the deep twilight of a narrow and incredibly old box-walk. The walk was just wide enough for one person to slip through, and its branches met overhead. It was like the ghost of a box-walk, its lustrous green all turning to the shadowy greyness of the avenues. I walked on and on, the branches hitting me in the face and springing back with a dry rattle; and at length I came out on the grassy top of the *chemin de ronde*. I walked along it to the gate-tower, looking down into the court, which was just below me. Not a human being was in sight; and neither were the dogs. I found a flight of steps in the thickness of the wall and went down them; and when I emerged again into the court, there stood the circle of dogs, the golden-brown one a little ahead of the others, the black greyhound shivering in the rear.

"Oh, hang it—you uncomfortable beasts, you!" I exclaimed, my voice startling me with a sudden echo. The dogs stood motionless, watching me. I knew by this time that they would not try to prevent my approaching the house, and the knowledge left me free to examine them. I had a feeling that they must be horribly cowed to be so silent and inert. Yet they did not look hungry or ill-treated. Their coats were smooth and they were not thin, except the shivering greyhound. It was more as if they had lived a long time with people who never spoke to them or looked at them: as though the silence of the place had gradually benumbed their busy inquisitive natures. And this strange passivity, this almost human lassitude, seemed to me sadder than the misery of starved and beaten animals.

I should have liked to rouse them for a minute, to coax them into a game or a scamper; but the longer I looked into their fixed and weary eyes the more preposterous the idea became. With the windows of that house looking down on us, how could I have imagined such a thing? The dogs knew better: *they* knew what the house would tolerate and what it would not. I even fancied that they knew what was passing through my mind, and pitied me for my frivolity. But even that feeling probably reached them through a thick fog of listlessness. I had an idea that their distance from me was as nothing to my remoteness from them. In the last analysis, the impression they produced was that of having in common one memory so deep and dark that nothing that had happened since was worth either a growl or a wag.

"I say," I broke out abruptly, addressing myself to the dumb circle, "do you know what you look like, the whole lot of you? You look as if you'd seen a ghost—that's how you look! I wonder if there *is* a ghost here, and nobody but you left for it to appear to?" The dogs continued to gaze at me without moving. . .

It was dark when I saw Lanrivain's motor lamps at the cross-roads—and I wasn't exactly sorry to see them. I had the sense of having escaped from the loneliest place in the whole world, and of not liking loneliness—to that degree—as much as I had imagined I should. My friend had brought his solicitor back from Quimper for the night, and seated beside a fat and affable stranger I felt no inclination to talk of Kerfol. . . .

But that evening, when Lanrivain and the solicitor were closeted in the study, Madame de Lanrivain began to question me in the drawing-room.

"Well—are you going to buy Kerfol?" she asked, tilting up her gay chin from her embroidery.

"I haven't decided yet. The fact is, I couldn't get into the house," I said, as if I had simply postponed my decision, and meant to go back for another look.

"You couldn't get in? Why, what happened? The family are mad to sell the place, and the old guardian has orders—"

"Very likely. But the old guardian wasn't there."

"What a pity! He must have gone to market. But his daughter—?"

"There was nobody about. At least I saw no one."

"How extraordinary! Literally nobody?"

"Nobody but a lot of dogs—a whole pack of them—who seemed to have the place to themselves."

Madame de Lanrivain let the embroidery slip to her knee and folded her hands on it. For several minutes she looked at me thoughtfully.

"A pack of dogs—you *saw* them?"

"Saw them? I saw nothing else!"

"How many?" She dropped her voice a little. "I've always wondered—"

I looked at her with surprise: I had supposed the place to be familiar to her. "Have you never been to Kerfol?" I asked.

"Oh, yes: often. But never on that day."

"What day?"

"I'd quite forgotten—and so had Herve, I'm sure. If we'd remembered, we never should have sent you today—but then, after all, one

155

doesn't half believe that sort of thing, does one?"

"What sort of thing?" I asked, involuntarily sinking my voice to the level of hers. Inwardly I was thinking: "I *knew* there was something. . ."

Madame de Lanrivain cleared her throat and produced a reassuring smile. "Didn't Herve tell you the story of Kerfol? An ancestor of his was mixed up in it. You know every Breton house has its ghost-story; and some of them are rather unpleasant."

"Yes—but those dogs?" I insisted.

"Well, those dogs are the ghosts of Kerfol. At least, the peasants say there's one day in the year when a lot of dogs appear there; and that day the keeper and his daughter go off to Morlaix and get drunk. The women in Brittany drink dreadfully." She stooped to match a silk; then she lifted her charming inquisitive Parisian face: "Did you *really* see a lot of dogs? There isn't one at Kerfol," she said.

2

Lanrivain, the next day, hunted out a shabby calf volume from the back of an upper shelf of his library.

"Yes—here it is. What does it call itself? *A History of the Assizes of the Duchy of Brittany. Quimper, 1702.* The book was written about a hundred years later than the Kerfol affair; but I believe the account is transcribed pretty literally from the judicial records. Anyhow, it's queer reading. And there's a Herve de Lanrivain mixed up in it—not exactly *my* style, as you'll see. But then he's only a collateral. Here, take the book up to bed with you. I don't exactly remember the details; but after you've read it I'll bet anything you'll leave your light burning all night!"

I left my light burning all night, as he had predicted; but it was chiefly because, till near dawn, I was absorbed in my reading. The account of the trial of Anne de Cornault, wife of the lord of Kerfol, was long and closely printed. It was, as my friend had said, probably an almost literal transcription of what took place in the court-room; and the trial lasted nearly a month. Besides, the type of the book was detestable. . .

At first I thought of translating the old record literally. But it is full of wearisome repetitions, and the main lines of the story are forever straying off into side issues. So I have tried to disentangle it, and give it here in a simpler form. At times, however, I have reverted to the text because no other words could have conveyed so exactly the sense of what I felt at Kerfol; and nowhere have I added anything of my own.

3

It was in the year 16— that Yves de Cornault, lord of the domain of Kerfol, went to the pardon of Locronan to perform his religious duties. He was a rich and powerful noble, then in his sixty-second year, but hale and sturdy, a great horseman and hunter and a pious man. So all his neighbours attested. In appearance he seems to have been short and broad, with a swarthy face, legs slightly bowed from the saddle, a hanging nose and broad hands with black hairs on them. He had married young and lost his wife and son soon after, and since then had lived alone at Kerfol. Twice a year he went to Morlaix, where he had a handsome house by the river, and spent a week or ten days there; and occasionally he rode to Rennes on business.

Witnesses were found to declare that during these absences he led a life different from the one he was known to lead at Kerfol, where he busied himself with his estate, attended mass daily, and found his only amusement in hunting the wild boar and water-fowl. But these rumours are not particularly relevant, and it is certain that among people of his own class in the neighbourhood he passed for a stern and even austere man, observant of his religious obligations, and keeping strictly to himself. There was no talk of any familiarity with the women on his estate, though at that time the nobility were very free with their peasants. Some people said he had never looked at a woman since his wife's death; but such things are hard to prove, and the evidence on this point was not worth much.

Well, in his sixty-second year, Yves de Cornault went to the *pardon* at Locronan, and saw there a young lady of Douarnenez, who had ridden over pillion behind her father to do her duty to the saint. Her name was Anne de Barrigan, and she came of good old Breton stock, but much less great and powerful than that of Yves de Cornault; and her father had squandered his fortune at cards, and lived almost like a peasant in his little granite manor on the moors. . . I have said I would add nothing of my own to this bald statement of a strange case; but I must interrupt myself here to describe the young lady who rode up to the lych-gate of Locronan at the very moment when the Baron de Cornault was also dismounting there.

I take my description from a rather rare thing: a faded drawing in red crayon, sober and truthful enough to be by a late pupil of the Clouets, which hangs in Lanrivain's study, and is said to be a portrait of Anne de Barrigan. It is unsigned and has no mark of identity but the initials A. B., and the date 16—, the year after her marriage. It represents a young woman with a small oval face, almost pointed, yet wide enough for a full mouth with a tender depression at the corners. The nose is small, and the eyebrows are set rather high, far apart, and as lightly pencilled as the eyebrows in a Chinese painting. The forehead is high and serious, and the hair, which one feels to be fine and thick and fair, drawn off it and lying close like a cap. The eyes are neither large nor small, hazel probably, with a look at once shy and steady. A pair of beautiful long hands are crossed below the lady's breast...

The chaplain of Kerfol, and other witnesses, averred that when the baron came back from Locronan he jumped from his horse, ordered another to be instantly saddled, called to a young page come with him, and rode away that same evening to the south. His steward followed the next morning with coffers laden on a pair of pack mules. The following week Yves de Cornault rode back to Kerfol, sent for his vassals and tenants, and told them he was to be married at All Saints to Anne de Barrigan of Douarnenez. And on All Saints' Day the marriage took place.

As to the next few years, the evidence on both sides seems to show that they passed happily for the couple. No one was found to say that Yves de Cornault had been unkind to his wife, and it was plain to all that he was content with his bargain. Indeed, it was admitted by the chaplain and other witnesses for the prosecution that the young lady had a softening influence on her husband, and that he became less exacting with his tenants, less harsh to peasants and dependents, and less subject to the fits of gloomy silence which had darkened his widow-hood. As to his wife, the only grievance her champions could call up in her behalf was that Kerfol was a lonely place, and that when her husband was away on business at Rennes or Morlaix—whither she was never taken—she was not allowed so much as to walk in the park unaccompanied.

But no one asserted that she was unhappy, though one servant-woman said she had surprised her crying, and had heard her say that she was a woman accursed to have no child, and nothing in life to call her own. But that was a natural enough feeling in a wife attached to her husband; and certainly it must have been a great grief to Yves de Cornault that she gave him no son. Yet he never made her feel her childlessness as a reproach—she herself admits this in her evidence— but seemed to try to make her forget it by showering gifts and favours on her. Rich though he was, he had never been open-handed; but nothing was too fine for his wife, in the way of silks or gems or linen, or whatever else she fancied. Every wandering merchant was welcome at Kerfol, and when the master was called away he never came back without bringing his wife a handsome present—something curious and particular—from Morlaix or Rennes or Quimper. One of the waiting-women gave, in cross-examination, an interesting list of one year's gifts, which I copy.

From Morlaix, a carved ivory *junk*, with Chinamen at the oars, that a strange sailor had brought back as a votive offering for Notre Dame de la Clarte, above Ploumanac'h; from Quimper, an embroidered gown, worked by the nuns of the Assumption; from Rennes, a silver rose that opened and showed an amber Virgin with a crown of garnets; from Morlaix, again, a length of Damascus velvet shot with gold, bought of a Jew from Syria; and for Michaelmas that same year, from Rennes, a necklet or bracelet of round stones—emeralds and pearls and rubies—strung like beads on a gold wire. This was the present that pleased the lady best, the woman said. Later on, as it happened, it was produced at the trial, and appears to have struck the Judges and the public as a curious and valuable jewel.

The very same winter, the baron absented himself again, this time as far as Bordeaux, and on his return he brought his wife something even odder and prettier than the bracelet. It was a winter evening when he rode up to Kerfol and, walking into the hall, found her sitting listlessly by the fire, her chin on her hand, looking into the fire. He carried a velvet box in his hand and, setting it down on the hearth, lifted the lid and let out a little golden-brown dog.

Anne de Cornault exclaimed with pleasure as the little creature bounded toward her. "Oh, it looks like a bird or a butterfly!" she cried as she picked it up; and the dog put its paws on her shoulders and looked at her with eyes "like a Christian's." After that she would never have it out of her sight, and petted and talked to it as if it had been a child—as indeed it was the nearest thing to a child she was to know. Yves de Cornault was much pleased with his purchase.

The dog had been brought to him by a sailor from an East India merchantman, and the sailor had bought it of a pilgrim in a bazaar at Jaffa, who had stolen it from a nobleman's wife in China: a perfectly permissible thing to do, since the pilgrim was a Christian and the nobleman a heathen doomed to hellfire. Yves de Cornault had paid a long price for the dog, for they were beginning to be in demand at the

French court, and the sailor knew he had got hold of a good thing; but Anne's pleasure was so great that, to see her laugh and play with the little animal, her husband would doubtless have given twice the sum.

So far, all the evidence is at one, and the narrative plain sailing; but now the steering becomes difficult. I will try to keep as nearly as possible to Anne's own statements; though toward the end, poor thing . . .

Well, to go back. The very year after the little brown dog was brought to Kerfol, Yves de Cornault, one winter night, was found dead at the head of a narrow flight of stairs leading down from his wife's rooms to a door opening on the court. It was his wife who found him and gave the alarm, so distracted, poor wretch, with fear and horror—for his blood was all over her—that at first the roused household could not make out what she was saying, and thought she had gone suddenly mad. But there, sure enough, at the top of the stairs lay her husband, stone dead, and head foremost, the blood from his wounds dripping down to the steps below him. He had been dreadfully scratched and gashed about the face and throat, as if with a dull weapon; and one of his legs had a deep tear in it which had cut an artery, and probably caused his death. But how did he come there, and who had murdered him?

His wife declared that she had been asleep in her bed, and hearing his cry had rushed out to find him lying on the stairs; but this was immediately questioned. In the first place, it was proved that from her room she could not have heard the struggle on the stairs, owing to the thickness of the walls and the length of the intervening passage; then it was evident that she had not been in bed and asleep, since she was dressed when she roused the house, and her bed had not been slept in.

Moreover, the door at the bottom of the stairs was ajar, and the key in the lock; and it was noticed by the chaplain (an observant man) that the dress she wore was stained with blood about the knees, and that there were traces of small bloodstained hands low down on the staircase walls, so that it was conjectured that she had really been at the postern-door when her husband fell and, feeling her way up to him in the darkness on her hands and knees, had been stained by his blood dripping down on her. Of course it was argued on the other side that the blood-marks on her dress might have been caused by her kneeling down by her husband when she rushed out of her room; but there was the open door below, and the fact that the finger-marks in the staircase all pointed upward.

The accused held to her statement for the first two days, in spite of its improbability; but on the third day word was brought to her that Herve de Lanrivain, a young nobleman of the neighbourhood, had been arrested for complicity in the crime. Two or three witnesses thereupon came forward to say that it was known throughout the country that Lanrivain had formerly been on good terms with the lady of Cornault; but that he had been absent from Brittany for over a year, and people had ceased to associate their names.

The witnesses who made this statement were not of a very reputable sort. One was an old herb-gatherer suspected of witchcraft, another a drunken clerk from a neighbouring parish, the third a half-witted shepherd who could be made to say anything; and it was clear that the prosecution was not satisfied with its case, and would have liked to find more definite proof of Lanrivain's complicity than the statement of the herb-gatherer, who swore to having seen him climbing the wall of the park on the night of the murder. One way of patching out incomplete proofs in those days was to put some sort of pressure, moral or physical, on the accused person.

It is not clear what pressure was put on Anne de Cornault; but on the third day, when she was brought into court, she "appeared weak and wandering," and after being encouraged to collect herself and speak the truth, on her honour and the wounds of her Blessed Redeemer, she confessed that she had in fact gone down the stairs to speak with Herve de Lanrivain (who denied everything), and had been surprised there by the sound of her husband's fall. That was better; and the prosecution rubbed its hands with satisfaction.

The satisfaction increased when various dependents living at Kerfol were induced to say—with apparent sincerity—that during the year or two preceding his death their master had once more grown uncertain and irascible, and subject to the fits of brooding silence which his household had learned to dread before his second marriage. This seemed to show that things had not been going well at Kerfol; though no one could be found to say that there had been any signs of open disagreement between husband and wife.

Anne de Cornault, when questioned as to her reason for going down at night to open the door to Herve de Lanrivain, made an answer which must have sent a smile around the court. She said it was because she was lonely and wanted to talk with the young man. Was this the only reason? she was asked; and replied: "Yes, by the Cross over your Lordships' heads."

"But why at midnight?" the court asked.

"Because I could see him in no other way." I can see the exchange of glances across the ermine collars under the Crucifix.

Anne de Cornault, further questioned, said that her married life had been extremely lonely: "desolate" was the word she used. It was true that her husband seldom spoke harshly to her; but there were days when he did not speak at all. It was true that he had never struck or threatened her; but he kept her like a prisoner at Kerfol, and when he rode away to Morlaix or Quimper or Rennes he set so close a watch on her that she could not pick a flower in the garden without having a waiting-woman at her heels. "I am no queen, to need such honours," she once said to him; and he had answered that a man who has a treasure does not leave the key in the lock when he goes out. "Then take me with you," she urged; but to this he said that towns were pernicious places, and young wives better off at their own firesides.

"But what did you want to say to Herve de Lanrivain?" the court asked; and she answered: "To ask him to take me away."

"Ah—you confess that you went down to him with adulterous thoughts?"

"No."

"Then why did you want him to take you away?"

"Because I was afraid for my life."

"Of whom were you afraid?"

"Of my husband."

"Why were you afraid of your husband?"

"Because he had strangled my little dog."

Another smile must have passed around the court-room: in days when any nobleman had a right to hang his peasants—and most of them exercised it—pinching a pet animal's wind-pipe was nothing to make a fuss about.

At this point one of the judges, who appears to have had a certain sympathy for the accused, suggested that she should be allowed to explain herself in her own way; and she thereupon made the following statement.

The first years of her marriage had been lonely; but her husband had not been unkind to her. If she had had a child she would not have been unhappy; but the days were long, and it rained too much.

It was true that her husband, whenever he went away and left her, brought her a handsome present on his return; but this did not make up for the loneliness. At least nothing had, till he brought her the little brown dog from the East: after that she was much less unhappy. Her husband seemed pleased that she was so fond of the dog; he gave her leave to put her jewelled bracelet around its neck, and to keep it always with her.

One day she had fallen asleep in her room, with the dog at her feet, as his habit was. Her feet were bare and resting on his back. Suddenly she was waked by her husband: he stood beside her, smiling not unkindly.

"You look like my great-grandmother, Juliane de Cornault, lying in the chapel with her feet on a little dog," he said.

The analogy sent a chill through her, but she laughed and answered: "Well, when I am dead you must put me beside her, carved in marble, with my dog at my feet."

"Oho—we'll wait and see," he said, laughing also, but with his black brows close together. "The dog is the emblem of fidelity."

"And do you doubt my right to lie with mine at my feet?"

"When I'm in doubt I find out," he answered. "I am an old man," he added, "and people say I make you lead a lonely life. But I swear you shall have your monument if you earn it."

"And I swear to be faithful," she returned, "if only for the sake of having my little dog at my feet."

Not long afterward he went on business to the Quimper Assizes; and while he was away his aunt, the widow of a great nobleman of the duchy, came to spend a night at Kerfol on her way to the *pardon* of Ste. Barbe. She was a woman of great piety and consequence, and much respected by Yves de Cornault, and when she proposed to Anne to go with her to Ste. Barbe no one could object, and even the chaplain declared himself in favour of the pilgrimage. So Anne set out for Ste. Barbe, and there for the first time she talked with Herve de Lanrivain. He had come once or twice to Kerfol with his father, but she had never before exchanged a dozen words with him. They did not talk for more than five minutes now: it was under the chestnuts, as the procession was coming out of the chapel. He said: "I pity you," and she was surprised, for she had not supposed that anyone thought her an object of pity. He added: "Call for me when you need me," and she smiled a little, but was glad afterward, and thought often of the meeting.

She confessed to having seen him three times afterward: not more. How or where she would not say—one had the impression that she feared to implicate someone. Their meetings had been rare and brief; and at the last he had told her that he was starting the next day for a foreign country, on a mission which was not without peril and might keep him for many months absent. He asked her for a remembrance, and she had none to give him but the collar about the little dog's neck. She was sorry afterward that she had given it, but he was so unhappy at going that she had not had the courage to refuse.

Her husband was away at the time. When he returned a few days later he picked up the little dog to pet it, and noticed that its collar was missing. His wife told him that the dog had lost it in the undergrowth of the park, and that she and her maids had hunted a whole day for it. It was true, she explained to the court, that she had made the maids search for the necklet—they all believed the dog had lost it in the park. . .

Her husband made no comment, and that evening at supper he was in his usual mood, between good and bad: you could never tell which. He talked a good deal, describing what he had seen and done at Rennes; but now and then he stopped and looked hard at her; and when she went to bed she found her little dog strangled on her pillow. The little thing was dead, but still warm; she stooped to lift it, and her distress turned to horror when she discovered that it had been strangled by twisting twice round its throat the necklet she had given to Lanrivain.

The next morning at dawn she buried the dog in the garden, and hid the necklet in her breast. She said nothing to her husband, then or later, and he said nothing to her; but that day he had a peasant hanged for stealing a faggot in the park, and the next day he nearly beat to death a young horse he was breaking.

Winter set in, and the short days passed, and the long nights, one by one; and she heard nothing of Herve de Lanrivain. It might be that her husband had killed him; or merely that he had been robbed of the necklet. Day after day by the hearth among the spinning maids, night after night alone on her bed, she wondered and trembled. Sometimes at table her husband looked across at her and smiled; and then she felt sure that Lanrivain was dead. She dared not try to get news of him, for she was sure her husband would find out if she did: she had an idea that he could find out anything.

Even when a witch-woman who was a noted seer, and could show you the whole world in her crystal, came to the castle for a night's shelter, and the maids flocked to her, Anne held back. The winter was long and black and rainy. One day, in Yves de Cornault's absence, some gypsies came to Kerfol with a troop of performing dogs. Anne bought the smallest and cleverest, a white dog with a feathery coat and one blue and one brown eye. It seemed to have been ill-treated by the gypsies, and clung to her plaintively when she took it from them. That evening her husband came back, and when she went to bed she found the dog strangled on her pillow.

After that she said to herself that she would never have another dog; but one bitter cold evening a poor lean greyhound was found whining at the castle-gate, and she took him in and forbade the maids to speak of him to her husband. She hid him in a room that no one went to, smuggled food to him from her own plate, made him a warm bed to lie on and petted him like a child.

Yves de Cornault came home, and the next day she found the greyhound strangled on her pillow. She wept in secret, but said nothing, and resolved that even if she met a dog dying of hunger she would never bring him into the castle; but one day she found a young sheepdog, a brindled puppy with good blue eyes, lying with a broken leg in the snow of the park. Yves de Cornault was at Rennes, and she brought the dog in, warmed and fed it, tied up its leg and hid it in the castle till her husband's return.

The day before, she gave it to a peasant woman who lived a long way off, and paid her handsomely to care for it and say nothing; but that night she heard a whining and scratching at her door, and when she opened it the lame puppy, drenched and shivering, jumped up on her with little sobbing barks. She hid him in her bed, and the next morning was about to have him taken back to the peasant woman when she heard her husband ride into the court. She shut the dog in a chest and went down to receive him. An hour or two later, when she returned to her room, the puppy lay strangled on her pillow. . .

After that she dared not make a pet of any other dog; and her loneliness became almost unendurable. Sometimes, when she crossed the court of the castle, and thought no one was looking, she stopped to pat the old pointer at the gate. But one day as she was caressing him her husband came out of the chapel; and the next day the old dog was gone. . .

This curious narrative was not told in one sitting of the court, or received without impatience and incredulous comment. It was plain that the judges were surprised by its puerility, and that it did not help the accused in the eyes of the public. It was an odd tale, certainly; but what did it prove? That Yves de Cornault disliked dogs, and that his wife, to gratify her own fancy, persistently ignored this dislike. As for pleading this trivial disagreement as an excuse for her relations—whatever their nature—with her supposed accomplice, the argument was so absurd that her own lawyer manifestly regretted having let her make use of it, and tried several times to cut short her story. But she went on to the end, with a kind of hypnotised insistence, as though the scenes she evoked were so real to her that she had forgotten where she was and imagined herself to be reliving them.

At length the judge who had previously shown a certain kindness to her said (leaning forward a little, one may suppose, from his row of dozing colleagues): "Then you would have us believe that you murdered your husband because he would not let you keep a pet dog?"

"I did not murder my husband."

"Who did, then? Herve de Lanrivain?"

"No."

"Who then? Can you tell us?"

"Yes, I can tell you. The dogs—" At that point she was carried out of the court in a swoon.

★★★★★★

It was evident that her lawyer tried to get her to abandon this line of defence. Possibly her explanation, whatever it was, had seemed convincing when she poured it out to him in the heat of their first private colloquy; but now that it was exposed to the cold daylight of judicial scrutiny, and the banter of the town, he was thoroughly ashamed of it, and would have sacrificed her without a scruple to save his professional reputation. But the obstinate judge—who perhaps, after all, was more inquisitive than kindly—evidently wanted to hear the story out, and she was ordered, the next day, to continue her deposition.

She said that after the disappearance of the old watchdog nothing particular happened for a month or two. Her husband was much as usual: she did not remember any special incident. But one evening a pedlar woman came to the castle and was selling trinkets to the maids. She had no heart for trinkets, but she stood looking on while the women made their choice. And then, she did not know how, but the pedlar coaxed her into buying for herself an odd pear-shaped pomander with a strong scent in it—she had once seen something of the kind on a gypsy woman. She had no desire for the pomander, and did not know why she had bought it.

The pedlar said that whoever wore it had the power to read the future; but she did not really believe that, or care much either. However, she bought the thing and took it up to her room, where she sat turning it about in her hand. Then the strange scent attracted her and she began to wonder what kind of spice was in the box. She opened it and found a grey bean rolled in a strip of paper; and on the paper she saw a sign she knew, and a message from Herve de Lanrivain, saying that he was at home again and would be at the door in the court that night after the moon had set. . .

She burned the paper and then sat down to think. It was nightfall, and her husband was at home. . . She had no way of warning Lanrivain, and there was nothing to do but to wait. . .

At this point I fancy the drowsy courtroom beginning to wake up. Even to the oldest hand on the bench there must have been a certain aesthetic relish in picturing the feelings of a woman on receiving such a message at nightfall from a man living twenty miles away, to whom she had no means of sending a warning. . .

She was not a clever woman, I imagine; and as the first result of her cogitation she appears to have made the mistake of being, that evening, too kind to her husband. She could not ply him with wine, according to the traditional expedient, for though he drank heavily at times he had a strong head; and when he drank beyond its strength it was because he chose to, and not because a woman coaxed him. Not his wife, at any rate—she was an old story by now. As I read the case, I fancy there was no feeling for her left in him but the hatred occasioned by his supposed dishonour.

At any rate, she tried to call up her old graces; but early in the evening he complained of pains and fever, and left the hall to go up to his room. His servant carried him a cup of hot wine, and brought back word that he was sleeping and not to be disturbed; and an hour later, when Anne lifted the tapestry and listened at his door, she heard his loud regular breathing. She thought it might be a feint, and stayed a long time barefooted in the cold passage, her ear to the crack; but the breathing went on too steadily and naturally to be other than that of a man in a sound sleep. She crept back to her room reassured, and stood in the window watching the moon set through the trees of the park.

The sky was misty and starless, and after the moon went down the night was pitch black. She knew the time had come, and stole along the passage, past her husband's door—where she stopped again to listen to his breathing—to the top of the stairs. There she paused a moment, and assured herself that no one was following her; then she began to go down the stairs in the darkness. They were so steep and winding that she had to go very slowly, for fear of stumbling. Her one thought was to get the door unbolted, tell Lanrivain to make his escape, and hasten back to her room. She had tried the bolt earlier in the evening, and managed to put a little grease on it; but nevertheless, when she drew it, it gave a squeak . . . not loud, but it made her heart stop; and the next minute, overhead, she heard a noise. . .

"What noise?" the prosecution interposed.

"My husband's voice calling out my name and cursing me."

"What did you hear after that?"

"A terrible scream and a fall."

"Where was Herve de Lanrivain at this time?"

"He was standing outside in the court. I just made him out in the darkness. I told him for God's sake to go, and then I pushed the door shut."

"What did you do next?"

"I stood at the foot of the stairs and listened."

"What did you hear?"

"I heard dogs snarling and panting." (Visible discouragement of the bench, boredom of the public, and exasperation of the lawyer for the defence. Dogs again—! But the inquisitive judge insisted.)

"What dogs?"

She bent her head and spoke so low that she had to be told to repeat her answer: "I don't know."

"How do you mean—you don't know?"

"I don't know what dogs. . ."

The judge again intervened: "Try to tell us exactly what happened. How long did you remain at the foot of the stairs?"

"Only a few minutes."

"And what was going on meanwhile overhead?"

"The dogs kept on snarling and panting. Once or twice he cried out. I think he moaned once. Then he was quiet."

"Then what happened?"

"Then I heard a sound like the noise of a pack when the wolf is thrown to them—gulping and lapping."

(There was a groan of disgust and repulsion through the court, and another attempted intervention by the distracted lawyer. But the inquisitive judge was still inquisitive.)

"And all the while you did not go up?"

"Yes—I went up then—to drive them off."

"The dogs?"

"Yes."

"Well—?"

"When I got there it was quite dark. I found my husband's flint and steel and struck a spark. I saw him lying there. He was dead."

"And the dogs?"

"The dogs were gone."

"Gone—where to?"

"I don't know. There was no way out—and there were no dogs at Kerfol."

She straightened herself to her full height, threw her arms above her head, and fell down on the stone floor with a long scream. There was a moment of confusion in the court-room. Someone on the bench was heard to say: "This is clearly a case for the ecclesiastical authorities"—and the prisoner's lawyer doubtless jumped at the suggestion.

After this, the trial loses itself in a maze of cross-questioning and squabbling. Every witness who was called corroborated Anne de Cornault's statement that there were no dogs at Kerfol: had been none for several months. The master of the house had taken a dislike to dogs, there was no denying it. But, on the other hand, at the inquest, there had been long and bitter discussion as to the nature of the dead man's wounds. One of the surgeons called in had spoken of marks that looked like bites. The suggestion of witchcraft was revived, and the opposing lawyers hurled tomes of necromancy at each other.

At last Anne de Cornault was brought back into court—at the instance of the same judge—and asked if she knew where the dogs she spoke of could have come from. On the body of her Redeemer she swore that she did not. Then the judge put his final question: "If the dogs you think you heard had been known to you, do you think you would have recognised them by their barking?"

"Yes."

"Did you recognise them?"

"Yes."

"What dogs do you take them to have been?"

"My dead dogs," she said in a whisper. . . She was taken out of court, not to reappear there again. There was some kind of ecclesiastical investigation, and the end of the business was that the judges disagreed with each other, and with the ecclesiastical committee, and that Anne de Cornault was finally handed over to the keeping of her husband's family, who shut her up in the keep of Kerfol, where she is said to have died many years later, a harmless madwoman.

So ends her story. As for that of Herve de Lanrivain, I had only to apply to his collateral descendant for its subsequent details. The evidence against the young man being insufficient, and his family influence in the duchy considerable, he was set free, and left soon afterward for Paris. He was probably in no mood for a worldly life, and he appears to have come almost immediately under the influence of the famous M. Arnauld d'Andilly and the gentlemen of Port Royal.

A year or two later he was received into their Order, and without achieving any particular distinction he followed its good and evil fortunes till his death some twenty years later. Lanrivain showed me a portrait of him by a pupil of Philippe de Champaigne: sad eyes, an impulsive mouth and a narrow brow. Poor Herve de Lanrivain: it was a grey ending. Yet as I looked at his stiff and sallow effigy, in the dark dress of the Jansenists, I almost found myself envying his fate. After all, in the course of his life two great things had happened to him: he had loved romantically, and he must have talked with Pascal. . .

Mrs. Manstey's View

The view from Mrs. Manstey's window was not a striking one, but to her at least it was full of interest and beauty. Mrs. Manstey occupied the back room on the third floor of a New York boarding- house, in a street where the ash-barrels lingered late on the sidewalk and the gaps in the pavement would have staggered a Quintus Curtius. She was the widow of a clerk in a large wholesale house, and his death had left her alone, for her only daughter had married in California, and could not afford the long journey to New York to see her mother. Mrs. Manstey, perhaps, might have joined her daughter in the West, but they had now been so many years apart that they had ceased to feel any need of each other's society, and their intercourse had long been limited to the exchange of a few perfunctory letters, written with indifference by the daughter, and with difficulty by Mrs. Manstey, whose right hand was growing stiff with gout.

Even had she felt a stronger desire for her daughter's companionship, Mrs. Manstey's increasing infirmity, which caused her to dread the three flights of stairs between her room and the street, would have given her pause on the eve of undertaking so long a journey; and without perhaps, formulating these reasons she had long since accepted as a matter of course her solitary life in New York. She was, indeed, not quite lonely, for a few friends still toiled up now and then to her room; but their visits grew rare as the years went by. Mrs. Manstey had never been a sociable woman, and during her husband's lifetime his companionship had been all-sufficient to her.

For many years she had cherished a desire to live in the country, to have a hen-house and a garden; but this longing had faded with age, leaving only in the breast of the uncommunicative old woman a vague tenderness for plants and animals. It was, perhaps, this tenderness which made her cling so fervently to her view from her window, a view in which the most optimistic eye would at first have failed to discover anything admirable.

Mrs. Manstey, from her coign of vantage (a slightly projecting bow-window where she nursed an ivy and a succession of unwholesome-looking bulbs), looked out first upon the yard of her own dwelling, of which, however, she could get but a restricted glimpse. Still, her gaze took in the topmost boughs of the ailanthus below her window, and she knew how early each year the clump of dicentra strung its bending stalk with hearts of pink. But of greater interest were the yards beyond. Being for the most part attached to boarding-houses they were in a state of chronic untidiness and fluttering, on certain days of the week, with miscellaneous garments and frayed tablecloths.

In spite of this Mrs. Manstey found much to admire in the long *vista* which she commanded. Some of the yards were, indeed, but stony wastes, with grass in the cracks of the pavement and no shade in spring save that afforded by the intermittent leafage of the clotheslines. These yards Mrs. Manstey disapproved of, but the others, the green ones, she loved. She had grown used to their disorder; the broken barrels, the empty bottles and paths unswept no longer annoyed her; hers was the happy faculty of dwelling on the pleasanter side of the prospect before her.

In the very next enclosure did not a magnolia open its hard white flowers against the watery blue of April? And was there not, a little way down the line, a fence foamed over every May by lilac waves of wistaria? Farther still, a horse-chestnut lifted its candelabra of buff and pink blossoms above broad fans of foliage; while in the opposite yard June was sweet with the breath of a neglected syringa, which persisted in growing in spite of the countless obstacles opposed to its welfare.

But if nature occupied the front rank in Mrs. Manstey's view, there was much of a more personal character to interest her in the aspect of the houses and their inmates. She deeply disapproved of the mustard-coloured curtains which had lately been hung in the doctor's window opposite; but she glowed with pleasure when the house farther down had its old bricks washed with a coat of paint. The occupants of the houses did not often show themselves at the back windows, but the servants were always in sight.

Noisy slatterns, Mrs. Manstey pronounced the greater number; she knew their ways and hated them. But to the quiet cook in the newly painted house, whose mistress bullied her, and who secretly fed the stray cats at nightfall, Mrs. Manstey's warmest sympathies were given.

On one occasion her feelings were racked by the neglect of a house-maid, who for two days forgot to feed the parrot committed to her care. On the third day, Mrs. Manstey, in spite of her gouty hand, had just penned a letter, beginning: "Madam, it is now three days since your parrot has been fed," when the forgetful maid appeared at the window with a cup of seed in her hand.

But in Mrs. Manstey's more meditative moods it was the narrowing perspective of far-off yards which pleased her best. She loved, at twilight, when the distant brown-stone spire seemed melting in the fluid yellow of the west, to lose herself in vague memories of a trip to Europe, made years ago, and now reduced in her mind's eye to a pale phantasmagoria of indistinct steeples and dreamy skies. Perhaps at heart Mrs. Manstey was an artist; at all events she was sensible of many changes of colour unnoticed by the average eye, and dear to her as the green of early spring was the black lattice of branches against a cold sulphur sky at the close of a snowy day.

She enjoyed, also, the sunny thaws of March, when patches of earth showed through the snow, like inkspots spreading on a sheet of white blotting-paper; and, better still, the haze of boughs, leafless but swollen, which replaced the clear-cut tracery of winter. She even watched with a certain interest the trail of smoke from a far-off factory chimney, and missed a detail in the landscape when the factory was closed and the smoke disappeared.

Mrs. Manstey, in the long hours which she spent at her window, was not idle. She read a little, and knitted numberless stockings; but the view surrounded and shaped her life as the sea does a lonely island. When her rare callers came it was difficult for her to detach herself from the contemplation of the opposite window-washing, or the scrutiny of certain green points in a neighbouring flower-bed which might, or might not, turn into hyacinths, while she feigned an interest in her visitor's anecdotes about some unknown grandchild. Mrs. Manstey's real friends were the denizens of the yards, the hyacinths, the magnolia, the green parrot, the maid who fed the cats, the doctor who studied late behind his mustard-colored curtains; and the confidant of her tenderer musings was the church-spire floating in the sunset.

One April day, as she sat in her usual place, with knitting cast aside and eyes fixed on the blue sky mottled with round clouds, a knock at the door announced the entrance of her landlady. Mrs. Manstey did not care for her landlady, but she submitted to her visits with ladylike resignation. Today, however, it seemed harder than usual to turn from the blue sky and the blossoming magnolia to Mrs. Sampson's unsuggestive face, and Mrs. Manstey was conscious of a distinct effort as she did so.

"The magnolia is out earlier than usual this year, Mrs. Sampson," she remarked, yielding to a rare impulse, for she seldom alluded to the absorbing interest of her life. In the first place it was a topic not likely to appeal to her visitors and, besides, she lacked the power of expression and could not have given utterance to her feelings had she wished to.

"The magnolia in the next yard—in Mrs. Black's yard," Mrs. Manstey repeated.

"Is it, indeed? I didn't know there was a magnolia there," said Mrs. Sampson, carelessly. Mrs. Manstey looked at her; she did not know that there was a magnolia in the next yard!

"By the way," Mrs. Sampson continued, "speaking of Mrs. Black reminds me that the work on the extension is to begin next week."

"The what?" it was Mrs. Manstey's turn to ask.

"The extension," said Mrs. Sampson, nodding her head in the direction of the ignored magnolia. "You knew, of course, that Mrs. Black was going to build an extension to her house? Yes, ma'am. I hear it is to run right back to the end of the yard. How she can afford to build an extension in these hard times I don't see; but she always was crazy about building. She used to keep a boarding-house in Seventeenth Street, and she nearly ruined herself then by sticking out bow-windows and what not; I should have thought that would have cured her of building, but I guess it's a disease, like drink. Anyhow, the work is to begin on Monday."

Mrs. Manstey had grown pale. She always spoke slowly, so the landlady did not heed the long pause which followed. At last Mrs. Manstey said: "Do you know how high the extension will be?"

"That's the most absurd part of it. The extension is to be built right up to the roof of the main building; now, did you ever?"

"Mrs. Manstey paused again. "Won't it be a great annoyance to you, Mrs. Sampson?" she asked.

"I should say it would. But there's no help for it; if people have got a mind to build extensions there's no law to prevent 'em, that I'm aware of." Mrs. Manstey, knowing this, was silent. "There is no help for it," Mrs. Sampson repeated, "but if I *am* a church member, I wouldn't be so sorry if it ruined Eliza Black. Well, good-day, Mrs. Manstey; I'm glad to find you so comfortable."

174

So comfortable—so comfortable! Left to herself the old woman turned once more to the window. How lovely the view was that day! The blue sky with its round clouds shed a brightness over everything; the ailanthus had put on a tinge of yellow-green, the hyacinths were budding, the magnolia flowers looked more than ever like rosettes carved in alabaster. Soon the wistaria would bloom, then the horse-chestnut; but not for her. Between her eyes and them a barrier of brick and mortar would swiftly rise; presently even the spire would disappear, and all her radiant world be blotted out. Mrs. Manstey sent away untouched the dinner-tray brought to her that evening. She lingered in the window until the windy sunset died in bat-coloured dusk; then, going to bed, she lay sleepless all night.

Early the next day she was up and at the window. It was raining, but even through the slanting grey gauze the scene had its charm— and then the rain was so good for the trees. She had noticed the day before that the ailanthus was growing dusty.

"Of course I might move," said Mrs. Manstey aloud, and turning from the window she looked about her room. She might move, of course; so might she be flayed alive; but she was not likely to survive either operation. The room, though far less important to her happiness than the view, was as much a part of her existence. She had lived in it seventeen years. She knew every stain on the wall-paper, every rent in the carpet; the light fell in a certain way on her engravings, her books had grown shabby on their shelves, her bulbs and ivy were used to their window and knew which way to lean to the sun. "We are all too old to move," she said.

That afternoon it cleared. Wet and radiant the blue reappeared through torn rags of cloud; the ailanthus sparkled; the earth in the flower-borders looked rich and warm. It was Thursday, and on Monday the building of the extension was to begin.

On Sunday afternoon a card was brought to Mrs. Black, as she was engaged in gathering up the fragments of the boarders' dinner in the basement. The card, black-edged, bore Mrs. Manstey's name.

"One of Mrs. Sampson's boarders; wants to move, I suppose. Well, I can give her a room next year in the extension. Dinah," said Mrs. Black, "tell the lady I'll be upstairs in a minute."

Mrs. Black found Mrs. Manstey standing in the long parlour garnished with statuettes and antimacassars; in that house she could not sit down.

Stooping hurriedly to open the register, which let out a cloud of dust, Mrs. Black advanced on her visitor.

"I'm happy to meet you, Mrs. Manstey; take a seat, please," the landlady remarked in her prosperous voice, the voice of a woman who can afford to build extensions. There was no help for it; Mrs. Manstey sat down.

"Is there anything I can do for you, ma'am?" Mrs. Black continued. "My house is full at present, but I am going to build an extension, and—"

"It is about the extension that I wish to speak," said Mrs. Manstey, suddenly. "I am a poor woman, Mrs. Black, and I have never been a happy one. I shall have to talk about myself first to—to make you understand."

Mrs. Black, astonished but imperturbable, bowed at this parenthesis.

"I never had what I wanted," Mrs. Manstey continued. "It was always one disappointment after another. For years I wanted to live in the country. I dreamed and dreamed about it; but we never could manage it. There was no sunny window in our house, and so all my plants died. My daughter married years ago and went away—besides, she never cared for the same things. Then my husband died and I was left alone. That was seventeen years ago. I went to live at Mrs. Sampson's, and I have been there ever since. I have grown a little infirm, as you see, and I don't get out often; only on fine days, if I am feeling very well. So you can understand my sitting a great deal in my window—the back window on the third floor—"

"Well, Mrs. Manstey," said Mrs. Black, liberally, "I could give you a back room, I dare say; one of the new rooms in the ex—"

"But I don't want to move; I can't move," said Mrs. Manstey, almost with a scream. "And I came to tell you that if you build that extension I shall have no view from my window—no view! Do you understand?"

Mrs. Black thought herself face to face with a lunatic, and she had always heard that lunatics must be humoured.

"Dear me, dear me," she remarked, pushing her chair back a little way, "that is too bad, isn't it? Why, I never thought of that. To be sure, the extension *will* interfere with your view, Mrs. Manstey."

"You do understand?" Mrs. Manstey gasped.

"Of course I do. And I'm real sorry about it, too. But there, don't you worry, Mrs. Manstey. I guess we can fix that all right."

Mrs. Manstey rose from her seat, and Mrs. Black slipped toward the door.

"What do you mean by fixing it? Do you mean that I can induce you to change your mind about the extension? Oh, Mrs. Black, listen to me. I have two thousand dollars in the bank and I could manage, I know I could manage, to give you a thousand if—"

Mrs. Manstey paused; the tears were rolling down her cheeks.

Her hand was on the door-knob, but with sudden vigour Mrs. Manstey seized her wrist.

"You are not giving me a definite answer. Do you mean to say that you accept my proposition?"

"Why, I'll think it over, Mrs. Manstey, certainly I will. I wouldn't annoy you for the world—"

"But the work is to begin tomorrow, I am told," Mrs. Manstey persisted.

Mrs. Black hesitated. "It shan't begin, I promise you that; I'll send word to the builder this very night."

Mrs. Manstey tightened her hold.

"You are not deceiving me, are you?" she said.

"No—no," stammered Mrs. Black. "How can you think such a thing of me, Mrs. Manstey?"

Slowly Mrs. Manstey's clutch relaxed, and she passed through the open door. "One thousand dollars," she repeated, pausing in the hall; then she let herself out of the house and hobbled down the steps, supporting herself on the cast-iron railing.

"My goodness," exclaimed Mrs. Black, shutting and bolting the hall-door, "I never knew the old woman was crazy! And she looks so quiet and ladylike, too."

Mrs. Manstey slept well that night, but early the next morning she was awakened by a sound of hammering. She got to her window with what haste she might and, looking out saw that Mrs. Black's yard was full of workmen. Some were carrying loads of brick from the kitchen to the yard, others beginning to demolish the oldfashioned wooden balcony which adorned each story of Mrs. Black's house. Mrs. Manstey saw that she had been deceived. At first she thought of confiding her trouble to Mrs. Sampson, but a settled discouragement soon took possession of her and she went back to bed, not caring to see what was going on.

Toward afternoon, however, feeling that she must know the worst, she rose and dressed herself. It was a laborious task, for her hands were stiffer than usual, and the hooks and buttons seemed to evade her.

When she seated herself in the window, she saw that the work-men had removed the upper part of the balcony, and that the bricks had multiplied since morning. One of the men, a coarse fellow with a bloated face, picked a magnolia blossom and, after smelling it, threw it to the ground; the next man, carrying a load of bricks, trod on the flower in passing.

"Look out, Jim," called one of the men to another who was smoking a pipe, "if you throw matches around near those barrels of paper you'll have the old tinder-box burning down before you know it."

And Mrs. Manstey, leaning forward, perceived that there were several barrels of paper and rubbish under the wooden balcony. At length the work ceased and twilight fell. The sunset was perfect and a roseate light, transfiguring the distant spire, lingered late in the west. When it grew dark Mrs. Manstey drew down the shades and proceeded, in her usual methodical manner, to light her lamp. She always filled and lit it with her own hands, keeping a kettle of kerosene on a zinc-covered shelf in a closet. As the lamp-light filled the room it assumed its usual peaceful aspect. The books and pictures and plants seemed, like their mistress, to settle themselves down for another quiet evening, and Mrs. Manstey, as was her wont, drew up her armchair to the table and began to knit.

That night she could not sleep. The weather had changed and a wild wind was abroad, blotting the stars with close-driven clouds. Mrs. Manstey rose once or twice and looked out of the window; but of the view nothing was discernible save a tardy light or two in the opposite windows. These lights at last went out, and Mrs. Manstey, who had watched for their extinction, began to dress herself. She was in evident haste, for she merely flung a thin dressing-gown over her nightdress and wrapped her head in a scarf; then she opened her closet and cautiously took out the kettle of kerosene.

Having slipped a bundle of wooden matches into her pocket she proceeded, with increasing precautions, to unlock her door, and a few moments later she was feeling her way down the dark staircase, led by a glimmer of gas from the lower hall. At length she reached the bottom of the stairs and began the more difficult descent into the utter darkness of the basement. Here, however, she could move more freely, as there was less danger of being overheard; and without much delay she contrived to unlock the iron door leading into the yard. A gust of cold wind smote her as she stepped out and groped shiveringly under the clotheslines.

That morning at three o'clock an alarm of fire brought the engines to Mrs. Black's door, and also brought Mrs. Sampson's startled boarders to their windows. The wooden balcony at the back of Mrs. Black's house was ablaze, and among those who watched the progress of the flames was Mrs. Manstey, leaning in her thin dressing-gown from the open window.

The fire, however, was soon put out, and the frightened occupants of the house, who had fled in scant attire, reassembled at dawn to find that little mischief had been done beyond the cracking of window panes and smoking of ceilings. In fact, the chief sufferer by the fire was Mrs. Manstey, who was found in the morning gasping with pneumonia, a not unnatural result, as everyone remarked, of her having hung out of an open window at her age in a dressing-gown. It was easy to see that she was very ill, but no one had guessed how grave the doctor's verdict would be, and the faces gathered that evening about Mrs. Sampson's table were awestruck and disturbed. Not that any of the boarders knew Mrs. Manstey well; she "kept to herself," as they said, and seemed to fancy herself too good for them; but then it is always disagreeable to have anyone dying in the house and, as one lady observed to another: "It might just as well have been you or me, my dear."

But it was only Mrs. Manstey; and she was dying, as she had lived, lonely if not alone. The doctor had sent a trained nurse, and Mrs. Sampson, with muffled step, came in from time to time; but both, to Mrs. Manstey, seemed remote and unsubstantial as the figures in a dream. All day she said nothing; but when she was asked for her daughter's address she shook her head. At times the nurse noticed that she seemed to be listening attentively for some sound which did not come; then again she dozed.

The next morning at daylight she was very low. The nurse called Mrs. Sampson and as the two bent over the old woman they saw her lips move.

"Lift me up—out of bed," she whispered.

They raised her in their arms, and with her stiff hand she pointed to the window.

"Oh, the window—she wants to sit in the window. She used to sit there all day," Mrs. Sampson explained. "It can do her no harm, I suppose?"

"Nothing matters now," said the nurse.

They carried Mrs. Manstey to the window and placed her in her chair. The dawn was abroad, a jubilant spring dawn; the spire had already caught a golden ray, though the magnolia and horsechestnut still slumbered in shadow. In Mrs. Black's yard all was quiet. The charred timbers of the balcony lay where they had fallen. It was evident that since the fire the builders had not returned to their work. The magnolia had unfolded a few more sculptural flowers; the view was undisturbed.

It was hard for Mrs. Manstey to breathe; each moment it grew more difficult. She tried to make them open the window, but they would not understand. If she could have tasted the air, sweet with the penetrating ailanthus savour, it would have eased her; but the view at least was there—the spire was golden now, the heavens had warmed from pearl to blue, day was alight from east to west, even the magnolia had caught the sun.

Mrs. Manstey's head fell back and smiling she died.

That day the building of the extension was resumed.

The Young Gentlemen

1

The uniform newness of a new country gives peculiar relief to its few relics of antiquity—a term which, in America, may fairly enough be applied to any building already above ground when the colony became a republic.

Groups of such buildings, little settlements almost unmarred by later accretions, are still to be found here and there in the Eastern states; and they are always productive of inordinate pride in those who discover and live in them. A place of the sort, twenty years ago, was Harpledon, on the New England coast, somewhere between Salem and Newburyport. How intolerantly proud we all were of inhabiting it! How we resisted modern improvements, ridiculed fashionable "summer resorts," fought trolley-lines, overhead wires and telephones, wrote to the papers denouncing municipal vandalism, and bought up (those of us who could afford it) one little heavy-roofed house after another, as the land-speculator threatened them!

All this, of course, was on a very small scale: Harpledon was, and is still, the smallest of towns, hardly more than a village, happily unmenaced by industry, and almost too remote for the week-end "flivver." And now that civic pride has taught Americans to preserve and adorn their modest monuments, setting them in smooth stretches of turf and nursing the elms of the village green, the place has become far more attractive, and far worthier of its romantic reputation, than when we artists and writers first knew it. Nevertheless, I hope I shall never see it again; certainly I shall not if I can help it. . . .

2

The elders of the tribe of summer visitors nearly all professed to have "discovered" Harpledon. The only one of the number who never, to my knowledge, put forth this claim was Waldo Cranch; and he had lived there longer than any of us.

The one person in the village who could remember his coming to Harpledon, and opening and repairing the old Cranch house (for his family had been India merchants when Harpledon was a thriving seaport)—the only person who went back far enough to antedate Waldo Cranch was an aunt of mine, old Miss Lucilla Selwick, who lived in the Selwick house, itself a stout relic of India merchant days, and who had been sitting at the same window, watching the main street of Harpledon, for seventy years and more to my knowledge. But unfortunately the long range of Aunt Lucilla's memory often made it hit rather wide of the mark. She remembered heaps and heaps of far-off things; but she almost always remembered them wrongly. For instance, she used to say: "Poor Polly Everitt! How well I remember her, coming up from the beach one day screaming, and saying she'd seen her husband drowning before her eyes"—whereas everyone knew that Mrs. Everitt was on a picnic when her husband was drowned at the other end of the world, and that no ghostly premonition of her loss had reached her.

And whenever Aunt Lucilla mentioned Mr. Cranch's coming to live at Harpledon she used to say: "Dear me, I can see him now, driving by on that rainy afternoon in Denny Brine's old carry-all, with a great pile of bags and bundles, and on top of them a black and white hobby-horse with a real mane—the very handsomest hobby-horse I ever saw." No persuasion could induce her to dissociate the image of this prodigious toy from her first sight of Waldo Cranch, most incurable of bachelors, and least concerned with the amusing of other people's children, even those of his best friends. In this case, to be sure, her power of evocation had a certain success. Someone told Cranch—Mrs. Durant I think it must have been—and I can still hear his hearty laugh.

"What could it have been that she saw?" Mrs. Durant questioned; and he responded gaily: "Why not simply the symbol of my numerous tastes?" Which—as Cranch painted and gardened and made music (even composed it)—seemed so happy an explanation that for long afterward the Cranch house was known to us as Hobby-Horse Hall.

It will be seen that Aunt Lucilla's reminiscences, though they sometimes provoked a passing amusement, were neither accurate nor illuminating. Naturally, nobody paid much attention to them, and we had to content ourselves with regarding Waldo Cranch, hale and hearty and social as he still was, as an Institution already venerable when the rest of us had first apprehended Harpledon. We knew, of course, the chief points in the family history: that the Cranches had been prosperous merchants for three centuries, and had intermarried with other prosperous families; that one of them, serving his business apprenticeship at Malaga in colonial days, had brought back a Spanish bride, to the bewilderment of Harpledon; and that Waldo Cranch himself had spent a studious and wandering youth in Europe. His Spanish great-grandmother's portrait still hung in the old house; and it was a long-standing joke at Harpledon that the young Cranch who went to Malaga, where he presumably had his pick of Spanish beauties, should have chosen so dour a specimen.

The lady was a forbidding character on the canvas: very short and thickset, with a huge wig of black ringlets, a long harsh nose, and one shoulder perceptibly above the other. It was characteristic of Aunt Lucilla Selwick that in mentioning this swart virago she always took the tone of elegy. "Ah, poor thing, they say she never forgot the sunshine and orange blossoms, and pined off early, when her queer son Calvert was hardly out of petticoats. A strange man Calvert Cranch was; but he married Euphemia Waldo of Wood's Hole, the beauty, and had two sons, one exactly like Euphemia, the other made in his own image. And they do say that one was so afraid of his own face that he went back to Spain and died a monk—if you'll believe it," she always concluded with a Puritan shudder.

This was all we knew of Waldo Cranch's past; and he had been so long a part of Harpledon that our curiosity seldom ranged beyond his coming there. He was our local ancestor; but it was a mark of his studied cordiality and his native tact that he never made us feel his priority. It was never he who embittered us with allusions to the picturesqueness of the old light-house before it was rebuilt, or the paintability of the vanished water-mill; he carried his distinction so far as to take Harpledon itself for granted, carelessly, almost condescendingly—as if there had been rows and rows of them strung along the Atlantic coast.

Yet the Cranch house was really something to brag about. Architects and photographers had come in pursuit of it long before the diffused quaintness of Harpledon made it the prey of the magazine illustrator. The Cranch house was not quaint; it owed little to the happy irregularities of later additions, and needed no such help. Foursquare and stern, built of a dark mountain granite (though all the other old houses in the place were of brick or wood), it stood at the far end of the green, where the elms were densest and the village street faded away between blueberry pastures and oakwoods.

A door with a white classical portico was the only eighteenth century addition. The house kept untouched its heavy slate roof, its low windows, its sober cornice and plain interior panelling—even the old box garden at the back, and the pagoda-roofed summer house, could not have been much later than the house. I have said that the latter owed little to later additions; yet some people thought the wing on the garden side was of more recent construction. If it was, its architect had respected the dimensions and detail of the original house, simply giving the wing one less story, and covering it with a lower-pitched roof.

The learned thought that the kitchen and offices, and perhaps the slaves' quarters, had originally been in this wing; they based their argument on the fact of there being no windows, but only blind arches, on the side toward the garden, Waldo Cranch said he didn't know; he had found the wing just as it was now, with a big empty room on the ground floor, that he used for storing things, and a few low-studded bedchambers above. The house was so big that he didn't need any of these rooms, and had never bothered about them. Once, I remember, I thought him a little short with a fashionable Boston architect who had insisted on Mrs. Durant's bringing him to see the house, and who wanted to examine the windows on the farther, the invisible, side of the wing.

"Certainly," Cranch had agreed. "But you see those windows look on the kitchen-court and the drying-ground. My old housekeeper and the faithful retainers generally sit there in the afternoons in hot weather, when their work is done, and they've been with me so long that I respect their habits. At some other hour, if you'll come again—. You're going back to Boston tomorrow? So sorry! Yes, of course, you can photograph the front as much as you like. It's used to it." And he showed out Mrs. Durant and her *protégé*.

When he came back a frown still lingered on his handsome brows. "I'm getting sick of having this poor old house lionized. No one bothered about it or me when I first came back to live here," he said. But a moment later he added, in his usual kindly tone: "After all, I suppose I ought to be pleased."

If anyone could have soothed his annoyance, and even made it appear unreasonable, it was Mrs. Durant. The fact that it was to her he had betrayed his impatience struck us all, and caused me to remark, for the first time, that she was the only person at Harpledon who was not afraid of him. Yes; we all were, though he came and went among us with such a show of good-fellowship that it took this trifling incident to remind me of his real aloofness. Not one of us but would have felt a slight chill at his tone to the Boston architect; but then I doubt if any of us but Mrs. Durant would have dared to bring a stranger to the house.

Mrs. Durant was a widow who combined gray hair with a still-youthful face at a time when this happy union was less generally fashionable than now. She had come to Harpledon among the earliest summer colonists, and had soon struck up a friendship with Waldo Cranch. At first Harpledon was sure they would marry; then it became sure they wouldn't; for a number of years now it had wondered why they hadn't. These conjectures, of which the two themselves could hardly have been unaware, did not seem to trouble the even tenor of their friendship. They continued to meet as often as before, and Mrs. Durant continued to be the channel for transmitting any request or inquiry that the rest of us hesitated to put to Cranch.

"We know he won't refuse you," I once said to her; and I recall the half-lift of her dark brows above a pinched little smile. "Perhaps," I thought, "he *has* refused her—once." If so, she had taken her failure gallantly, and Cranch appeared to find an undiminished pleasure in her company. Indeed, as the years went on their friendship grew closer; one would have said he was dependent on her if one could have pictured Cranch as dependent on anybody. But whenever I tried to do this I was driven back to the fundamental fact of his isolation.

"He could get on well enough without any of us," I thought to myself, wondering if this remoteness were inherited from the homesick Spanish ancestress. Yet I have seldom known a more superficially sociable man than Cranch. He had many talents, none of which perhaps went as far as he had once confidently hoped; but at least he used them as links with his kind instead of letting them seclude him in their jealous hold. He was always eager to show his sketches, to read aloud his occasional articles in the lesser literary reviews, and above all to play his new compositions to the musically-minded among us; or rather, since "eager" is hardly the term to apply to his calm balanced manner, I should say that he was affably ready to show off his accomplishments.

But then he may have regarded doing so as one of the social obligations: I had felt from the first that, whatever Cranch did, he was always living up to some self-imposed and complicated standard. Even his way of taking off his hat struck me as the result of more thought than most people give to the act; his very absence of flourish lent it an odd importance.

3

It was the year of Harpledon's first "jumble sale" that all these odds and ends of observation first began to connect themselves in my mind.

Harpledon had decided that it ought to have a village hospital and dispensary, and Cranch was among the first to promise a subscription and to join the committee. A meeting was called at Mrs. Durant's and after much deliberation it was decided to hold a village fair and jumble sale in somebody's grounds; but whose? We all hoped Cranch would lend his garden; but no one dared to ask him. We sounded each other cautiously, before he arrived, and each tried to shift the enterprise to his neighbour; till at last Homer Davids, our chief celebrity as a painter, and one of the shrewdest heads in the community, said drily: "Oh, Cranch wouldn't care about it."

"How do you know he wouldn't?" someone queried.

"Just as you all do; if not, why is it that you all want someone else to ask him?"

Mrs. Durant hesitated. "I'm sure—" she began.

"Oh, well, all right, then! *You* ask him," rejoined Davids cheerfully.

"I can't always be the one—"

I saw her embarrassment, and volunteered: "If you think there's enough shade in my garden. . . ."

By the way their faces lit up I saw the relief it was to them all not to have to tackle Cranch. Yet why, having a garden he was proud of, need he have been displeased at the request?

"Men don't like the bother," said one of our married ladies; which occasioned the proper outburst of praise for my unselfishness, and the observation that Cranch's maids, who had all been for years in his service, were probably set in their ways, and wouldn't care for the confusion and extra work. "Yes, old Catherine especially; she guards the place like a dragon," one of the ladies remarked; and at that moment Cranch appeared. Having been told what had been settled he joined with the others in complimenting me; and we began to plan for the jumble sale.

The men needed enlightenment on this point, I as much as the rest, but the prime mover immediately explained: "Oh, you just send

186

any old rubbish you've got in the house."

We all welcomed this novel way of clearing out our cupboards, except Cranch who, after a moment, and with a whimsical wrinkling of his brows, said: "But I haven't got any old rubbish."

"Oh, well, children's cast-off toys for instance," a newcomer threw out at random.

There was a general smile, to which Cranch responded with one of his rare expressive gestures, as who should say: "*Toys*—in my house? But whose?"

I laughed, and one of the ladies, remembering our old joke, cried out: "Why, but the hobby-horse!"

Cranch's face became a well-bred blank. Long-suffering courtesy was the note of the voice in which he echoed: "Hobbyhorse—?"

"Don't you remember?" It was Mrs. Durant who prompted him. "Our old joke? The wonderful black-and-white hobby-horse that Miss Lucilla Selwick said she saw you driving home with when you first arrived here? It had a real mane." Her colour rose a little as she spoke.

There was a moment's pause, while Cranch's brow remained puzzled; then a smile slowly cleared his face. "Of course!" he said. "I'd forgotten. Well, I feel now that I *was* young enough for toys thirty years ago; but I didn't feel so then. And we should have to apply to Miss Selwick to know what became of that hobby-horse. Meanwhile," he added, putting his hand in his pocket, "here's a small offering to supply some new ones for the fair."

The offering was not small: Cranch always gave liberally, yet always produced the impression of giving indifferently. Well, one couldn't have it both ways; some of our most gushing givers were the least lavish. The committee was delighted. . . .

"It was queer," I said afterward to Mrs. Durant. "Why did the hobby-horse joke annoy Cranch? He used to like it."

She smiled. "He may think it's lasted long enough. Harpledon jokes *do* last, you know."

Yes; perhaps they did, though I had never thought of it before.

"There's one thing that puzzles me," I went on; "I never know beforehand what is going to annoy him."

She pondered. "I'll tell you, then," she said suddenly. "It has annoyed him that no one thought of asking him to give one of his water-colours to the sale."

"Didn't we?"

"No. Homer Davids was asked, and that made it...rather more marked..."

"Oh, of course! I suppose we all forgot—"

She looked away. "Well," she said, "I don't suppose he likes to be forgotten."

"You mean: to have his accomplishments forgotten?"

"Isn't that a little condescending? I should say, his *gifts*," she corrected a trifle sharply. Sharpness was so unusual in her that she may have seen my surprise, for she added, in her usual tone: "After all, I suppose he's our most brilliant man, isn't he?" She smiled a little, as if to take the sting from my doing so.

"Of course he is," I rejoined. "But all the more reason—how could a man of his kind resent such a trifling oversight? I'll write at once—"

"Oh, *don't!*" she cut me short, almost pleadingly.

Mrs. Durant's word was law: Cranch was not asked for a watercolour. Homer Davids's, I may add, sold for two thousand dollars, and paid for a heating-system for our hospital. A Boston millionaire came down on purpose to buy the picture. It was a great day for Harpledon.

4

About a week after the fair I went one afternoon to call on Mrs. Durant, and found Cranch just leaving. His greeting, as he hurried by, was curt and almost hostile, and his handsome countenance so disturbed and pale that I hardly recognised him. I was sure there could be nothing personal in his manner; we had always been on good terms, and, next to Mrs. Durant, I suppose I was his nearest friend at Harpledon—if ever one could be said to get near Waldo Cranch!

After he had passed me I stood hesitating at Mrs. Durant's open door—front doors at Harpledon were always open in those friendly days, except, by the way, Cranch's own, which the stern Catherine kept chained and bolted. Since meeting me could not have been the cause of his anger, it might have been excited by something which had passed between Mrs. Durant and himself; and if that were so, my call was probably inopportune. I decided not to go in, and was turning away when I heard hurried steps, and Mrs. Durant's voice. "Waldo!" she said.

I suppose I had always assumed that she called him so; yet the familiar appellation startled me, and made me feel more than ever in the way. None of us had ever given Cranch his Christian name.

Mrs. Durant checked her steps, perceiving that the back in the doorway was not Cranch's but mine. "Oh, do come in," she murmured, with an attempt at ease.

In the little drawing-room I turned and looked at her. She, too, was visibly disturbed; not angry, as he had been, but showing, on her white face and reddened lids, the pained reflection of his anger. Was it against her, then, that he had manifested it? Probably she guessed my thought, or felt her appearance needed to be explained, for she added quickly: "Mr. Cranch has just gone. Did he speak to you?"

"No. He seemed in a great hurry."

"Yes. . . I wanted to beg him to come back. . . .to try to quiet him. . . . ."

She saw my bewilderment, and picked up a copy of an illustrated magazine which had been tossed on the sofa. "It's that—" she said.

The pages fell apart at an article entitled: "Colonial Harpledon," the greater part of which was taken up by a series of clever sketches signed by the Boston architect whom she had brought to Cranch's a few months earlier.

Of the six or seven drawings, four were devoted to the Cranch house. One represented the facade and its pillared gates, a second the garden front with the windowless side of the wing, the third a corner of the box garden surrounding the Chinese summer-house; while the fourth, a full-page drawing, was entitled: "The back of the slaves' quarters and service-court: quaint window-grouping."

On that picture the magazine had opened; it was evidently the one which had been the subject of discussion between my hostess and her visitor.

"You see. . . .you see. . . ." she cried.

"This picture? Well, what of it? I suppose it's the far side of the wing—the side we've never any of us seen."

"Yes; that's just it. He's horribly upset. . . ."

"Upset about what? I heard him tell the architect he could come back some other day and see the wing. . . .some day when the maids were not sitting in the court; wasn't that it?"

She shook her head tragically. "He didn't mean it. Couldn't you tell by the sound of his voice that he didn't?"

Her tragedy airs were beginning to irritate me. "I don't know that I pay as much attention as all that to the sound of his voice."

She coloured, and choked back her tears. "I know him so well; I'm always sorry to see him lose his self-control. And then he considers me responsible."

"You?"

189

"It was I who took the wretched man there. And of course it was an indiscretion to do that drawing; he was never really authorized to come back. In fact, Mr. Cranch gave orders to Catherine and all the other servants not to let him in if he did."

"Well—?"

"One of the maids seems to have disobeyed the order; Mr. Cranch imagines she was bribed. He has been staying in Boston, and this morning, on the way back, he saw this magazine at the book-stall at the station. He was so horrified that he brought it to me. He came straight from the train without going home, so he doesn't yet know how the thing happened."

"It doesn't take much to horrify him," I said, again unable to restrain a faint sneer.

"What's the harm in the man's having made that sketch?"

"Harm?" She looked surprised at my lack of insight. "No actual harm, I suppose; but it was very impertinent; and Mr. Cranch resents such liberties intensely. He's so punctilious."

"Well, we Americans are not punctilious, and being one himself, he ought to know it by this time."

She pondered again. "It's his Spanish blood, I suppose. . . .he's frightfully proud." As if this were a misfortune, she added: "I'm very sorry for him."

"So am I, if such trifles upset him."

Her brows lightened. "Ah, that's what I tell him—such things *are* trifles, aren't they? As I said just now: 'Your life's been too fortunate, too prosperous. That's why you're so easily put out.'"

"And what did he answer?"

"Oh, it only made him angrier. He said: 'I never expected that from *you*'—that was when he rushed out of the house." Her tears flowed over, and seeing her so genuinely perturbed I restrained my impatience, and took leave after a few words of sympathy.

Never had Harpledon seemed to me more like a tea-cup than with that silly tempest convulsing it. That there should be grownup men who could lose their self-command over such rubbish, and women to tremble and weep with them! For a moment I felt the instinctive irritation of normal man at such foolishness; yet before I reached my own door I was as mysteriously perturbed as Mrs. Durant.

The truth was, I had never thought of Cranch as likely to lose his balance over trifles. He had never struck me as unmanly; his quiet manner, his even temper, showed a sound sense of the relative importance of things. How then could so petty an annoyance have thrown him into such disorder?

I stopped short on my threshold, remembering his face as he brushed past me. "Something *is* wrong; really wrong," I thought. But what? Could it be jealousy of Mrs. Durant and the Boston architect? The idea would not bear a moment's consideration, for I remembered *her* face too.

"Oh, well, if it's his silly *punctilio*," I grumbled, trying to reassure myself, and remaining, after all, as much perplexed as before.

All the next day it poured, and I sat at home among my books. It must have been after ten in the evening when I was startled by a ring. The maids had gone to bed, and I went to the door, and opened it to Mrs. Durant. Surprised at the lateness of her visit, I drew her in out of the storm. She had flung a cloak over her light dress, and the lace scarf on her head dripped with rain. Our houses were only a few hundred yards apart, and she had brought no umbrella, nor even exchanged her evening slippers for heavier shoes.

I took her wet cloak and scarf and led her into the library. She stood trembling and staring at me, her face like a marble mask in which the lips were too rigid for speech; then she laid a sheet of note-paper on the table between us. On it was written, in Waldo Cranch's beautiful hand: "My dear friend, I am going away on a journey. You will hear from me," with his initials beneath. Nothing more. The letter bore no date.

I looked at her, waiting for an explanation. None came. The first word she said was: "Will you come with me—now, at once?"

"Come with you—where?"

"To his house—before he leaves. I've only just got the letter, and I daren't go alone.. . . ."

"Go to Cranch's house? But!. . . .at this hour. . . .What is it you are afraid of?" I broke out, suddenly looking into her eyes.

She gave me back my look, and her rigid face melted. "I don't know—any more than you do—That's why I'm afraid."

"But I know nothing. What on earth has happened since I saw you yesterday?"

"Nothing till I got this letter."

"You haven't seen him?"

"Not since you saw him leave my house yesterday."

"Or had any message—any news of him?"

"Absolutely nothing. I've just sat and remembered his face."

My perplexity grew. "But surely you can't imagine. . . .If you're as frightened as that you must have some other reason for it," I insisted.

She shook her head wearily. "It's the having none that frightens me. Oh, do come!"

"You think his leaving in this way means that he's in some kind of trouble?"

"In dreadful trouble."

"And you don't know why?"

"No more than you do!" she repeated.

I pondered, trying to avoid her entreating eyes. "But at this hour— come, do consider! I don't know Cranch so awfully well. How will he take it? You say he made a scene yesterday about that silly business of the architect's going to his house without leave..."

"That's just it. I feel as if his going away might be connected with that."

"But then he's mad!" I exclaimed. "No; not mad. Only—desperate."

I stood irresolute. It was evident that I had to do with a woman whose nerves were in fiddle-strings. What had reduced them to that state I could not conjecture, unless, indeed, she were keeping back the vital part of her confession. But that, queerly enough, was not what I suspected. For some reason I felt her to be as much in the dark over the whole business as I was; and that added to the strangeness of my dilemma.

"Do you know in the least what you're going for?" I asked at length.

"No, no, no—but come!"

"If he's there, he'll kick us out, most likely; kick *me* out, at any rate."

She did not answer; I saw that in her anguish she was past speaking. "Wait till I get my coat," I said.

She took my arm, and side by side we hurried in the rain through the shuttered village. As we passed the Selwick house I saw a light burning in old Miss Selwick's bedroom window. It was on the tip of my tongue to say: "Hadn't we better stop and ask Aunt Lucilla what's wrong? She knows more about Cranch than any of us!"

Then I remembered Cranch's expression the last time Aunt Lucilla's legend of the hobby-horse had been mentioned before him—the day we were planning the jumble sale—and a sudden shiver checked my pleasantry. "He looked then as he did when he passed me in the doorway yesterday," I thought; and I had a vision of my ancient relative, sitting there propped up in her bed and looking quietly into the unknown while all the village slept. Was she aware, I wondered, that we were passing under her window at that moment, and did she know what would await us when we reached our destination?

5

Mrs. Durant, in her thin slippers, splashed on beside me through the mud.

"Oh," she exclaimed, stopping short with a gasp, "look at the lights!"

We had crossed the green, and were groping our way under the dense elm-shadows, and there before us stood the Cranch house, all its windows illuminated. It was the only house in the village except Miss Selwick's that was not darkened and shuttered.

"Well, he can't be gone; he's giving a party, you see," I said derisively.

My companion made no answer. She only pulled me forward, and yielding once more I pushed open the tall entrance gates. In the brick path I paused. "Do you still want to go in?" I asked.

"More than ever!" She kept her tight clutch on my arm, and I walked up the path at her side and rang the bell.

The sound went on jangling for a long time through the stillness; but no one came to the door. At length Mrs. Durant laid an impatient hand on the door-panel. "But it's open!" she exclaimed.

It was probably the first time since Waldo Cranch had come back to live in the house that unbidden visitors had been free to enter it. We looked at each other in surprise and I followed Mrs. Durant into the lamplit hall. It was empty.

With a common accord we stood for a moment listening; but not a sound came to us, though the doors of library and drawing-room stood open, and there were lighted lamps in both rooms.

"It's queer," I said, "all these lights, and no one about."

My companion had walked impulsively into the drawing-room and stood looking about at its familiar furniture. From the panelled wall, distorted by the wavering lamp-light, the old Spanish ancestress glared down duskily at us out of the shadows. Mrs. Durant had stopped short—a sound of voices, agitated, discordant, a strange man's voice among them, came to us from across the hall. Silently we retraced our steps, opened the dining-room door, and went in. But here also we found emptiness; the talking came from beyond, came, as we

193

now perceived, from the wing which none of us had ever entered. Again we hesitated and looked at each other. Then "Come!" said Mrs. Durant in a resolute tone; and again I followed her.

She led the way into a large pantry, airy, orderly, well-stocked with china and glass. That too was empty; and two doors opened from it. Mrs. Durant passed through the one on the right, and we found ourselves, not, as I had expected, in the kitchen, but in a kind of vague unfurnished anteroom. The quarrelling voices had meanwhile died out; we seemed once more to have the mysterious place to ourselves. Suddenly, beyond another closed door, we heard a shrill crowing laugh. Mrs. Durant dashed at this last door and it let us into a large high-studded room. We paused and looked about us. Evidently we were in what Cranch had always described as the lumber-room on the ground floor of the wing. But there was no lumber in it now. It was scrupulously neat, and fitted up like a big and rather bare nursery; and in the middle of the floor, on a square of drugget, stood a great rearing black and white animal: my Aunt Lucilla's hobby-horse. . . .

I gasped at the sight; but in spite of its strangeness it did not detain me long, for at the farther end of the room, before a fire protected by a tall nursery fender, I had seen something stranger still. Two little boys in old-fashioned round jackets and knickerbockers knelt by the hearth, absorbed in the building of a house of blocks. Mrs. Durant saw them at the same moment. She caught my arm as if she were about to fall, and uttered a faint cry.

The sound, low as it was, produced a terrifying effect on the two children. Both of them dropped their blocks, turned around as if to dart at us, and then stopped short, holding each other by the hand, and staring and trembling as if we had been ghosts.

At the opposite end of the room, we stood staring and trembling also; for it was they who were the ghosts to our terrified eyes. It must have been Mrs. Durant who spoke first.

"Oh. . . .the poor things. . . ." she said in a low choking voice.

The little boys stood there, motionless and far off, among the ruins of their house of blocks. But, as my eyes grew used to the faint light—there was only one lamp in the big room—and as my shaken nerves adjusted themselves to the strangeness of the scene, I perceived the meaning of Mrs. Durant's cry.

The children before us were not children; they were two tiny withered men, with frowning foreheads under their baby curls, and heavy-shouldered middle-aged bodies. The sight was horrible, and rendered more so by the sameness of their size and by their old-fashioned childish dress. I recoiled; but Mrs. Durant had let my arm go, and was moving softly forward. Her own arms outstretched, she advanced toward the two strange beings. "You poor poor things, you," she repeated, the tears running down her face.

I thought her tender tone must have drawn the little creatures; but as she advanced they continued to stand motionless, and then suddenly—each with the same small *falsetto* scream—turned and dashed toward the door. As they reached it, old Catherine appeared and held out her arms to them.

"Oh, my God—how dare you, madam? My young gentlemen!" she cried.

They hid their dreadful little faces in the folds of her skirt, and kneeling down she put her arms about them and received them on her bosom. Then, slowly, she lifted up her head and looked at us.

I had always, like the rest of Harpledon, thought of Catherine as a morose old Englishwoman, civil enough in her cold way, but yet forbidding. Now it seemed to me that her worn brown face, in its harsh folds of grey hair, was the saddest I had ever looked upon.

"How could you, madam; oh, how could you? Haven't we got enough else to bear?" she asked, speaking low above the cowering heads on her breast. Her eyes were on Mrs. Durant.

The latter, white and trembling, gave back the look. "Enough else? Is there *more*, then?"

"There's everything—." The old servant got to her feet, keeping her two charges by the hand. She put her finger to her lips, and stooped again to the dwarfs. "Master Waldo, Master Donald, you'll come away now with your old Catherine. No one's going to harm us, my dears; you'll just go upstairs and let Janey Sampson put you to bed, for it's very late; and presently Catherine'll come up and hear your prayers like every night." She moved to the door; but one of the dwarfs hung back, his forehead puckering, his eyes still fixed on Mrs. Durant in indescribable horror.

"Good Dobbin," cried he abruptly, in a piercing pipe.

"No, dear, no; the lady won't touch good Dobbin," said Catherine. "It's the young gentlemen's great pet," she added, glancing at the Roman steed in the middle of the floor. She led the changelings away, and a moment later returned. Her face was ashen-white under its swarthiness, and she stood looking at us like a figure of doom.

"And now, perhaps," she said, "you'll be good enough to go away too."

195

"Go away?" Mrs. Durant, instead, came closer to her. "How can I—when I've just had this from your master?" She held out the letter she had brought to my house.

Catherine glanced coldly at the page and returned it to her.

"He says he's going on a journey. Well, he's been, madam; been and come back," she said.

"Come back? Already? He's in the house, then? Oh, do let me—" Mrs. Durant dropped back before the old woman's frozen gaze.

"He's lying overhead, dead on his bed, madam—just as they carried him up from the beach. Do you suppose, else, you'd have ever got in here and seen the young gentlemen? He rushed out and died sooner than have them seen, the poor lambs; him that was their father, madam. And here you and this gentleman come thrusting yourselves in. . . . ."

I thought Mrs. Durant would reel under the shock; but she stood quiet, very quiet—it was almost as if the blow had mysteriously strengthened her.

"He's dead? He's killed himself?" She looked slowly about the trivial tragic room. "Oh, now I understand," she said.

Old Catherine faced her with grim lips. "It's a pity you didn't understand sooner, then; you and the others, whoever they was, forever poking and prying; till at last that miserable girl brought in the police on us—"

"The police?"

"They was here, madam, in this house, not an hour ago, frightening my young gentlemen out of their senses. When word came that my master had been found on the beach they went down there to bring him back. Now they've gone to Hingham to report his death to the coroner. But there's one of them in the kitchen, mounting guard. Over what, I wonder? As if my young gentlemen could run away! Where in God's pity would they go? Wherever it is, I'll go with them; I'll never leave them. . . . And here we were at peace for thirty years, till you brought that man to draw the pictures of the house. . . ."

For the first time Mrs. Durant's strength seemed to fail her; her body drooped, and she leaned her weight against the door. She and the housekeeper stood confronted, two stricken old women staring at each other; then Mrs. Durant's agony broke from her. "Don't say I did it—don't say that!"

But the other was relentless. As she faced us, her arms outstretched, she seemed still to be defending her two charges. "What else would you have me say, madam? You brought that man here, didn't you? And he was determined to see the other side of the wing, and my poor master was determined he shouldn't." She turned to me for the first time. "It was plain enough to you, sir, wasn't it? To me it was, just coming and going with the tea-things. And the minute your backs was turned, Mr. Cranch rang, and gave me the order: 'That man's never to set foot here again, you understand.'

"And I went out and told the other three; the cook, and Janey, and Hannah Oast, the parlour-maid. I was as sure of the cook and Janey as I was of myself; but Hannah was new, she hadn't been with us not above a year, and though I knew all about her, and had made sure before she came that she was a decent close-mouthed girl, and one that would respect our. . . . our misfortune. . . . yet I couldn't feel as safe about her as the others, and of her temper I wasn't sure from the first. I told Mr. Cranch so, often enough; I said: 'Remember, now, sir, not to put her pride up, won't you?' For she was jealous, and angry, I think, at never being allowed to see the young gentlemen, yet knowing they were there, as she had to know. But their father would never have any but me and Janey Sampson about them.

"Well—and then, in he came yesterday with those accursed pictures. And however had the man got in? And where was Hannah? And it must have been her doing. . . . nd swearing and cursing at her. . . . and me crying to him and saying: 'For God's sake, sir, let be, let be. . . . don't stir the matter up...just let me talk to her. . . . And I went in to my little boys, to see about their supper; and before I was back, I heard a trunk bumping down the stairs, and the gardener's lad outside with a wheel-barrow, and Hannah Oast walking away out of the gate like a ramrod. 'Oh, sir, what have you done? Let me go after her!' I begged and besought him; but my master, very pale, but as calm as possible, held me back by the arm, and said: 'Don't you worry, Catherine. It passed off very quietly. We'll have no trouble from her.'

'No trouble, sir, from Hannah Oast? Oh, for pity's sake, call her back and let me smooth it over, sir!'

"But the girl was gone, and he wouldn't leave go of my arm nor yet listen to me, but stood there like a marble stone and saw her drive away, and wouldn't stop her. 'I'd die first, Catherine,' he said, his kind face all changed to me, and looking like that old Spanish she-devil on the parlour wall, that brought the curse on us. . . . And this morning the police came. The gardener got wind of it, and let us know they was on the way; and my master sat and wrote a long time in his room, and then walked out, looking very quiet, and saying to me he was going to the post office, and would be back before they got here. And the next we knew of him was when they carried him up to his bed just now. . . . And perhaps we'd best give thanks that he's at rest in it. But, oh, my young gentlemen. . . . my young gentlemen!"

6

I never saw the "young gentlemen" again. I suppose most men are cowards about calamities of that sort, the irremediable kind that have to be faced anew every morning. It takes a woman to shoulder such a lasting tragedy, and hug it to her. . . . as I had seen Catherine doing; as I saw Mrs. Durant yearning to do. . . .

It was about that very matter that I interviewed the old housekeeper the day after the funeral. Among the papers which the police found on poor Cranch's desk was a letter addressed to me. Like his message to Mrs. Durant it was of the briefest. "I have appointed no one to care for my sons; I expected to outlive them. Their mother would have wished Catherine to stay with them. Will you try to settle all this mercifully? There is plenty of money, but my brain won't work. Goodbye."

It was a matter, first of all, for the law; but before we entered on that phase I wanted to have a talk with old Catherine. She came to me, very decent in her new black; I hadn't the heart to go to that dreadful house again, and I think perhaps it was easier for her to speak out under another roof. At any rate, I soon saw that, after all the years of silence, speech was a relief; as it might have been to him too, poor fellow, if only he had dared! But he couldn't; there was that pride of his, his "Spanish pride" as she called it.

"Not but what he would have hated me to say so, sir; for the Spanish blood in him, and all that went with it, was what he most abominated. . . . But there it was, closer to him than his marrow. . . . Oh, what that old woman done to us! He told me why, once, long ago—it was about the time when he began to understand that our little boys were never going to grow up like other young gentlemen. 'It's her doing, the devil,' he said to me; and then he told me how she'd been a great Spanish heiress, a rich merchant's daughter, and had been promised, in that foreign way they have, to a young nobleman who'd never set eyes on her; and when the bridegroom came to the city where she lived, and saw her sitting in her father's box across the theatre, he turned about and mounted his horse and rode off the same night; and never a word came from him—the shame of it!

"It nigh killed her, I believe, and she swore then and there she'd marry a foreigner and leave Spain; and that was how she took up with young Mr. Cranch that was in her father's bank; and the old gentleman put a big sum into the Cranch shipping business, and packed off the young couple to Harpledon. . . .But the poor misbuilt thing, it seems, couldn't ever rightly get over the hurt to her pride, nor get used to the cold climate, and the snow and the strange faces; she would go about pining for the orange-flowers and the sunshine; and though she brought her husband a son, I do believe she hated him, and was glad to die and get out of Harpledon. . . .That was my Mr. Cranch's story. . . .

"Well, sir, he despised his great-grandfather more than he hated the Spanish woman. 'Marry that twisted stick for her money, and put her poisoned blood in us I' He used to put it that way, sir, in his bad moments. And when he was twenty-one, and travelling abroad, he met the young English lady I was maid to, the loveliest soundest young creature you ever set eyes on. They loved and married, and the next year—oh, the pity—the next year she brought him our young gentlemen...twins, they were. . . .When she died, a few weeks after, he was desperate. . . .more desperate than I've ever seen him till the other day. But as the years passed, and he began to understand about our little boys—well, then he was thankful she was gone. And that thankfulness was the bitterest part of his grief.

"It was when they was about nine or ten that *he* first saw it; though I'd been certain long before that. We were living in Italy then. And one day—oh, what a day, sir!—he got a letter, Mr. Cranch did, from a circus-man who'd heard somehow of our poor little children. . . .Oh, sir! . . . .Then it was that he decided to leave Europe, and come back to Harpledon to live. It was a lonely lost place at that time; and there was all the big wing for our little gentlemen. We were happy in the old house, in our way; but it was a solitary life for so young a man as Mr. Cranch was then, and when the summer folk began to settle here I was glad of it, and I said to him: 'You go out, sir, now, and make friends, and invite your friends here. I'll see to it that our secret is kept.'

"And so I did, sir, so I did. . . .and he always trusted me. He needed life and company himself; but he would never separate himself from the little boys. He was so proud—and yet so soft-hearted! And where could he have put the little things? They never grew past their toys—there's the worst of it. Heaps and heaps of them he brought home to them, year after year. Pets he tried too. . . .but animals were afraid of them—just as I expect you were, sir, when you saw them," she added suddenly, "but with no reason; there were never gentler beings. Little Waldo especially—it's as if they were trying to make up for being a burden. . . .Oh, for pity's sake, let them stay on in their father's house, and me with them, won't you, sir?"

As she wished it, so it was. The legal side of the matter did not take long to settle, for the Cranches were almost extinct; there were only some distant cousins, long since gone from Harpledon. Old Catherine was suffered to remain on with her charges in the Cranch house, and one of the guardians appointed by the courts was Mrs. Durant.

Would you have believed it? She wanted it—the horror, the responsibility and all. After that she lived all the year round at Harpledon; I believe she saw Cranch's sons every day. I never went back there; but she used sometimes to come up and see me in Boston. The first time she appeared—it must have been about a year after the events I have related—I scarcely knew her when she walked into my library. She was an old bent woman; her white hair now seemed an attribute of age, not a form of *coquetry*. After that, each time I saw her she seemed older and more bowed. But she told me once she was not unhappy—"not as unhappy as I used to be," she added, qualifying the phrase.

On the same occasion—it was only a few months ago—she also told me that one of the twins was ill. She did not think he would last long, she said; and old Catherine did not think so either. "It's little Waldo; he was the one who felt his father's death the most; the dark one; I really think he understands. And when he goes, Donald won't last long either." Her eyes filled with tears. "Presently I shall be alone again," she added.

I asked her then how old they were; and she thought for a moment, murmuring the years over slowly under her breath. "Only forty-one," she said at length—as if she had said "Only four."

Women are strange. I am their other guardian; and I have never yet had the courage to go down to Harpledon and see them.

Afterward

1

"Oh, there *is* one, of course, but you'll never know it."

The assertion, laughingly flung out six months earlier in a bright June garden, came back to Mary Boyne with a sharp perception of its latent significance as she stood, in the December dusk, waiting for the lamps to be brought into the library.

The words had been spoken by their friend Alida Stair, as they sat at tea on her lawn at Pangbourne, in reference to the very house of which the library in question was the central, the pivotal "feature." Mary Boyne and her husband, in quest of a country place in one of the southern or southwestern counties, had, on their arrival in England, carried their problem straight to Alida Stair, who had successfully solved it in her own case; but it was not until they had rejected, almost capriciously, several practical and judicious suggestions that she threw it out: "Well, there's Lyng, in Dorsetshire. It belongs to Hugo's cousins, and you can get it for a song."

The reasons she gave for its being obtainable on these terms—its remoteness from a station, its lack of electric light, hot-water pipes, and other vulgar necessities—were exactly those pleading in its favour with two romantic Americans perversely in search of the economic drawbacks which were associated, in their tradition, with unusual architectural felicities.

"I should never believe I was living in an old house unless I was thoroughly uncomfortable," Ned Boyne, the more extravagant of the two, had jocosely insisted; "the least hint of 'convenience' would make me think it had been bought out of an exhibition, with the pieces numbered, and set up again." And they had proceeded to enumerate, with humorous precision, their various suspicions and exactions, refusing to believe that the house their cousin recommended was *really*

Tudor till they learned it had no heating system, or that the village church was literally in the grounds till she assured them of the deplorable uncertainty of the water-supply.

"It's too uncomfortable to be true!" Edward Boyne had continued to exult as the avowal of each disadvantage was successively wrung from her; but he had cut short his rhapsody to ask, with a sudden relapse to distrust: "And the ghost? You've been concealing from us the fact that there is no ghost!"

Mary, at the moment, had laughed with him, yet almost with her laugh, being possessed of several sets of independent perceptions, had noted a sudden flatness of tone in Alida's answering hilarity.

"Oh, Dorsetshire's full of ghosts, you know."

"Yes, yes; but that won't do. I don't want to have to drive ten miles to see somebody else's ghost. I want one of my own on the premises. *Is* there a ghost at Lyng?"

His rejoinder had made Alida laugh again, and it was then that she had flung back tantalizingly: "Oh, there *is* one, of course, but you'll never know it."

"Never know it?" Boyne pulled her up. "But what in the world constitutes a ghost except the fact of its being known for one?"

"I can't say. But that's the story."

"That there's a ghost, but that nobody knows it's a ghost?"

"Well—not till afterward, at any rate."

"Till afterward?"

"Not till long, long afterward."

"But if it's once been identified as an unearthly visitant, why hasn't its *signalement* been handed down in the family? How has it managed to preserve its *incognito?*"

Alida could only shake her head. "Don't ask me. But it has."

"And then suddenly—" Mary spoke up as if from some cavernous depth of divination—"suddenly, long afterward, one says to one's self, '*That was* it?'"

She was oddly startled at the sepulchral sound with which her question fell on the banter of the other two, and she saw the shadow of the same surprise flit across Alida's clear pupils. "I suppose so. One just has to wait."

"Oh, hang waiting!" Ned broke in. "Life's too short for a ghost who can only be enjoyed in retrospect. Can't we do better than that, Mary?"

But it turned out that in the event they were not destined to, for within three months of their conversation with Mrs. Stair they were established at Lyng, and the life they had yearned for to the point of planning it out in all its daily details had actually begun for them.

It was to sit, in the thick December dusk, by just such a wide-hooded fireplace, under just such black oak rafters, with the sense that beyond the mullioned panes the downs were darkening to a deeper solitude: it was for the ultimate indulgence in such sensations that Mary Boyne had endured for nearly fourteen years the soul-deadening ugliness of the Middle West, and that Boyne had ground on doggedly at his engineering till, with a suddenness that still made her blink, the prodigious windfall of the Blue Star Mine had put them at a stroke in possession of life and the leisure to taste it. They had never for a moment meant their new state to be one of idleness; but they meant to give themselves only to harmonious activities. She had her vision of painting and gardening (against a background of grey walls), he dreamed of the production of his long-planned book on the "Economic Basis of Culture"; and with such absorbing work ahead no existence could be too sequestered; they could not get far enough from the world, or plunge deep enough into the past.

Dorsetshire had attracted them from the first by a semblance of remoteness out of all proportion to its geographical position. But to the Boynes it was one of the ever-recurring wonders of the whole incredibly compressed island—a nest of counties, as they put it—that for the production of its effects so little of a given quality went so far: that so few miles made a distance, and so short a distance a difference.

"It's that," Ned had once enthusiastically explained, "that gives such depth to their effects, such relief to their least contrasts. They've been able to lay the butter so thick on every exquisite mouthful."

The butter had certainly been laid on thick at Lyng: the old grey house, hidden under a shoulder of the downs, had almost all the finer marks of commerce with a protracted past. The mere fact that it was neither large nor exceptional made it, to the Boynes, abound the more richly in its special sense—the sense of having been for centuries a deep, dim reservoir of life. The life had probably not been of the most vivid order: for long periods, no doubt, it had fallen as noiselessly into the past as the quiet drizzle of autumn fell, hour after hour, into the green fish-pond between the yews; but these back-waters of existence sometimes breed, in their sluggish depths, strange acuities of emotion, and Mary Boyne had felt from the first the occasional brush of an intenser memory.

The feeling had never been stronger than on the December afternoon when, waiting in the library for the belated lamps, she rose from her seat and stood among the shadows of the hearth. Her husband had gone off, after luncheon, for one of his long tramps on the downs. She had noticed of late that he preferred to be unaccompanied on these occasions; and, in the tried security of their personal relations, had been driven to conclude that his book was bothering him, and that he needed the afternoons to turn over in solitude the problems left from the morning's work. Certainly the book was not going as smoothly as she had imagined it would, and the lines of perplexity between his eyes had never been there in his engineering days. Then he had often looked fagged to the verge of illness, but the native demon of "worry" had never branded his brow. Yet the few pages he had so far read to her—the introduction, and a synopsis of the opening chapter—gave evidences of a firm possession of his subject, and a deepening confidence in his powers.

The fact threw her into deeper perplexity, since, now that he had done with "business" and its disturbing contingencies, the one other possible element of anxiety was eliminated. Unless it were his health, then? But physically he had gained since they had come to Dorsetshire, grown robuster, ruddier, and fresher-eyed. It was only within a week that she had felt in him the undefinable change that made her restless in his absence, and as tongue-tied in his presence as though it were *she* who had a secret to keep from him!

The thought that there *was* a secret somewhere between them struck her with a sudden smart rap of wonder, and she looked about her down the dim, long room.

"Can it be the house?" she mused.

The room itself might have been full of secrets. They seemed to be piling themselves up, as evening fell, like the layers and layers of velvet shadow dropping from the low ceiling, the dusky walls of books, the smoke-blurred sculpture of the hooded hearth.

"Why, of course—the house is haunted!" she reflected.

The ghost—Alida's imperceptible ghost—after figuring largely in the banter of their first month or two at Lyng, had been gradually discarded as too ineffectual for imaginative use. Mary had, indeed, as became the tenant of a haunted house, made the customary inquiries among her few rural neighbours, but, beyond a vague, "They do say so, Ma'am," the villagers had nothing to impart. The elusive spectre had apparently never had sufficient identity for a legend to crystallize about it, and after a time the Boynes had laughingly set the matter down to their profit-and-loss account, agreeing that Lyng was one of the few houses good enough in itself to dispense with supernatural enhancements.

"And I suppose, poor, ineffectual demon, that's why it beats its beautiful wings in vain in the void," Mary had laughingly concluded.

"Or, rather," Ned answered, in the same strain, "why, amid so much that's ghostly, it can never affirm its separate existence as *the* ghost." And thereupon their invisible housemate had finally dropped out of their references, which were numerous enough to make them promptly unaware of the loss.

Now, as she stood on the hearth, the subject of their earlier curiosity revived in her with a new sense of its meaning—a sense gradually acquired through close daily contact with the scene of the lurking mystery. It was the house itself, of course, that possessed the ghost-seeing faculty, that communed visually but secretly with its own past; and if one could only get into close enough communion with the house, one might surprise its secret, and acquire the ghost-sight on one's own account. Perhaps, in his long solitary hours in this very room, where she never trespassed till the afternoon, her husband *had* acquired it already, and was silently carrying the dread weight of whatever it had revealed to him.

Mary was too well-versed in the code of the spectral world not to know that one could not talk about the ghosts one saw: to do so was almost as great a breach of good-breeding as to name a lady in a club. But this explanation did not really satisfy her. "What, after all, except for the fun of the *frisson*," she reflected, "would he really care for any of their old ghosts?" And thence she was thrown back once more on the fundamental dilemma: the fact that one's greater or less susceptibility to spectral influences had no particular bearing on the case, since, when one *did* see a ghost at Lyng, one did not know it.

"Not till long afterward," Alida Stair had said. Well, supposing Ned *had* seen one when they first came, and had known only within the last week what had happened to him? More and more under the spell of the hour, she threw back her searching thoughts to the early days of their tenancy, but at first only to recall a gay confusion of unpacking, settling, arranging of books, and calling to each other from remote corners of the house as treasure after treasure of their habitation revealed itself to them. It was in this particular connection that she presently recalled a certain soft afternoon of the previous October, when, passing from the first rapturous flurry of exploration to a detailed inspection of the old house, she had pressed (like a novel heroine) a panel that opened at her touch, on a narrow flight of stairs leading to an unsuspected flat ledge of the roof—the roof which, from below, seemed to slope away on all sides too abruptly for any but practised feet to scale.

The view from this hidden coign was enchanting, and she had flown down to snatch Ned from his papers and give him the freedom of her discovery. She remembered still how, standing on the narrow ledge, he had passed his arm about her while their gaze flew to the long, tossed horizon-line of the downs, and then dropped contentedly back to trace the arabesque of yew hedges about the fish-pond, and the shadow of the cedar on the lawn.

"And now the other way," he had said, gently turning her about within his arm; and closely pressed to him, she had absorbed, like some long, satisfying draft, the picture of the gray-walled court, the squat lions on the gates, and the lime-avenue reaching up to the high-road under the downs.

It was just then, while they gazed and held each other, that she had felt his arm relax, and heard a sharp "Hullo!" that made her turn to glance at him.

Distinctly, yes, she now recalled she had seen, as she glanced, a shadow of anxiety, of perplexity, rather, fall across his face; and, following his eyes, had beheld the figure of a man—a man in loose, greyish clothes, as it appeared to her—who was sauntering down the lime-avenue to the court with the tentative gait of a stranger seeking his way. Her short-sighted eyes had given her but a blurred impression of slightness and greyness, with something foreign, or at least unlocal, in the cut of the figure or its garb; but her husband had apparently seen more—seen enough to make him push past her with a sharp "Wait!" and dash down the twisting stairs without pausing to give her a hand for the descent.

A slight tendency to dizziness obliged her, after a provisional clutch at the chimney against which they had been leaning, to follow him down more cautiously; and when she had reached the attic landing she paused again for a less definite reason, leaning over the oak banister to strain her eyes through the silence of the brown, sun-flecked depths below. She lingered there till, somewhere in those depths, she heard the closing of a door; then, mechanically impelled, she went down the shallow flights of steps till she reached the lower hall.

The front door stood open on the mild sunlight of the court, and hall and court were empty. The library door was open, too, and after listening in vain for any sound of voices within, she quickly crossed the threshold, and found her husband alone, vaguely fingering the papers on his desk.

He looked up, as if surprised at her precipitate entrance, but the shadow of anxiety had passed from his face, leaving it even, as she fancied, a little brighter and clearer than usual.

"What was it? Who was it?" she asked.

"Who?" he repeated, with the surprise still all on his side.

"The man we saw coming toward the house." Boyne shrugged his shoulders. "So I thought; but he must have got up steam in the interval. What do you say to our trying a scramble up Meldon Steep before sunset?"

That was all. At the time the occurrence had been less than nothing, had, indeed, been immediately obliterated by the magic of their first vision from Meldon Steep, a height which they had dreamed of climbing ever since they had first seen its bare spine heaving itself above the low roof of Lyng. Doubtless it was the mere fact of the other incident's having occurred on the very day of their ascent to Meldon that had kept it stored away in the unconscious fold of association from which it now emerged; for in itself it had no mark of the portentous. At the moment there could have been nothing more natural than that Ned should dash himself from the roof in the pursuit of dilatory tradesmen. It was the period when they were always on the watch for one or the other of the specialists employed about the place; always lying in wait for them, and dashing out at them with questions, reproaches, or reminders. And certainly in the distance the grey figure had looked like Peters.

Yet now, as she reviewed the rapid scene, she felt her husband's explanation of it to have been invalidated by the look of anxiety on his face. Why had the familiar appearance of Peters made him anxious? Why, above all, if it was of such prime necessity to confer with that authority on the subject of the stable-drains, had the failure to find him produced such a look of relief? Mary could not say that any one of these considerations had occurred to her at the time, yet, from the promptness with which they now marshalled themselves at her summons, she had a sudden sense that they must all along have been there, waiting their hour.

207

Weary with her thoughts, she moved toward the window. The library was now completely dark, and she was surprised to see how much faint light the outer world still held.

As she peered out into it across the court, a figure shaped itself in the tapering perspective of bare lines: it looked a mere blot of deeper grey in the greyness, and for an instant, as it moved toward her, her heart thumped to the thought, "It's the ghost!"

She had time, in that long instant, to feel suddenly that the man of whom, two months earlier, she had a brief distant vision from the roof was now, at his predestined hour, about to reveal himself as *not* having been Peters; and her spirit sank under the impending fear of the disclosure. But almost with the next tick of the clock the ambiguous figure, gaining substance and character, showed itself even to her weak sight as her husband's; and she turned away to meet him, as he entered, with the confession of her folly.

"It's really too absurd," she laughed out from the threshold, "but I never *can* remember!"

"Remember what?" Boyne questioned as they drew together.

"That when one sees the Lyng ghost one never knows it."

Her hand was on his sleeve, and he kept it there, but with no response in his gesture or in the lines of his fagged, preoccupied face.

"Did you think you'd seen it?" he asked, after an appreciable interval.

"Why, I actually took *you* for it, my dear, in my mad determination to spot it!"

"Me—just now?" His arm dropped away, and he turned from her with a faint echo of her laugh. "Really, dearest, you'd better give it up, if that's the best you can do."

"Yes, I give it up—I give it up. Have *you?*" she asked, turning round on him abruptly.

The parlour-maid had entered with letters and a lamp, and the light struck up into Boyne's face as he bent above the tray she presented.

"Have *you?*" Mary perversely insisted, when the servant had disappeared on her errand of illumination.

"Have I what?" he rejoined absently, the light bringing out the sharp stamp of worry between his brows as he turned over the letters.

"I never tried," he said, tearing open the wrapper of a newspaper.

"Well, of course," Mary persisted, "the exasperating thing is that there's no use trying, since one can't be sure till so long afterward."

He was unfolding the paper as if he had hardly heard her; but after a pause, during which the sheets rustled spasmodically between his hands, he lifted his head to say abruptly, "Have you any idea *how long?*"

Mary had sunk into a low chair beside the fireplace. From her seat she looked up, startled, at her husband's profile, which was darkly projected against the circle of lamplight.

"No; none. Have *you*" she retorted, repeating her former phrase with an added keenness of intention.

Boyne crumpled the paper into a bunch, and then inconsequently turned back with it toward the lamp.

"Lord, no! I only meant," he explained, with a faint tinge of impatience, "is there any legend, any tradition, as to that?"

"Not that I know of," she answered; but the impulse to add, "What makes you ask?" was checked by the reappearance of the parlour-maid with tea and a second lamp.

With the dispersal of shadows, and the repetition of the daily domestic office, Mary Boyne felt herself less oppressed by that sense of something mutely imminent which had darkened her solitary afternoon. For a few moments she gave herself silently to the details of her task, and when she looked up from it she was struck to the point of bewilderment by the change in her husband's face. He had seated himself near the farther lamp, and was absorbed in the perusal of his letters; but was it something he had found in them, or merely the shifting of her own point of view, that had restored his features to their normal aspect? The longer she looked, the more definitely the change affirmed itself. The lines of painful tension had vanished, and such traces of fatigue as lingered were of the kind easily attributable to steady mental effort. He glanced up, as if drawn by her gaze, and met her eyes with a smile.

"I'm dying for my tea, you know; and here's a letter for you," he said.

She took the letter he held out in exchange for the cup she proffered him, and, returning to her seat, broke the seal with the languid gesture of the reader whose interests are all enclosed in the circle of one cherished presence.

Her next conscious motion was that of starting to her feet, the letter falling to them as she rose, while she held out to her husband a long newspaper clipping.

"Ned! What's this? What does it mean?"

209

He had risen at the same instant, almost as if hearing her cry before she uttered it; and for a perceptible space of time he and she studied each other, like adversaries watching for an advantage, across the space between her chair and his desk.

"What's what? You fairly made me jump!" Boyne said at length, moving toward her with a sudden, half-exasperated laugh. The shadow of apprehension was on his face again, not now a look of fixed foreboding, but a shifting vigilance of lips and eyes that gave her the sense of his feeling himself invisibly surrounded.

Her hand shook so that she could hardly give him the clipping.

"This article—from the *Waukesha Sentinel*—that a man named Elwell has brought suit against you—that there was something wrong about the Blue Star Mine. I can't understand more than half."

They continued to face each other as she spoke, and to her astonishment, she saw that her words had the almost immediate effect of dissipating the strained watchfulness of his look.

"Oh, *that!*" He glanced down the printed slip, and then folded it with the gesture of one who handles something harmless and familiar. "What's the matter with you this afternoon, Mary? I thought you'd got bad news."

She stood before him with her undefinable terror subsiding slowly under the reassuring touch of his composure.

"You knew about this, then—it's all right?"

"Certainly I knew about it; and it's all right."

"But what *is* it? I don't understand. What does this man accuse you of?"

"Oh, pretty nearly every crime in the calendar." Boyne had tossed the clipping down, and thrown himself comfortably into an arm-chair near the fire. "Do you want to hear the story? It's not particularly interesting—just a squabble over interests in the Blue Star."

"But who is this Elwell? I don't know the name."

"Oh, he's a fellow I put into it—gave him a hand up. I told you all about him at the time."

"I daresay. I must have forgotten." Vainly she strained back among her memories. "But if you helped him, why does he make this return?"

"Oh, probably some shyster lawyer got hold of him and talked him over. It's all rather technical and complicated. I thought that kind of thing bored you."

His wife felt a sting of compunction. Theoretically, she deprecated the American wife's detachment from her husband's professional interests, but in practice she had always found it difficult to fix her attention on Boyne's report of the transactions in which his varied interests involved him. Besides, she had felt from the first that, in a community where the amenities of living could be obtained only at the cost of efforts as arduous as her husband's professional labours, such brief leisure as they could command should be used as an escape from immediate preoccupations, a flight to the life they always dreamed of living. Once or twice, now that this new life had actually drawn its magic circle about them, she had asked herself if she had done right; but hitherto such conjectures had been no more than the retrospective excursions of an active fancy. Now, for the first time, it startled her a little to find how little she knew of the material foundation on which her happiness was built.

She glanced again at her husband, and was reassured by the composure of his face; yet she felt the need of more definite grounds for her reassurance.

"But doesn't this suit worry you? Why have you never spoken to me about it?"

He answered both questions at once: "I didn't speak of it at first because it *did* worry me—annoyed me, rather. But it's all ancient history now. Your correspondent must have got hold of a back number of the *Sentinel*."

She felt a quick thrill of relief. "You mean it's over? He's lost his case?"

There was a just perceptible delay in Boyne's reply. "The suit's been withdrawn—that's all."

But she persisted, as if to exonerate herself from the inward charge of being too easily put off. "Withdrawn because he saw he had no chance?"

"Oh, he had no chance," Boyne answered.

She was still struggling with a dimly felt perplexity at the back of her thoughts.

"How long ago was it withdrawn?"

He paused, as if with a slight return of his former uncertainty. "I've just had the news now; but I've been expecting it."

"Just now—in one of your letters?"

"Yes; in one of my letters."

She made no answer, and was aware only, after a short interval of waiting, that he had risen, and strolling across the room, had placed himself on the sofa at her side. She felt him, as he did so, pass an arm about her, she felt his hand seek hers and clasp it, and turning slowly, drawn by the warmth of his cheek, she met the smiling clearness of his eyes.

"It's all right—it's all right?" she questioned, through the flood of her dissolving doubts; and "I give you my word it never was righter!" he laughed back at her, holding her close.

3

One of the strangest things she was afterward to recall out of all the next day's incredible strangeness was the sudden and complete recovery of her sense of security.

It was in the air when she woke in her low-ceilinged, dusky room; it accompanied her downstairs to the breakfast-table, flashed out at her from the fire, and re-duplicated itself brightly from the flanks of the urn and the sturdy flutings of the Georgian teapot. It was as if, in some roundabout way, all her diffused apprehensions of the previous day, with their moment of sharp concentration about the newspaper article,—as if this dim questioning of the future, and startled return upon the past,—had between them liquidated the arrears of some haunting moral obligation. If she had indeed been careless of her husband's affairs, it was, her new state seemed to prove, because her faith in him instinctively justified such carelessness; and his right to her faith had overwhelmingly affirmed itself in the very face of menace and suspicion. She had never seen him more untroubled, more naturally and unconsciously in possession of himself, than after the cross-examination to which she had subjected him: it was almost as if he had been aware of her lurking doubts, and had wanted the air cleared as much as she did.

It was as clear, thank Heaven! as the bright outer light that surprised her almost with a touch of summer when she issued from the house for her daily round of the gardens. She had left Boyne at his desk, indulging herself, as she passed the library door, by a last peep at his quiet face, where he bent, pipe in his mouth, above his papers, and now she had her own morning's task to perform. The task involved on such charmed winter days almost as much delighted loitering about the different quarters of her demesne as if spring were already at work on shrubs and borders. There were such inexhaustible possibilities still before her, such opportunities to bring out the latent graces of the old place, without a single irreverent touch of alteration, that the winter months were all too short to plan what spring and autumn executed. And her recovered sense of safety gave, on this particular morning, a peculiar zest to her progress through the sweet, still place. She went first to the kitchen-garden, where the espaliered pear-trees drew complicated patterns on the walls, and pigeons were fluttering and preening about the silvery-slated roof of their cot. There was something wrong about the piping of the hothouse, and she was expecting an authority from Dorchester, who was to drive out between trains and make a diagnosis of the boiler.

But when she dipped into the damp heat of the greenhouses, among the spiced scents and waxy pinks and reds of old-fashioned exotics,—even the flora of Lyng was in the note!—she learned that the great man had not arrived, and the day being too rare to waste in an artificial atmosphere, she came out again and paced slowly along the springy turf of the bowling-green to the gardens behind the house. At their farther end rose a grass terrace, commanding, over the fish-pond and the yew hedges, a view of the long house-front, with its twisted chimney-stacks and the blue shadows of its roof angles, all drenched in the pale gold moisture of the air.

Seen thus, across the level tracery of the yews, under the suffused, mild light, it sent her, from its open windows and hospitably smoking chimneys, the look of some warm human presence, of a mind slowly ripened on a sunny wall of experience. She had never before had so deep a sense of her intimacy with it, such a conviction that its secrets were all beneficent, kept, as they said to children, "for one's good," so complete a trust in its power to gather up her life and Ned's into the harmonious pattern of the long, long story it sat there weaving in the sun.

She heard steps behind her, and turned, expecting to see the gardener, accompanied by the engineer from Dorchester. But only one figure was in sight, that of a youngish, slightly built man, who, for reasons she could not on the spot have specified, did not remotely resemble her preconceived notion of an authority on hot-house boilers. The newcomer, on seeing her, lifted his hat, and paused with the air of a gentleman—perhaps a traveller—desirous of having it immediately known that his intrusion is involuntary. The local fame of Lyng occasionally attracted the more intelligent sight-seer, and Mary half-expected to see the stranger dissemble a camera, or justify his presence by producing it. But he made no gesture of any sort, and after a moment she asked, in a tone responding to the courteous deprecation of his attitude: "Is there anyone you wish to see?"

"I came to see Mr. Boyne," he replied. His intonation, rather than his accent, was faintly American, and Mary, at the familiar note, looked at him more closely. The brim of his soft felt hat cast a shade on his face, which, thus obscured, wore to her short-sighted gaze a look of seriousness, as of a person arriving "on business," and civilly but firmly aware of his rights.

Past experience had made Mary equally sensible to such claims; but she was jealous of her husband's morning hours, and doubtful of his having given anyone the right to intrude on them.

"Have you an appointment with Mr. Boyne?" she asked.

He hesitated, as if unprepared for the question.

"Not exactly an appointment," he replied.

"Then I'm afraid, this being his working-time, that he can't receive you now. Will you give me a message, or come back later?"

The visitor, again lifting his hat, briefly replied that he would come back later, and walked away, as if to regain the front of the house. As his figure receded down the walk between the yew hedges, Mary saw him pause and look up an instant at the peaceful house-front bathed in faint winter sunshine; and it struck her, with a tardy touch of compunction, that it would have been more humane to ask if he had come from a distance, and to offer, in that case, to inquire if her husband could receive him. But as the thought occurred to her he passed out of sight behind a pyramidal yew, and at the same moment her attention was distracted by the approach of the gardener, attended by the bearded pepper-and-salt figure of the boiler-maker from Dorchester.

The encounter with this authority led to such far-reaching issues that they resulted in his finding it expedient to ignore his train, and beguiled Mary into spending the remainder of the morning in absorbed confabulation among the greenhouses. She was startled to find, when the colloquy ended, that it was nearly luncheon-time, and she half expected, as she hurried back to the house, to see her husband coming out to meet her. But she found no one in the court but an under-gardener raking the gravel, and the hall, when she entered it, was so silent that she guessed Boyne to be still at work behind the closed door of the library.

Not wishing to disturb him, she turned into the drawing-room, and there, at her writing-table, lost herself in renewed calculations of the outlay to which the morning's conference had committed her. The knowledge that she could permit herself such follies had not yet lost its novelty; and somehow, in contrast to the vague apprehensions of the previous days, it now seemed an element of her recovered security, of the sense that, as Ned had said, things in general had never been "righter."

She was still luxuriating in a lavish play of figures when the parlour-maid, from the threshold, roused her with a dubiously worded inquiry as to the expediency of serving luncheon. It was one of their jokes that Trimmle announced luncheon as if she were divulging a state secret, and Mary, intent upon her papers, merely murmured an absent-minded assent.

She felt Trimmle wavering expressively on the threshold as if in rebuke of such offhand acquiescence; then her retreating steps sounded down the passage, and Mary, pushing away her papers, crossed the hall, and went to the library door. It was still closed, and she wavered in her turn, disliking to disturb her husband, yet anxious that he should not exceed his normal measure of work. As she stood there, balancing her impulses, the esoteric Trimmle returned with the announcement of luncheon, and Mary, thus impelled, opened the door and went into the library.

Boyne was not at his desk, and she peered about her, expecting to discover him at the bookshelves, somewhere down the length of the room; but her call brought no response, and gradually it became clear to her that he was not in the library.

She turned back to the parlour-maid.

"Mr. Boyne must be upstairs. Please tell him that luncheon is ready."

The parlour-maid appeared to hesitate between the obvious duty of obeying orders and an equally obvious conviction of the foolishness of the injunction laid upon her. The struggle resulted in her saying doubtfully, "If you please, Madam, Mr. Boyne's not upstairs."

"Not in his room? Are you sure?"

"I'm sure, Madam."

Mary consulted the clock. "Where is he, then?"

"He's gone out," Trimmle announced, with the superior air of one who has respectfully waited for the question that a well-ordered mind would have first propounded.

Mary's previous conjecture had been right, then. Boyne must have gone to the gardens to meet her, and since she had missed him, it was clear that he had taken the shorter way by the south door, instead of going round to the court. She crossed the hall to the glass portal opening directly on the yew garden, but the parlour-maid, after another

215

moment of inner conflict, decided to bring out recklessly, "Please, Madam, Mr. Boyne didn't go that way."

Mary turned back. "Where *did* he go? And when?"

"He went out of the front door, up the drive, Madam." It was a matter of principle with Trimmle never to answer more than one question at a time.

"Up the drive? At this hour?" Mary went to the door herself, and glanced across the court through the long tunnel of bare limes. But its perspective was as empty as when she had scanned it on entering the house.

"Did Mr. Boyne leave no message?" she asked.

Trimmle seemed to surrender herself to a last struggle with the forces of chaos.

"No, Madam. He just went out with the gentleman."

"The gentleman? What gentleman?" Mary wheeled about, as if to front this new factor.

"The gentleman who called, Madam," said Trimmle, resignedly.

"When did a gentleman call? Do explain yourself, Trimmle!"

Only the fact that Mary was very hungry, and that she wanted to consult her husband about the greenhouses, would have caused her to lay so unusual an injunction on her attendant; and even now she was detached enough to note in Trimmle's eye the dawning defiance of the respectful subordinate who has been pressed too hard.

"I couldn't exactly say the hour, Madam, because I didn't let the gentleman in," she replied, with the air of magnanimously ignoring the irregularity of her mistress's course.

"You didn't let him in?"

"No, Madam. When the bell rang I was dressing, and Agnes—"

"Go and ask Agnes, then," Mary interjected. Trimmle still wore her look of patient magnanimity. "Agnes would not know, Madam, for she had unfortunately burnt her hand in trying the wick of the new lamp from town—"Trimmle, as Mary was aware, had always been opposed to the new lamp—"and so Mrs. Dockett sent the kitchen-maid instead."

Mary looked again at the clock. "It's after two! Go and ask the kitchen-maid if Mr. Boyne left any word."

She went into luncheon without waiting, and Trimmle presently brought her there the kitchen-maid's statement that the gentleman had called about one o'clock, that Mr. Boyne had gone out with him without leaving any message. The kitchen-maid did not even know the caller's name, for he had written it on a slip of paper, which he had folded and handed to her, with the injunction to deliver it at once to Mr. Boyne.

Mary finished her luncheon, still wondering, and when it was over, and Trimmle had brought the coffee to the drawing-room, her wonder had deepened to a first faint tinge of disquietude. It was unlike Boyne to absent himself without explanation at so unwonted an hour, and the difficulty of identifying the visitor whose summons he had apparently obeyed made his disappearance the more unaccountable. Mary Boyne's experience as the wife of a busy engineer, subject to sudden calls and compelled to keep irregular hours, had trained her to the philosophic acceptance of surprises; but since Boyne's withdrawal from business he had adopted a Benedictine regularity of life. As if to make up for the dispersed and agitated years, with their "stand-up" lunches and dinners rattled down to the joltings of the dining-car, he cultivated the last refinements of punctuality and monotony, discouraging his wife's fancy for the unexpected; and declaring that to a delicate taste there were infinite gradations of pleasure in the fixed recurrences of habit.

Still, since no life can completely defend itself from the unforeseen, it was evident that all Boyne's precautions would sooner or later prove unavailable, and Mary concluded that he had cut short a tiresome visit by walking with his caller to the station, or at least accompanying him for part of the way.

This conclusion relieved her from farther preoccupation, and she went out herself to take up her conference with the gardener. Thence she walked to the village post-office, a mile or so away; and when she turned toward home, the early twilight was setting in.

She had taken a foot-path across the downs, and as Boyne, meanwhile, had probably returned from the station by the highroad, there was little likelihood of their meeting on the way. She felt sure, however, of his having reached the house before her; so sure that, when she entered it herself, without even pausing to inquire of Trimmle, she made directly for the library. But the library was still empty, and with an unwonted precision of visual memory she immediately observed that the papers on her husband's desk lay precisely as they had lain when she had gone in to call him to luncheon.

Then of a sudden she was seized by a vague dread of the unknown. She had closed the door behind her on entering, and as she stood alone in the long, silent, shadowy room, her dread seemed to take shape and sound, to be there audibly breathing and lurking among the shadows. Her short-sighted eyes strained through them, half-discerning an actual presence, something aloof, that watched and knew; and in the recoil from that intangible propinquity she threw herself suddenly on the bell-rope and gave it a desperate pull.

The long, quavering summons brought Trimmle in precipitately with a lamp, and Mary breathed again at this sobering reappearance of the usual.

"You may bring tea if Mr. Boyne is in," she said, to justify her ring.

"Very well, Madam. But Mr. Boyne is not in," said Trimmle, putting down the lamp.

"Not in? You mean he's come back and gone out again?"

"No, Madam. He's never been back."

The dread stirred again, and Mary knew that now it had her fast.

"Not since he went out with—the gentleman?"

"Not since he went out with the gentleman."

"But who *was* the gentleman?" Mary gasped out, with the sharp note of someone trying to be heard through a confusion of meaningless noises.

"That I couldn't say, Madam." Trimmle, standing there by the lamp, seemed suddenly to grow less round and rosy, as though eclipsed by the same creeping shade of apprehension.

"But the kitchen-maid knows—wasn't it the kitchen-maid who let him in?"

"She doesn't know either, Madam, for he wrote his name on a folded paper."

Mary, through her agitation, was aware that they were both designating the unknown visitor by a vague pronoun, instead of the conventional formula which, till then, had kept their allusions within the bounds of custom. And at the same moment her mind caught at the suggestion of the folded paper.

"But he must have a name! Where is the paper?"

She moved to the desk, and began to turn over the scattered documents that littered it. The first that caught her eye was an unfinished letter in her husband's hand, with his pen lying across it, as though dropped there at a sudden summons.

"My dear Parvis,"—who was Parvis?—"I have just received your letter announcing Elwell's death, and while I suppose there is now no farther risk of trouble, it might be safer—"

She tossed the sheet aside, and continued her search; but no folded paper was discoverable among the letters and pages of manuscript which had been swept together in a promiscuous heap, as if by a hurried or a startled gesture.

"But the kitchen-maid *saw* him. Send her here," she commanded, wondering at her dullness in not thinking sooner of so simple a solution.

Trimmle, at the behest, vanished in a flash, as if thankful to be out of the room, and when she reappeared, conducting the agitated underling, Mary had regained her self-possession, and had her questions pat.

The gentleman was a stranger, yes—that she understood. But what had he said? And, above all, what had he looked like? The first question was easily enough answered, for the disconcerting reason that he had said so little—had merely asked for Mr. Boyne, and, scribbling something on a bit of paper, had requested that it should at once be carried in to him.

"Then you don't know what he wrote? You're not sure it *was* his name?"

The kitchen-maid was not sure, but supposed it was, since he had written it in answer to her inquiry as to whom she should announce.

"And when you carried the paper in to Mr. Boyne, what did he say?"

The kitchen-maid did not think that Mr. Boyne had said anything, but she could not be sure, for just as she had handed him the paper and he was opening it, she had become aware that the visitor had followed her into the library, and she had slipped out, leaving the two gentlemen together.

"But then, if you left them in the library, how do you know that they went out of the house?"

This question plunged the witness into momentary inarticulateness, from which she was rescued by Trimmle, who, by means of ingenious circumlocutions, elicited the statement that before she could cross the hall to the back passage she had heard the gentlemen behind her, and had seen them go out of the front door together.

"Then, if you saw the gentleman twice, you must be able to tell me what he looked like."

But with this final challenge to her powers of expression it became clear that the limit of the kitchen-maid's endurance had been reached. The obligation of going to the front door to "show in" a visitor was in itself so subversive of the fundamental order of things that it had thrown her faculties into hopeless disarray, and she could only stammer out, after various panting efforts at evocation, "His hat, mum, was different-like, as you might say—"

"Different? How different?" Mary flashed out at her, her own mind, in the same instant, leaping back to an image left on it that morning, but temporarily lost under layers of subsequent impressions. "His hat had a wide brim, you mean? and his face was pale—a youngish face?" Mary pressed her, with a white-lipped intensity of interrogation. But if the kitchen-maid found any adequate answer to this challenge, it was swept away for her listener down the rushing current of her own convictions. The stranger—the stranger in the garden! Why had Mary not thought of him before? She needed no one now to tell her that it was he who had called for her husband and gone away with him. But who was he, and why had Boyne obeyed his call?

4

It leaped out at her suddenly, like a grin out of the dark, that they had often called England so little—"such a confoundedly hard place to get lost in."

A confoundedly hard place to get lost in! That had been her husband's phrase. And now, with the whole machinery of official investigation sweeping its flash-lights from shore to shore, and across the dividing straits; now, with Boyne's name blazing from the walls of every town and village, his portrait (how that wrung her!) hawked up and down the country like the image of a hunted criminal; now the little compact, populous island, so policed, surveyed, and administered, revealed itself as a Sphinx-like guardian of abysmal mysteries, staring back into his wife's anguished eyes as if with the malicious joy of knowing something they would never know!

In the fortnight since Boyne's disappearance there had been no word of him, no trace of his movements. Even the usual misleading reports that raise expectancy in tortured bosoms had been few and fleeting. No one but the bewildered kitchen-maid had seen him leave the house, and no one else had seen "the gentleman" who accompanied him. All inquiries in the neighbourhood failed to elicit the memory of a stranger's presence that day in the neighbourhood of Lyng. And no one had met Edward Boyne, either alone or in company, in any of the neighbouring villages, or on the road across the downs, or at either of the local railway-stations. The sunny English noon had swallowed him as completely as if he had gone out into Cimmerian night.

Mary, while every external means of investigation was working at its highest pressure, had ransacked her husband's papers for any trace of antecedent complications, of entanglements or obligations unknown to her, that might throw a faint ray into the darkness. But if any such had existed in the background of Boyne's life, they had disappeared as completely as the slip of paper on which the visitor had written his name. There remained no possible thread of guidance except—if it were indeed an exception—the letter which Boyne had apparently been in the act of writing when he received his mysterious summons. That letter, read and reread by his wife, and submitted by her to the police, yielded little enough for conjecture to feed on.

"I have just heard of Elwell's death, and while I suppose there is now no farther risk of trouble, it might be safer—" That was all. The "risk of trouble" was easily explained by the newspaper clipping which had apprised Mary of the suit brought against her husband by one of his associates in the Blue Star enterprise. The only new information conveyed in the letter was the fact of its showing Boyne, when he wrote it, to be still apprehensive of the results of the suit, though he had assured his wife that it had been withdrawn, and though the letter itself declared that the plaintiff was dead. It took several weeks of exhaustive cabling to fix the identity of the "Parvis" to whom the fragmentary communication was addressed, but even after these inquiries had shown him to be a Waukesha lawyer, no new facts concerning the Elwell suit were elicited. He appeared to have had no direct concern in it, but to have been conversant with the facts merely as an acquaintance, and possible intermediary; and he declared himself unable to divine with what object Boyne intended to seek his assistance.

This negative information, sole fruit of the first fortnight's feverish search, was not increased by a jot during the slow weeks that followed. Mary knew that the investigations were still being carried on, but she had a vague sense of their gradually slackening, as the actual march of time seemed to slacken. It was as though the days, flying horror-struck from the shrouded image of the one inscrutable day, gained assurance as the distance lengthened, till at last they fell back into their normal gait. And so with the human imaginations at work on the dark event. No doubt it occupied them still, but week by week and hour by hour it grew less absorbing, took up less space, was slowly but inevitably crowded out of the foreground of consciousness by the new problems perpetually bubbling up from the vaporous caldron of human experience.

Even Mary Boyne's consciousness gradually felt the same lowering of velocity. It still swayed with the incessant oscillations of conjecture; but they were slower, more rhythmical in their beat. There were moments of overwhelming lassitude when, like the victim of some poison which leaves the brain clear, but holds the body motionless, she saw herself domesticated with the Horror, accepting its perpetual presence as one of the fixed conditions of life.

These moments lengthened into hours and days, till she passed into a phase of stolid acquiescence. She watched the familiar routine of life with the incurious eye of a savage on whom the meaningless processes of civilization make but the faintest impression. She had come to regard herself as part of the routine, a spoke of the wheel, revolving with its motion; she felt almost like the furniture of the room in which she sat, an insensate object to be dusted and pushed about with the chairs and tables. And this deepening apathy held her fast at Lyng, in spite of the urgent entreaties of friends and the usual medical recommendation of "change."

Her friends supposed that her refusal to move was inspired by the belief that her husband would one day return to the spot from which he had vanished, and a beautiful legend grew up about this imaginary state of waiting. But in reality she had no such belief: the depths of anguish inclosing her were no longer lighted by flashes of hope. She was sure that Boyne would never come back, that he had gone out of her sight as completely as if Death itself had waited that day on the threshold. She had even renounced, one by one, the various theories as to his disappearance which had been advanced by the press, the police, and her own agonised imagination. In sheer lassitude her mind turned from these alternatives of horror, and sank back into the blank fact that he was gone.

No, she would never know what had become of him—no one would ever know. But the house *knew*; the library in which she spent her long, lonely evenings knew. For it was here that the last scene had been enacted, here that the stranger had come, and spoken the word which had caused Boyne to rise and follow him. The floor she trod had felt his tread; the books on the shelves had seen his face; and there were moments when the intense consciousness of the old, dusky walls seemed about to break out into some audible revelation of their secret. But the revelation never came, and she knew it would never come. Lyng was not one of the garrulous old houses that betray the secrets intrusted to them. Its very legend proved that it had always been the mute accomplice, the incorruptible custodian of the mysteries it had surprised. And Mary Boyne, sitting face to face with its portentous silence, felt the futility of seeking to break it by any human means.

5

"I don't say it *wasn't* straight, yet don't say it *was* straight. It was business."

Mary, at the words, lifted her head with a start, and looked intently at the speaker.

When, half an hour before, a card with "Mr. Parvis" on it had been brought up to her, she had been immediately aware that the name had been a part of her consciousness ever since she had read it at the head of Boyne's unfinished letter. In the library she had found awaiting her a small neutral-tinted man with a bald head and gold eye-glasses, and it sent a strange tremor through her to know that this was the person to whom her husband's last known thought had been directed.

Parvis, civilly, but without vain preamble,—in the manner of a man who has his watch in his hand,—had set forth the object of his visit. He had "run over" to England on business, and finding himself in the neighbourhood of Dorchester, had not wished to leave it without paying his respects to Mrs. Boyne; without asking her, if the occasion offered, what she meant to do about Bob Elwell's family.

The words touched the spring of some obscure dread in Mary's bosom. Did her visitor, after all, know what Boyne had meant by his unfinished phrase? She asked for an elucidation of his question, and noticed at once that he seemed surprised at her continued ignorance of the subject. Was it possible that she really knew as little as she said?

"I know nothing—you must tell me," she faltered out; and her visitor thereupon proceeded to unfold his story. It threw, even to her confused perceptions, and imperfectly initiated vision, a lurid glare on the whole hazy episode of the Blue Star Mine. Her husband had made his money in that brilliant speculation at the cost of "getting ahead" of someone less alert to seize the chance; the victim of his ingenuity was young Robert Elwell, who had "put him on" to the Blue Star scheme.

Parvis, at Mary's first startled cry, had thrown her a sobering glance through his impartial glasses.

"Bob Elwell wasn't smart enough, that's all; if he had been, he might have turned round and served Boyne the same way. It's the kind of thing that happens every day in business. I guess it's what the scientists call the survival of the fittest," said Mr. Parvis, evidently pleased with the aptness of his analogy.

Mary felt a physical shrinking from the next question she tried to frame; it was as though the words on her lips had a taste that nauseated her.

"But then—you accuse my husband of doing something dishonourable?"

Mr. Parvis surveyed the question dispassionately. "Oh, no, I don't. I don't even say it wasn't straight." He glanced up and down the long lines of books, as if one of them might have supplied him with the definition he sought. "I don't say it *wasn't* straight, and yet I don't say it *was* straight. It was business." After all, no definition in his category could be more comprehensive than that.

Mary sat staring at him with a look of terror. He seemed to her like the indifferent, implacable emissary of some dark, formless power.

"But Mr. Elwell's lawyers apparently did not take your view, since I suppose the suit was withdrawn by their advice."

"Oh, yes, they knew he hadn't a leg to stand on, technically. It was when they advised him to withdraw the suit that he got desperate. You see, he'd borrowed most of the money he lost in the Blue Star, and he was up a tree. That's why he shot himself when they told him he had no show."

The horror was sweeping over Mary in great, deafening waves.

"He shot himself? He killed himself because of *that?*"

"Well, he didn't kill himself, exactly. He dragged on two months before he died." Parvis emitted the statement as unemotionally as a gramophone grinding out its "record."

"You mean that he tried to kill himself, and failed? And tried again?"

"Oh, he didn't have to try again," said Parvis, grimly.

They sat opposite each other in silence, he swinging his eye-glass thoughtfully about his finger, she, motionless, her arms stretched along her knees in an attitude of rigid tension.

"But if you knew all this," she began at length, hardly able to force her voice above a whisper, "how is it that when I wrote you at the time of my husband's disappearance you said you didn't understand his letter?"

Parvis received this without perceptible discomfiture. "Why, I didn't understand it—strictly speaking. And it wasn't the time to talk about it, if I had. The Elwell business was settled when the suit was withdrawn. Nothing I could have told you would have helped you to find your husband."

Mary continued to scrutinize him. "Then why are you telling me now?"

Still Parvis did not hesitate. "Well, to begin with, I supposed you knew more than you appear to—I mean about the circumstances of Elwell's death. And then people are talking of it now; the whole matter's been raked up again. And I thought, if you didn't know, you ought to."

She remained silent, and he continued: "You see, it's only come out lately what a bad state Elwell's affairs were in. His wife's a proud woman, and she fought on as long as she could, going out to work, and taking sewing at home, when she got too sick—something with the heart, I believe. But she had his bedridden mother to look after, and the children, and she broke down under it, and finally had to ask for help. That attracted attention to the case, and the papers took it up, and a subscription was started. Everybody out there liked Bob Elwell, and most of the prominent names in the place are down on the list, and people began to wonder why—"

Parvis broke off to fumble in an inner pocket. "Here," he continued, "here's an account of the whole thing from the *Sentinel*—a little sensational, of course. But I guess you'd better look it over."

He held out a newspaper to Mary, who unfolded it slowly, remembering, as she did so, the evening when, in that same room, the perusal of a clipping from the *Sentinel* had first shaken the depths of her security.

As she opened the paper, her eyes, shrinking from the glaring headlines, "Widow of Boyne's Victim Forced to Appeal for Aid," ran down the column of text to two portraits inserted in it. The first was her husband's, taken from a photograph made the year they had come to England. It was the picture of him that she liked best, the one that stood on the writing-table upstairs in her bedroom. As the eyes in the photograph met hers, she felt it would be impossible to read what was said of him, and closed her lids with the sharpness of the pain.

"I thought if you felt disposed to put your name down—" she heard Parvis continue.

She opened her eyes with an effort, and they fell on the other portrait. It was that of a youngish man, slightly built, in rough clothes, with features somewhat blurred by the shadow of a projecting hat-brim. Where had she seen that outline before? She stared at it confusedly, her heart hammering in her throat and ears. Then she gave a cry. "This is the man—the man who came for my husband!"

She heard Parvis start to his feet, and was dimly aware that she had slipped backward into the corner of the sofa, and that he was bending above her in alarm. With an intense effort she straightened herself, and reached out for the paper, which she had dropped.

"It's the man! I should know him anywhere!" she cried in a voice that sounded in her own ears like a scream.

Parvis's voice seemed to come to her from far off, down endless, fog-muffled windings.

"Mrs. Boyne, you're not very well. Shall I call somebody? Shall I get a glass of water?"

"No, no, no!" She threw herself toward him, her hand frantically clenching the newspaper. "I tell you, it's the man! I *know* him! He spoke to me in the garden!"

Parvis took the journal from her, directing his glasses to the portrait. "It can't be, Mrs. Boyne. It's Robert Elwell."

"Robert Elwell?" Her white stare seemed to travel into space. "Then it was Robert Elwell who came for him."

"Came for Boyne? The day he went away?" Parvis's voice dropped as hers rose. He bent over, laying a fraternal hand on her, as if to coax her gently back into her seat. "Why, Elwell was dead! Don't you remember?"

Mary sat with her eyes fixed on the picture, unconscious of what he was saying.

"Don't you remember Boyne's unfinished letter to me—the one you found on his desk that day? It was written just after he'd heard of Elwell's death." She noticed an odd shake in Parvis's unemotional voice. "Surely you remember that!" he urged her.

Yes, she remembered: that was the profoundest horror of it. Elwell had died the day before her husband's disappearance; and this was Elwell's portrait; and it was the portrait of the man who had spoken to her in the garden. She lifted her head and looked slowly about the library. The library could have borne witness that it was also the portrait of the man who had come in that day to call Boyne from his unfinished letter. Through the misty surgings of her brain she heard the faint boom of half-forgotten words—words spoken by Alida Stair on the lawn at Pangbourne before Boyne and his wife had ever seen the house at Lyng, or had imagined that they might one day live there.

"This was the man who spoke to me," she repeated.

She looked again at Parvis. He was trying to conceal his disturbance under what he imagined to be an expression of indulgent commiseration; but the edges of his lips were blue. "He thinks me mad; but I'm not mad," she reflected; and suddenly there flashed upon her a way of justifying her strange affirmation.

She sat quiet, controlling the quiver of her lips, and waiting till she could trust her voice to keep its habitual level; then she said, looking straight at Parvis: "Will you answer me one question, please? When was it that Robert Elwell tried to kill himself?"

"When—when?" Parvis stammered.

"Yes; the date. Please try to remember."

She saw that he was growing still more afraid of her. "I have a reason," she insisted gently.

"Yes, yes. Only I can't remember. About two months before, I should say."

"I want the date," she repeated.

Parvis picked up the newspaper. "We might see here," he said, still humouring her. He ran his eyes down the page. "Here it is. Last October—the—"

She caught the words from him. "The 20th, wasn't it?" With a sharp look at her, he verified. "Yes, the 20th. Then you *did* know?"

"I know now." Her white stare continued to travel past him. "Sunday, the 20th—that was the day he came first."

Parvis's voice was almost inaudible. "Came *here* first?"

"Yes."

"You saw him twice, then?"

"Yes, twice." She breathed it at him with dilated eyes. "He came first on the 20th of October. I remember the date because it was the day we went up Meldon Steep for the first time." She felt a faint gasp of inward laughter at the thought that but for that she might have forgotten.

Parvis continued to scrutinise her, as if trying to intercept her gaze.

"We saw him from the roof," she went on. "He came down the lime-avenue toward the house. He was dressed just as he is in that picture. My husband saw him first. He was frightened, and ran down ahead of me; but there was no one there. He had vanished."

"Elwell had vanished?" Parvis faltered.

"Yes." Their two whispers seemed to grope for each other. "I couldn't think what had happened. I see now. He *tried* to come then; but he wasn't dead enough—he couldn't reach us. He had to wait for two months; and then he came back again—and Ned went with him."

She nodded at Parvis with the look of triumph of a child who has successfully worked out a difficult puzzle. But suddenly she lifted her hands with a desperate gesture, pressing them to her bursting temples. "Oh, my God! I sent him to Ned—I told him where to go! I sent him to this room!" she screamed out.

She felt the walls of the room rush toward her, like inward falling ruins; and she heard Parvis, a long way off, as if through the ruins, crying to her, and struggling to get at her. But she was numb to his touch, she did not know what he was saying. Through the tumult she heard but one clear note, the voice of Alida Stair, speaking on the lawn at Pangbourne.

"You won't know till afterward," it said. "You won't know till long, long afterward.

A Journey

As she lay in her berth, staring at the shadows overhead, the rush of the wheels was in her brain, driving her deeper and deeper into circles of wakeful lucidity. The sleeping-car had sunk into its night-silence. Through the wet window-pane she watched the sudden lights, the long stretches of hurrying blackness. Now and then she turned her head and looked through the opening in the hangings at her husband's curtains across the aisle. . . .

She wondered restlessly if he wanted anything and if she could hear him if he called. His voice had grown very weak within the last months and it irritated him when she did not hear. This irritability, this increasing childish petulance seemed to give expression to their imperceptible estrangement. Like two faces looking at one another through a sheet of glass they were close together, almost touching, but they could not hear or feel each other: the conductivity between them was broken. She, at least, had this sense of separation, and she fancied sometimes that she saw it reflected in the look with which he supplemented his failing words.

Doubtless the fault was hers. She was too impenetrably healthy to be touched by the irrelevancies of disease. Her self-reproachful tenderness was tinged with the sense of his irrationality: she had a vague feeling that there was a purpose in his helpless tyrannies. The suddenness of the change had found her so unprepared. A year ago their pulses had beat to one robust measure; both had the same prodigal confidence in an exhaustless future. Now their energies no longer kept step: hers still bounded ahead of life, pre-empting unclaimed regions of hope and activity, while his lagged behind, vainly struggling to overtake her.

When they married, she had such arrears of living to make up: her days had been as bare as the whitewashed school-room where she forced innutritious facts upon reluctant children. His coming had broken in on the slumber of circumstance, widening the present till it became the encloser of remotest chances. But imperceptibly the horizon narrowed. Life had a grudge against her: she was never to be allowed to spread her wings.

At first the doctors had said that six weeks of mild air would set him right; but when he came back this assurance was explained as having of course included a winter in a dry climate. They gave up their pretty house, storing the wedding presents and new furniture, and went to Colorado. She had hated it there from the first. Nobody knew her or cared about her; there was no one to wonder at the good match she had made, or to envy her the new dresses and the visiting-cards which were still a surprise to her.

And he kept growing worse. She felt herself beset with difficulties too evasive to be fought by so direct a temperament. She still loved him, of course; but he was gradually, undefinably ceasing to be himself. The man she had married had been strong, active, gently masterful: the male whose pleasure it is to clear a way through the material obstructions of life; but now it was she who was the protector, he who must be shielded from importunities and given his drops or his beef-juice though the skies were falling. The routine of the sick-room bewildered her; this punctual administering of medicine seemed as idle as some uncomprehended religious mummery.

There were moments, indeed, when warm gushes of pity swept away her instinctive resentment of his condition, when she still found his old self in his eyes as they groped for each other through the dense medium of his weakness. But these moments had grown rare. Sometimes he frightened her: his sunken expressionless face seemed that of a stranger; his voice was weak and hoarse; his thin-lipped smile a mere muscular contraction. Her hand avoided his damp soft skin, which had lost the familiar roughness of health: she caught herself furtively watching him as she might have watched a strange animal. It frightened her to feel that this was the man she loved; there were hours when to tell him what she suffered seemed the one escape from her fears.

But in general she judged herself more leniently, reflecting that she had perhaps been too long alone with him, and that she would feel differently when they were at home again, surrounded by her robust and buoyant family. How she had rejoiced when the doctors at last gave their consent to his going home! She knew, of course, what the decision meant; they both knew. It meant that he was to die; but they dressed the truth in hopeful euphuisms, and at times, in the joy of preparation, she really forgot the purpose of their journey, and slipped into an eager allusion to next year's plans.

At last the day of leaving came. She had a dreadful fear that they would never get away; that somehow at the last moment he would fail her; that the doctors held one of their accustomed treacheries in reserve; but nothing happened. They drove to the station, he was installed in a seat with a rug over his knees and a cushion at his back, and she hung out of the window waving unregretful farewells to the acquaintances she had really never liked till then.

The first twenty-four hours had passed off well. He revived a little and it amused him to look out of the window and to observe the humours of the car. The second day he began to grow weary and to chafe under the dispassionate stare of the freckled child with the lump of chewing-gum. She had to explain to the child's mother that her husband was too ill to be disturbed: a statement received by that lady with a resentment visibly supported by the maternal sentiment of the whole car. . . .

That night he slept badly and the next morning his temperature frightened her: she was sure he was growing worse. The day passed slowly, punctuated by the small irritations of travel. Watching his tired face, she traced in its contractions every rattle and jolt of the tram, till her own body vibrated with sympathetic fatigue. She felt the others observing him too, and hovered restlessly between him and the line of interrogative eyes. The freckled child hung about him like a fly; offers of candy and picture-books failed to dislodge her: she twisted one leg around the other and watched him imperturbably. The porter, as he passed, lingered with vague proffers of help, probably inspired by philanthropic passengers swelling with the sense that "something ought to be done;" and one nervous man in a skull-cap was audibly concerned as to the possible effect on his wife's health.

The hours dragged on in a dreary inoccupation. Towards dusk she sat down beside him and he laid his hand on hers. The touch startled her. He seemed to be calling her from far off. She looked at him helplessly and his smile went through her like a physical pang.

"Are you very tired?" she asked.

"No, not very."

"We'll be there soon now."

"Yes, very soon."

"This time tomorrow—"

He nodded and they sat silent. When she had put him to bed and crawled into her own berth she tried to cheer herself with the thought that in less than twenty-four hours they would be in New York. Her people would all be at the station to meet her—she pictured their round unanxious faces pressing through the crowd. She only hoped they would not tell him too loudly that he was looking splendidly and would be all right in no time: the subtler sympathies developed by long contact with suffering were making her aware of a certain coarseness of texture in the family sensibilities.

Suddenly she thought she heard him call. She parted the curtains and listened. No, it was only a man snoring at the other end of the car. His snores had a greasy sound, as though they passed through tallow. She lay down and tried to sleep....Had she not heard him move? She started up trembling. . . .The silence frightened her more than any sound. He might not be able to make her hear—he might be calling her now....What made her think of such things? It was merely the familiar tendency of an over-tired mind to fasten itself on the most intolerable chance within the range of its forebodings....

Putting her head out, she listened; but she could not distinguish his breathing from that of the other pairs of lungs about her. She longed to get up and look at him, but she knew the impulse was a mere vent for her restlessness, and the fear of disturbing him restrained her. . . The regular movement of his curtain reassured her, she knew not why; she remembered that he had wished her a cheerful goodnight; and the sheer inability to endure her fears a moment longer made her put them from her with an effort of her whole sound tired body. She turned on her side and slept.

She sat up stiffly, staring out at the dawn. The train was rushing through a region of bare hillocks huddled against a lifeless sky. It looked like the first day of creation. The air of the car was close, and she pushed up her window to let in the keen wind. Then she looked at her watch: it was seven o'clock, and soon the people about her would be stirring. She slipped into her clothes, smoothed her dishevelled hair and crept to the dressing-room. When she had washed her face and adjusted her dress she felt more hopeful. It was always a struggle for her not to be cheerful in the morning. Her cheeks burned deliciously under the coarse towel and the wet hair about her temples broke into strong upward tendrils. Every inch of her was full of life and elasticity. And in ten hours they would be at home!

She stepped to her husband's berth: it was time for him to take his early glass of milk. The window-shade was down, and in the dusk of the curtained enclosure she could just see that he lay sideways, with his face away from her. She leaned over him and drew up the shade. As she did so she touched one of his hands. It felt cold. . . .

She bent closer, laying her hand on his arm and calling him by name. He did not move. She spoke again more loudly; she grasped his shoulder and gently shook it. He lay motionless. She caught hold of his hand again: it slipped from her limply, like a dead thing. A dead thing?. . . . Her breath caught. She must see his face. She leaned forward, and hurriedly, shrinkingly, with a sickening reluctance of the flesh, laid her hands on his shoulders and turned him over. His head fell back; his face looked small and smooth; he gazed at her with steady eyes.

She remained motionless for a long time, holding him thus; and they looked at each other. Suddenly she shrank back: the longing to scream, to call out, to fly from him, had almost overpowered her. But a strong hand arrested her. Good God! If it were known that he was dead, they would be put off the train at the next station—

In a terrifying flash of remembrance there arose before her a scene she had once witnessed in travelling, when a husband and wife, whose child had died in the train, had been thrust out at some chance station. She saw them standing on the platform with the child's body between them; she had never forgotten the dazed look with which they followed the receding train. And this was what would happen to her. Within the next hour she might find herself on the platform of some strange station, alone with her husband's body. . . . Anything but that! It was too horrible—She quivered like a creature at bay.

As she cowered there, she felt the train moving more slowly. It was coming then—they were approaching a station! She saw again the husband and wife standing on the lonely platform; and with a violent gesture she drew down the shade to hide her husband's face.

Feeling dizzy, she sank down on the edge of the berth, keeping away from his outstretched body, and pulling the curtains close, so that he and she were shut into a kind of sepulchral twilight. She tried to think. At all costs she must conceal the fact that he was dead. But how? Her mind refused to act: she could not plan, combine. She could think of no way but to sit there, clutching the curtains, all day long. . . .

She heard the porter making up her bed; people were beginning to move about the car; the dressing-room door was being opened and shut. She tried to rouse herself. At length with a supreme effort she rose to her feet, stepping into the aisle of the car and drawing the curtains tight behind her. She noticed that they still parted slightly with the motion of the car, and finding a pin in her dress she fastened them together. Now she was safe. She looked round and saw the porter. She fancied he was watching her.

"Ain't he awake yet?" he enquired.

"No," she faltered.

"I got his milk all ready when he wants it. You know you told me to have it for him by seven."

She nodded silently and crept into her seat.

At half-past eight the train reached Buffalo. By this time the other passengers were dressed and the berths had been folded back for the day. The porter, moving to and fro under his burden of sheets and pillows, glanced at her as he passed. At length he said: "Ain't he going to get up? You know we're ordered to make up the berths as early as we can."

She turned cold with fear. They were just entering the station.

"Oh, not yet," she stammered. "Not till he's had his milk. Won't you get it, please?"

"All right. Soon as we start again."

When the train moved on he reappeared with the milk. She took it from him and sat vaguely looking at it: her brain moved slowly from one idea to another, as though they were stepping-stones set far apart across a whirling flood. At length she became aware that the porter still hovered expectantly.

"Will I give it to him?" he suggested.

"Oh, no," she cried, rising. "He—he's asleep yet, I think—"

She waited till the porter had passed on; then she unpinned the curtains and slipped behind them. In the semi-obscurity her husband's face stared up at her like a marble mask with agate eyes. The eyes were dreadful. She put out her hand and drew down the lids. Then she remembered the glass of milk in her other hand: what was she to do with it? She thought of raising the window and throwing it out; but to do so she would have to lean across his body and bring her face close to his. She decided to drink the milk.

She returned to her seat with the empty glass and after a while the porter came back to get it.

"When'll I fold up his bed?" he asked.

"Oh, not now—not yet; he's ill—he's very ill. Can't you let him stay as he is? The doctor wants him to lie down as much as possible."

He scratched his head. "Well, if he's *really* sick—"

He took the empty glass and walked away, explaining to the passengers that the party behind the curtains was too sick to get up just yet.

She found herself the centre of sympathetic eyes. A motherly woman with an intimate smile sat down beside her.

"I'm real sorry to hear your husband's sick. I've had a remarkable amount of sickness in my family and maybe I could assist you. Can I take a look at him?"

"Oh, no—no, please! He mustn't be disturbed."

The lady accepted the rebuff indulgently.

"Well, it's just as you say, of course, but you don't look to me as if you'd had much experience in sickness and I'd have been glad to assist you. What do you generally do when your husband's taken this way?"

"I—I let him sleep."

"Too much sleep ain't any too healthful either. Don't you give him any medicine?"

"Y—yes."

"Don't you wake him to take it?"

"Yes."

"When does he take the next dose?"

"Not for—two hours—"

The lady looked disappointed. "Well, if I was you I'd try giving it oftener. That's what I do with my folks."

After that many faces seemed to press upon her. The passengers were on their way to the dining-car, and she was conscious that as they passed down the aisle they glanced curiously at the closed curtains. One lantern-jawed man with prominent eyes stood still and tried to shoot his projecting glance through the division between the folds. The freckled child, returning from breakfast, waylaid the passers with a buttery clutch, saying in a loud whisper, "He's sick;" and once the conductor came by, asking for tickets. She shrank into her corner and looked out of the window at the flying trees and houses, meaningless hieroglyphs of an endlessly unrolled papyrus.

Now and then the train stopped, and the newcomers on entering the car stared in turn at the closed curtains. More and more people seemed to pass—their faces began to blend fantastically with the images surging in her brain. . . .

Later in the day a fat man detached himself from the mist of faces. He had a creased stomach and soft pale lips. As he pressed himself into the seat facing her she noticed that he was dressed in black broadcloth, with a soiled white tie.

"Husband's pretty bad this morning, is he?"

"Yes."

"Dear, dear! Now that's terribly distressing, ain't it?" An apostolic smile revealed his gold-filled teeth.

"Of course you know there's no sech thing as sickness. Ain't that a lovely thought? Death itself is but a deloosion of our grosser senses. On'y lay yourself open to the influx of the sperrit, submit yourself passively to the action of the divine force, and disease and dissolution will cease to exist for you. If you could indooce your husband to read this little pamphlet—"

The faces about her again grew indistinct. She had a vague recollection of hearing the motherly lady and the parent of the freckled child ardently disputing the relative advantages of trying several medicines at once, or of taking each in turn; the motherly lady maintaining that the competitive system saved time; the other objecting that you couldn't tell which remedy had effected the cure; their voices went on and on, like bell-buoys droning through a fog.... The porter came up now and then with questions that she did not understand, but that somehow she must have answered since he went away again without repeating them; every two hours the motherly lady reminded her that her husband ought to have his drops; people left the car and others replaced them...

Her head was spinning and she tried to steady herself by clutching at her thoughts as they swept by, but they slipped away from her like bushes on the side of a sheer precipice down which she seemed to be falling. Suddenly her mind grew clear again and she found herself vividly picturing what would happen when the train reached New York. She shuddered as it occurred to her that he would be quite cold and that someone might perceive he had been dead since morning.

She thought hurriedly:—"If they see I am not surprised they will suspect something. They will ask questions, and if I tell them the truth they won't believe me—no one would believe me! It will be terrible"—and she kept repeating to herself:—"I must pretend I don't know. I must pretend I don't know. When they open the curtains I must go up to him quite naturally—and then I must scream." .... She had an idea that the scream would be very hard to do.

Gradually new thoughts crowded upon her, vivid and urgent: she tried to separate and restrain them, but they beset her clamorously, like her schoolchildren at the end of a hot day, when she was too tired to silence them. Her head grew confused, and she felt a sick fear of forgetting her part, of betraying herself by some unguarded word or look.

"I must pretend I don't know," she went on murmuring. The words had lost their significance, but she repeated them mechanically, as though they had been a magic formula, until suddenly she heard herself saying: "I can't remember, I can't remember!"

Her voice sounded very loud, and she looked about her in terror; but no one seemed to notice that she had spoken.

As she glanced down the car her eye caught the curtains of her husband's berth, and she began to examine the monotonous arabesques woven through their heavy folds. The pattern was intricate and difficult to trace; she gazed fixedly at the curtains and as she did so the thick stuff grew transparent and through it she saw her husband's face—his dead face. She struggled to avert her look, but her eyes refused to move and her head seemed to be held in a vice. At last, with an effort that left her weak and shaking, she turned away; but it was of no use; close in front of her, small and smooth, was her husband's face. It seemed to be suspended in the air between her and the false braids of the woman who sat in front of her.

With an uncontrollable gesture she stretched out her hand to push the face away, and suddenly she felt the touch of his smooth skin. She repressed a cry and half started from her seat. The woman with the false braids looked around, and feeling that she must justify her movement in some way she rose and lifted her travelling-bag from the opposite seat. She unlocked the bag and looked into it; but the first object her hand met was a small flask of her husband's, thrust there at the last moment, in the haste of departure. She locked the bag and closed her eyes. . . .his face was there again, hanging between her eyeballs and lids like a waxen mask against a red curtain. . . .

She roused herself with a shiver. Had she fainted or slept? Hours seemed to have elapsed; but it was still broad day, and the people about her were sitting in the same attitudes as before.

A sudden sense of hunger made her aware that she had eaten nothing since morning. The thought of food filled her with disgust, but she dreaded a return of faintness, and remembering that she had some biscuits in her bag she took one out and ate it. The dry crumbs choked her, and she hastily swallowed a little brandy from her husband's flask. The burning sensation in her throat acted as a counter-irritant, momentarily relieving the dull ache of her nerves. Then she felt a gently-stealing warmth, as though a soft air fanned her, and the swarming fears relaxed their clutch, receding through the stillness that enclosed her, a stillness soothing as the spacious quietude of a summer day. She slept.

Through her sleep she felt the impetuous rush of the train. It seemed to be life itself that was sweeping her on with headlong inexorable force—sweeping her into darkness and terror, and the awe of unknown days.—Now all at once everything was still—not a sound, not a pulsation... She was dead in her turn, and lay beside him with smooth upstaring face. How quiet it was!—and yet she heard feet coming, the feet of the men who were to carry them away. . . .She could feel too—she felt a sudden prolonged vibration, a series of hard shocks, and then another plunge into darkness: the darkness of death this time—a black whirlwind on which they were both spinning like leaves, in wild uncoiling spirals, with millions and millions of the dead....

★★★★★★

She sprang up in terror. Her sleep must have lasted a long time, for the winter day had paled and the lights had been lit. The car was in confusion, and as she regained her self-possession she saw that the passengers were gathering up their wraps and bags. The woman with the false braids had brought from the dressing-room a sickly ivy-plant in a bottle, and the Christian Scientist was reversing his cuffs. The porter passed down the aisle with his impartial brush. An impersonal figure with a gold-banded cap asked for her husband's ticket. A voice shouted "Baig-gage express!" and she heard the clicking of metal as the passengers handed over their checks.

Presently her window was blocked by an expanse of sooty wall, and the train passed into the Harlem tunnel. The journey was over; in a few minutes she would see her family pushing their joyous way through the throng at the station. Her heart dilated. The worst terror was past. . . .

"We'd better get him up now, hadn't we?" asked the porter, touching her arm.

He had her husband's hat in his hand and was meditatively revolving it under his brush.

She looked at the hat and tried to speak; but suddenly the car grew dark. She flung up her arms, struggling to catch at something, and fell face downward, striking her head against the dead man's berth.

The Duchess at Prayer

1

Have you ever questioned the long shuttered front of an old Italian house, that motionless mask, smooth, mute, equivocal as the face of a priest behind which buzz the secrets of the confessional? Other houses declare the activities they shelter; they are the clear expressive cuticle of a life flowing close to the surface; but the old palace in its narrow street, the villa on its cypress-hooded hill, are as impenetrable as death. The tall windows are like blind eyes, the great door is a shut mouth. Inside there may be sunshine, the scent of myrtles, and a pulse of life through all the arteries of the huge frame; or a mortal solitude, where bats lodge in the disjointed stones and the keys rust in unused doors. .. . .

2

From the loggia, with its vanishing *frescoes*, I looked down an avenue barred by a ladder of cypress-shadows to the ducal escutcheon and mutilated vases of the gate. Flat noon lay on the gardens, on fountains, porticoes and grottoes. Below the terrace, where a chrome-coloured lichen had sheeted the balustrade as with fine *laminae* of gold, vineyards stooped to the rich valley clasped in hills. The lower slopes were strewn with white villages like stars spangling a summer dusk; and beyond these, fold on fold of blue mountain, clear as gauze against the sky. The August air was lifeless, but it seemed light and vivifying after the atmosphere of the shrouded rooms through which I had been led. Their chill was on me and I hugged the sunshine.

"The duchess's apartments are beyond," said the old man.

He was the oldest man I had ever seen; so sucked back into the past that he seemed more like a memory than a living being. The one trait linking him with the actual was the fixity with which his small

239

saurian eye held the pocket that, as I entered, had yielded a *lira* to the gate-keeper's child. He went on, without removing his eye:

"For two hundred years nothing has been changed in the apartments of the duchess."

"And no one lives here now?"

"No one, sir. The duke, goes to Como for the summer season."

I had moved to the other end of the loggia. Below me, through hanging groves, white roofs and domes flashed like a smile.

"And that's Vicenza?"

"*Proprio!*" The old man extended fingers as lean as the hands fading from the walls behind us. "You see the palace roof over there, just to the left of the Basilica? The one with the row of statues like birds taking flight? That's the duke's town palace, built by Palladio."

"And does the duke come there?"

"Never. In winter he goes to Rome."

"And the palace and the villa are always closed?"

"As you see—always."

"How long has this been?"

"Since I can remember."

I looked into his eyes: they were like tarnished metal mirrors reflecting nothing. "That must be a long time," I said involuntarily.

"A long time," he assented.

I looked down on the gardens. An opulence of dahlias overran the box-borders, between cypresses that cut the sunshine like basalt shafts. Bees hung above the lavender; lizards sunned themselves on the benches and slipped through the cracks of the dry basins. Everywhere were vanishing traces of that fantastic horticulture of which our dull age has lost the art. Down the alleys maimed statues stretched their arms like rows of whining beggars; faun-eared terms grinned in the thickets, and above the laurustinus walls rose the mock ruin of a temple, falling into real ruin in the bright disintegrating air. The glare was blinding.

"Let us go in," I said.

The old man pushed open a heavy door, behind which the cold lurked like a knife.

"The duchess's apartments," he said.

Overhead and around us the same evanescent *frescoes*, underfoot the same *scagliola* volutes, unrolled themselves interminably. Ebony cabinets, with inlay of precious marbles in cunning perspective, alternated down the room with the tarnished efflorescence of gilt consoles supporting Chinese monsters; and from the chimney-panel a gentle-man in the Spanish habit haughtily ignored us.

"Duke Ercole II.," the old man explained, "by the Genoese Priest."

It was a narrow-browed face, sallow as a wax effigy, high-nosed and cautious-lidded, as though modelled by priestly hands; the lips weak and vain rather than cruel; a quibbling mouth that would have snapped at verbal errors like a lizard catching flies, but had never learned the shape of a round yes or no. One of the duke's hands rested on the head of a dwarf, a simian creature with pearl ear-rings and fantastic dress; the other turned the pages of a folio propped on a skull.

"Beyond is the duchess's bedroom," the old man reminded me.

Here the shutters admitted but two narrow shafts of light, gold bars deepening the subaqueous gloom. On a dais the bedstead, grim, nuptial, official, lifted its baldachin; a yellow Christ agonised between the curtains, and across the room a lady smiled at us from the chimney-breast.

The old man unbarred a shutter and the light touched her face. Such a face it was, with a flicker of laughter over it like the wind on a June meadow, and a singular tender pliancy of mien, as though one of Tiepolo's lenient goddesses had been busked into the stiff sheath of a seventeenth century dress!

"No one has slept here," said the old man, "since the Duchess Violante."

"And she was —?"

"The lady there—first Duchess of Duke Ercole II."

He drew a key from his pocket and unlocked a door at the farther end of the room. "The chapel," he said. "This is the duchess's balcony." As I turned to follow him the duchess tossed me a sidelong smile.

I stepped into a grated tribune above a chapel festooned with *stucco*. Pictures of bituminous saints mouldered between the pilasters; the artificial roses in the altar-vases were gray with dust and age, and under the cobwebby rosettes of the vaulting a bird's nest clung. Before the altar stood a row of tattered armchairs, and I drew back at sight of a figure kneeling near them.

"The duchess," the old man whispered. "By the Cavaliere Bernini."

It was the image of a woman in furred robes and spreading fraise, her hand lifted, her face addressed to the tabernacle. There was a strangeness in the sight of that immovable presence locked in prayer before an abandoned shrine. Her face was hidden, and I wondered whether it were grief or gratitude that raised her hands and drew her eyes to the altar, where no living prayer joined her marble invocation. I followed my guide down the tribune steps, impatient to see what mystic version of such terrestrial graces the ingenious artist had found—the *Cavaliere* was master of such arts. The duchess's attitude was one of transport, as though heavenly airs fluttered her laces and the love-locks escaping from her coif. I saw how admirably the sculptor had caught the poise of her head, the tender slope of the shoulder; then I crossed over and looked into her face—it was a frozen horror. Never have hate, revolt and agony so possessed a human countenance.

The old man crossed himself and shuffled his feet on the marble.

"The Duchess Violante," he repeated.

"The same as in the picture?"

"Eh—the same."

"But the face—what does it mean?"

He shrugged his shoulders and turned deaf eyes on me. Then he shot a glance round the sepulchral place, clutched my sleeve and said, close to my ear: "It was not always so."

"What was not?"

"The face—so terrible."

"The duchess's face?"

"The statue's. It changed after—"

"After?"

"It was put here."

"The statue's face *changed*—?"

He mistook my bewilderment for incredulity and his confidential finger dropped from my sleeve. "Eh, that's the story. I tell what I've heard. What do I know?" He resumed his senile shuffle across the marble. "This is a bad place to stay in—no one comes here. It's too cold. But the gentleman said, *I must see everything!*"

I let the *lire* sound. "So I must—and hear everything. This story, now—from whom did you have it?"

His hand stole back. "One that saw it, by God!"

"That saw it?"

"My grandmother, then. I'm a very old man."

"Your grandmother? Your grandmother was —?"

"The Duchess's serving girl, with respect to you."

"Your grandmother? Two hundred years ago?"

"Is it too long ago? That's as God pleases. I am a very old man and she was a very old woman when I was born. When she died she was as black as a miraculous Virgin and her breath whistled like the wind in a keyhole. She told me the story when I was a little boy. She told it to me out there in the garden, on a bench by the fish-pond, one summer night of the year she died. It must be true, for I can show you the very bench we sat on. . . . ”

3

Noon lay heavier on the gardens; not our live humming warmth but the stale exhalation of dead summers. The very statues seemed to drowse like watchers by a death-bed. Lizards shot out of the cracked soil like flames and the bench in the laurustinus-niche was strewn with the blue varnished bodies of dead flies. Before us lay the fish-pond, a yellow marble slab above rotting secrets. The villa looked across it, composed as a dead face, with the cypresses flanking it for candles. . . .

4

“Impossible, you say, that my mother’s mother should have been the duchess’s maid? What do I know? It is so long since anything has happened here that the old things seem nearer, perhaps, than to those who live in cities. . . . . But how else did she know about the statue then? Answer me that, sir! That she saw with her eyes, I can swear to, and never smiled again, so she told me, till they put her first child in her arms . . . . for she was taken to wife by the steward’s son, Antonio, the same who had carried the letters. . . . But where am I? Ah, well . . . she was a mere slip, you understand, my grandmother, when the duchess died, a niece of the upper maid, Nencia, and suffered about the duchess because of her pranks and the funny songs she knew. It’s possible, you think, she may have heard from others what she afterward fancied she had seen herself? How that is, it’s not for an unlettered man to say; though indeed I myself seem to have seen many of the things she told me. This is a strange place. No one comes here, nothing changes, and the old memories stand up as distinct as the statues in the garden. . . .

“It began the summer after they came back from the Brenta. Duke Ercole had married the lady from Venice, you must know; it was a gay city, then, I’m told, with laughter and music on the water, and the days slipped by like boats running with the tide. Well, to humour her he took her back the first autumn to the Brenta. Her father, it appears, had a grand palace there, with such gardens, bowling-alleys, grottoes and casinos as never were; *gondolas* bobbing at the water-gates, a stable full of gilt coaches, a theatre full of players, and kitchens and offices full of cooks and lackeys to serve up chocolate all day long to the fine ladies in masks and furbelows, with their pet dogs and their blacka-moors and their *abates*. Eh! I know it all as if I'd been there, for Nencia, you see, my grandmother's aunt, travelled with the duchess, and came back with her eyes round as platters, and not a word to say for the rest of the year to any of the lads who'd courted her here in Vicenza.

"What happened there I don't know—my grandmother could never get at the rights of it, for Nencia was mute as a fish where her lady was concerned—but when they came back to Vicenza the duke ordered the villa set in order; and in the spring he brought the duch-ess here and left her. She looked happy enough, my grandmother said, and seemed no object for pity. Perhaps, after all, it was better than be-ing shut up in Vicenza, in the tall painted rooms where priests came and went as softly as cats prowling for birds, and the duke was forever closeted in his library, talking with learned men.

"The duke was a scholar; you noticed he was painted with a book? Well, those that can read 'em make out that they're full of wonderful things; as a man that's been to a fair across the mountains will always tell his people at home it was beyond anything *they'll* ever see. As for the duchess, she was all for music, play-acting and young company. The duke was a silent man, stepping quietly, with his eyes down, as though he'd just come from confession; when the duchess's lap-dog yapped at his heels he danced like a man in a swarm of hornets; when the duchess laughed he winced as if you'd drawn a diamond across a window-pane. And the duchess was always laughing.

"When she first came to the villa she was very busy laying out the gardens, designing grottoes, planting groves and planning all man-ner of agreeable surprises in the way of water-jets that drenched you unexpectedly, and hermits in caves, and wild men that jumped at you out of thickets. She had a very pretty taste in such matters, but after a while she tired of it, and there being no one for her to talk to but her maids and the chaplain—a clumsy man deep in his books—why, she would have strolling players out from Vicenza, mountebanks and fortune-tellers from the market-place, travelling doctors and astrolo-gers, and all manner of trained animals. Still it could be seen that the poor lady pined for company, and her waiting women, who loved her, were glad when the Cavaliere Ascanio, the duke's cousin, came to live at the vineyard across the valley—you see the pinkish house over there in the mulberries, with a red roof and a pigeon-cote?

"The Cavaliere Ascanio was a cadet of one of the great Venetian houses, *pezzi grossi* of the Golden Book. He had been' meant for the Church, I believe, but what! he set fighting above praying and cast in his lot with the captain of the Duke of Mantua's *bravi*, himself a Venetian of good standing, but a little at odds with the law. Well, the next I know, the *Cavaliere* was in Venice again, perhaps not in good odour on account of his connection with the gentleman I speak of. Some say he tried to carry off a nun from the convent of Santa Croce; how that may be I can't say; but my grandmother declared he had enemies there, and the end of it was that on some pretext or other the Ten banished him to Vicenza. There, of course, the duke, being his kinsman, had to show him a civil face; and that was how he first came to the villa.

"He was a fine young man, beautiful as a Saint Sebastian, a rare musician, who sang his own songs to the lute in a way that used to make my grandmother's heart melt and run through her body like mulled wine. He had a good word for everybody, too, and was always dressed in the French fashion, and smelt as sweet as a bean-field; and every soul about the place welcomed the sight of him.

"Well, the duchess, it seemed, welcomed it too; youth will have youth, and laughter turns to laughter; and the two matched each other like the candlesticks on an altar. The duchess—you've seen her portrait—but to hear my grandmother, sir, it no more approached her than a weed comes up to a rose. The *Cavaliere*, indeed, as became a poet, paragoned her in his song to all the pagan goddesses of antiquity; and doubtless these were finer to look at than mere women; but so, it seemed, was she; for, to believe my grandmother, she made other women look no more than the big French fashion-doll that used to be shown on Ascension days in the *piazza*. She was one, at any rate, that needed no outlandish finery to beautify her; whatever dress she wore became her as feathers fit the bird; and her hair didn't get its colour by bleaching on the housetop. It glittered of itself like the threads in an Easter chasuble, and her skin was whiter than fine wheaten bread and her mouth as sweet as a ripe fig. . . . . .

"Well, sir, you could no more keep them apart than the bees and the lavender. They were always together, singing, bowling, playing cup and ball, walking in the gardens, visiting the aviaries and petting her grace's trick-dogs and monkeys. The duchess was as gay as a foal, always playing pranks and laughing, tricking out her animals like comedians, disguising herself as a peasant or a nun (you should have seen her one day pass herself off to the chaplain as a mendicant sister), or teaching the lads and girls of the vineyards to dance and sing madrigals together. The *Cavaliere* had a singular ingenuity in planning such entertainments and the days were hardly long enough for their diversions. But toward the end of the summer the duchess fell quiet and would hear only sad music, and the two sat much together in the gazebo at the end of the garden. It was there the duke found them one day when he drove out from Vicenza in his gilt coach. He came but once or twice a year to the villa, and it was, as my grandmother said, just a part of her poor lady's ill-luck to be wearing that day the Venetian habit, which uncovered the shoulders in a way the duke always scowled at, and her curls loose and powdered with gold. Well, the three drank chocolate in the gazebo, and what happened no one knew, except that the duke, on taking leave, gave his cousin a seat in his carriage; but the *Cavaliere* never returned.

"Winter approaching, and the poor lady thus finding herself once more alone, it was surmised among her women that she must fall into a deeper depression of spirits. But far from this being the case, she displayed such cheerfulness and equanimity of humour that my grandmother, for one, was half-vexed with her for giving no more thought to the poor young man who, all this time, was eating his heart out in the house across the valley. It is true she quitted her gold-laced gowns and wore a veil over her head; but Nencia would have it she looked the lovelier for the change and so gave the duke greater displeasure. Certain it is that the duke drove out oftener to the villa, and though he found his lady always engaged in some innocent pursuit, such as embroidery or music, or playing games with her young women, yet he always went away with a sour look and a whispered word to the chaplain.

Now as to the chaplain, my grandmother owned there had been a time when her grace had not handled him over-wisely. For, according to Nencia, it seems that his reverence, who seldom approached the duchess, being buried in his library like a mouse in a cheese—well, one day he made bold to appeal to her for a sum of money, a large sum, Nencia said, to buy certain tall books, a chest full of them, that a foreign pedlar had brought him; whereupon the duchess, who could never abide a book, breaks out at him with a laugh and a flash of her old spirit—'Holy Mother of God, must I have more books about me? I was nearly smothered with them in the first year of my marriage;' and the chaplain turning red at the affront, she added: 'You may buy them and welcome, my good chaplain, if you can find the money; but as for me, I am yet seeking a way to pay for my turquoise necklace, and the statue of Daphne at the end of the bowling-green, and the Indian parrot that my black boy brought me last Michaelmas from the Bohemians—so you see I've no money to waste on trifles;' and as he backs out awkwardly she tosses at him over her shoulder: 'You should pray to Saint Blandina to open the duke's pocket!' to which he returned, very quietly, 'Your Excellency's suggestion is an admirable one, and I have already entreated that blessed martyr to open the duke's understanding.'

"Thereat, Nencia said (who was standing by), the duchess flushed wonderfully red and waved him out of the room; and then 'Quick!' she cried to my grandmother (who was too glad to run on such errands), 'Call me Antonio, the gardener's boy, to the box-garden; I've a word to say to him about the new clove-carnations. . . .'

"Now I may not have told you, sir, that in the crypt under the chapel there has stood, for more generations than a man can count, a stone coffin containing a thighbone of the blessed Saint Blandina of Lyons, a relic offered, I've been told, by some great Duke of France to one of our own dukes when they fought the Turk together; and the object, ever since, of particular veneration in this illustrious family. Now, since the duchess had been left to herself, it was observed she affected a fervent devotion to this relic, praying often in the chapel and even causing the stone slab that covered the entrance to the crypt to be replaced by a wooden one, that she might at will descend and kneel by the coffin. This was matter of edification to all the household and should have been peculiarly pleasing to the chaplain; but, with respect to you, he was the kind of man who brings a sour mouth to the eating of the sweetest apple.

"However that may be, the duchess, when she dismissed him, was seen running to the garden, where she talked earnestly with the boy Antonio about the new clove-carnations; and the rest of the day she sat indoors and played sweetly on the virginal. Now Nencia always had it in mind that her grace had made a mistake in refusing that request of the chaplain's; but she said nothing, for to talk reason to the duchess was of no more use than praying for rain in a drought.

"Winter came early that year, there was snow on the hills by All Souls, the wind stripped the gardens, and the lemon-trees were nipped in the lemon-house. The duchess kept her room in this black season, sitting over the fire, embroidering, reading books of devotion (which was a thing she had never done) and praying frequently in the chapel.

As for the chaplain, it was a place he never set foot in but to say mass in the morning, with the duchess overhead in the tribune, and the servants aching with rheumatism on the marble floor. The chaplain himself hated the cold, and galloped through the mass like a man with witches after him. The rest of the day he spent in his library, over a brazier, with his eternal books. . . . .

"You'll wonder, sir, if I'm ever to get to the gist of the story; and I've gone slowly, I own, for fear of what's coming. Well, the winter was long and hard. When it fell cold the duke ceased to come out from Vicenza, and not a soul had the duchess to speak to but her maid-servants and the gardeners about the place. Yet it was wonderful, my grandmother said, how she kept her brave colours and her spirits; only it was remarked that she prayed longer in the chapel, where a brazier was kept burning for her all day. When the young are denied their natural pleasures they turn often enough to religion; and it was a mercy, as my grandmother said, that she, who had scarce a live sinner to speak to, should take such comfort in a dead saint.

"My grandmother seldom saw her that winter, for though she showed a brave front to all she kept more and more to herself, choosing to have only Nencia about her and dismissing even her when she went to pray. For her devotion had that mark of true piety, that she wished it not to be observed; so that Nencia had strict orders, on the chaplain's approach, to warn her mistress if she happened to be in prayer.

"Well, the winter passed, and spring was well forward, when my grandmother one evening had a bad fright. That it was her own fault I won't deny, for she'd been down the lime-walk with Antonio when her aunt fancied her to be stitching in her chamber; and seeing a sudden light in Nencia's window, she took fright lest her disobedience be found out, and ran up quickly through the laurel-grove to the house. Her way lay by the chapel, and as she crept past it, meaning to slip in through the scullery, and groping her way, for the dark had fallen and the moon was scarce up, she heard a crash close behind her, as though someone had dropped from a window of the chapel. The young fool's heart turned over, but she looked round as she ran, and there, sure enough, was a man scuttling across the terrace; and as he doubled the corner of the house my grandmother swore she caught the whisk of the chaplain's skirts.

Now that was a strange thing, certainly; for why should the chap-lain be getting out of the chapel window when he might have passed through the door? For you may have noticed, sir, there's a door leads from the chapel into the saloon on the ground floor; the only other way out being through the duchess's tribune.

"Well, my grandmother turned the matter over, and next time she met Antonio in the lime-walk (which, by reason of her fright, was not for some days) she laid before him what had happened; but to her surprise he only laughed and said, 'You little simpleton, he wasn't getting out of the window, he was trying to look in'; and not another word could she get from him.

"So the season moved on to Easter, and news came the duke had gone to Rome for that holy festivity. His comings and goings made no change at the villa, and yet there was no one there but felt easier to think his yellow face was on the far side of the Apennines, unless perhaps it was the chaplain.

"Well, it was one day in May that the duchess, who had walked long with Nencia on the terrace, rejoicing at the sweetness of the prospect and the pleasant scent of the gilly-flowers in the stone vases, the duchess toward midday withdrew to her rooms, giving orders that her dinner should be served in her bed-chamber. My grandmother helped to carry in the dishes, and observed, she said, the singular beauty of the duchess, who in honour of the fine weather had put on a gown of shot-silver and hung her bare shoulders with pearls, so that she looked fit to dance at court with an emperor. She had ordered, too, a rare repast for a lady that heeded so little what she ate—jellies, game-pasties, fruits in syrup, spiced cakes and a flagon of Greek wine; and she nodded and clapped her hands as the women set it before her, saying again and again, 'I shall eat well today.'

"But presently another mood seized her; she turned from the table, called for her rosary, and said to Nencia: 'The fine weather has made me neglect my devotions. I must say a litany before I dine.'

"She ordered the women out and barred the door, as her custom was; and Nencia and my grandmother went downstairs to work in the linen-room.

"Now the linen-room gives on the courtyard, and suddenly my grandmother saw a strange sight approaching. First up the avenue came the duke's carriage (whom all thought to be in Rome), and after it, drawn by a long string of mules and oxen, a cart carrying what looked like a kneeling figure wrapped in death-clothes. The strangeness of it struck the girl dumb and the duke's coach was at the door before she had the wit to cry out that it was coming. Nencia, when she saw it, went white and ran out of the room. My grandmother followed, scared by her face, and the two fled along the corridor to the chapel. On the way they met the chaplain, deep in a book, who asked in surprise where they were running, and when they said, to announce the duke's arrival, he fell into such astonishment and asked them so many questions and uttered such ohs and ahs, that by the time he let them by the duke was at their heels. Nencia reached the chapel-door first and cried out that the duke was coming; and before she had a reply he was at her side, with the chaplain following.

"A moment later the door opened and there stood the duchess. She held her rosary in one hand and had drawn a scarf over her shoulders; but they shone through it like the moon in a mist, and her countenance sparkled with beauty.

"The duke took her hand with a bow. 'Madam,' he said, 'I could have had no greater happiness than thus to surprise you at your devotions.'

"'My own happiness,' she replied, 'would have been greater had your excellency prolonged it by giving me notice of your arrival.'

"'Had you expected me, Madam,' said he, 'your appearance could scarcely have been more fitted to the occasion. Few ladies of your youth and beauty array themselves to venerate a saint as they would to welcome a lover.'

"'Sir,' she answered, 'having never enjoyed the latter opportunity, I am constrained to make the most of the former.—What's that?' she cried, falling back, and the rosary dropped from her hand.

"There was a loud noise at the other end of the saloon, as of a heavy object being dragged down the passage; and presently a dozen men were seen hauling across the threshold the shrouded thing from the oxcart. The duke waved his hand toward it. 'That,' said he, 'Madam, is a tribute to your extraordinary piety. I have heard with peculiar satisfaction of your devotion to the blessed relics in this chapel, and to commemorate a zeal which neither the rigors of winter nor the sultriness of summer could abate I have ordered a sculptured image of you, marvellously executed by the Cavaliere Bernini, to be placed before the altar over the entrance to the crypt.'

"The duchess, who had grown pale, nevertheless smiled playfully at this. 'As to commemorating my piety,' she said, 'I recognise there one of your Excellency's pleasantries—'

"'A pleasantry?' the duke interrupted; and he made a sign to the men, who had now reached the threshold of the chapel. In an instant the wrappings fell from the figure, and there knelt the duchess to the life. A cry of wonder rose from all, but the duchess herself stood whiter than the marble.

"'You will see,' says the duke, 'this is no pleasantry, but a triumph of the incomparable Bernini's chisel. The likeness was done from your miniature portrait by the divine Elisabetta Sirani, which I sent to the master some six months ago, with what results all must admire.'

"'Six months!' cried the duchess, and seemed about to fall; but his excellency caught her by the hand.

"'Nothing,' he said, 'could better please me than the excessive emotion you display, for true piety is ever modest, and your thanks could not take a form that better became you. And now,' says he to the men, 'let the image be put in place.'

"By this, life seemed to have returned to the duchess, and she answered him with a deep reverence. 'That I should be overcome by so unexpected a grace, your excellency admits to be natural; but what honours you accord it is my privilege to accept, and I entreat only that in mercy to my modesty the image be placed in the remotest part of the chapel.'

"At that the duke darkened. 'What! You would have this masterpiece of a renowned chisel, which, I disguise not, cost me the price of a good vineyard in gold pieces, you would have it thrust out of sight like the work of a village stonecutter?'

"'It is my semblance, not the sculptor's work, I desire to conceal.'

"'It you are fit for my house, Madam, you are fit for God's, and entitled to the place of honour in both. Bring the statue forward, you dawdlers!' he called out to the men.

"The duchess fell back submissively. 'You are right, sir, as always; but I would at least have the image stand on the left of the altar, that, looking up, it may behold your Excellency's seat in the tribune.'

"'A pretty thought, Madam, for which I thank you; but I design before long to put my companion image on the other side of the altar; and the wife's place, as you know, is at her husband's right hand.'

"'True, my lord—but, again, if my poor presentment is to have the unmerited honour of kneeling beside yours, why not place both before the altar, where it is our habit to pray in life?'

"'And where, Madam, should we kneel if they took our places? Besides,' says the duke, still speaking very blandly, 'I have a more particular purpose in placing your image over the entrance to the crypt; for not only would I thereby mark your special devotion to the blessed saint who rests there, but, by sealing up the opening in the pavement, would assure the perpetual preservation of that holy martyr's bones, which hitherto have been too thoughtlessly exposed to sacrilegious attempts.'

"'What attempts, my lord?' cries the duchess. 'No one enters this chapel without my leave.'

"'So I have understood, and can well believe from what I have learned of your piety; yet at night a malefactor might break in through a window, Madam, and your excellency not know it.'

"'I'm a light sleeper,' said the duchess.

"The duke looked at her gravely. 'Indeed?' said he. 'A bad sign at your age. I must see that you are provided with a sleeping-draught.'

"The duchess's eyes filled. 'You would deprive me, then, of the consolation of visiting those venerable relics?'

"'I would have you keep eternal guard over them, knowing no one to whose care they may more fittingly be entrusted.'

"By this the image was brought close to the wooden slab that covered the entrance to the crypt, when the duchess, springing forward, placed herself in the way.

"'Sir, let the statue be put in place tomorrow, and suffer me, to-night, to say a last prayer beside those holy bones.'

"The duke stepped instantly to her side. 'Well thought, Madam; I will go down with you now, and we will pray together.'

"'Sir, your long absences have, alas! given me the habit of solitary devotion, and I confess that any presence is distracting.'

"'Madam, I accept your rebuke. Hitherto, it is true, the duties of my station have constrained me to long absences; but henceforward I remain with you while you live. Shall we go down into the crypt together?"

"'No; for I fear for your Excellency's ague. The air there is excessively damp.'

"'The more reason you should no longer be exposed to it; and to prevent the intemperance of your zeal I will at once make the place inaccessible.'

"The duchess at this fell on her knees on the slab, weeping excessively and lifting her hands to heaven.

"'Oh,' she cried, 'you are cruel, sir, to deprive me of access to the sacred relics that have enabled me to support with resignation the solitude to which your Excellency's duties have condemned me; and if prayer and meditation give me any authority to pronounce on such matters, suffer me to warn you, sir, that I fear the blessed Saint Blandina will punish us for thus abandoning her venerable remains!'

"The duke at this seemed to pause, for he was a pious man, and my grandmother thought she saw him exchange a glance with the chaplain; who, stepping timidly forward, with his eyes on the ground, said, 'There is indeed much wisdom in her Excellency's words, but I would suggest, sir, that her pious wish might be met, and the saint more conspicuously honoured, by transferring the relics from the crypt to a place beneath the altar.'

"'True!' cried the duke, 'and it shall be done at once.'

"But thereat the duchess rose to her feet with a terrible look.

"'No,' she cried, 'by the body of God! For it shall not be said that, after your excellency has chosen to deny every request I addressed to him, I owe his consent to the solicitation of another!'

"The chaplain turned red and the duke yellow, and for a moment neither spoke.

"Then the duke said, 'Here are words enough, Madam. Do you wish the relics brought up from the crypt?'

"'I wish nothing that I owe to another's intervention!'

"'Put the image in place then,' says the duke furiously; and handed her grace to a chair.

"She sat there, my grandmother said, straight as an arrow, her hands locked, her head high, her eyes on the duke, while the statue was dragged to its place; then she stood up and turned away. As she passed by Nencia, 'Call me Antonio,' she whispered; but before the words were out of her mouth the duke stepped between them.

"'Madam,' says he, all smiles now, 'I have travelled straight from Rome to bring you the sooner this proof of my esteem. I lay last night at Monselice and have been on the road since daybreak. Will you not invite me to supper?'

"'Surely, my lord,' said the duchess. 'It shall be laid in the dining-parlour within the hour.'

"'Why not in your chamber and at once, Madam? Since I believe it is your custom to sup there.'

"'In my chamber?' says the duchess, in disorder.

"'Have you anything against it?' he asked.

"'Assuredly not, sir, if you will give me time to prepare myself.'

"'I will wait in your cabinet,' said the duke.

"At that, said my grandmother, the duchess gave one look, as the souls in hell may have looked when the gates closed on our Lord; then

253

she called Nencia and passed to her chamber.

"What happened there my grandmother could never learn, but that the duchess, in great haste, dressed herself with extraordinary splendour, powdering her hair with gold, painting her face and bosom, and covering herself with jewels till she shone like our Lady of Loreto; and hardly were these preparations complete when the duke entered from the cabinet, followed by the servants carrying supper. Thereupon the duchess dismissed Nencia, and what follows my grandmother learned from a pantry-lad who brought up the dishes and waited in the cabinet; for only the duke's body-servant entered the bed-chamber.

"Well, according to this boy, sir, who was looking and listening with his whole body, as it were, because he had never before been suffered so near the duchess, it appears that the noble couple sat down in great good humour, the duchess playfully reproving her husband for his long absence, while the duke swore that to look so beautiful was the best way of punishing him. In this tone the talk continued, with such gay sallies on the part of the duchess, such tender advances on the duke's, that the lad declared they were for all the world like a pair of lovers courting on a summer's night in the vineyard; and so it went till the servant brought in the mulled wine.

"'Ah,' the duke was saying at that moment, 'this agreeable evening repays me for the many dull ones I have spent away from you; nor do I remember to have enjoyed such laughter since the afternoon last year when we drank chocolate in the gazebo with my cousin Ascanio. And that reminds me,' he said, 'is my cousin in good health?'

"'I have no reports of it,' says the duchess. 'But your Excellency should taste these figs stewed in malmsey—'

"'I am in the mood to taste whatever you offer,' said he; and as she helped him to the figs he added, 'If my enjoyment were not complete as it is, I could almost wish my Cousin Ascanio were with us. The fellow is rare good company at supper. What do you say, Madam? I hear he's still in the country; shall we send for him to join us?'

"'Ah,' said the duchess, with a sigh and a languishing look, 'I see your excellency wearies of me already.'

"'I, Madam? Ascanio is a capital good fellow, but to my mind his chief merit at this moment is his absence. It inclines me so tenderly to him that, by God, I could empty a glass to his good health.'

"With that the duke caught up his goblet and signed to the servant to fill the duchess's.

"'Here's to the cousin,' he cried, standing, 'who has the good taste to stay away when he's not wanted. I drink to his very long life—and you, Madam?'

"At this the duchess, who had sat staring at him with a changed face, rose also and lifted her glass to her lips.

"'And I to his happy death,' says she in a wild voice; and as she spoke the empty goblet dropped from her hand and she fell face down on the floor.

"The duke shouted to her women that she had swooned, and they came and lifted her to the bed. . . . She suffered horribly all night, Nencia said, twisting herself like a heretic at the stake, but without a word escaping her. The duke watched by her, and toward daylight sent for the chaplain; but by this she was unconscious and, her teeth being locked, our Lord's body could not be passed through them.

"The duke announced to his relations that his lady had died after partaking too freely of spiced wine and an omelet of carp's roe, at a supper she had prepared in honour of his return; and the next year he brought home a new duchess, who gave him a son and five daughters. . . . ."

5

The sky had turned to a steel grey, against which the villa stood out sallow and inscrutable. A wind strayed through the gardens, loosening here and there a yellow leaf from the sycamores; and the hills across the valley were purple as thunder-clouds.

"And the statue —?" I asked.

"Ah, the statue. Well, sir, this is what my grandmother told me, here on this very bench where we're sitting. The poor child, who worshipped the duchess as a girl of her years will worship a beautiful kind mistress, spent a night of horror, you may fancy, shut out from her lady's room, hearing the cries that came from it, and seeing, as she crouched in her corner, the women rush to and fro with wild looks, the duke's lean face in the door, and the chaplain skulking in the antechamber with his eyes on his breviary. No one minded her that night or the next morning; and toward dusk, when it became known the duchess was no more, the poor girl felt the pious wish to say a prayer for her dead mistress. She crept to the chapel and stole in unobserved.

"The place was empty and dim, but as she advanced she heard a low moaning, and coming in front of the statue she saw that its face, the day before so sweet and smiling, had the look on it that you know—and the moaning seemed to come from its lips. My grandmother turned cold, but something, she said afterward, kept her from calling or shrieking out, and she turned and ran from the place. In the passage she fell in a swoon; and when she came to her senses, in her own chamber, she heard that the duke had locked the chapel door and forbidden any to set foot there. . . . The place was never opened again till the duke died, some ten years later; and then it was that the other servants, going in with the new heir, saw for the first time the horror that my grandmother had kept in her bosom. . . ."

"And the crypt?" I asked. "Has it never been opened?"

"Heaven forbid, sir!" cried the old man, crossing himself. "Was it not the duchess's express wish that the relics should not be disturbed?"

Coming Home

The young men of our American Relief Corps are beginning to come back from the front with stories.

There was no time to pick them up during the first months—the whole business was too wild and grim. The horror has not decreased, but nerves and sight are beginning to be disciplined to it. In the earlier days, moreover, such fragments of experience as one got were torn from their setting like bits of flesh scattered by shrapnel. Now things that seemed disjointed are beginning to link themselves together, and the broken bones of history are rising from the battlefields.

I can't say that, in this respect, all the members of the Relief Corps have made the most of their opportunity. Some are unobservant, or perhaps simply inarticulate; others, when going beyond the bald statistics of their job, tend to drop into sentiment and cinema scenes; and none but H. Macy Greer has the gift of making the thing told seem as true as if one had seen it. So it is on H. Macy Greer that I depend, and when his motor dashes him back to Paris for supplies I never fail to hunt him down and coax him to my rooms for dinner and a long cigar.

Greer is a small hard-muscled youth, with pleasant manners, a sallow face, straight hemp-coloured hair and grey eyes of unexpected inwardness. He has a voice like thick soup, and speaks with the slovenly drawl of the new generation of Americans, dragging his words along like reluctant dogs on a string, and depriving his narrative of every shade of expression that intelligent intonation gives. But his eyes see so much that they make one see even what his foggy voice obscures.

Some of his tales are dark and dreadful, some are unutterably sad, and some end in a huge laugh of irony. I am not sure how I ought to classify the one I have written down here.

2

On my first dash to the Northern fighting line—Greer told me the other night—I carried supplies to an ambulance where the surgeon asked me to have a talk with an officer who was badly wounded and fretting for news of his people in the east of France.

He was a young Frenchman, a cavalry lieutenant, trim and slim, with a pleasant smile and obstinate blue eyes that I liked. He looked as if he could hold on tight when it was worth his while. He had had a leg smashed, poor devil, in the first fighting in Flanders, and had been dragging on for weeks in the squalid camp-hospital where I found him. He didn't waste any words on himself, but began at once about his family. They were living, when the war broke out, at their country-place in the Vosges; his father and mother, his sister, just eighteen, and his brother Alain, two years younger.

His father, the Comte de Réchamp, had married late in life, and was over seventy: his mother, a good deal younger, was crippled with rheumatism; and there was, besides—to round off the group—a help-less but intensely alive and domineering old grandmother about whom all the others revolved. You know how French families hang together, and throw out branches that make new roots but keep hold of the central trunk, like that tree—what's it called?—that they give pictures of in books about the East.

Jean de Réchamp—that was my lieutenant's name—told me his family was a typical case. "We're very province," he said. "My people live at Réchamp all the year. We have a house at Nancy—rather a fine old *hôtel*—but my parents go there only once in two or three years, for a few weeks. That's our 'season.'. . . .Imagine the point of view! Or rather don't, because you couldn't. . . . " (He had been about the world a good deal, and known something of other angles of vision.)

Well, of this helpless exposed little knot of people he had had no word—simply nothing—since the first of August. He was at home, staying with them at Réchamp, when war broke out. He was mobilised the first day, and had only time to throw his traps into a cart and dash to the station. His depot was on the other side of France, and communications with the East by mail and telegraph were completely interrupted during the first weeks. His regiment was sent at once to the fighting line, and the first news he got came to him in October, from a *communiqué* in a Paris paper a month old, saying: "The enemy yesterday retook Réchamp." After that, dead silence: and the poor devil left in the trenches to digest that "retook"!

There are thousands and thousands of just such cases; and men bearing them, and cracking jokes, and hitting out as hard as they can. Jean de Réchamp knew this, and tried to crack jokes too—but he got his leg smashed just afterward, and ever since he'd been lying on a straw pallet under a horse-blanket, saying to himself: "Réchamp re-taken."

"Of course," he explained with a weary smile, "as long as you can tot up your daily bag in the trenches it's a sort of satisfaction—though I don't quite know why; anyhow, you're so dead-beat at night that no dreams come. But lying here staring at the ceiling one goes through the whole business once an hour, at the least: the attack, the slaughter, the ruins. . . . and worse. . . . Haven't I seen and heard things enough on this side to know what's been happening on the other? Don't try to sugar the dose. I like it bitter."

I was three days in the neighbourhood, and I went back every day to see him. He liked to talk to me because he had a faint hope of my getting news of his family when I returned to Paris. I hadn't much myself, but there was no use telling him so. Besides, things change from day to day, and when we parted I promised to get word to him as soon as I could find out anything. We both knew, of course, that that would not be till Réchamp was taken a third time—by his own troops; and perhaps soon after that, I should be able to get there, or near there, and make enquiries myself.

To make sure that I should forget nothing, he drew the family photographs from under his pillow, and handed them over: the little witch-grandmother, with a face like a withered walnut, the father, a fine broken-looking old boy with a Roman nose and a weak chin, the mother, in crape, simple, serious and provincial, the little sister *ditto*, and Alain, the young brother—just the age the brutes have been carrying off to German prisons—an over-grown thread-paper boy with too much forehead and eyes, and not a muscle in his body. A charming-looking family, distinguished and amiable; but all, except the grandmother, rather usual. The kind of people who come in sets.

As I pocketed the photographs I noticed that another lay face down by his pillow. "Is that for me too?" I asked.

He coloured and shook his head, and I felt I had blundered. But after a moment he turned the photograph over and held it out.

"It's the young girl I am engaged to. She was at Réchamp visiting my parents when war was declared; but she was to leave the day after I did. . . ." He hesitated. "There may have been some difficulty about her going. . . .I should like to be sure she got away. . . .Her name is Yvonne Malo."

He did not offer me the photograph, and I did not need it. That girl had a face of her own! Dark and keen and splendid: a type so different from the others that I found myself staring. If he had not said "*ma fiancée*" I should have understood better. After another pause he went on: "I will give you her address in Paris. She has no family: she lives alone—she is a musician. Perhaps you may find her there." His colour deepened again as he added: "But I know nothing—I have had no news of her either."

To ease the silence that followed I suggested: "But if she has no family, wouldn't she have been likely to stay with your people, and wouldn't that be the reason of your not hearing from her?"

"Oh, no—I don't think she stayed." He seemed about to add: "If she could help it," but shut his lips and slid the picture out of sight.

As soon as I got back to Paris I made enquiries, but without result. The Germans had been pushed back from that particular spot after a fortnight's intermittent occupation; but their lines were close by, across the valley, and Réchamp was still in a net of trenches. No one could get to it, and apparently no news could come from it. For the moment, at any rate, I found it impossible to get in touch with the place.

My enquiries about Mlle. Malo were equally unfruitful. I went to the address Réchamp had given me, somewhere off in Passy, among gardens, in what they call a "Square," no doubt because it's oblong: a kind of long narrow court with aesthetic-looking studio buildings round it. Mlle. Malo lived in one of them, on the top floor, the *concierge* said, and I looked up and saw a big studio window, and a roof-terrace with dead gourds dangling from a pergola. But she wasn't there, she hadn't been there, and they had no news of her. I wrote to Réchamp of my double failure, he sent me back a line of thanks; and after that for a long while I heard no more of him.

By the beginning of November, the enemy's hold had begun to loosen in the Argonne and along the Vosges, and one day we were sent off to the East with a couple of ambulances. Of course we had to have military chauffeurs, and the one attached to my ambulance happened to be a fellow I knew. The day before we started, in talking over our route with him, I said: "I suppose we can manage to get to Réchamp now?"

He looked puzzled—it was such a little place that he'd forgotten the name. "Why do you want to get there?" he wondered. I told him, and he gave an exclamation. "Good God! Of course—but how extraordinary! Jean de Réchamp's here now, in Paris, too lame for the front, and driving a motor." We stared at each other, and he went on: "He must take my place—he must go with you. I don't know how it can be done; but done it shall be."

Done it was, and the next morning at daylight I found Jean de Réchamp at the wheel of my car. He looked another fellow from the wreck I had left in the Flemish hospital; all made over, and burning with activity, but older, and with lines about his eyes. He had had news from his people in the interval, and had learned that they were still at Réchamp, and well. What was more surprising was that Mlle. Malo was with them—had never left. Alain had been got away to England, where he remained; but none of the others had budged. They had fitted up an ambulance in the *château*, and Mlle. Malo and the little sister were nursing the wounded. There were not many details in the letters, and they had been a long time on the way; but their tone was so reassuring that Jean could give himself up to unclouded anticipation. You may fancy if he was grateful for the chance I was giving him; for of course he couldn't have seen his people in any other way.

Our permits, as you know, don't as a rule let us into the firing-line: we only take supplies to second-line ambulances, and carry back the badly wounded in need of delicate operations. So I wasn't in the least sure we should be allowed to go to Réchamp—though I had made up my mind to get there, anyhow.

We were about a fortnight on the way, coming and going in Champagne and the Argonne, and that gave us time to get to know each other. It was bitter cold, and after our long runs over the lonely frozen hills we used to crawl into the *café* of the inn—if there was one—and talk and talk. We put up in fairly rough places, generally in a farm house or a cottage packed with soldiers; for the villages have all remained empty since the autumn, except when troops are quartered in them. Usually, to keep warm, we had to go up after supper to the room we shared, and get under the blankets with our clothes on. Once some jolly Sisters of Charity took us in at their Hospice, and we slept two nights in an ice-cold whitewashed cell—but what tales we heard around their kitchen-fire! The Sisters had stayed alone to face the Germans, had seen the town burn, and had made the Teutons turn the hose on the singed roof of their Hospice and beat the fire back from it. It's a pity those Sisters of Charity can't marry. . . .

Réchamp told me a lot in those days. I don't believe he was talkative before the war, but his long weeks in hospital, starving for news, had unstrung him. And then he was mad with excitement at getting back to his own place. In the interval he'd heard how other people caught in their country-houses had fared—you know the stories we all refused to believe at first, and that we now prefer not to think about. . . . Well, he'd been thinking about those stories pretty steadily for some months; and he kept repeating: "My people say they're all right—but they give no details."

"You see," he explained, "there never were such helpless beings. Even if there had been time to leave, they couldn't have done it. My mother had been having one of her worst attacks of rheumatism—she was in bed, helpless, when I left. And my grandmother, who is a demon of activity in the house, won't stir out of it. We haven't been able to coax her into the garden for years. She says it's draughty; and you know how we all feel about draughts! As for my father, he hasn't had to decide anything since the Comte de Chambord refused to adopt the tricolour. My father decided that he was right, and since then there has been nothing particular for him to take a stand about. But I know how he behaved just as well as if I'd been there—he kept saying: 'One must act—one must act!' and sitting in his chair and doing nothing. Oh, I'm not disrespectful: they were like that in his generation! Besides—it's better to laugh at things, isn't it?" And suddenly his face would darken. . . .

On the whole, however, his spirits were good till we began to traverse the line of ruined towns between Sainte Menehould and Bar-le-Duc. "This is the way the devils came," he kept saying to me; and I saw he was hard at work picturing the work they must have done in his own neighbourhood.

"But since your sister writes that your people are safe!"

"They may have made her write that to reassure me. They'd heard I was badly wounded. And, mind you, there's never been a line from my mother."

"But you say your mother's hands are so lame that she can't hold a pen. And wouldn't Mlle. Malo have written you the truth?"

At that his frown would lift. "Oh, yes. She would despise any attempt at concealment."

"Well, then—what the deuce is the matter?"

"It's when I see these devils' traces—" he could only mutter.

One day, when we had passed through a particularly devastated little place, and had got from the *curé* some more than usually abominable details of things done there, Réchamp broke out to me over the kitchen-fire of our night's lodging. "When I hear things like that I don't believe anybody who tells me my people are all right!"

"But you know well enough," I insisted, "that the Germans are not all alike—that it all depends on the particular officer...."

"Yes, yes, I know," he assented, with a visible effort at impartiality. "Only, you see—as one gets nearer. . . ." He went on to say that, when he had been sent from the ambulance at the front to a hospital at Moulins, he had been for a day or two in a ward next to some wounded German soldiers—bad cases, they were—and had heard them talking. They didn't know he knew German, and he had heard things. . . . There was one name always coming back in their talk, von Scharlach, Oberst von Scharlach.

One of them, a young fellow, said: "I wish now I'd cut my hand off rather than do what he told us to that night. . . . Every time the fever comes I see it all again. I wish I'd been struck dead first." They all said "Scharlach" with a kind of terror in their voices, as if he might hear them even there, and come down on them horribly. Réchamp had asked where their regiment came from, and had been told: From the Vosges. That had set his brain working, and whenever he saw a ruined village, or heard a tale of savagery, the Scharlach nerve began to quiver. At such times it was no use reminding him that the Germans had had at least three hundred thousand men in the East in August. He simply didn't listen. . . .

3

The day before we started for Réchamp his spirits flew up again, and that night he became confidential. "You've been such a friend to me that there are certain things—seeing what's ahead of us—that I should like to explain"; and, noticing my surprise, he went on: "I mean about my people. The state of mind in my *milieu* must be so remote from anything you're used to in your happy country.... But perhaps I can make you understand. . . . "

I saw that what he wanted was to talk to me of the girl he was engaged to. Mlle. Malo, left an orphan at ten, had been the ward of a neighbour of the Réchamps', a chap with an old name and a starred *château*, who had lost almost everything else at baccarat before he was forty, and had repented, had the gout and studied agriculture for the rest of his life. The girl's father was a rather brilliant painter, who

263

died young, and her mother, who followed him in a year or two, was a Pole: you may fancy that, with such antecedents, the girl was just the mixture to shake down quietly into French country life with a gouty and repentant guardian. The Marquis de Corvenaire—that was his name—brought her down to his place, got an old maid sister to come and stay, and really, as far as one knows, brought his ward up rather decently.

Now and then she used to be driven over to play with the young Réchamps, and Jean remembered her as an ugly little girl in a plaid frock, who used to invent wonderful games and get tired of playing them just as the other children were beginning to learn how. But her domineering ways and searching questions did not meet with his mother's approval, and her visits were not encouraged. When she was seventeen her guardian died and left her a little money. The maiden sister had gone dotty, there was nobody to look after Yvonne, and she went to Paris, to an aunt, broke loose from the aunt when she came of age, set up her studio, travelled, painted, played the violin, knew lots of people; and never laid eyes on Jean de Réchamp till about a year before the war, when her guardian's place was sold, and she had to go down there to see about her interest in the property.

The old Réchamps heard she was coming, but didn't ask her to stay. Jean drove over to the shut-up *château*, however, and found Mlle. Malo lunching on a corner of the kitchen table. She exclaimed: "My little Jean!" flew to him with a kiss for each cheek, and made him sit down and share her omelet. . . . The ugly little girl had shed her chrysalis—and you may fancy if he went back once or twice!

Mlle. Malo was staying at the *château* all alone, with the farmer's wife to come in and cook her dinner: not a soul in the house at night but herself and her brindled sheep dog. She had to be there a week, and Jean suggested to his people to ask her to Réchamp. But at Réchamp they hesitated, coughed, looked away, said the spare rooms were all upside down, and the *valet-de-chambre* laid up with the mumps, and the cook short-handed—till finally the irrepressible grandmother broke out: "A young girl who chooses to live alone—probably prefers to live alone!"

There was a deadly silence, and Jean did not raise the question again; but I can imagine his blue eyes getting obstinate.

Soon after Mlle. Malo's return to Paris he followed her and began to frequent the Passy studio. The life there was unlike anything he had ever seen—or conceived as possible, short of the prairies. He had sampled the usual varieties of French womankind, and explored most of the social layers; but he had missed the newest, that of the artistic-emancipated. I don't know much about that set myself, but from his descriptions I should say they were a good deal like intelligent Americans, except that they don't seem to keep art and life in such watertight compartments. But his great discovery was the new girl.

Apparently he had never before known any but the traditional type, which predominates in the provinces, and still persists, he tells me, in the last fastnesses of the Faubourg St. Germain. The girl who comes and goes as she pleases, reads what she likes, has opinions about what she reads, who talks, looks, behaves with the independence of a married woman—and yet has kept the Diana-freshness—think how she must have shaken up such a man's inherited view of things! Mlle. Malo did far more than make Réchamp fall in love with her: she turned his world topsy-turvy, and prevented his ever again squeezing himself into his little old pigeon-hole of prejudices.

Before long they confessed their love—just like any young couple of Anglo-Saxons—and Jean went down to Réchamp to ask permission to marry her. Neither you nor I can quite enter into the state of mind of a young man of twenty-seven who has knocked about all over the globe, and been in and out of the usual sentimental coils—and who has to ask his parents' leave to get married! Don't let us try: it's no use. We should only end by picturing him as an incorrigible ninny. But there isn't a man in France who wouldn't feel it his duty to take that step, as Jean de Réchamp did. All we can do is to accept the premise and pass on.

Well—Jean went down and asked his father and his mother and his old grandmother if they would permit him to marry Mlle. Malo; and they all with one voice said they wouldn't. There was an uproar, in fact; and the old grandmother contributed the most piercing note to the concert. Marry Mlle. Malo! A young girl who lived alone! Travelled! Spent her time with foreigners—with musicians and painters! A young girl! Of course, if she had been a married woman—that is, a widow—much as they would have preferred a young girl for Jean, or even, if widow it had to be, a widow of another type—still, it was conceivable that, out of affection for him, they might have resigned themselves to his choice. But a young girl—bring such a young girl to Réchamp! Ask them to receive her under the same roof with their little Simone, their innocent Alain. . . . .

He had a bad hour of it; but he held his own, keeping silent while

265

they screamed, and stiffening as they began to wobble from exhaustion. Finally, he took his mother apart, and tried to reason with her. His arguments were not much use, but his resolution impressed her, and he saw it. As for his father, nobody was afraid of Monsieur de Réchamp. When he said: "Never—never while I live, and there is a roof on Réchamp!" they all knew he had collapsed inside.

But the grandmother was terrible. She was terrible because she was so old, and so clever at taking advantage of it. She could bring on a valvular heart attack by just sitting still and holding her breath, as Jean and his mother had long since found out; and she always treated them to one when things weren't going as she liked. Madame de Réchamp promised Jean that she would intercede with her mother-in-law; but she hadn't much faith in the result, and when she came out of the old lady's room she whispered: "She's just sitting there holding her breath."

The next day Jean himself advanced to the attack. His grandmother was the most intelligent member of the family, and she knew he knew it, and liked him for having found it out; so when he had her alone she listened to him without resorting to any valvular tricks. "Of course," he explained, "you're much too clever not to understand that the times have changed, and manners with them, and that what a woman was criticised for doing yesterday she is ridiculed for not doing today. Nearly all the old social thou-shalt-nots have gone: intelligent people nowadays don't give a fig for them, and that simple fact has abolished them. They only existed as long as there was some one left for them to scare." His grandmother listened with a sparkle of admiration in her ancient eyes.

"And of course," Jean pursued, "that can't be the real reason for your opposing my marriage—a marriage with a young girl you've always known, who has been received here—"

"Ah, that's it—we've always known her!" the old lady snapped him up.

"What of that? I don't see—"

"Of course you don't. You're here so little: you don't hear things....."

"What things?"

"Things in the air. . . .that blow about. . . .You were doing your military service at the time. . . . "

"At what time?"

She leaned forward and laid a warning hand on his arm. "Why did Corvenaire leave her all that money—why?"

"But why not—why shouldn't he?" Jean stammered, indignant.

Then she unpacked her bag—a heap of vague insinuations, baseless conjectures, village tattle, all, at the last analysis, based, as he succeeded in proving, and making her own, on a word launched at random by a discharged maid-servant who had retailed her grievance to the cure's housekeeper. "Oh, she does what she likes with Monsieur le Marquis, the young miss! She knows how. . . ." On that single phrase the neighbourhood had raised a slander built of adamant.

Well, I'll give you an idea of what a determined fellow Réchamp is, when I tell you he pulled it down—or thought he did. He kept his temper, hunted up the servant's record, proved her a liar and dishonest, cast grave doubts on the discretion of the cure's housekeeper, and poured such a flood of ridicule over the whole flimsy fable, and those who had believed in it, that in sheer shamefacedness at having based her objection on such grounds, his grandmother gave way, and brought his parents toppling down with her.

All this happened a few weeks before the war, and soon afterward Mlle. Malo came down to Réchamp. Jean had insisted on her coming: he wanted her presence there, as his betrothed, to be known to the neighbourhood. As for her, she seemed delighted to come. I could see from Rechamp's tone, when he reached this part of his story, that he rather thought I should expect its heroine to have shown a becoming reluctance—to have stood on her dignity. He was distinctly relieved when he found I expected no such thing.

"She's simplicity itself—it's her great quality. Vain complications don't exist for her, because she doesn't see them. . . . that's what my people can't be made to understand. . . . . "

I gathered from the last phrase that the visit had not been a complete success, and this explained his having let out, when he first told me of his fears for his family, that he was sure Mlle. Malo would not have remained at Réchamp if she could help it. Oh, no, decidedly, the visit was not a success. . . .

"You see," he explained with a half-embarrassed smile, "it was partly her fault. Other girls as clever, but less—how shall I say?—less proud, would have adapted themselves, arranged things, avoided startling allusions. She wouldn't stoop to that; she talked to my family as naturally as she did to me. You can imagine for instance, the effect of her saying: 'One night, after a supper at Montmartre, I was walking home with two or three pals'—. It was her way of affirming her convictions, and I adored her for it—but I wished she wouldn't!"

And he depicted, to my joy, the neighbours rumbling over to call in heraldic barouches (the mothers alone—with embarrassed excuses for not bringing their daughters), and the agony of not knowing, till they were in the room, if Yvonne would receive them with lowered lids and folded hands, sitting by in a *pose de fiancée* while the elders talked; or if she would take the opportunity to air her views on the separation of Church and State, or the necessity of making divorce easier. "It's not," he explained, "that she really takes much interest in such questions: she's much more absorbed in her music and painting. But anything her eye lights on sets her mind dancing—as she said to me once: 'It's your mother's friends' bonnets that make me stand up for divorce!'" He broke off abruptly to add: "Good God, how far off all that nonsense seems!"

4

The next day we started for Réchamp, not sure if we could get through, but bound to, anyhow! It was the coldest day we'd had, the sky steel, the earth iron, and a snow-wind howling down on us from the north. The Vosges are splendid in winter. In summer they are just plump puddingy hills; when the wind strips them they turn to mountains. And we seemed to have the whole country to ourselves—the black firs, the blue shadows, the beech-woods cracking and groaning like rigging, the bursts of snowy sunlight from cold clouds. Not a soul in sight except the sentinels guarding the railways, muffled to the eyes, or peering out of their huts of pine-boughs at the cross-roads. Every now and then we passed a long string of seventy-fives, or a train of supply waggons or army ambulances, and at intervals a cavalryman cantered by, his cloak bellied out by the gale; but of ordinary people about the common jobs of life, not a sign.

The sense of loneliness and remoteness that the absence of the civil population produces everywhere in eastern France is increased by the fact that all the names and distances on the mile-stones have been scratched out and the sign-posts at the cross-roads thrown down. It was done, presumably, to throw the enemy off the track in September: and the signs have never been put back. The result is that one is forever losing one's way, for the soldiers quartered in the district know only the names of their particular villages, and those on the march can tell you nothing about the places they are passing through. We had got badly off our road several times during the trip, but on the last day's run Réchamp was in his own country, and knew every yard of the way—or thought he did. We had turned off the main road, and were running along between rather featureless fields and woods, crossed by a good many wood-roads with nothing to distinguish them; but he continued to push ahead, saying:

"We don't turn till we get to a manor-house on a stream, with a big paper-mill across the road." He went on to tell me that the mill-owners lived in the manor, and were old friends of his people: good old local stock, who had lived there for generations and done a lot for the neighbourhood.

"It's queer I don't see their village-steeple from this rise. The village is just beyond the house. How the devil could I have missed the turn?" We ran on a little farther, and suddenly he stopped the motor with a jerk. We were at a cross-road, with a stream running under the bank on our right. The place looked like an abandoned stoneyard. I never saw completer ruin. To the left, a fortified gate gaped on empti-ness; to the right, a mill-wheel hung in the stream. Everything else was as flat as your dinner-table.

"Was this what you were trying to see from that rise?" I asked; and I saw a tear or two running down his face.

"They were the kindest people: their only son got himself shot the first month in Champagne—"

He had jumped out of the car and was standing staring at the level waste. "The house was there—there was a splendid lime in the court. I used to sit under it and have a glass of *vin cris de Lorraine* with the old people. . . . Over there, where that cinder-heap is, all their children are buried." He walked across to the grave-yard under a blackened wall—a bit of the apse of the vanished church—and sat down on a grave-stone. "If the devils have done this here—so close to us," he burst out, and covered his face.

An old woman walked toward us down the road. Réchamp jumped up and ran to meet her. "Why, Marie Jeanne, what are you doing in these ruins?"

The old woman looked at him with unastonished eyes. She seemed incapable of any surprise. "They left my house standing. I'm glad to see *Monsieur*," she simply said.

We followed her to the one house left in the waste of stones. It was a two-roomed cottage, propped against a cow-stable, but fairly decent, with a curtain in the window and a cat on the sill.

Réchamp caught me by the arm and pointed to the door-panel. "Oberst von Scharlach" was scrawled on it. He turned as white as your table-cloth, and hung on to me a minute; then he spoke to the old woman. "The officers were quartered here: that was the reason they spared your house?"

She nodded. "Yes: I was lucky. But the gentlemen must come in and have a mouthful."

Réchamp's finger was on the name. "And this one—this was their commanding officer?"

"I suppose so. Is it somebody's name?" She had evidently never speculated on the meaning of the scrawl that had saved her.

"You remember him—their captain? Was his name Scharlach?" Réchamp persisted.

Under its rich weathering the old woman's face grew as pale as his. "Yes, that was his name—I heard it often enough."

"Describe him, then. What was he like? Tall and fair? They're all that—but what else? What in particular?"

She hesitated, and then said: "This one wasn't fair. He was dark, and had a scar that drew up the left corner of his mouth."

Réchamp turned to me. "It's the same. I heard the men describing him at Moulins."

We followed the old woman into the house, and while she gave us some bread and wine she told us about the wrecking of the village and the factory. It was one of the most damnable stories I've heard yet. Put together the worst of the typical horrors and you'll have a fair idea of it. Murder, outrage, torture: Scharlach's programme seemed to be fairly comprehensive. She ended off by saying: "His orderly showed me a silver-mounted flute he always travelled with, and a beautiful paint-box mounted in silver too. Before he left he sat down on my door-step and made a painting of the ruins. . . ."

Soon after leaving this place of death we got to the second lines and our troubles began. We had to do a lot of talking to get through the lines, but what Réchamp had just seen had made him eloquent. Luckily, too, the ambulance doctor, a charming fellow, was short of tetanus-serum, and I had some left; and while I went over with him to the pine-branch hut where he hid his wounded I explained Réchamp's case, and implored him to get us through.

Finally, it was settled that we should leave the ambulance there—for in the lines the ban against motors is absolute—and drive the remaining twelve miles. A sergeant fished out of a farmhouse a toothless old woman with a furry horse harnessed to a two-wheeled trap, and we started off by round-about wood-tracks. The horse was in no hurry, nor the old lady either; for there were bits of road that were pretty steadily currycombed by shell, and it was to everybody's interest not to cross them before twilight. Jean de Réchamp's excitement seemed to have dropped: he sat beside me dumb as a fish, staring straight ahead of him. I didn't feel talkative either, for a word the doctor had let drop had left me thinking.

"That poor old granny mind the shells? Not she!" he had said when our crazy chariot drove up. "She doesn't know them from snow-flakes any more. Nothing matters to her now, except trying to outwit a German. They're all like that where Scharlach's been—you've heard of him? She had only one boy—half-witted: he cocked a broom handle at them, and they burnt him. Oh, she'll take you to Réchamp safe enough."

"Where Scharlach's been"—so he had been as close as this to Réchamp! I was wondering if Jean knew it, and if that had sealed his lips and given him that flinty profile. The old horse's woolly flanks jogged on under the bare branches and the old woman's bent back jogged in time with it She never once spoke or looked around at us. "It isn't the noise we make that'll give us away," I said at last; and just then the old woman turned her head and pointed silently with the osier-twig she used as a whip. Just ahead of us lay a heap of ruins: the wreck, apparently, of a great *château* and its dependencies. "Lermont!" Réchamp exclaimed, turning white. He made a motion to jump out and then dropped back into the seat. "What's the use?" he muttered. He leaned forward and touched the old woman's shoulder.

"I hadn't heard of this—when did it happen?"

"In September."

"They did it?"

"Yes. Our wounded were there. It's like this everywhere in our country."

I saw Jean stiffening himself for the next question. "At Réchamp, too?"

She relapsed into indifference. "I haven't been as far as Réchamp."

"But you must have seen people who'd been there—you must have heard."

"I've heard the masters were still there—so there must be something standing. Maybe though," she reflected, "they're in the cellars. . . .."

We continued to jog on through the dusk.

5

"There's the steeple!" Réchamp burst out.

Through the dimness I couldn't tell which way to look; but I suppose in the thickest midnight he would have known where he was. He jumped from the trap and took the old horse by the bridle. I made out that he was guiding us into a long village street edged by houses in which every light was extinguished. The snow on the ground sent up a pale reflection, and I began to see the gabled outline of the houses and the steeple at the head of the street. The place seemed as calm and unchanged as if the sound of war had never reached it. In the open space at the end of the village Réchamp checked the horse.

"The elm—there's the old elm in front of the church!" he shouted in a voice like a boy's. He ran back and caught me by both hands. "It was true, then—nothing's touched!" The old woman asked: "Is this Réchamp?" and he went back to the horse's head and turned the trap toward a tall gate between park walls. The gate was barred and padlocked, and not a gleam showed through the shutters of the porter's lodge; but Réchamp, after listening a minute or two, gave a low call twice repeated, and presently the lodge door opened, and an old man peered out. Well—I leave you to brush in the rest. Old family servant, tears and hugs and so on. I know you affect to scorn the cinema, and this was it, *tremolo* and all. Hang it! This war's going to teach us not to be afraid of the obvious.

We piled into the trap and drove down a long avenue to the house. Black as the grave, of course; but in another minute the door opened, and there, in the hall, was another servant, screening a light—and then more doors opened on another cinema-scene: fine old drawing-room with family portraits, shaded lamp, domestic group about the fire. They evidently thought it was the servant coming to announce dinner, and not a head turned at our approach. I could see them all over Jean's shoulder: a grey-haired lady knitting with stiff fingers, an old gentleman with a high nose and a weak chin sitting in a big carved armchair and looking more like a portrait than the portraits; a pretty girl at his feet, with a dog's head in her lap, and another girl, who had a Red Cross on her sleeve, at the table with a book. She had been reading aloud in a rich veiled voice, and broke off her last phrase to say: "Dinner. . . . " Then she looked up and saw Jean. Her dark face remained perfectly calm, but she lifted her hand in a just perceptible gesture of warning, and instantly understanding he drew back and pushed the servant forward in his place.

"Madame la Comtesse—it is someone outside asking for *Mademoiselle*."

The dark girl jumped up and ran out into the hall. I remember wondering: "Is it because she wants to have him to herself first—or because she's afraid of their being startled?" I wished myself out of the way, but she took no notice of me, and going straight to Jean flung her arms about him. I was behind him and could see her hands about his neck, and her brown fingers tightly locked. There wasn't much doubt about those two. . . . .

The next minute she caught sight of me, and I was being rapidly tested by a pair of the finest eyes I ever saw—I don't apply the term to their setting, though that was fine too, but to the look itself, a look at once warm and resolute, all-promising and all-penetrating. I really can't do with fewer adjectives. . . .

Réchamp explained me, and she was full of thanks and welcome; not excessive, but—well, I don't know—eloquent! She gave every intonation all it could carry, and without the least emphasis: that's the wonder.

She went back to "prepare" the parents, as they say in melodrama; and in a minute or two we followed. What struck me first was that these insignificant and inadequate people had the command of the grand gesture—had *la ligne*. The mother had laid aside her knitting—not dropped it—and stood waiting with open arms. But even in clasping her son she seemed to include me in her welcome. I don't know how to describe it; but they never let me feel I was in the way. I suppose that's part of what you call distinction; knowing instinctively how to deal with unusual moments.

All the while, I was looking about me at the fine secure old room, in which nothing seemed altered or disturbed, the portraits smiling from the walls, the servants beaming in the doorway—and wondering how such things could have survived in the trail of death and havoc we had been following.

The same thought had evidently struck Jean, for he dropped his sister's hand and turned to gaze about him too.

"Then nothing's touched—nothing? I don't understand," he stammered.

Monsieur de Réchamp raised himself majestically from his chair, crossed the room and lifted Yvonne Malo's hand to his lips. "Nothing is touched—thanks to this hand and this brain."

Madame de Réchamp was shining on her son through tears. "Ah, yes—we owe it all to Yvonne."

"All, all! Grandmamma will tell you!" Simone chimed in; and

273

Yvonne, brushing aside their praise with a half-impatient laugh, said to her betrothed: "But your grandmother! You must go up to her at once."

A wonderful specimen, that grandmother: I was taken to see her after dinner. She sat by the fire in a bare panelled bedroom, bolt up-right in an armchair with ears, a knitting-table at her elbow with a shaded candle on it.

She was even more withered and ancient than she looked in her photograph, and I judge she'd never been pretty; but she somehow made me feel as if I'd got through with prettiness. I don't know exactly what she reminded me of: a dried bouquet, or something rich and clovy that had turned brittle through long keeping in a sandal-wood box. I suppose her sandal-wood box had been Good Society. Well, I had a rare evening with her. Jean and his parents were called down to see the *curé*, who had hurried over to the *château* when he heard of the young man's arrival; and the old lady asked me to stay on and chat with her.

She related their experiences with uncanny detachment, seeming chiefly to resent the indignity of having been made to descend into the cellar—"to avoid French shells, if you'll believe it: the Germans had the decency not to bombard us," she observed impartially. I was so struck by the absence of rancour in her tone that finally, out of sheer curiosity, I made an allusion to the horror of having the enemy under one's roof.

"Oh, I might almost say I didn't see them," she returned. "I never go downstairs any longer; and they didn't do me the honour of com-ing beyond my door. A glance sufficed them—an old woman like me!" she added with a phosphorescent gleam of *coquetry*.

"But they searched the *château*, surely?"

"Oh, a mere form; they were very decent—very decent," she al-most snapped at me. "There was a first moment, of course, when we feared it might be hard to get Monsieur de Réchamp away with my young grandson; but Mlle. Malo managed that very cleverly. They slipped off while the officers were dining." She looked at me with the smile of some arch old lady in a Louis XV pastel. "My grandson Jean's *fiancée* is a very clever young woman: in my time no young girl would have been so sure of herself, so cool and quick. After all, there is something to be said for the new way of bringing up girls. My poor daughter-in-law, at Yvonne's age, was a bleating baby: she is so still, at times. The convent doesn't develop character. I'm glad Yvonne was not brought up in a convent." And this champion of tradition smiled on me more intensely.

Little by little I got from her the story of the German approach: the distracted fugitives pouring in from the villages north of Réchamp, the sound of distant cannonading, and suddenly, the next afternoon, after a reassuring lull, the sight of a single spiked helmet at the end of the drive. In a few minutes a dozen followed: mostly officers; then all at once the place hummed with them. There were supply waggons and motors in the court, bundles of hay, stacks of rifles, artillery-men unharnessing and rubbing down their horses. The crowd was hot and thirsty, and in a moment the old lady, to her amazement, saw wine and cider being handed about by the Réchamp servants. "Or so at least I was told," she added, correcting herself, "for it's not my habit to look out of the window. I simply sat here and waited." Her seat, as she spoke, might have been a curule chair.

Downstairs, it appeared, Mlle. Malo had instantly taken her measures. She didn't sit and wait. Surprised in the garden with Simone, she had made the girl walk quietly back to the house and receive the officers with her on the doorstep. The officer in command—captain, or whatever he was—had arrived in a bad temper, cursing and swearing, and growling out menaces about spies. The day was intensely hot, and possibly he had had too much wine. At any rate Mlle. Malo had known how to "put him in his place"; and when he and the other officers entered they found the dining-table set out with refreshing drinks and cigars, melons, strawberries and iced coffee. "The clever creature! She even remembered that they liked whipped cream with their coffee!"

The effect had been miraculous. The captain—what was his name? Yes, Chariot, Chariot—Captain Chariot had been specially complimentary on the subject of the whipped cream and the cigars. Then he asked to see the other members of the family, and Mlle. Malo told him there were only two—"two old women!" He made a face at that, and said all the same he should like to meet them; and she answered: "'One is your hostess, the Comtesse de Réchamp, who is ill in bed'—for my poor daughter-in-law was lying in bed paralyzed with rheumatism—'and the other her mother-in-law, a very old lady who never leaves her room.'"

"But aren't there any men in the family?" he had then asked; and she had said: "Oh yes—two. The Comte de Réchamp and his son."

"And where are they?"

"In England. Monsieur de Réchamp went a month ago to take his son on a trip."

The officer said: "I was told they were here today"; and Mlle. Malo replied: "You had better have the house searched and satisfy yourself."

He laughed and said: "The idea had occurred to me."

She laughed also, and sitting down at the piano struck a few chords. Captain Chariot, who had his foot on the threshold, turned back—Simone had described the scene to her grandmother afterward.

"Some of the brutes, it seems, are musical," the old lady explained; "and this was one of them. While he was listening, some soldiers appeared in the court carrying another who seemed to be wounded. It turned out afterward that he'd been climbing a garden wall after fruit, and cut himself on the broken glass at the top; but the blood was enough—they raised the usual dreadful outcry about an ambush, and a lieutenant clattered into the room where Mlle. Malo sat playing Stravinsky." The old lady paused for her effect, and I was conscious of giving her all she wanted.

"Well—?"

"Will you believe it? It seems she looked at her watch-bracelet and said: 'Do you gentlemen dress for dinner? I do—but we've still time for a little Moussorgsky'—or whatever wild names they call themselves—'if you'll make those people outside hold their tongues.' Our captain looked at her again, laughed, gave an order that sent the lieutenant right about, and sat down beside her at the piano. Imagine my stupor, dear sir: the drawing-room is directly under this room, and in a moment I heard two voices coming up to me. Well, I won't conceal from you that his was the finest. But then I always adored a *baritone*." She folded her shrivelled hands among their laces.

"After that, the Germans were *très bien—très bien*. They stayed two days, and there was nothing to complain of. Indeed, when the second detachment came, a week later, they never even entered the gates. Orders had been left that they should be quartered elsewhere. Of course we were lucky in happening on a man of the world like Captain Chariot."

"Yes, very lucky. It's odd, though, his having a French name."

"Very. It probably accounts for his breeding," she answered placidly; and left me marvelling at the happy remoteness of old age.

6

The next morning early Jean de Réchamp came to my room. I

was struck at once by the change in him: he had lost his first glow, and seemed nervous and hesitating. I knew what he had come for: to ask me to postpone our departure for another twenty-four hours. By rights we should have been off that morning; but there had been a sharp brush a few *kilometres* away, and a couple of poor devils had been brought to the *château* whom it would have been death to carry farther that day and criminal not to hurry to a base hospital the next morning. "We've simply got to stay till tomorrow: you're in luck," I said laughing.

He laughed back, but with a frown that made me feel I had been a brute to speak in that way of a respite due to such a cause.

"The men will pull through, you know—trust Mlle. Malo for that!" I said.

His frown did not lift. He went to the window and drummed on the pane.

"Do you see that breach in the wall, down there behind the trees? It's the only scratch the place has got. And think of Lennont! It's incredible—simply incredible!"

"But it's like that everywhere, isn't it? Everything depends on the officer in command."

"Yes: that's it, I suppose. I haven't had time to get a consecutive account of what happened: they're all too excited. Mlle. Malo is the only person who can tell me exactly how things went." He swung about on me. "Look here, it sounds absurd, what I'm asking; but try to get me an hour alone with her, will you?"

I stared at the request, and he went on, still half-laughing: "You see, they all hang on me; my father and mother, Simone, the *curé*, the servants. The whole village is coming up presently: they want to stuff their eyes full of me. It's natural enough, after living here all these long months cut off from everything. But the result is I haven't said two words to her yet."

"Well, you shall," I declared; and with an easier smile he turned to hurry down to a mass of thanksgiving which the *curé* was to celebrate in the private chapel. "My parents wanted it," he explained; "and after that the whole village will be upon us. But later—"

"Later I'll effect a diversion; I swear I will," I assured him.

★★★★★★

By daylight, decidedly, Mlle. Malo was less handsome than in the evening. It was my first thought as she came toward me, that afternoon, under the limes. Jean was still indoors, with his people, receiving the village; I rather wondered she hadn't stayed there with him. Theoretically, her place was at his side; but I knew she was a young woman who didn't live by rule, and she had already struck me as having a distaste for superfluous expenditures of feeling.

Yes, she was less effective by day. She looked older for one thing; her face was pinched, and a little sallow and for the first time I noticed that her cheek-bones were too high. Her eyes, too, had lost their velvet depth: fine eyes still, but not unfathomable. But the smile with which she greeted me was charming: it ran over her tired face like a lamp-lighter kindling flames as he runs.

"I was looking for you," she said. "Shall we have a little talk? The reception is sure to last another hour: every one of the villagers is going to tell just what happened to him or her when the Germans came."

"And you've run away from the ceremony?"

"I'm a trifle tired of hearing the same adventures retold," she said, still smiling.

"But I thought there were no adventures—that that was the wonder of it?"

She shrugged. "It makes their stories a little dull, at any rate; we've not a hero or a martyr to show." She had strolled farther from the house as we talked, leading me in the direction of a bare horse-chestnut walk that led toward the park.

"Of course Jean's got to listen to it all, poor boy; but I needn't," she explained.

I didn't know exactly what to answer and we walked on a little way in silence; then she said: "If you'd carried him off this morning he would have escaped all this fuss." After a pause she added slowly: "On the whole, it might have been as well."

"To carry him off?"

"Yes." She stopped and looked at me. "I wish you would."

"Would?—Now?"

"Yes, now: as soon as you can. He's really not strong yet—he's drawn and nervous." ("So are you," I thought.) "And the excitement is greater than you can perhaps imagine—"

I gave her back her look. "Why, I think I can imagine. . . . ."

She coloured up through her sallow skin and then laughed away her blush. "Oh, I don't mean the excitement of seeing me! But his parents, his grandmother, the *curé*, all the old associations—"

I considered for a moment; then I said: "As a matter of fact, you're about the only person he hasn't seen."

She checked a quick answer on her lips, and for a moment or two we faced each other silently. A sudden sense of intimacy, of complicity almost, came over me. What was it that the girl's silence was crying out to me?

"If I take him away now he won't have seen you at all," I continued.

She stood under the bare trees, keeping her eyes on me. "Then take him away now!" she retorted; and as she spoke I saw her face change, decompose into deadly apprehension and as quickly regain its usual calm. From where she stood she faced the courtyard, and glancing in the same direction I saw the throng of villagers coming out of the *château*. "Take him away—take him away at once!" she passionately commanded; and the next minute Jean de Réchamp detached himself from the group and began to limp down the walk in our direction.

What was I to do? I can't exaggerate the sense of urgency Mlle. Malo's appeal gave me, or my faith in her sincerity. No one who had seen her meeting with Réchamp the night before could have doubted her feeling for him: if she wanted him away it was not because she did not delight in his presence. Even now, as he approached, I saw her face veiled by a faint mist of emotion: it was like watching a fruit ripen under a midsummer sun. But she turned sharply from the house and began to walk on.

"Can't you give me a hint of your reason?" I suggested as I followed.

"My reason? I've given it!" I suppose I looked incredulous, for she added in a lower voice: "I don't want him to hear—yet—about all the horrors."

"The horrors? I thought there had been none here."

"All around us—" Her voice became a whisper. "Our friends. . . our neighbours. . . .everyone. . . ."

"He can hardly avoid hearing of that, can he? And besides, since you're all safe and happy . . . . Look here," I broke off, "he's coming after us. Don't we look as if we were running away?"

She turned around, suddenly paler; and in a stride or two Réchamp was at our side. He was pale too; and before I could find a pretext for slipping away he had begun to speak. But I saw at once that he didn't know or care if I was there.

"What was the name of the officer in command who was quartered here?" he asked, looking straight at the girl.

She raised her eyebrows slightly. "Do you mean to say that after listening for three hours to every inhabitant of Béchamp you haven't found that out?"

"They all call him something different. My grandmother says he had a French name: she calls him Chariot."

"Your grandmother was never taught German: his name was the Oberst von Scharlach." She did not remember my presence either: the two were still looking straight in each other's eyes.

Béchamp had grown white to the lips: he was rigid with the effort to control himself.

"Why didn't you tell me it was Scharlach who was here?" he brought out at last in a low voice.

She turned her eyes in my direction. "I was just explaining to Mr. Greer—"

"To Mr. Greer?" He looked at me too, half-angrily.

"I know the stories that are about," she continued quietly; "and I was saying to your friend that, since we had been so happy as to be spared, it seemed useless to dwell on what has happened elsewhere."

"Damn what happened elsewhere! I don't yet know what happened here."

I put a hand on his arm. Mlle. Malo was looking hard at me, but I wouldn't let her see I knew it. "I'm going to leave you to hear the whole story now," I said to Réchamp.

"But there isn't any story for him to hear!" she broke in. She pointed at the serene front of the *château*, looking out across its gardens to the unscarred fields. "We're safe; the place is untouched. Why brood on other horrors—horrors we were powerless to help?"

Réchamp held his ground doggedly. "But the man's name is a curse and an abomination. Wherever he went he spread ruin."

"So they say. Mayn't there be a mistake? Legends grow up so quickly in these dreadful times. Here—" she looked about her again at the peaceful scene—"here he behaved as you see. For heaven's sake be content with that!"

"Content?" He passed his hand across his forehead. "I'm blind with joy. . . .or should be, if only. . . ."

She looked at me entreatingly, almost desperately, and I took hold of Réchamp's arm with a warning pressure.

"My dear fellow, don't you see that Mlle. Malo has been under a great strain? *La joie fait peur*—that's the trouble with both of you!"

He lowered his head. "Yes, I suppose it is." He took her hand and kissed it. "I beg your pardon. Greer's right: we're both on edge."

"Yes: I'll leave you for a little while, if you and Mr Greer will excuse me." She included us both in a quiet look that seemed to me extremely noble, and walked lowly away toward the *château*. Réchamp stood gazing after her for a moment; then he dropped down on one of benches at the edge of the path. He covered his face with his hands. "Scharlach—Scharlach!" I heard him say.

We sat there side by side for ten minutes or more without speaking. Finally, I said: "Look here, Réchamp—she's right and you're wrong. I shall be sorry I brought you here if you don't see it before it's too late."

His face was still hidden; but presently he dropped his hands and answered me. "I do see. She's saved everything for me—my, people and my house, and the ground we're standing on. And I worship it because she walks on it!"

"And so do your people: the war's done that for you, anyhow," I reminded him.

7

The morning after we were off before dawn. Our time allowance was up, and it was thought advisable, on account of our wounded, to slip across the exposed bit of road in the dark.

Mlle. Malo was downstairs when we started, pale in her white dress, but calm and active. We had borrowed a farmer's cart in which our two men could be laid on a mattress, and she had stocked our trap with food and remedies. Nothing seemed to have been forgotten. While I was settling the men I suppose Réchamp turned back into the hall to bid her goodbye; anyhow, when she followed him out a moment later he looked quieter and less strained. He had taken leave of his parents and his sister upstairs, and Yvonne Malo stood alone in the dark driveway, watching us as we drove away.

There was not much talk between us during our slow drive back to the lines. We had to go it a snail's pace, for the roads were rough; and there was time for meditation. I knew well enough what my companion was thinking about and my own thoughts ran on the same lines. Though the story of the German occupation of Réchamp had been retold to us a dozen times the main facts did not vary. There were little discrepancies of detail, and gaps in the narrative here and there; but all the household, from the astute ancestress to the last bewildered pantry-boy, were at one in saying that Mlle. Malo's coolness and courage had saved the *chateau* and the village. The officer in command had arrived full of threats and insolence: Mlle. Malo had placated and disarmed him, turned his suspicions to ridicule, entertained him and his comrades at dinner, and contrived during that time—or rather while they were making music afterward (which they did for half the night, it seemed)—that Monsieur de Réchamp and Alain should slip out of the cellar in which they had been hidden, gain the end of the gardens through an old hidden passage, and get off in the darkness.

Meanwhile Simone had been safe upstairs with her mother and grandmother, and none of the officers lodged in the *château* had—after a first hasty inspection—set foot in any part of the house but the wing assigned to them. On the third morning they had left, and Scharlach, before going, had put in Mlle. Malo's hands a letter requesting whatever officer should follow him to show every consideration to the family of the Comte de Réchamp, and if possible—owing to the grave illness of the countess—avoid taking up quarters in the *château*: a request which had been scrupulously observed.

Such were the amazing but undisputed facts over which Réchamp and I, in our different ways, were now pondering. He hardly spoke, and when he did it was only to make some casual reference to the road or to our wounded soldiers; but all the while I sat at his side I kept hearing the echo of the question he was inwardly asking himself, and hoping to God he wouldn't put it to me. . . .

It was nearly noon when we finally reached the lines, and the men had to have a rest before we could start again; but a couple of hours later we landed them safely at the base hospital. From there we had intended to go back to Paris; but as we were starting there came an unexpected summons to another point of the front, where there had been a successful night-attack, and a lot of Germans taken in a blown-up trench. The place was fifty miles away, and off my beat, but the number of wounded on both sides was exceptionally heavy, and all the available ambulances had already started. An urgent call had come for more, and there was nothing for it but to go; so we went.

We found things in a bad mess at the second line shanty-hospital where they were dumping the wounded as fast as they could bring them in. At first we were told that none were fit to be carried farther that night; and after we had done what we could we went off to hunt up a shake-down in the village. But a few minutes later an orderly overtook us with a message from the surgeon. There was a German with an abdominal wound who was in a bad way, but might be saved by an operation if he could be got back to the base before midnight.

Would we take him at once and then come back for others?

There is only one answer to such requests, and a few minutes later we were back at the hospital, and the wounded man was being carried out on a stretcher. In the shaky lantern gleam I caught a glimpse of a livid face and a torn uniform, and saw that he was an officer, and nearly done for. Réchamp had climbed to the box, and seemed not to be noticing what was going on at the back of the motor. I understood that he loathed the job, and wanted not to see the face of the man we were carrying; so when we had got him settled I jumped into the ambulance beside him and called out to Béchamp that we were ready. A second later an *infirmier* ran up with a little packet and pushed it into my hand. "His papers," he explained. I pocketed them and pulled the door shut, and we were off.

The man lay motionless on his back, conscious, but desperately weak. Once I turned my pocket-lamp on him and saw that he was young—about thirty—with damp dark hair and a thin face. He had received a flesh-wound above the eyes, and his forehead was bandaged, but the rest of the face uncovered. As the light fell on him he lifted his eyelids and looked at me: his look was inscrutable.

For half an hour or so I sat there in the dark, the sense of that face pressing close on me. It was a damnable face—meanly handsome, basely proud. In my one glimpse of it I had seen that the man was suffering atrociously, but as we slid along through the night he made no sound. At length the motor stopped with a violent jerk that drew a single moan from him. I turned the light on him, but he lay perfectly still, lips and lids shut, making no sign; and I jumped out and ran round to the front to see what had happened.

The motor had stopped for lack of gasoline and was stock still in the deep mud. Réchamp muttered something about a leak in his tank. As he bent over it, the lantern flame struck up into his face, which was set and businesslike. It struck me vaguely that he showed no particular surprise.

"What's to be done?" I asked.

"I think I can tinker it up; but we've got to have more essence to go on with."

I stared at him in despair: it was a good hour's walk back to the lines, and we weren't so sure of getting any gasoline when we got there! But there was no help for it; and as Réchamp was dead lame, no alternative but for me to go.

I opened the ambulance door, gave another look at the motionless man inside and took out a remedy which I handed over to Réchamp with a word of explanation. "You know how to give a hypo? Keep a close eye on him and pop this in if you see a change—not otherwise."

He nodded. "Do you suppose he'll die?" he asked below his breath.

"No, I don't. If we get him to the hospital before morning I think he'll pull through."

"Oh, all right." He unhooked one of the motor lanterns and handed it over to me. "I'll do my best," he said as I turned away.

Getting back to the lines through that pitch-black forest, and finding somebody to bring the gasoline back for me was about the weariest job I ever tackled. I couldn't imagine why it wasn't daylight when we finally got to the place where I had left the motor. It seemed to me as if I had been gone twelve hours when I finally caught sight of the grey bulk of the car through the thinning darkness.

Réchamp came forward to meet us, and took hold of my arm as I was opening the door of the car. "The man's dead," he said.

I had lifted up my pocket-lamp, and its light fell on Réchamp's face, which was perfectly composed, and seemed less gaunt and drawn than at any time since we had started on our trip.

"Dead? Why—how? What happened? Did you give him the hypodermic?" I stammered, taken aback.

"No time to. He died in a minute."

"How do you know he did? Were you with him?"

"Of course I was with him," Réchamp retorted, with a sudden harshness which made me aware that I had grown harsh myself. But I had been almost sure the man wasn't anywhere near death when I left him. I opened the door of the ambulance and climbed in with my lantern. He didn't appear to have moved, but he was dead sure enough—had been for two or three hours, by the feel of him. It must have happened not long after I left. . . . . Well, I'm not a doctor, anyhow. . . . .

I don't think Réchamp and I exchanged a word during the rest of that run. But it was my fault and not his if we didn't. By the mere rub of his sleeve against mine as we sat side by side on the motor I knew he was conscious of no bar between us: he had somehow got back, in the night's interval, to a state of wholesome stolidity, while I, on the contrary, was tingling all over with exposed nerves.

I was glad enough when we got back to the base at last, and the grim load we carried was lifted out and taken into the hospital. Réchamp waited in the courtyard beside his car, lighting a cigarette in the cold early sunlight; but I followed the bearers and the surgeon into the whitewashed room where the dead man was laid out to be undressed. I had a burning spot at the pit of my stomach while his clothes were ripped off him and the bandages undone: I couldn't take my eyes from the surgeon's face. But the surgeon, with a big batch of wounded on his hands, was probably thinking more of the living than the dead; and besides, we were near the front, and the body before him was an enemy's.

He finished his examination and scribbled something in a note-book. "Death must have taken place nearly five hours ago," he merely remarked: it was the conclusion I had already come to myself.

"And how about the papers?" the surgeon continued. "You have them, I suppose? This way, please."

We left the half-stripped body on the bloodstained oil-cloth, and he led me into an office where a functionary sat behind a littered desk.

"The papers? Thank you. You haven't examined them? Let us see, then."

I handed over the leather note-case I had thrust into my pocket the evening before, and saw for the first time its silver-edged corners and the coronet in one of them. The official took out the papers and spread them on the desk between us. I watched him absently while he did so.

Suddenly he uttered an exclamation. "Ah—that's a haul!" he said, and pushed a bit of paper toward me. On it was engraved the name: Oberst Graf Benno von Scharlach. . . .

"A good riddance," said the surgeon over my shoulder.

I went back to the courtyard and saw Réchamp still smoking his cigarette in the cold sunlight. I don't suppose I'd been in the hospital ten minutes; but I felt as old as Methuselah.

My friend greeted me with a smile. "Ready for breakfast?" he said, and a little chill ran down my spine.. . . .But I said: "Oh, all right—come along. . . . ."

For, after all, I knew there wasn't a paper of any sort on that man when he was lifted into my ambulance the night before: the French officials attend to their business too carefully for me not to have been sure of that. And there wasn't the least shred of evidence to prove that he hadn't died of his wounds during the unlucky delay in the forest; or that Réchamp had known his tank was leaking when we started out from the lines.

"I could do with *a café complet*, couldn't you?" Réchamp suggested, looking straight at me with his good blue eyes; and arm in arm we started off to hunt for the inn. . . .

The Portrait

It was at Mrs. Mellish's, one Sunday afternoon last spring. We were talking over George Lillo's portraits—a collection of them was being shown at Durand-Ruel's—and a pretty woman had emphatically declared:—

"Nothing on earth would induce me to sit to him!"

There was a chorus of interrogations.

"Oh, because—he makes people look so horrid; the way one looks on board ship, or early in the morning, or when one's hair is out of curl and one knows it. I'd so much rather be done by Mr. Cumberton!"

Little Cumberton, the fashionable purveyor of rose-water pastels, stroked his moustache to hide a conscious smile.

"Lillo is a genius—that we must all admit," he said indulgently, as though condoning a friend's weakness; "but he has an unfortunate temperament. He has been denied the gift—so precious to an artist—of perceiving the ideal. He sees only the defects of his sitters; one might almost fancy that he takes a morbid pleasure in exaggerating their weak points, in painting them on their worst days; but I honestly believe he can't help himself. His peculiar limitations prevent his seeing anything but the most prosaic side of human nature—"*A primrose by the river's brim. . . . A yellow primrose is to him. . . . And it is nothing more.*"

Cumberton looked round to surprise an order in the eye of the lady whose sentiments he had so deftly interpreted, but poetry always made her uncomfortable, and her nomadic attention had strayed to other topics. His glance was tripped up by Mrs. Mellish.

"Limitations? But, my dear man, it's because he hasn't any limitations, because he doesn't wear the portrait-painter's conventional blinders, that we're all so afraid of being painted by him. It's not because he sees only one aspect of his sitters, it's because he selects the real, the typical one, as instinctively as a detective collars a pick-pocket in a crowd. If there's nothing to paint—no real person—he paints nothing; look at the sumptuous emptiness of his portrait of Mrs. Guy Awdrey"—("Why," the pretty woman perplexedly interjected, "that's the only nice picture he ever did!") "If there's one positive trait in a negative whole he brings it out in spite of himself; if it isn't a nice trait, so much the worse for the sitter; it isn't Lillo's fault: he's no more to blame than a mirror. Your other painters do the surface—he does the depths; they paint the ripples on the pond, he drags the bottom. He makes flesh seem as fortuitous as clothes.

"When I look at his portraits of fine ladies in pearls and velvet I seem to see a little naked cowering wisp of a soul sitting beside the big splendid body, like a poor relation in the darkest corner of an opera-box. But look at his pictures of really great people— how great *they* are! There's plenty of ideal there. Take his Professor Clyde; how clearly the man's history is written in those broad steady strokes of the brush: the hard work, the endless patience, the fearless imagination of the great *savant!* Or the picture of Mr. Domfrey—the man who has felt beauty without having the power to create it.

"The very brushwork expresses the difference between the two; the crowding of nervous tentative lines, the subtler gradations of colour, somehow convey a suggestion of dilettantism. You feel what a delicate instrument the man is, how every sense has been tuned to the finest responsiveness." Mrs. Mellish paused, blushing a little at the echo of her own eloquence. "My advice is, don't let George Lillo paint you if you don't want to be found out—or to find yourself out. That's why I've never let him do *me*; I'm waiting for the day of judgment," she ended with a laugh.

Everyone but the pretty woman, whose eyes betrayed a quivering impatience to discuss clothes, had listened attentively to Mrs. Mellish. Lillo's presence in New York—he had come over from Paris for the first time in twelve years, to arrange the exhibition of his pictures—gave to the analysis of his methods as personal a flavour as though one had been furtively dissecting his domestic relations.

The analogy, indeed, is not unapt; for in Lillo's curiously detached existence it is difficult to figure any closer tie than that which unites him to his pictures. In this light, Mrs. Mellish's flushed harangue seemed not unfitted to the trivialities of the tea hour, and someone almost at once carried on the argument by saying:—"But according to your theory—that the significance of his work depends on the significance of the sitter—his portrait of Vard ought to be a master-piece; and it's his biggest failure."

Alonzo Vard's suicide—he killed himself, strangely enough, the day that Lillo's pictures were first shown—had made his portrait the chief feature of the exhibition. It had been painted ten or twelve years earlier, when the terrible "Boss" was at the height of his power; and if ever man presented a type to stimulate such insight as Lillo's, that man was Vard; yet the portrait was a failure. It was magnificently composed; the technique was dazzling; but the face had been—well, expurgated. It was Vard as Cumberton might have painted him—a common man trying to look at ease in a good coat. The picture had never before been exhibited, and there was a general outcry of disappointment. It wasn't only the critics and the artists who grumbled.

Even the big public, which had gaped and shuddered at Vard, revelling in his genial villainy, and enjoying in his death that succumbing to divine wrath which, as a spectacle, is next best to its successful defiance—even the public felt itself defrauded. What had the painter done with their hero? Where was the big sneering domineering face that figured so convincingly in political cartoons and patent-medicine advertisements, on cigar-boxes and electioneering posters? They had admired the man for looking his part so boldly; for showing the undisguised blackguard in every line of his coarse body and cruel face; the pseudo-gentleman of Lillo's picture was a poor thing compared to the real Vard.

It had been vaguely expected that the great boss's portrait would have the zest of an incriminating document, the scandalous attraction of secret memoirs; and instead, it was as insipid as an obituary. It was as though the artist had been in league with his sitter, had pledged himself to oppose to the lust for post-mortem "revelations" an impassable blank wall of negation. The public was resentful; the critics were aggrieved. Even Mrs. Mellish had to lay down her arms.

"Yes, the portrait of Vard *is* a failure," she admitted, "and I've never known why. If he'd been an obscure elusive type of villain, one could understand Lillo's missing the mark for once; but with that face from the pit—!"

She turned at the announcement of a name which our discussion had drowned, and found herself shaking hands with Lillo.

The pretty woman started and put her hands to her curls; Cumberton dropped a condescending eyelid (he never classed himself by recognising degrees in the profession), and Mrs. Mellish, cheerfully aware that she had been overheard, said, as she made room for Lillo— "I wish you'd explain it."

Lillo smoothed his beard and waited for a cup of tea. Then, "Would there be any failures," he said, "if one could explain them?"

"Ah, in some cases I can imagine it's impossible to seize the type— or to say why one has missed it. Some people are like daguerreotypes; in certain lights one can't see them at all. But surely Vard was obvious enough. What I want to know is, what became of him? What did you do with him? How did you manage to shuffle him out of sight?"

"It was much easier than you think. I simply missed an opportunity—"

"That a sign-painter would have seen!"

"Very likely. In fighting shy of the obvious one may miss the significant—"

"—And when I got back from Paris," the pretty woman was heard to wail, "I found all the women here were wearing the very models I'd brought home with me!"

Mrs. Mellish, as became a vigilant hostess, got up and shuffled her guests; and the question of Vard's portrait was dropped.

I left the house with Lillo; and on the way down Fifth Avenue, after one of his long silences, he suddenly asked:

"Is that what is generally said of my picture of Vard? I don't mean in the newspapers, but by the fellows who know?"

I said it was.

He drew a deep breath. "Well," he said, "it's good to know that when one tries to fail one can make such a complete success of it."

"Tries to fail?"

"Well, no; that's not quite it, either; I didn't want to make a failure of Vard's picture, but I did so deliberately, with my eyes open, all the same. It was what one might call a lucid failure."

"But why—?"

"The why of it is rather complicated. I'll tell you some time—" He hesitated. "Come and dine with me at the club by and by, and I'll tell you afterwards. It's a nice morsel for a psychologist."

At dinner he said little; but I didn't mind that. I had known him for years, and had always found something soothing and companionable in his long abstentions from speech. His silence was never unsocial; it was bland as a natural hush; one felt one's self included in it, not left out. He stroked his beard and gazed absently at me; and when we had finished our coffee and liqueurs we strolled down to his studio.

At the studio—which was less draped, less posed, less consciously "artistic" than those of the smaller men—he handed me a cigar, and fell to smoking before the fire. When he began to talk it was of indifferent matters, and I had dismissed the hope of hearing more of Vard's portrait, when my eye lit on a photograph of the picture. I walked across the room to look at it, and Lillo presently followed with a light.

"It certainly is a complete disguise," he muttered over my shoulder; then he turned away and stooped to a big portfolio propped against the wall.

"Did you ever know Miss Vard?" he asked, with his head in the portfolio; and without waiting for my answer he handed me a crayon sketch of a girl's profile.

I had never seen a crayon of Lillo's, and I lost sight of the sitter's personality in the interest aroused by this new aspect of the master's complex genius. The few lines—faint, yet how decisive!—flowered out of the rough paper with the lightness of opening petals. It was a mere hint of a picture, but vivid as some word that wakens long reverberations in the memory.

I felt Lillo at my shoulder again.

"You knew her, I suppose?"

I had to stop and think. Why, of course I'd known her: a silent handsome girl, showy yet ineffective, whom I had seen without seeing the winter that society had capitulated to Vard. Still looking at the crayon, I tried to trace some connection between the Miss Vard I recalled and the grave young seraph of Lillo's sketch. Had the Vards bewitched him? By what masterstroke of suggestion had he been beguiled into drawing the terrible father as a barber's block, the commonplace daughter as this memorable creature?

"You don't remember much about her? No, I suppose not. She was a quiet girl and nobody noticed her much, even when—" he paused with a smile— "you were all asking Vard to dine."

I winced. Yes, it was true—we had all asked Vard to dine. It was some comfort to think that fate had made him expiate our weakness.

Lillo put the sketch on the mantel-shelf and drew his armchair to the fire.

"It's cold tonight. Take another cigar, old man; and some whiskey? There ought to be a bottle and some glasses in that cupboard behind you. . . . help yourself. . . ."

2

About Vard's portrait? (he began.) Well, I'll tell you. It's a queer story, and most people wouldn't see anything in it. My enemies might say it was a roundabout way of explaining a failure; but you know better than that. Mrs. Mellish was right. Between me and Vard there could be no question of failure. The man was made for me—I felt that the first time I clapped eyes on him. I could hardly keep from asking him to sit to me on the spot; but somehow one couldn't ask favours of the fellow. I sat still and prayed he'd come to me, though; for I was looking for something big for the next salon.

It was twelve years ago—the last time I was out ere—and I was ravenous for an opportunity. I had the feeling—do you writer-fellows have it too?—that there was something tremendous in me if it could only be got out; and I felt Vard was the Moses to strike the rock. There were vulgar reasons, too, that made me hunger for a victim. I'd been grinding on obscurely for a good many years, without gold or glory, and the first thing of mine that had made a noise was my picture of Pepita, exhibited the year before. There'd been a lot of talk about that, orders were beginning to come in, and I wanted to follow it up with a rousing big thing at the next salon.

Then the critics had been insinuating that I could do only Spanish things—I suppose I *had* overdone the castanet business; it's a nursery-disease we all go through—and I wanted to show that I had plenty more shot in my locker. Don't you get up every morning meaning to prove you're equal to Balzac or Thackeray? That's the way I felt then; *only give me a chance*, I wanted to shout out to them; and I saw at once that Vard was my chance.

I had come over from Paris in the autumn to paint Mrs. Clingsborough, and I met Vard and his daughter at one of the first dinners I went to. After that I could think of nothing but that man's head. What a type! I raked up all the details of his scandalous history; and there were enough to fill an encyclopaedia. The papers were full of him just then; he was mud from head to foot; it was about the time of the big viaduct steal, and irreproachable citizens were forming ineffectual leagues to put him down. And all the time one kept meeting him at dinners—that was the beauty of it!

Once I remember seeing him next to the Bishop's wife; I've got a little sketch of that duet somewhere... Well, he was simply magnificent, a born ruler; what a splendid condottiere he would have made, in gold armour, with a griffin grinning on his casque! You remember those drawings of Leonardo's, where the knight's face and the outline of his helmet combine in one monstrous saurian profile? He always reminded me of that. . . . .

But how was I to get at him?—One day it occurred to me to try talking to Miss Vard. She was a monosyllabic person, who didn't seem to see an inch beyond the last remark one had made; but suddenly I found myself blurting out, "I wonder if you know how extraordinarily paintable your father is?" and you should have seen the change that came over her. Her eyes lit up and she looked—well, as I've tried to make her look there. (He glanced up at the sketch.) Yes, she said, *wasn't* her father splendid, and didn't I think him one of the handsomest men I'd ever seen?

That rather staggered me, I confess; I couldn't think her capable of joking on such a subject, yet it seemed impossible that she should be speaking seriously. But she was. I knew it by the way she looked at Vard, who was sitting opposite, his wolfish profile thrown back, the shaggy locks tossed off his narrow high white forehead. The girl worshipped him.

She went on to say how glad she was that I saw him as she did. So many artists admired only regular beauty, the stupid Greek type that was made to be done in marble; but she'd always fancied from what she'd seen of my work—she knew everything I'd done, it appeared—that I looked deeper, cared more for the way in which faces are modelled by temperament and circumstance; "and of course in that sense," she concluded, "my father's face *is* beautiful."

This was even more staggering; but one couldn't question her divine sincerity. I'm afraid my one thought was to take advantage of it; and I let her go on, perceiving that if I wanted to paint Vard all I had to do was to listen.

She poured out her heart. It was a glorious thing for a girl, she said, wasn't it, to be associated with such a life as that? She felt it so strongly, sometimes, that it oppressed her, made her shy and stupid. She was so afraid people would expect her to live up to *him*. But that was absurd, of course; brilliant men so seldom had clever children. Still—did I know?—she would have been happier, much happier, if he hadn't been in public life; if he and she could have hidden themselves away somewhere, with their books and music, and she could have had it all to herself: his cleverness, his learning, his immense unbounded goodness. For no one knew how good he was; no one but herself. Everybody recognized his cleverness, his brilliant abilities; even his enemies had to admit his extraordinary intellectual gifts, and hated him the worse, of course, for the admission; but no one, no one could guess what he was at home.

She had heard of great men who were always giving gala performances in public, but whose wives and daughters saw only the empty theatre, with the footlights out and the scenery stacked in the wings; but with him it was just the other way: wonderful as he was in public, in society, she sometimes felt he wasn't doing himself justice—he was so much more wonderful at home. It was like carrying a guilty secret about with her: his friends, his admirers, would never forgive her if they found out that he kept all his best things for *her!*

I don't quite know what I felt in listening to her. I was chiefly taken up with leading her on to the point I had in view; but even through my personal preoccupation I remember being struck by the fact that, though she talked foolishly, she didn't talk like a fool. She was not stupid; she was not obtuse; one felt that her impassive surface was alive with delicate points of perception; and this fact, coupled with her crystalline frankness, flung me back on a startled revision of my impressions of her father. He came out of the test more monstrous than ever, as an ugly image reflected in clear water is made uglier by the purity of the medium.

Even then I felt a pang at the use to which fate had put the mountain-pool of Miss Vard's spirit, and an uneasy sense that my own reflection there was not one to linger over. It was odd that I should have scrupled to deceive, on one small point, a girl already so hugely cheated; perhaps it was the completeness of her delusion that gave it the sanctity of a religious belief. At any rate, a distinct sense of discomfort tempered the satisfaction with which, a day or two later, I heard from her that her father had consented to give me a few sittings.

I'm afraid my scruples vanished when I got him before my easel. He was immense, and he was unexplored. From my point of view, he'd never been done before—I was his Cortez. As he talked the wonder grew. His daughter came with him, and I began to think she was right in saying that he kept his best for her. It wasn't that she drew him out, or guided the conversation; but one had a sense of delicate vigilance, hardly more perceptible than one of those atmospheric influences that give the pulses a happier turn. She was a vivifying climate. I had meant to turn the talk to public affairs, but it slipped toward books and art, and I was faintly aware of its being kept there without undue pressure. Before long I saw the value of the diversion.

It was easy enough to get at the political Vard: the other aspect was rarer and more instructive. His daughter had described him as a scholar. He wasn't that, of course, in any intrinsic sense: like most men of his type he had gulped his knowledge standing, as he had snatched his food from lunch-counters; the wonder of it lay in his extraordinary power of assimilation. It was the strangest instance of a mind to which erudition had given force and fluency without culture; his learning had not educated his perceptions: it was an implement serving to slash others rather than to polish himself. I have said that at first sight he was immense; but as I studied him he began to lessen under my scrutiny. His depth was a false perspective painted on a wall.

It was there that my difficulty lay: I had prepared too big a can-vas for him. Intellectually his scope was considerable, but it was like the digital reach of a mediocre pianist—it didn't make him a great musician. And morally he wasn't bad enough; his corruption wasn't sufficiently imaginative to be interesting. It was not so much a means to an end as a kind of virtuosity practised for its own sake, like a highly-developed skill in cannoning billiard balls. After all, the point of view is what gives distinction to either vice or virtue: a morality with ground-glass windows is no duller than a narrow cynicism.

His daughter's presence—she always came with him—gave unin-tentional emphasis to these conclusions; for where she was richest he was naked. She had a deep-rooted delicacy that drew colour and per-fume from the very centre of her being: his sentiments, good or bad, were as detachable as his cuffs. Thus her nearness, planned, as I guessed, with the tender intention of displaying, elucidating him, of making him accessible in detail to my dazzled perceptions—this pious design in fact defeated itself. She made him appear at his best, but she cheap-ened that best by her proximity. For the man was vulgar to the core; vulgar in spite of his force and magnitude; thin, hollow, spectacular; a lath-and-plaster bogey—

Did she suspect it? I think not—then. He was wrapped in her im-pervious faith. . . . The papers? Oh, their charges were set down to po-litical rivalry; and the only people she saw were his hangers-on, or the fashionable set who had taken him up for their amusement. Besides, she would never have found out in that way: at a direct accusation her resentment would have flamed up and smothered her judgment. If the truth came to her, it would come through knowing intimately someone—different; through—how shall I put it?—an imperceptible shifting of her centre of gravity. My besetting fear was that I couldn't count on her obtuseness. She wasn't what is called clever; she left that to him; but she was exquisitely good; and now and then she had intuitive felicities that frightened me. Do I make you see her? We fellows can explain better with the brush; I don't know how to mix my words or lay them on. She wasn't clever; but her heart thought— that's all I can say.. . . .

If she'd been stupid, it would have been easy enough: I could have painted him as he was. Could have? I did—brushed the face in one day from memory; it was the very man! I painted it out before she came: I couldn't bear to have her see it. I had the feeling that I held her faith in him in my hands, carrying it like a brittle object through a jostling mob; a hair's- breadth swerve and it was in splinters.

When she wasn't there I tried to reason myself out of these subtleties. My business was to paint Vard as he was—if his daughter didn't mind his looks, why should I? The opportunity was magnificent—I knew that by the way his face had leapt out of the canvas at my first touch. It would have been a big thing. Before every sitting I swore to myself I'd do it; then she came, and sat near him, and I—didn't.

I knew that before long she'd notice I was shirking the face. Vard himself took little interest in the portrait, but she watched me closely, and one day when the sitting was over she stayed behind and asked me when I meant to begin what she called "the likeness." I guessed from her tone that the embarrassment was all on my side, or that if she felt any it was at having to touch a vulnerable point in my pride. Thus far the only doubt that troubled her was a distrust of my ability. Well, I put her off with any rot you please: told her she must trust me, must let me wait for the inspiration; that someday the face would come; I should see it suddenly— feel it under my brush... The poor child believed me: you can make a woman believe almost anything she doesn't quite understand. She was abashed at her philistinism, and begged me not to tell her father—he would make such fun of her!

After that—well, the sittings went on. Not many, of course; Vard was too busy to give me much time. Still, I could have done him ten times over. Never had I found my formula with such ease, such assurance; there were no hesitations, no obstructions—the face was *there*, waiting for me; at times it almost shaped itself on the canvas. Unfortunately, Miss Vard was there too. . . .

All this time the papers were busy with the viaduct scandal. The outcry was getting louder. You remember the circumstances? One of Vard's associates—Bardwell, wasn't it?—threatened disclosures. The rival machine got hold of him, the Independents took him to their bosom, and the press shrieked for an investigation. It was not the first storm Vard had weathered, and his face wore just the right shade of cool vigilance; he wasn't the man to fall into the mistake of appearing too easy. His demeanour would have been superb if it had been inspired by a sense of his own strength; but it struck me rather as based on contempt for his antagonists. Success is an inverted telescope through which one's enemies are apt to look too small and too remote. As for Miss Vard, her serenity was undiminished; but I half-detected a defiance in her unruffled sweetness, and during the last sittings I had the factitious vivacity of a hostess who hears her best china crashing.

One day it *did* crash: the headlines of the morning papers shouted the catastrophe at me:—"The Monster forced to disgorge—Warrant out against Vard—Bardwell the Boss's Boomerang"—you know the kind of thing.

When I had read the papers I threw them down and went out. As it happened, Vard was to have given me a sitting that morning; but there would have been a certain irony in waiting for him. I wished I had finished the picture—I wished I'd never thought of painting it. I wanted to shake off the whole business, to put it out of my mind, if I could: I had the feeling—I don't know if I can describe it—that there was a kind of disloyalty to the poor girl in my even acknowledging to myself that I knew what all the papers were howling from the housetops. . . .

I had walked for an hour when it suddenly occurred to me that Miss Vard might, after all, come to the studio at the appointed hour. Why should she? I could conceive of no reason; but the mere thought of what, if she *did* come, my absence would imply to her, sent me bolting back to Twelfth Street. It was a presentiment, if you like, for she was there.

As she rose to meet me a newspaper slipped from her hand: I'd been fool enough, when I went out, to leave the damned things lying all over the place.

I muttered some apology for being late, and she said reassuringly:
"But my father's not here yet."

"Your father—?" I could have kicked myself for the way I bungled it!

"He went out very early this morning, and left word that he would meet me here at the usual hour."

She faced me, with an eye full of bright courage, across the newspaper lying between us.

"He ought to be here in a moment now—he's always so punctual. But my watch is a little fast, I think."

She held it out to me almost gaily, and I was just pretending to compare it with mine, when there was a smart rap on the door and Vard stalked in. There was always a civic majesty in his gait, an air of having just stepped off his pedestal and of dissembling an oration in his umbrella; and that day he surpassed himself. Miss Vard had turned pale at the knock; but the mere sight of him replenished her veins, and if she now avoided my eye, it was in mere pity for my discomfiture.

I was in fact the only one of the three who didn't instantly "play up"; but such virtuosity was inspiring, and by the time Vard had thrown off his coat and dropped into a senatorial pose, I was ready to pitch into my work. I swore I'd do his face then and there; do it as she saw it; she sat close to him, and I had only to glance at her while I painted—

Vard himself was masterly: his talk rattled through my hesitations and embarrassments like a brisk northwester sweeping the dry leaves from its path. Even his daughter showed the sudden brilliance of a lamp from which the shade has been removed. We were all surprisingly vivid—it felt, somehow, as though we were being photographed by flashlight. . . .

It was the best sitting we'd ever had—but unfortunately it didn't last more than ten minutes.

It was Vard's secretary who interrupted us—a slinking chap called Cornley, who burst in, as white as sweetbread, with the face of a depositor who hears his bank has stopped payment. Miss Vard started up as he entered, but caught herself together and dropped back into her chair. Vard, who had taken out a cigarette, held the tip tranquilly to his *fusee*.

"You're here, thank God!" Cornley cried. "There's no time to be lost, Mr. Vard. I've got a carriage waiting round the corner in Thirteenth Street—"

Vard looked at the tip of his cigarette.

"A carriage in Thirteenth Street? My good fellow, my own brougham is at the door."

"I know, I know—but _they're there too, sir; or they will be, inside of a minute. For God's sake, Mr. Vard, don't trifle!—There's a way out by Thirteenth Street, I tell you"—

"Bardwell's myrmidons, eh?" said Vard. "Help me on with my overcoat, Cornley, will you?"

Cornley's teeth chattered.

"Mr. Vard, your best friends.. . . . Miss Vard, won't you speak to your father?" He turned to me haggardly;—"We can get out by the back way?"

I nodded.

Vard stood towering—in some infernal way he seemed literally to rise to the situation—one hand in the bosom of his coat, in the attitude of patriotism in bronze. I glanced at his daughter: she hung on him with a drowning look. Suddenly she straightened herself; there was something of Vard in the way she faced her fears—a kind of primitive calm we drawing- room folk don't have. She stepped to him and laid her hand on his arm. The pause hadn't lasted ten seconds.

"Father—" she said.

Vard threw back his head and swept the studio with a sovereign eye.

"The back way, Mr. Vard, the back way," Cornley whimpered. "For God's sake, sir, don't lose a minute."

Vard transfixed his abject henchman.

"I have never yet taken the back way," he enunciated; and, with a gesture matching the words, he turned to me and bowed.

"I regret the disturbance"—and he walked to the door. His daughter was at his side, alert, transfigured.

"Stay here, my dear."

"Never!"

They measured each other an instant; then he drew her arm in his. She flung back one look at me—a *paean* of victory—and they passed out with Cornley at their heels.

I wish I'd finished the face then; I believe I could have caught something of the look she had tried to make me see in him. Unluckily I was too excited to work that day or the next, and within the week the whole business came out. If the indictment wasn't a put-up job—and on that I believe there were two opinions—all that followed was. You remember the farcical trial, the packed jury, the compliant judge, the triumphant acquittal?. . . . . It's a spectacle that always carries conviction to the voter: Vard was never more popular than after his "exoneration". . . . .

I didn't see Miss Vard for weeks. It was she who came to me at length; came to the studio alone, one afternoon at dusk. She had—what shall I say?—a veiled manner; as though she had dropped a fine gauze between us. I waited for her to speak.

She glanced about the room, admiring a hawthorn vase I had picked up at auction. Then, after a pause, she said:

"You haven't finished the picture?"

"Not quite," I said.

She asked to see it, and I wheeled out the easel and threw the drapery back.

"Oh," she murmured, "you haven't gone on with the face?"

I shook my head.

She looked down on her clasped hands and up at the picture; not once at me.

"You—you're going to finish it?"

"Of course," I cried, throwing the revived purpose into my voice. By God, I would finish it!

The merest tinge of relief stole over her face, faint as the first thin chirp before daylight.

"Is it so very difficult?" she asked tentatively.

"Not insuperably, I hope."

She sat silent, her eyes on the picture. At length, with an effort, she brought out: "Shall you want more sittings?"

For a second I blundered between two conflicting conjectures; then the truth came to me with a leap, and I cried out, "No, no more sittings!"

She looked up at me then for the first time; looked too soon, poor child; for in the spreading light of reassurance that made her eyes like a rainy dawn, I saw, with terrible distinctness, the rout of her disbanded hopes. I knew that she knew ...

I finished the picture and sent it home within a week. I tried to make it —what you see.—Too late, you say? Yes—for her; but not for me or for the public. If she could be made to feel, for a day longer, for an hour even, that her miserable secret *was* a secret—why, she'd made it seem worthwhile to me to chuck my own ambitions for that. . . . .

★★★★★★

Lillo rose, and taking down the sketch stood looking at it in silence. After a while I ventured, "And Miss Vard—?"

He opened the portfolio and put the sketch back, tying the strings with deliberation. Then, turning to relight his cigar at the lamp, he said: "She died last year, thank God."

The Legend

1

Arthur Bernald could never afterward recall just when the first conjecture flashed on him: oddly enough, there was no record of it in the agitated jottings of his diary. But, as it seemed to him in retrospect, he had always felt that the queer man at the Wades' must be John Pellerin, if only for the negative reason that he couldn't imaginably be anyone else. It was impossible, in the confused pattern of the century's intellectual life, to fit the stranger in anywhere, save in the big gap which, some five and twenty years earlier, had been left by Pellerin's unaccountable disappearance; and conversely, such a man as the Wades' visitor couldn't have lived for sixty years without filling, somewhere in space, a nearly equivalent void.

At all events, it was certainly not to Doctor Wade or to his mother that Bernald owed the hint: the good unconscious Wades, one of whose chief charms in the young man's eyes was that they remained so robustly untainted by Pellerinism, in spite of the fact that Doctor Wade's younger brother, Howland, was among its most impudently flourishing high-priests.

The incident had begun by Bernald's running across Doctor Robert Wade one hot summer night at the University Club, and by Wade's saying, in the tone of unprofessional laxity which the shadowy stillness of the place invited:

I got hold of a queer fish at St. Martin's the other day—case of heat-prostration picked up in Central Park. When we'd patched him up I found he had nowhere to go, and not a dollar in his pocket, and I sent him down to our place at Portchester to rebuild.

The opening roused his hearer's attention. Bob Wade had an odd unformulated sense of values that Bernald had learned to trust.

"What sort of chap? Young or old?"

"Oh, every age—full of years, and yet with a lot left. He called himself sixty on the books."

"Sixty's a good age for some kinds of living. And age is of course purely subjective. How has he used his sixty years?"

"Well—part of them in educating himself, apparently. He's a scholar—humanities, languages, and so forth."

"Oh—decayed gentleman," Bernald murmured, disappointed.

"Decayed? Not much!" cried the doctor with his accustomed literalness. "I only mentioned that side of Winterman—his name's Winterman—because it was the side my mother noticed first. I suppose women generally do. But it's only a part—a small part. The man's the big thing."

"Really big?"

"Well—there again..... When I took him down to the country, looking rather like a tramp from a 'Shelter,' with an untrimmed beard, and a suit of reach-me-downs he'd slept round the Park in for a week, I felt sure my mother'd carry the silver up to her room, and send for the gardener's dog to sleep in the hall the first night. But she didn't."

"I see. 'Women and children love him.' Oh, Wade!" Bernald groaned.

"Not a bit of it! You're out again. We don't love him, either of us. But we *feel* him—the air's charged with him. You'll see."

And Bernald agreed that he *would* see, the following Sunday. Wade's inarticulate attempts to characterize the stranger had struck his friend. The human revelation had for Bernald a poignant and ever-renewed interest, which his trade, as the dramatic critic of a daily paper, had hitherto failed to discourage. And he knew that Bob Wade, simple and undefiled by literature—Bernald's specific affliction—had a free and personal way of judging men, and the diviner's knack of reaching their hidden springs. During the days that followed, the young doctor gave Bernald farther details about John Winterman: details not of fact—for in that respect his visitor's reticence was baffling—but of impression. It appeared that Winterman, while lying insensible in the Park, had been robbed of the few dollars he possessed; and on leaving the hospital, still weak and half-blind, he had quite simply and unprotestingly accepted the Wades' offer to give him shelter till such time as he should be strong enough to go to work.

"But what's his work?" Bernald interjected. "Hasn't he at least told you that?"

"Well, writing. Some kind of writing." Doctor Bob always became vague and clumsy when he approached the confines of literature. "He means to take it up again as soon as his eyes get right."

Bernald groaned. "Oh, Lord—that finishes him; and *me!* He's looking for a publisher, of course—he wants a 'favourable notice.' I won't come!"

"He hasn't written a line for twenty years."

"A line of *what?* What kind of literature can one keep corked up for twenty years?"

Wade surprised him. "The real kind, I should say. But I don't know Winterman's line," the doctor added. "He speaks of the things he used to write merely as 'stuff that wouldn't sell.' He has a wonderfully confidential way of *not* telling one things. But he says he'll have to do something for his living as soon as his eyes are patched up, and that writing is the only trade he knows. The queer thing is that he seems pretty sure of selling *now.* He even talked of buying the bungalow of us, with an acre or two about it."

"The bungalow? What's that?"

"The studio down by the shore that we built for Howland when he thought he meant to paint." (Howland Wade, as Bernald knew, had experienced various "calls.") "Since he's taken to writing nobody's been near it. I offered it to Winterman, and he camps there—cooks his meals, does his own house-keeping, and never comes up to the house except in the evenings, when he joins us on the verandah, in the dark, and smokes while my mother knits."

"A discreet visitor, eh?"

"More than he need be. My mother actually wanted him to stay on in the house—in her pink chintz room. Think of it! But he says houses smother him. I take it he's lived for years in the open."

"In the open where?"

"I can't make out, except that it was somewhere in the East. 'East of everything—beyond the day-spring. In places not on the map.' That's the way he put it; and when I said: 'You've been an explorer, then?' he smiled in his beard, and answered: 'Yes; that's it—an explorer.' Yet he doesn't strike me as a man of action: hasn't the hands or the eyes."

"What sort of hands and eyes has he?"

Wade reflected. His range of observation was not large, but within its limits it was exact and could give an account of itself.

"He's worked a lot with his hands, but that's not what they were made for. I should say they were extraordinarily delicate conductors of sensation. And his eye—his eye too. He hasn't used it to dominate people: he didn't care to. He simply looks through 'em all like windows. Makes me feel like the fellows who think they're made of glass. The mitigating circumstance is that he seems to see such a glorious landscape through me." Wade grinned at the thought of serving such a purpose.

"I see. I'll come on Sunday and be looked through!" Bernald cried.

2

Bernald came on two successive Sundays; and the second time he lingered till the Tuesday.

"Here he comes!" Wade had said, the first evening, as the two young men, with Wade's mother sat in the sultry dusk, with the Virginian creeper drawing, between the verandah arches, its black arabesques against a moon-lined sky.

In the darkness Bernald heard a step on the gravel, and saw the red flit of a cigar through the shrubs. Then a loosely-moving figure obscured the patch of sky between the creepers, and the red spark became the centre of a dim bearded face, in which Bernald discerned only a broad white gleam of forehead.

It was the young man's subsequent impression that Winterman had not spoken much that first evening; at any rate, Bernald himself remembered chiefly what the Wades had said. And this was the more curious because he had come for the purpose of studying their visitor, and because there was nothing to divert him from that purpose in Wade's halting communications or his mother's artless comments. He reflected afterward that there must have been a mysteriously fertilizing quality in the stranger's silence: it had brooded over their talk like a large moist cloud above a dry country.

Mrs. Wade, apparently apprehensive lest her son should have given Bernald an exaggerated notion of their visitor's importance, had hastened to qualify it before the latter appeared.

"He's not what you or Howland would call intellectual—"(Bernald writhed at the coupling of the names)—"not in the least *literary;* though he told Bob he used to write. I don't think, though, it could have been what Howland would call writing." Mrs. Wade always mentioned her younger son with a reverential drop of the voice. She viewed literature much as she did Providence, as an inscrutably mystery; and she spoke of Howland as a dedicated being, set apart to perform secret rites within the veil of the sanctuary.

"I shouldn't say he had a quick mind," she continued, reverting apologetically to Winterman. "Sometimes he hardly seems to follow what we're saying. But he's got such sound ideas—when he does speak he's never silly. And clever people sometimes *are*, don't you think so?" Bernald groaned an unqualified assent. "And he's so capable. The other day something went wrong with the kitchen range, just as I was expecting some friends of Bob's for dinner; and do you know, when Mr. Winterman heard we were in trouble, he came and took a look, and knew at once what to do? I told him it was a dreadful pity he wasn't married!"

Close on midnight, when the session on the verandah ended, and the two young men were strolling down to the bungalow at Winterman's side, Bernald's mind reverted to the image of the fertilizing cloud. There was something brooding, pregnant, in the silent presence beside him: he had, in place of any circumscribing impression of the individual, a large hovering sense of manifold latent meanings. And he felt a distinct thrill of relief when, half-way down the lawn, Doctor Bob was checked by a voice that called him back to the telephone.

"Now I'll be with him alone!" thought Bernald, with a throb like a lover's.

In the low-ceilinged bungalow Winterman had to grope for the lamp on his desk, and as its light struck up into his face Bernald's sense of the rareness of his opportunity increased. He couldn't have said why, for the face, with its ridged brows, its shabby greyish beard and blunt Socratic nose, made no direct appeal to the eye. It seemed rather like a stage on which remarkable things might be enacted, like some shaggy moorland landscape dependent for form and expression on the clouds rolling over it, and the bursts of light between; and one of these flashed out in the smile with which Winterman, as if in answer to his companion's thought, said simply, as he turned to fill his pipe: "Now we'll talk."

So he'd known all along that they hadn't yet—and had guessed that, with Bernald, one might!

The young man's glow of pleasure was so intense that it left him for a moment unable to meet the challenge; and in that moment he felt the brush of something winged and summoning. His spirit rose to it with a rush; but just as he felt himself poised between the ascending pinions, the door opened and Bob Wade plunged in.

"Too bad! I'm so sorry! It was from Howland, to say he can't come tomorrow after all." The doctor panted out his news with honest grief.

"I tried my best to pull it off for you; and my brother *wants* to come—he's keen to talk to you and see what he can do. But you see he's so tremendously in demand. He'll try for another Sunday later on."

Winterman nodded with a whimsical gesture. "Oh, he'll find me here. I shall work my time out slowly." He pointed to the scattered sheets on the kitchen table which formed his writing desk.

"Not slowly enough to suit us," Wade answered hospitably. "Only, if Howland could have come he might have given you a tip or two— put you on the right track—shown you how to get in touch with the public."

Winterman, his hands in his sagging pockets, lounged against the bare pine walls, twisting his pipe under his beard. "Does your brother enjoy the privilege of that contact?" he questioned gravely.

Wade stared a little. "Oh, of course Howland's not what you'd call a *popular* writer; he despises that kind of thing. But whatever he says goes with—well, with the chaps that count; and everyone tells me he's written *the* book on Pellerin. You must read it when you get back your eyes." He paused, as if to let the name sink in, but Winterman drew at his pipe with a blank face.

"You must have heard of Pellerin, I suppose?" the doctor continued. "I've never read a word of him myself: he's too big a proposition for *me*. But one can't escape the talk about him. I have him crammed down my throat even in hospital. The internes read him at the clinics. He tumbles out of the nurses' pockets. The patients keep him under their pillows. Oh, with most of them, of course, it's just a craze, like the last new game or puzzle: they don't understand him in the least. Howland says that even now, twenty-five years after his death, and with his books in everybody's hands, there are not twenty people who really understand Pellerin; and Howland ought to know, if anybody does. He's—what's their great word?—*interpreted* him. You must get Howland to put you through a course of Pellerin."

And as the young men, having taken leave of Winterman, retraced their way across the lawn, Wade continued to develop the theme of his brother's accomplishments.

"I wish I *could* get Howland to take an interest in Winterman: this is the third Sunday he's chucked us. Of course he does get bored with people consulting him about their writings—but I believe if he could only talk to Winterman he'd see something in him, as we do. And it would be such a god-send to the poor man to have someone to advise him about his work. I'm going to make a desperate effort to get Howland here next Sunday."

It was then that Bernald vowed to himself that he would return the next Sunday at all costs. He hardly knew whether he was prompted by the impulse to shield Winterman from Howland Wade's ineptitude, or by the desire to see the latter abandon himself to the full shamelessness of its display; but of one fact he was blissfully assured—and that was of the existence in Winterman of some quality which would provoke Howland to the amplest exercise of his fatuity. "How he'll draw him—how he'll draw him!" Bernald chuckled, with a security the more unaccountable that his one glimpse of Winterman had shown the latter only as a passive subject for experimentation; and he felt himself avenged in advance for the injury of Howland Wade's existence.

3

That this hope was to be frustrated Bernald learned from Howland Wade's own lips, the day before the two young men were to meet at Portchester.

"I can't really, my dear fellow," the Interpreter lisped, passing a polished hand over the faded smoothness of his face. "Oh, an authentic engagement, I assure you: otherwise, to oblige old Bob I'd submit cheerfully to looking over his foundling's literature. But I'm pledged this week to the Pellerin Society of Kenosha: I had a hand in founding it, and for two years now they've been patiently waiting for a word from me—the *Fiat Lux*, so to speak. You see it's a ministry, Bernald—I assure you, I look upon my calling quite religiously."

As Bernald listened, his disappointment gradually changed to relief. Howland, on trial, always turned out to be too insufferable, and the pleasure of watching his antics was invariably lost in the impulse to put a sanguinary end to them.

"If he'd only keep his beastly pink hands off Pellerin," Bernald groaned, thinking of the thick manuscript condemned to perpetual incarceration in his own desk by the publication of Howland's "definitive" work on the great man. One couldn't, *after* Howland Wade, expose one's self to the derision of writing about Pellerin: the eagerness with which Wade's book had been devoured proved, not that the public had enough appetite for another, but simply that, for a stomach so undiscriminating, anything better than Wade had given it would

307

be too good. And Bernald, in the confidence that his own work was open to this objection, had stoically locked it up. Yet if he had resigned his exasperated intelligence to the fact that Wade's book existed, and was already passing into the immortality of perpetual republication, he could not, after repeated trials, adjust himself to the author's talk about Pellerin. When Wade wrote of the great dead he was egregious, but in conversation he was familiar and fond.

It might have been supposed that one of the beauties of Pellerin's hidden life and mysterious taking off would have been to guard him from the fingering of anecdote; but biographers like Howland Wade were born to rise above such obstacles. He might be vague or inaccurate in dealing with the few recorded events of his subject's life; but when he left fact for conjecture no one had a firmer footing. Whole chapters in his volume were constructed in the conditional mood and packed with hypothetical detail; and in talk, by the very law of the process, hypothesis became affirmation, and he was ready to tell you confidentially the exact circumstances of Pellerin's death, and of the "distressing incident" leading up to it.

Bernald himself not only questioned the form under which this incident was shaping itself before posterity, but the mere radical fact of its occurrence: he had never been able to discover any break in the dense cloud enveloping Pellerin's later life and its mysterious termination. He had gone away—that was all that any of them knew: he who had so little, at any time, been with them or of them; and his going had so slightly stirred the public consciousness that even the subsequent news of his death, laconically imparted from afar, had dropped unheeded into the universal scrap-basket, to be long afterward fished out, with all its details missing, when some enquiring spirit first became aware, by chance encounter with a two-penny volume in a London book-stall, not only that such a man as John Pellerin had died, but that he had ever lived, or written.

It need hardly be noted that Howland Wade had not been the pioneer in question: his had been the wiser part of swelling the chorus when it rose, and gradually drowning the other voices by his own insistent note. He had pitched the note so screamingly, and held it so long, that he was now the accepted authority on Pellerin, not only in the land which had given birth to his genius but in the Europe which had first acclaimed it; and it was the central point of pain in Bernald's sense of the situation that a man who had so yearned for silence as Pellerin should have his grave piped over by such a voice as Wade's.

Bernald's talk with the Interpreter had revived this ache to the momentary exclusion of other sensations; and he was still sore with it when, the next afternoon, he arrived at Portchester for his second Sunday with the Wades.

At the station he had the surprise of seeing Winterman's face on the platform, and of hearing from him that Doctor Bob had been called away to assist at an operation in a distant town.

"Mrs. Wade wanted to put you off, but I believe the message came too late; so she sent me down to break the news to you," said Winterman, holding out his hand.

Perhaps because they were the first conventional words that Bernald had heard him speak, the young man was struck by the relief his intonation gave them.

"She wanted to send a carriage," Winterman added, "but I told her we'd walk back through the woods." He looked at Bernald with a sudden kindness that flushed the young man with pleasure.

"Are you strong enough? It's not too far?"

"Oh, no. I'm pulling myself together. Getting back to work is the slowest part of the business: not on account of my eyes—I can use them now, though not for reading; but some of the links between things are missing. It's a kind of broken spectrum. . . . . here, that boy will look after your bag."

The walk through the woods remained in Bernald's memory as an enchanted hour. He used the word literally, as descriptive of the way in which Winterman's contact changed the face of things, or perhaps restored them to their primitive meanings. And the scene they traversed—one of those little untended woods that still, in America, fringe the tawdry skirts of civilization—acquired, as a background to Winterman, the hush of a spot aware of transcendent visitings. Did he talk, or did he make Bernald talk? The young man never knew. He recalled only a sense of lightness and liberation, as if the hard walls of individuality had melted, and he were merged in the poet's deeper interfusion, yet without losing the least sharp edge of self.

This general impression resolved itself afterward into the sense of Winterman's wide elemental range. His thought encircled things like the horizon at sea. He didn't, as it happened, touch on lofty themes— Bernald was gleefully aware that, to Howland Wade, their talk would hardly have been talk at all—but Winterman's mind, applied to lowly topics, was like a powerful lens that brought out microscopic delicacies and differences.

The lack of Sunday trains kept Doctor Bob for two days on the scene of his surgical duties, and during those two days Bernald seized every moment of communion with his friend's guest. Winterman, as Wade had said, was reticent as to his personal affairs, or rather as to the practical and material conditions to which the term is generally applied. But it was evident that, in Winterman's case, the usual classification must be reversed, and that the discussion of ideas carried one much farther into his intimacy than any specific acquaintance with the incidents of his life.

"That's exactly what Howland Wade and his tribe have never understood about Pellerin: that it's much less important to know how, or even why, he disapp—"

Bernald pulled himself up with a jerk, and turned to look full at his companion. It was late on the Monday evening, and the two men, after an hour's chat on the verandah to the tune of Mrs. Wade's knitting-needles, had bidden their hostess goodnight and strolled back to the bungalow together.

"Come and have a pipe before you turn in," Winterman had said; and they had sat on together till midnight, with the door of the bungalow open on a heaving moonlit bay, and summer insects bumping against the chimney of the lamp. Winterman had just bent down to re-fill his pipe from the jar on the table, and Bernald, jerking about to catch him in the yellow circle of lamplight, sat speechless, staring at a fact that seemed suddenly to have substituted itself for Winterman's face, or rather to have taken on its features.

"No, they never saw that Pellerin's ideas *were* Pellerin. . . . ." He continued to stare at Winterman. "Just as this man's ideas are—why, *are* Pellerin!"

The thought uttered itself in a kind of inner shout, and Bernald started upright with the violent impact of his conclusion. Again and again in the last forty-eight hours he had exclaimed to himself: "This is as good as Pellerin." Why hadn't he said till now: "This *is* Pellerin"? . . . . . Surprising as the answer was, he had no choice but to take it. He hadn't said so simply because Winterman was *better than Pellerin*—that there was so much more of him, so to speak. Yes; but—it came to Bernald in a flash—wouldn't there by this time have been any amount more of Pellerin? . . . . . The young man felt actually dizzy with the thought. That was it—there was the solution of the haunting problem! This man was Pellerin, and more than Pellerin! It was so fantastic and yet so unanswerable that he burst into a sudden startled laugh.

Winterman, at the same moment, brought his palm down with a sudden crash on the pile of manuscript covering the desk.

"What's the matter?" Bernald gasped.

"My match wasn't out. In another minute the destruction of the library of Alexandria would have been a trifle compared to what you'd have seen." Winterman, with his large deep laugh, shook out the smouldering sheets. "And I should have been a pensioner on Doctor Bob the Lord knows how much longer!"

Bernald pulled himself together. "You've really got going again? The thing's actually getting into shape?"

"This particular thing *is* in shape. I drove at it hard all last week, thinking our friend's brother would be down on Sunday, and might look it over."

Bernald had to repress the tendency to another wild laugh.

"Howland—you meant to show *Howland* what you've done?"

Winterman, looming against the moonlight, slowly turned a dusky shaggy head toward him.

"Isn't it a good thing to do?"

Bernald wavered, torn between loyalty to his friends and the grotesqueness of answering in the affirmative. After all, it was none of his business to furnish Winterman with an estimate of Howland Wade.

"Well, you see, you've never told me what your line *is*," he answered, temporising.

"No, because nobody's ever told *me*. It's exactly what I want to find out," said the other genially.

"And you expect Wade—?"

"Why, I gathered from our good doctor that it's his trade. Doesn't he explain—interpret?"

"In his own domain—which is Pellerinism."

Winterman gazed out musingly upon the moon-touched dusk of waters. "And what *is* Pellerinism?" he asked.

Bernald sprang to his feet with a cry. "Ah, I don't know—but you're Pellerin!"

They stood for a minute facing each other, among the uncertain swaying shadows of the room, with the sea breathing through it as something immense and inarticulate breathed through young Bernald's thoughts; then Winterman threw up his arms with a humorous gesture.

"Don't shoot!" he said.

Dawn found them there, and the risen sun laid its beams on the rough floor of the bungalow, before either of the men was conscious of the passage of time. Bernald, vaguely trying to define his own state in retrospect, could only phrase it: "I floated..... floated....."

The gist of fact at the core of the extraordinary experience was simply that John Pellerin, twenty-five years earlier, had voluntarily disappeared, causing the rumour of his death to be reported to an inattentive world; and that now he had come back to see what that world had made of him.

"You'll hardly believe it of me; I hardly believe it of myself; but I went away in a rage of disappointment, of wounded pride—no, vanity! I don't know which cut deepest—the sneers or the silence—but between them, there wasn't an inch of me that wasn't raw. I had just the one thing in me: the message, the cry, the revelation. But nobody saw and nobody listened. Nobody wanted what I had to give. I was like a poor devil of a tramp looking for shelter on a bitter night, in a town with every door bolted and all the windows dark. And suddenly I felt that the easiest thing would be to lie down and go to sleep in the snow. Perhaps I'd a vague notion that if they found me there at daylight, frozen stiff, the pathetic spectacle might produce a reaction, a feeling of remorse..... So I took care to be found!

"Well, a good many thousand people die every day on the face of the globe; and I soon discovered that I was simply one of the thousands; and when I made that discovery I really died—and stayed dead a year or two.....When I came to life again I was off on the underside of the world, in regions unaware of what we know as 'the public.' Have you any notion how it shifts the point of view to wake under new constellations? I advise any who's been in love with a woman under Cassiopeia to go and think about her under the Southern Cross.. ... It's the only way to tell the pivotal truths from the others..... I didn't believe in my theory any less—there was my triumph and my vindication! It held out, resisted, measured itself with the stars. But I didn't care a snap of my finger whether anybody else believed in it, or even knew it had been formulated.

"It escaped out of my books—my poor still-born books—like Psyche from the chrysalis and soared away into the blue, and lived there. I knew then how it frees an idea to be ignored; how apprehension circumscribes and deforms it..... Once I'd learned that, it was easy enough to turn to and shift for myself. I was sure now that my idea would live: the good ones are self-supporting. I had to learn to be so; and I tried my hand at a number of things ... adventurous, menial, commercial.. . . . It's not a bad thing for a man to have to live his life—and we nearly all manage to dodge it. Our first round with the Sphinx may strike something out of us—a book or a picture or a symphony; and we're amazed at our feat, and go on letting that first work breed others, as some animal forms reproduce each other without renewed fertilization. So there we are, committed to our first guess at the riddle; and our works look as like as successive impressions of the same plate, each with the lines a little fainter; whereas they ought to be—if we touch earth between times—as different from each other as those other creatures—jellyfish, aren't they, of a kind?—where successive generations produce new forms, and it takes a zoologist to see the hidden likeness.. . . .

"Well, I proved my first guess, off there in the wilds, and it lived, and grew, and took care of itself. And I said 'Someday it will make itself heard; but by that time my atoms will have waltzed into a new pattern.' Then, in Cashmere one day, I met a fellow in a caravan, with a dog-eared book in his pocket. He said he never stirred without it—wanted to know where I'd been, never to have heard of it. It was *my guess*—in its twentieth edition! . . . . . The globe spun round at that, and all of a sudden I was under the old stars. That's the way it happens when the ballast of vanity shifts! I'd lived a third of a life out there, unconscious of human opinion—because I supposed it was unconscious of *me*. But now—now! Oh, it was different. I wanted to know what they said.. . . . Not exactly that, either: I wanted to know *what I'd made them say*. There's a difference. ... And here I am," said John Pellerin, with a pull at his pipe.

So much Bernald retained of his companion's actual narrative; the rest was swept away under the tide of wonder that rose and submerged him as Pellerin—at some indefinitely later stage of their talk—picked up his manuscript and began to read. Bernald sat opposite, his elbows propped on the table, his eyes fixed on the swaying waters outside, from which the moon gradually faded, leaving them to make a denser blackness in the night. As Pellerin read, this density of blackness—which never for a moment seemed inert or unalive—was attenuated by imperceptible degrees, till a greyish pallor replaced it; then the pallor breathed and brightened, and suddenly dawn was on the sea.

Something of the same nature went on in the young man's mind while he watched and listened. He was conscious of a gradually withdrawing light, of an interval of obscurity full of the stir of invisible forces, and then of the victorious flush of day. And as the light rose, he saw how far he had travelled and what wonders the night had prepared. Pellerin had been right in saying that his first idea had survived, had borne the test of time; but he had given his hearer no hint of the extent to which it had been enlarged and modified, of the fresh implications it now unfolded. In a brief flash of retrospection Bernald saw the earlier books dwindle and fall into their place as mere precursors of this fuller revelation; then, with a leap of helpless rage, he pictured Howland Wade's pink hands on the new treasure, and his prophetic feet upon the lecture platform.

5

"It won't do—oh, he let him down as gently as possible; but it appears it simply won't do."

Doctor Bob imparted the ineluctable fact to Bernald while the two men, accidentally meeting at their club a few nights later, sat together over the dinner they had immediately agreed to consume in company.

Bernald had left Portchester the morning after his strange discovery, and he and Bob Wade had not seen each other since. And now Bernald, moved by an irresistible instinct of postponement, had waited for his companion to bring up Winterman's name, and had even executed several conversational diversions in the hope of delaying its mention. For how could one talk of Winterman with the thought of Pellerin swelling one's breast?

"Yes; the very day Howland got back from Kenosha I brought the manuscript to town, and got him to read it. And yesterday evening I nailed him, and dragged an answer out of him."

"Then Howland hasn't seen Winterman yet?"

"No. He said: 'Before you let him loose on me I'll go over the stuff, and see if it's at all worthwhile.'"

Bernald drew a freer breath. "And he found it wasn't?"

"Between ourselves, he found it was of no account at all. Queer, isn't it, when the *man*. . . . but of course literature's another proposition. Howland says it's one of the cases where an idea might seem original and striking if one didn't happen to be able to trace its descent. And this is straight out of bosh—by Pellerin. . . . . Yes: Pellerin. It seems that everything in the article that isn't pure nonsense is just Pellerinism. Howland thinks poor Winterman must have been tremendously struck by Pellerin's writings, and have lived too much out of the world to know that they've become the text-books of modern thought. Otherwise, of course, he'd have taken more trouble to disguise his plagiarisms."

"I see," Bernald mused. "Yet you say there *is* an original element?"

"Yes; but unluckily it's no good."

"It's not—conceivably—in any sense a development of Pellerin's idea: a logical step farther?"

"*Logical?* Howland says it's twaddle at white heat."

Bernald sat silent, divided between the fierce satisfaction of seeing the Interpreter rush upon his fate, and the despair of knowing that the state of mind he represented was indestructible. Then both emotions were swept away on a wave of pure joy, as he reflected that now, at last, Howland Wade had given him back John Pellerin.

The possession was one he did not mean to part with lightly; and the dread of its being torn from him constrained him to extraordinary precautions.

"You've told Winterman, I suppose? How did he take it?"

"Why, unexpectedly, as he does most things. You can never tell which way he'll jump. I thought he'd take a high tone, or else laugh it off; but he did neither. He seemed awfully cast down. I wished myself well out of the job when I saw how cut up he was." Bernald thrilled at the words. Pellerin had shared his pang, then—the "old woe of the world" at the perpetuity of human dullness!

"But what did he say to the charge of plagiarism—if you made it?"

"Oh, I told him straight out what Howland said. I thought it fairer. And his answer to that was the rummest part of all."

"What was it?" Bernald questioned, with a tremor.

"He said: 'That's queer, for I've never read Pellerin.'"

Bernald drew a deep breath of ecstasy. "Well—and I suppose you believed him?"

"I believed him, because I know him. But the public won't—the critics won't. And if it's a pure coincidence it's just as bad for him as if it were a straight steal—isn't it?"

Bernald sighed his acquiescence.

"It bothers me awfully," Wade continued, knitting his kindly brows, "because I could see what a blow it was to him. He's got to earn his living, and I don't suppose he knows how to do anything else. At his age it's hard to start fresh. I put that to Howland—asked him if there wasn't a chance he might do better if he only had a little encouragement. I can't help feeling he's got the essential thing in him. But of course I'm no judge when it comes to books. And Howland says it would be cruel to give him any hope." Wade paused, turned his wineglass about under a meditative stare, and then leaned across the table toward Bernald. "Look here—do you know what I've proposed to Winterman? That he should come to town with me tomorrow and go in the evening to hear Howland lecture to the Uplift Club. They're to meet at Mrs. Beecher Bain's, and Howland is to repeat the lecture that he gave the other day before the Pellerin Society at Kenosha.

"It will give Winterman a chance to get some notion of what Pellerin *was:* he'll get it much straighter from Howland than if he tried to plough through Pellerin's books. And then afterward—as if accidentally—I thought I might bring him and Howland together. If Howland could only see him and hear him talk, there's no knowing what might come of it. He couldn't help feeling the man's force, as we do; and he might give him a pointer—tell him what line to take. Anyhow, it would please Winterman, and take the edge off his disappointment. I saw that as soon as I proposed it."

"Someone who's never heard of Pellerin?"

Mrs. Beecher Bain, large, smiling, diffuse, reached out parenthetically from the incoming throng on her threshold to waylay Bernald with the question as he was about to move past her in the wake of his companion.

"Oh, keep straight on, Mr. Winterman!" she interrupted herself to call after the latter. "Into the back drawing-room, please! And remember, you're to sit next to me—in the corner on the left, close under the platform."

She renewed her interrogative clutch on Bernald's sleeve. "Most curious! Doctor Wade has been telling me all about him—how remarkable you all think him. And it's actually true that he's never heard of Pellerin? Of course as soon as Doctor Wade told me *that*, I said 'Bring him!' It will be so extraordinarily interesting to watch the first impression.—Yes, do follow him, dear Mr. Bernald, and be sure that you and he secure the seats next to me. Of course Alice Fosdick insists on being with us. She was wild with excitement when I told her she was to meet someone who'd never heard of Pellerin!"

On the indulgent lips of Mrs. Beecher Bain conjecture speedily passed into affirmation; and as Bernald's companion, broad and shaggy in his visibly new evening clothes, moved down the length of the crowded rooms, he was already, to the ladies drawing aside their skirts to let him pass, the interesting Huron of the fable.

How far he was aware of the character ascribed to him it was impossible for Bernald to discover. He was as unconscious as a tree or a cloud, and his observer had never known anyone so alive to human contacts and yet so secure from them. But the scene was playing such a lively tune on Bernald's own sensibilities that for the moment he could not adjust himself to the probable effect it produced on his companion. The young man, of late, had made but rare appearances in the group of which Mrs. Beecher Bain was one of the most indefatigable hostesses, and the Uplift Club the chief medium of expression. To a critic, obliged by his trade to cultivate convictions, it was the essence of luxury to leave them at home in his hours of ease; and Bernald gave his preference to circles in which less finality of judgment prevailed, and it was consequently less embarrassing to be caught without an opinion.

But in his fresher days he had known the spell of the Uplift Club and the thrill of moving among the Emancipated; and he felt an odd sense of rejuvenation as he looked at the rows of faces packed about the embowered platform from which Howland Wade was presently to hand down the eternal verities. Many of these countenances belonged to the old days, when the gospel of Pellerin was unknown, and it required considerable intellectual courage to avow one's acceptance of the very doctrines he had since demolished. The latter moral revolution seemed to have been accepted as submissively as a change in hairdressing; and it even struck Bernald that, in the case of many of the assembled ladies, their convictions were rather newer than their clothes.

One of the most interesting examples of this facility of adaptation was actually, in the person of Miss Alice Fosdick, brushing his elbow with exotic amulets, and enveloping him in Arabian odours, as she leaned forward to murmur her sympathetic sense of the situation. Miss Fosdick, who was one of the most advanced exponents of Pellerinism, had large eyes and a plaintive mouth, and Bernald had always fancied that she might have been pretty if she had not been perpetually explaining things.

"Yes, I know—Isabella Bain told me all about him. (He can't hear us, can he?) And I wonder if you realise how remarkably interesting it is that we should have such an opportunity *now*—I mean the opportunity to see the impression of Pellerinism on a perfectly fresh mind. (You must introduce him as soon as the lecture's over.) I explained that to Isabella as soon as she showed me Doctor Wade's note.

Of course you see why, don't you?" Bernald made a faint motion of acquiescence, which she instantly swept aside. "At least I think I can *make you see why*. (If you're sure he can't hear?) Why, it's just this—Pellerinism is in danger of becoming a truism. Oh, it's an awful thing to say! But then I'm not afraid of saying awful things! I rather believe it's my mission. What I mean is, that we're getting into the way of taking Pellerin for granted—as we do the air we breathe. We don't sufficiently lead our *conscious life* in him—we're gradually letting him become subliminal." She swayed closer to the young man, and he saw that she was making a graceful attempt to throw her explanatory net over his companion, who, evading Mrs. Bain's hospitable signal, had cautiously wedged himself into a seat between Bernald and the wall.

"*Did* you hear what I was saying, Mr. Winterman? (Yes, I know who you are, of course!) Oh, well, I don't really mind if you did. I was talking about you—about you and Pellerin. I was explaining to Mr. Bernald that what we need at this very minute is a Pellerin revival; and we need someone like you—to whom his message comes as a wonderful new interpretation of life—to lead the revival, and rouse us out of our apathy. ...

"You see," she went on winningly, "it's not only the big public that needs it (of course *their* Pellerin isn't ours!) It's we, his disciples, his interpreters, who discovered him and gave him to the world—we, the Chosen People, the Custodians of the Sacred Books, as Howland Wade calls us—it's *we*, who are in perpetual danger of sinking back into the old stagnant ideals, and practising the Seven Deadly Virtues; it's *we* who need to count our mercies, and realize anew what he's done for us, and what we ought to do for him! And it's for that reason that I urged Mr. Wade to speak here, in the very inner sanctuary of Pellerinism, exactly as he would speak to the uninitiated—to repeat, simply, his Kenosha lecture, 'What Pellerinism means'; and we ought all, I think, to listen to him with the hearts of little children—just as *you* will, Mr. Winterman—as if he were telling us new things, and we—"

"Alice, *dear*—" Mrs. Bain murmured with a deprecating gesture; and Howland Wade, emerging between the palms, took the centre of the platform.

A pang of commiseration shot through Bernald as he saw him there, so innocent and so exposed. His plump pulpy body, which made his evening dress fall into intimate and wrapper-like folds, was like a wide surface spread to the shafts of irony; and the mild ripples of his voice seemed to enlarge the vulnerable area as he leaned forward, poised on confidential finger-tips, to say persuasively: "Let me try to tell you what Pellerinism means."

Bernald moved restlessly in his seat. He had the obscure sense of being a party to something not wholly honourable. He ought not to have come; he ought not to have let his companion come. Yet how could he have done otherwise? John Pellerin's secret was his own. As long as he chose to remain John Winterman it was no one's business to gainsay him; and Bernald's scruples were really justifiable only in respect of his own presence on the scene. But even in this connection he ceased to feel them as soon as Howland Wade began to speak.

6

It had been arranged that Pellerin, after the meeting of the Uplift Club, should join Bernald at his rooms and spend the night there, instead of returning to Portchester. The plan had been eagerly elaborated by the young man, but he had been unprepared for the alacrity with which his wonderful friend accepted it. He was beginning to see that it was a part of Pellerin's wonderfulness to fall in, quite simply and naturally, with any arrangements made for his convenience, or tending to promote the convenience of others. Bernald felt that his extreme docility in such matters was proportioned to the force of resistance which, for nearly half a life-time, had kept him, with his back to the wall, fighting alone against the powers of darkness. In such a scale of values how little the small daily alternatives must weigh!

At the close of Howland Wade's discourse, Bernald, charged with his prodigious secret, had felt the need to escape for an instant from the liberated rush of talk. The interest of watching Pellerin was so perilously great that the watcher felt it might, at any moment, betray him. He lingered in the crowded drawing-room long enough to see his friend enclosed in a mounting tide, above which Mrs. Beecher Bain and Miss Fosdick actively waved their conversational tridents; then he took refuge, at the back of the house, in a small dim library where, in his younger days, he had discussed personal immortality and the problem of consciousness with beautiful girls whose names he could not remember.

In this retreat he surprised Mr. Beecher Bain, a quiet man with a mild brow, who was smoking a surreptitious cigar over the last number of the *Strand*. Mr. Bain, at Bernald's approach, dissembled the *Strand* under a copy of the *Hibbert Journal*, but tendered his cigar-case with the remark that stocks were heavy again; and Bernald blissfully abandoned himself to this unexpected contact with reality.

On his return to the drawing-room he found that the tide had set toward the supper-table, and when it finally carried him thither it was to land him in the welcoming arms of Bob Wade.

"Hullo, old man! Where have you been all this time?—Winterman? Oh, *he's* talking to Howland: yes, I managed it finally. I believe Mrs. Bain has steered them into the library, so that they shan't be disturbed. I gave her an idea of the situation, and she was awfully kind. We'd better leave them alone, don't you think? I'm trying to get a croquette for Miss Fosdick."

Bernald's secret leapt in his bosom, and he devoted himself to the task of distributing sandwiches and champagne while his pulses danced to the tune of the cosmic laughter. The vision of Pellerin and his Interpreter, face to face at last, had a Cyclopean grandeur that dwarfed all other comedy. "And I shall hear of it presently; in an hour or two he'll be telling me about it. And that hour will be all mine—mine and his!" The dizziness of the thought made it difficult for Bernald to preserve the balance of the supper-plates he was distributing. Life had for him at that moment the completeness which seems to defy disintegration.

The throng in the dining-room was thickening, and Bernald's efforts as purveyor were interrupted by frequent appeals, from ladies who had reached repleteness, that he should sit down a moment and tell them all about his interesting friend. Winterman's fame, trumpeted abroad by Miss Fosdick, had reached the four corners of the Uplift Club, and Bernald found himself fabricating *de toutes pieces* a Winterman legend which should in some degree respond to the Club's demand for the human document. When at length he had acquitted himself of this obligation, and was free to work his way back through the lessening groups into the drawing-room, he was at last rewarded by a glimpse of his friend, who, still densely encompassed, towered in the centre of the room in all his Sovran ugliness.

Their eyes met across the crowd; but Bernald gathered only perplexity from the encounter. What were Pellerin's eyes saying to him? What orders, what confidences, what indefinable apprehension did their long look impart? The young man was still trying to decipher their complex message when he felt a tap on the arm, and turned to encounter the rueful gaze of Bob Wade, whose meaning lay clearly enough on the surface of his good blue stare.

"Well, it won't work—it won't work," the doctor groaned.

"What won't?"

"I mean with Howland. Winterman won't. Howland doesn't take to him. Says he's crude—frightfully crude. And you know how Howland hates crudeness."

"Oh, I know," Bernald exulted. It was the word he had waited for—he saw it now! Once more he was lost in wonder at Howland's miraculous faculty for always, as the naturalists said, being true to type.

"So I'm afraid it's all up with his chance of writing. At least *I* can do no more," said Wade, discouraged.

Bernald pressed him for farther details. "Does Winterman seem to mind much? Did you hear his version?"

"His version?"

"I mean what he said to Howland."

"Why no. What the deuce was there for him to say?"

"What indeed? I think I'll take him home," said Bernald gaily.

He turned away to join the circle from which, a few minutes before, Pellerin's eyes had vainly and enigmatically signalled to him; but the circle had dispersed, and Pellerin himself was not in sight.

Bernald, looking about him, saw that during his brief aside with Wade the party had passed into the final phase of dissolution. People still delayed, in diminishing groups, but the current had set toward the doors, and every moment or two it bore away a few more lingerers. Bernald, from his post, commanded the clearing perspective of the two drawing-rooms, and a rapid survey of their length sufficed to assure him that Pellerin was not in either. Taking leave of Wade, the young man made his way back to the drawing-room, where only a few hardened feasters remained, and then passed on to the library which had been the scene of the late momentous colloquy. But the library too was empty, and drifting back uncertainly to the inner drawing-room Bernald found Mrs. Beecher Bain domestically putting out the wax candles on the mantel-piece.

"Dear Mr. Bernald! Do sit down and have a little chat. What a wonderful privilege it has been! I don't know when I've had such an intense impression."

She made way for him, hospitably, in a corner of the sofa to which she had sunk; and he echoed her vaguely: "You *were* impressed, then?"

"I can't express to you how it affected me! As Alice said, it was a resurrection—it was as if John Pellerin were actually here in the room with us!"

321

Bernald turned on her with a half-audible gasp. "You felt that, dear Mrs. Bain?"

"We all felt it—every one of us! I don't wonder the Greeks—it *was* the Greeks?—regarded eloquence as a supernatural power. As Alice says, when one looked at Howland Wade one understood what they meant by the Afflatus."

Bernald rose and held out his hand. "Oh, I see—it was Howland who made you feel as if Pellerin were in the room? And he made Miss Fosdick feel so too?"

"Why, of course. But why are you rushing off?"

"Because I must hunt up my friend, who's not used to such late hours."

"Your friend?" Mrs. Bain had to collect her thoughts. "Oh, Mr. Winterman, you mean? But he's gone already."

"Gone?" Bernald exclaimed, with an odd twinge of foreboding. Remembering Pellerin's signal across the crowd, he reproached himself for not having answered it more promptly. Yet it was certainly strange that his friend should have left the house without him.

"Are you quite sure?" he asked, with a startled glance at the clock.

"Oh, perfectly. He went half an hour ago. But you needn't hurry home on his account, for Alice Fosdick carried him off with her. I saw them leave together."

"Carried him off? She took him home with her, you mean?"

"Yes. You know what strange hours she keeps. She told me she was going to give him a Welsh rabbit, and explain Pellerinism to him."

"Oh, *if* she's going to explain—" Bernald murmured. But his amazement at the news struggled with a confused impatience to reach his rooms in time to be there for his friend's arrival. There could be no stranger spectacle beneath the stars than that of John Pellerin carried off by Miss Fosdick, and listening, in the small hours, to her elucidation of his doctrines; but Bernald knew enough of his sex to be aware that such an experiment may present a less humorous side to its subject than to an impartial observer. Even the Uplift Club and its connotations might benefit by the attraction of the unknown; and it was conceivable that to a traveller from Mesopotamia Miss Fosdick might present elements of interest which she had lost for the frequenters of Fifth Avenue. There was, at any rate, no denying that the affair had become unexpectedly complex, and that its farther development promised to be rich in comedy.

In the charmed contemplation of these possibilities Bernald sat over his fire, listening for Pellerin's ring. He had arranged his modest quarters with the reverent care of a celebrant awaiting the descent of his deity. He guessed Pellerin to be unconscious of visual detail, but sensitive to the happy blending of sensuous impressions: to the intimate spell of lamplight on books, and of a deep chair placed where one could watch the fire. The chair was there, and Bernald, facing it across the hearth, already saw it filled by Pellerin's lounging figure. The autumn dawn came late, and even now they had before them the promise of some untroubled hours.

Bernald, sitting there alone in the warm stillness of his room, and in the profounder hush of his expectancy, was conscious of gathering up all his sensibilities and perceptions into one exquisitely-adjusted instrument of notation. Until now he had tasted Pellerin's society only in unpremeditated snatches, and had always left him with a sense, on his own part, of waste and shortcoming. Now, in the lull of this dedicated hour, he felt that he should miss nothing, and forget nothing, of the initiation that awaited him. And catching sight of Pellerin's pipe, he rose and laid it carefully on a table by the armchair.

"No. I've never had any news of him," Bernald heard himself repeating. He spoke in a low tone, and with the automatic utterance that alone made it possible to say the words.

They were addressed to Miss Fosdick, into whose neighbourhood chance had thrown him at a dinner, a year or so later than their encounter at the Uplift Club. Hitherto he had successfully, and intentionally, avoided Miss Fosdick, not from any animosity toward that unconscious instrument of fate, but from an intense reluctance to pronounce the words which he knew he should have to speak if they met.

Now, as it turned out, his chief surprise was that she should wait so long to make him speak them. All through the dinner she had swept him along on a rapid current of talk which showed no tendency to linger or turn back upon the past. At first he ascribed her reserve to a sense of delicacy with which he reproached himself for not having previously credited her; then he saw that she had been carried so far beyond the point at which they had last faced each other, that it was by the merest hazard of associated ideas that she was now finally borne back to it. For it appeared that the very next evening, at Mrs. Beecher Bain's, a Hindu *Mahatma* was to lecture to the Uplift Club on the Limits of the Subliminal; and it was owing to no less a person than Howland Wade that this exceptional privilege had been obtained.

"Of course Howland's known all over the world as the interpreter of Pellerinism, and the Aga Gautch, who had absolutely declined to speak anywhere in public, wrote to Isabella that he could not refuse anything that Mr. Wade asked. Did you know that Howland's lecture, 'What Pellerinism Means,' has been translated into twenty-two languages, and gone into a fifth edition in Icelandic? Why, that reminds me," Miss Fosdick broke off—"I've never heard what became of your queer friend—what was his name?—whom you and Bob Wade accused me of spiriting away after that very lecture. And I've never seen *you* since you rushed into the house the next morning, and dragged me out of bed to know what I'd done with him!"

With a sharp effort Bernald gathered himself together to have it out. "Well, what *did* you do with him?" he retorted.

She laughed her appreciation of his humour. "Just what I told you, of course. I said goodbye to him on Isabella's doorstep."

Bernald looked at her. "It's really true, then, that he didn't go home with you?"

She bantered back: "Have you suspected me, all this time, of hiding his remains in the cellar?" And with a droop of her fine lids she added: "I wish he *had* come home with me, for he was rather interesting, and there were things I think I could have explained to him."

Bernald helped himself to a nectarine, and Miss Fosdick continued on a note of amused curiosity: "So you've really never had any news of him since that night?"

"No—I've never had any news of him."

"Not the least little message?"

"Not the least little message."

"Or a rumour or report of any kind?"

"Or a rumour or report of any kind."

Miss Fosdick's interest seemed to be revived by the strangeness of the case. "It's rather creepy, isn't it? What *could* have happened? You don't suppose he could have been waylaid and murdered?" she asked with brightening eyes.

Bernald shook his head serenely. "No. I'm sure he's safe—quite safe."

"But if you're sure, you must know something."

"No. I know nothing," he repeated.

She scanned him incredulously. "But what's your theory—for you must have a theory? What in the world can have become of him?"

Bernald returned her look and hesitated. "Do you happen to remember the last thing he said to you—the very last, on the doorstep, when he left you?"

"The last thing?" She poised her fork above the peach on her plate. "I don't think he said anything. Oh, yes—when I reminded him that he'd solemnly promised to come back with me and have a little talk he said he couldn't because he was going home."

"Well, then, I suppose," said Bernald, "he went home."

She glanced at him as if suspecting a trap. "Dear me, how flat! I always inclined to a mysterious murder. But of course you know more of him than you say."

She began to cut her peach, but paused above a lifted bit to ask, with a renewal of animation in her expressive eyes: "By the way, had you heard that Howland Wade has been gradually getting farther and farther away from Pellerinism? It seems he's begun to feel that there's a Positivist element in it which is narrowing to anyone who has gone at all deeply into the Wisdom of the East. He was intensely interesting about it the other day, and of course I *do* see what he feels. . . . . Oh, it's too long to tell you now; but if you could manage to come in to tea some afternoon soon—any day but Wednesday—I should so like to explain—"

The Pretext

1

Mrs. Ransom, when the front door had closed on her visitor, passed with a spring from the drawing-room to the narrow hall, and thence up the narrow stairs to her bedroom. Though slender, and still light of foot, she did not always move so quickly: hitherto, in her life, there had not been much to hurry for, save the recurring domestic tasks that compel haste without fostering elasticity; but some impetus of youth revived, communicated to her by her talk with Guy Dawnish, now found expression in her girlish flight upstairs, her girlish impatience to bolt herself into her room with her throbs and her blushes.

Her blushes? Was she really blushing?

She approached the cramped eagle-topped mirror above her plain prim dressing-table: just such a meagre concession to the weakness of the flesh as every old-fashioned house in Wentworth counted among its relics. The face reflected in this unflattering surface—for even the mirrors of Wentworth erred on the side of depreciation—did not seem, at first sight, a suitable theatre for the display of the tenderer emotions, and its owner blushed more deeply as the fact was forced upon her.

Her fair hair had grown too thin—it no longer quite hid the blue veins in her candid forehead—a forehead that one seemed to see turned toward professorial desks, in large bare halls where a snowy winter light fell uncompromisingly on rows of "thoughtful women." Her mouth was thin, too, and a little strained; her lips were too pale; and there were lines in the corners of her eyes. It was a face which had grown middle-aged while it waited for the joys of youth.

Well—but if she could still blush? Instinctively she drew back a little, so that her scrutiny became less microscopic, and the pretty lingering pink threw a veil over her pallor, the hollows in her temples, the faint wrinkles of inexperience about her lips and eyes. How a little colour helped! It made her eyes so deep and shining. She saw now why bad women rouged. . . . Her redness deepened at the thought.

But suddenly she noticed for the first time that the collar of her dress was cut too low. It showed the shrunken lines of the throat. She rummaged feverishly in a tidy scentless drawer, and snatching out a bit of black velvet, bound it about her neck. Yes—that was better. It gave her the relief she needed. Relief—contrast—that was it! She had never had any, either in her appearance or in her setting. She was as flat as the pattern of the wallpaper—and so was her life. And all the people about her had the same look. Wentworth was the kind of place where husbands and wives gradually grew to resemble each other—one or two of her friends, she remembered, had told her lately that she and Ransom were beginning to look alike. . . . .

But why had she always, so tamely, allowed her aspect to conform to her situation? Perhaps a gayer exterior would have provoked a brighter fate. Even now—she turned back to the glass, loosened the tight strands of hair above her brow, ran the fine end of the comb under them with a rapid frizzing motion, and then disposed them, more lightly and amply, above her eager face. Yes—it was really better; it made a difference. She smiled at herself with a timid *coquetry*, and her lips seemed rosier as she smiled. Then she laid down the comb and the smile faded. It made a difference, certainly—but was it right to try to make one's hair look thicker and wavier than it really was? Between that and rouging the ethical line seemed almost impalpable, and the spectre of her rigid New England ancestry rose reprovingly before her. She was sure that none of her grandmothers had ever simulated a curl or encouraged a blush.

A blush, indeed! What had any of them ever had to blush for in all their frozen lives? And what, in Heaven's name, had she? She sat down in the stiff mahogany rocking-chair beside her work-table and tried to collect herself. From childhood she had been taught to "collect herself"—but never before had her small sensations and aspirations been so widely scattered, diffused over so vague and uncharted an expanse. Hitherto they had lain in neatly sorted and easily accessible bundles on the high shelves of a perfectly ordered moral consciousness. And now—now that for the first time they *needed* collecting—now that the little winged and scattered bits of self were dancing madly down the vagrant winds of fancy, she knew no spell to call them to the fold again. The best way, no doubt—if only her bewilderment permitted—was to go back to the beginning—the beginning, at least, of today's visit—to recapitulate, word for word and look for look. . . .

She clasped her hands on the arms of the chair, checked its swaying with a firm thrust of her foot, and fixed her eyes upon the inward vision. . . .

To begin with, what had made today's visit so different from the others? It became suddenly vivid to her that there had been many, almost daily, others, since Guy Dawnish's coming to Wentworth. Even the previous winter—the winter of his arrival from England—his visits had been numerous enough to make Wentworth aware that—very naturally—Mrs. Ransom was "looking after" the stray young Englishman committed to her husband's care by an eminent Q. C. whom the Ransoms had known on one of their brief London visits, and with whom Ransom had since maintained professional relations. All this was in the natural order of things, as sanctioned by the social code of Wentworth.

Everyone was kind to Guy Dawnish—some rather importunately so, as Margaret Ransom had smiled to observe—but it was recognized as fitting that she should be kindest, since he was in a sense her property, since his people in England, by profusely acknowledging her kindness, had given it the domestic sanction without which, to Wentworth, any social relation between the sexes remained unhallowed and to be viewed askance. Yes! And even this second winter, when the visits had become so much more frequent, so admitted a part of the day's routine, there had not been, from anyone, a hint of surprise or of conjecture. . . . .

Mrs. Ransom smiled with a faint bitterness. She was protected by her age, no doubt—her age and her past, and the image her mirror gave back to her. . . .

Her door-handle turned suddenly, and the bolt's resistance was met by an impatient knock.

"Margaret!"

She started up, her brightness fading, and unbolted the door to admit her husband.

"Why are you locked in? Why, you're not dressed yet!" he exclaimed.

It was possible for Ransom to reach his dressing-room by a slight circuit through the passage; but it was characteristic of the relentless domesticity of their relation that he chose, as a matter of course, the directer way through his wife's bedroom. She had never before been disturbed by this practice, which she accepted as inevitable, but had merely adapted her own habits to it, delaying her hasty toilet till he was safely in his room, or completing it before she heard his step on the stair; since a scrupulous traditional prudery had miraculously survived this massacre of all the privacies.

"Oh, I shan't dress this evening—I shall just have some tea in the library after you've gone," she answered absently. "Your things are laid out," she added, rousing herself.

He looked surprised. "The dinner's at seven. I suppose the speeches will begin at nine. I thought you were coming to hear them."

She wavered. "I don't know. I think not. Mrs. Sperry's ill, and I've no one else to go with."

He glanced at his watch. "Why not get hold of Dawnish? Wasn't he here just now? Why didn't you ask him?"

She turned toward her dressing-table, and straightened the comb and brush with a nervous hand. Her husband had given her, that morning, two tickets for the ladies' gallery in Hamblin Hall, where the great public dinner of the evening was to take place—a banquet offered by the faculty of Wentworth to visitors of academic eminence—and she had meant to ask Dawnish to go with her: it had seemed the most natural thing to do, till the end of his visit came, and then, after all, she had not spoken. . . .

"It's too late now," she murmured, bending over her pin cushion.

"Too late? Not if you telephone him."

Her husband came toward her, and she turned quickly to face him, lest he should suspect her of trying to avoid his eye. To what duplicity was she already committed!

Ransom laid a friendly hand on her arm: "Come along, Margaret. You know I speak for the bar." She was aware, in his voice, of a little note of surprise at his having to remind her of this.

"Oh, yes. I meant to go, of course—"

"Well, then—" He opened his dressing-room door, and caught a glimpse of the retreating house-maid's skirt. "Here's Maria now. Maria! Call up Mr. Dawnish—at Mrs. Creswell's, you know. Tell him Mrs. Ransom wants him to go with her to hear the speeches this evening—the *speeches*, you understand?—and he's to call for her at a quarter before nine."

Margaret heard the Irish "Yessir" on the stairs, and stood motionless, while her husband added loudly: "And bring me some towels when you come up." Then he turned back into his wife's room.

"Why, it would be a thousand pities for Guy to miss this. He's so interested in the way we do things over here—and I don't know that he's ever heard me speak in public." Again the slight note of fatuity! Was it possible that Ransom was a fatuous man?

He paused in front of her, his short-sighted unobservant glance concentrating itself unexpectedly on her face.

"You're not going like that, are you?" he asked, with glaring eye-glasses.

"Like what?" she faltered, lifting a conscious hand to the velvet at her throat.

"With your hair in such a fearful mess. Have you been shampooing it? You look like the Brant girl at the end of a tennis-match."

The Brant girl was their horror—the horror of all right-thinking Wentworth; a laced, whale-boned, frizzle-headed, high-heeled daughter of iniquity, who came—from New York, of course—on long, disturbing, tumultuous visits to a Wentworth aunt, working havoc among the freshmen, and leaving, when she departed, an angry wake of criticism that ruffled the social waters for weeks. *She*, too, had tried her hand at Guy—with ludicrous unsuccess. And now, to be compared to her—to be accused of looking "New Yorky!" Ah, there are times when husbands are obtuse; and Ransom, as he stood there, thick and yet juiceless, in his dry legal middle age, with his wiry dust-coloured beard, and his perpetual *pince-nez*, seemed to his wife a sudden embodiment of this traditional attribute.

Not that she had ever fancied herself, poor soul, a *"femme incomprise."* She had, on the contrary, prided herself on being understood by her husband, almost as much as on her own complete comprehension of him. Wentworth laid a good deal of stress on "motives"; and Margaret Ransom and her husband had dwelt in a complete community of motive. It had been the proudest day of her life when, without consulting her, he had refused an offer of partnership in an eminent New York firm because he preferred the distinction of practising in Wentworth, of being known as the legal representative of the University. Wentworth, in fact, had always been the bond between the two; they were united in their veneration for that estimable seat of learning, and in their modest yet vivid consciousness of possessing its tone.

The Wentworth "tone" is unmistakable: it permeates every part of the social economy, from the *coiffure* of the ladies to the preparation of the food. It has its sumptuary laws as well as its curriculum of learning. It sits in judgment not only on its own townsmen but on the rest of the world—enlightening, criticising, ostracizing a heedless universe—and non-conformity to Wentworth standards involves obliteration from Wentworth's consciousness.

In a world without traditions, without reverence, without stability, such little expiring centres of prejudice and precedent make an irresistible appeal to those instincts for which a democracy has neglected to provide. Wentworth, with its "tone," its backward references, its inflexible aversions and condemnations, its hard moral outline preserved intact against a whirling background of experiment, had been all the poetry and history of Margaret Ransom's life. Yes, what she had really esteemed in her husband was the fact of his being so intense an embodiment of Wentworth; so long and closely identified, for instance, with its legal affairs, that he was almost a part of its university existence, that of course, at a college banquet, he would inevitably speak for the bar!

It was wonderful of how much consequence all this had seemed till now. . . .

2

When, punctually at ten minutes to seven, her husband had emerged from the house, Margaret Ransom remained seated in her bedroom, addressing herself anew to the difficult process of self-collection. As an aid to this endeavour, she bent forward and looked out of the window, following Ransom's figure as it receded down the elm-shaded street. He moved almost alone between the prim flowerless grass-plots, the white porches, the protrusion of irrelevant shingled gables, which stamped the empty street as part of an American college town. She had always been proud of living in Hill Street, where the university people congregated, proud to associate her husband's retreating back, as he walked daily to his office, with backs literary and pedagogic, backs of which it was whispered, for the edification of duly-impressed visitors: "Wait till that old boy turns—that's so-and-so."

This had been her world, a world destitute of personal experience, but filled with a rich sense of privilege and distinction, of being not as those millions were who, denied the inestimable advantage of living at Wentworth, pursued elsewhere careers foredoomed to futility by that very fact.

And now—!

She rose and turned to her work-table where she had dropped, on entering, the handful of photographs that Guy Dawnish had left with her. While he sat so close, pointing out and explaining, she had hardly taken in the details; but now, on the full tones of his low young voice, they came back with redoubled distinctness. This was Guise Abbey, his uncle's place in Wiltshire, where, under his grandfather's rule, Guy's own boyhood had been spent: a long gabled Jacobean facade, many-chimneyed, ivy-draped, overhung (she felt sure) by the boughs of a venerable rookery.

And in this other picture—the walled garden at Guise—that was his uncle, Lord Askern, a hale gouty-looking figure, planted robustly on the terrace, a gun on his shoulder and a couple of setters at his feet. And here was the river below the park, with Guy "punting" a girl in a flapping hat—how Margaret hated the flap that hid the girl's face! And here was the tennis-court, with Guy among a jolly cross-legged group of youths in flannels, and pretty girls about the tea-table under the big lime: in the centre the curate handing bread and butter, and in the middle distance a footman approaching with more cups.

Margaret raised this picture closer to her eyes, puzzling, in the diminished light, over the face of the girl nearest to Guy Dawnish—bent above him in profile, while he laughingly lifted his head. No hat hid this profile, which stood out clearly against the foliage behind it.

"And who is that handsome girl?" Margaret had said, detaining the photograph as he pushed it aside, and struck by the fact that, of the whole group, he had left only this member unnamed.

"Oh, only Gwendolen Matcher—I've always known her—. Look at this: the alms-houses at Guise. Aren't they jolly?"

And then—without her having had the courage to ask if the girl in the punt were also Gwendolen Matcher—they passed on to pho-tographs of his rooms at Oxford, of a cousin's studio in London—one of Lord Askern's grandsons was "artistic"—of the rose-hung cottage in Wales to which, on the old Earl's death, his daughter-in-law, Guy's mother, had retired.

Every one of the photographs opened a window on the life Mar-garet had been trying to picture since she had known him—a life so rich, so romantic, so packed—in the mere casual vocabulary of daily life—with historic reference and poetic allusion, that she felt almost oppressed by this distant whiff of its air. The very words he used fasci-nated and bewildered her. He seemed to have been born into all sorts of connections, political, historical, official, that made the Ransom situation at Wentworth as featureless as the top shelf of a dark closet.

Someone in the family had "asked for the Chiltern Hundreds"—one uncle was an Elder Brother of the Trinity House—someone else was the Master of a College—someone was in command at Devonport—the Army, the Navy, the House of Commons, the House of Lords, the most venerable seats of learning, were all woven into the dense background of this young man's light unconscious talk. For the unconsciousness was unmistakable.

Margaret was not without experience of the transatlantic visitor who sounds loud names and evokes reverberating connections. The poetry of Guy Dawnish's situation lay in the fact that it was so completely a part of early associations and accepted facts. Life was like that in England—in Wentworth of course (where he had been sent, through his uncle's influence, for two years' training in the neighbouring electrical works at Smedden)—in Wentworth, though "immensely jolly," it was different. The fact that he was qualifying to be an electrical engineer—with the hope of a secretaryship at the London end of the great Smedden Company—that, at best, he was returning home to a life of industrial "grind," this fact, though avowedly a bore, did not disconnect him from that brilliant pinnacled past, that many-faceted life in which the brightest episodes of the whole body of English fiction seemed collectively reflected.

Of course he would have to work—younger sons' sons almost always had to—but his uncle Askern (like Wentworth) was "immensely jolly," and Guise always open to him, and his other uncle, the Master, a capital old boy too—and in town he could always put up with his clever aunt, Lady Caroline Duckett, who had made a "beastly marriage" and was horribly poor, but who knew everybody jolly and amusing, and had always been particularly kind to him.

It was not—and Margaret had not, even in her own thoughts, to defend herself from the imputation—it was not what Wentworth would have called the "material side" of her friend's situation that captivated her. She was austerely proof against such appeals: her enthusiasms were all of the imaginative order. What subjugated her was the unexampled prodigality with which he poured for her the same draught of tradition of which Wentworth held out its little teacupful. He besieged her with a million Wentworths in one—saying, as it were: "All these are mine for the asking—and I choose you instead!"

For this, she told herself somewhat dizzily, was what it came to—the summing-up toward which her conscientious efforts at self-collection had been gradually pushing her: with all this in reach, Guy

Dawnish was leaving Wentworth reluctantly.

"I *was* a bit lonely here at first—but *now!*" And again: "It will be jolly, of course, to see them all again—but there are some things one doesn't easily give up. . . ."

If he had known only Wentworth, it would have been wonderful enough that he should have chosen her out of all Wentworth—but to have known that other life, and to set her in the balance against it— poor Margaret Ransom, in whom, at the moment, nothing seemed of weight but her years! Ah, it might well produce, in nerves and brain, and poor unpractised pulses, a flushed tumult of sensation, the rush of a great wave of life, under which memory struggled in vain to reassert itself, to particularize again just what his last words—the very last—had been. . . .

When consciousness emerged, quivering, from this retrospective assault, it pushed Margaret Ransom—feeling herself a mere leaf in the blast—toward the writing-table from which her innocent and voluminous correspondence habitually flowed. She had a letter to write now—much shorter but more difficult than any she had ever been called on to indite.

"Dear Mr. Dawnish," she began, "since telephoning you just now I have decided not—"

Maria's voice, at the door, announced that tea was in the library: "And I s'pose it's the brown silk you'll wear to the speaking?"

In the usual order of the Ransom existence, its mistress's toilet was performed unassisted; and the mere enquiry—at once friendly and deferential—projected, for Margaret, a strong light on the importance of the occasion. That she should answer: "But I am not going," when the going was so manifestly part of a household solemnity about which the thoughts below stairs fluttered in proud participation; that in face of such participation she should utter a word implying indifference or hesitation—nay, revealing herself the transposed, uprooted thing she had been on the verge of becoming; to do this was—well! infinitely harder than to perform the alternative act of tearing up the sheet of note-paper under her reluctant pen.

Yes, she said, she would wear the brown silk. . . .

3

All the heat and glare from the long illuminated table, about which the fumes of many courses still hung in a savoury fog, seemed to surge up to the ladies' gallery, and concentrate themselves in the burning cheeks of a slender figure withdrawn behind the projection of a pillar.

It never occurred to Margaret Ransom that she was sitting in the shade. She supposed that the full light of the chandeliers was beating on her face—and there were moments when it seemed as though all the heads about the great horse-shoe below, bald, shaggy, sleek, close-thatched, or thinly latticed, were equipped with an additional pair of eyes, set at an angle which enabled them to rake her face as relentlessly as the electric burners.

In the lull after a speech, the gallery was fluttering with the rustle of programmes consulted, and Mrs. Sheff (the Brant girl's aunt) leaned forward to say enthusiastically: "And now we're to hear Mr. Ransom!"

A louder buzz rose from the table, and the heads (without relaxing their upward vigilance) seemed to merge, and flow together, like an attentive flood, toward the upper end of the horse-shoe, where all the threads of Margaret Ransom's consciousness were suddenly drawn into what seemed a small speck, no more—a black speck that rose, hung in air, dissolved into gyrating gestures, became distended, enormous, preponderant—became her husband "speaking."

"It's the heat—" Margaret gasped, pressing her handkerchief to her whitening lips, and finding just strength enough left to push back farther into the shadow.

She felt a touch on her arm. "It *is* horrible—shall we go?" a voice suggested; and, "Yes, yes, let us go," she whispered, feeling, with a great throb of relief, *that* to be the only possible, the only conceivable, solution. To sit and listen to her husband *now*—how could she ever have thought she could survive it? Luckily, under the lingering hubbub from below, his opening words were inaudible, and she had only to run the gauntlet of sympathetic feminine glances, shot after her between waving fans and programmes, as, guided by Guy Dawnish, she managed to reach the door. It was really so hot that even Mrs. Sheff was not much surprised—till long afterward. . . . .

The winding staircase was empty, half dark and blessedly silent. In a committee room below Dawnish found the inevitable water jug, and filled a glass for her, while she leaned back, confronted only by a frowning college President in an emblazoned frame. The academic frown descended on her like an anathema when she rose and followed her companion out of the building.

Hamblin Hall stands at the end of the long green "Campus" with its sextuple line of elms—the boast and the singularity of Wentworth. A pale spring moon, rising above the dome of the University library at the opposite end of the elm-walk, diffused a pearly mildness in the sky, melted to thin haze the shadows of the trees, and turned to golden yellow the lights of the college windows. Against this soft suffusion of light the Library cupola assumed a Bramantesque grace, the white steeple of the congregational church became a campanile topped by a winged spirit, and the scant porticoes of the older halls the colonnades of classic temples.

"This is better—" Dawnish said, as they passed down the steps and under the shadow of the elms.

They moved on a little way in silence before he began again: "You're too tired to walk. Let us sit down a few minutes."

Her feet, in truth, were leaden, and not far off a group of park benches, encircling the pedestal of a patriot in bronze, invited them to rest. But Dawnish was guiding her toward a lateral path which bent, through shrubberies, toward a strip of turf between two of the buildings.

"It will be cooler by the river," he said, moving on without waiting for a possible protest. None came: it seemed easier, for the moment, to let herself be led without any conventional feint of resistance. And besides, there was nothing wrong about *this*—the wrong would have been in sitting up there in the glare, pretending to listen to her husband, a dutiful wife among her kind. . . .

The path descended, as both knew, to the chosen, the inimitable spot of Wentworth: that fugitive curve of the river, where, before hurrying on to glut the brutal industries of South Wentworth and Smedden, it simulated for a few hundred yards the leisurely pace of an ancient university stream, with willows on its banks and a stretch of turf extending from the grounds of Hamblin Hall to the boat houses at the farther bend. Here too were benches, beneath the willows, and so close to the river that the voice of its gliding softened and filled out the reverberating silence between Margaret and her companion, and made her feel that she knew why he had brought her there.

"Do you feel better?" he asked gently as he sat down beside her.

"Oh, yes. I only needed a little air."

"I'm so glad you did. Of course the speeches were tremendously interesting—but I prefer this. What a good night!"

"Yes."

There was a pause, which now, after all, the soothing accompaniment of the river seemed hardly sufficient to fill.

"I wonder what time it is. I ought to be going home," Margaret began at length.

"Oh, it's not late. They'll be at it for hours in there—yet."

She made a faint inarticulate sound. She wanted to say: "No—Robert's speech was to be the last—" but she could not bring herself to pronounce Ransom's name, and at the moment no other way of refuting her companion's statement occurred to her.

The young man leaned back luxuriously, reassured by her silence.

"You see it's my last chance—and I want to make the most of it."

"Your last chance?" How stupid of her to repeat his words on that cooing note of interrogation! It was just such a lead as the Brant girl might have given him.

"To be with you—like this. I haven't had so many. And there's less than a week left."

She attempted to laugh. "Perhaps it will sound longer if you call it five days."

The flatness of that, again! And she knew there were people who called her intelligent. Fortunately, he did not seem to notice it; but her laugh continued to sound in her own ears—the *coquettish* chirp of middle age! She decided that if he spoke again—if he *said anything*—she would make no farther effort at evasion: she would take it directly, seriously, frankly—she would not be doubly disloyal.

"Besides," he continued, throwing his arm along the back of the bench, and turning toward her so that his face was like a dusky bas-relief with a silver rim—"besides, there's something I've been wanting to tell you."

The sound of the river seemed to cease altogether: the whole world became silent.

Margaret had trusted her inspiration farther than it appeared likely to carry her. Again she could think of nothing happier than to repeat, on the same witless note of interrogation: "To tell me?"

"You only."

The constraint, the difficulty, seemed to be on his side now: she divined it by the renewed shifting of his attitude—he was capable, usually, of such fine intervals of immobility—and by a confusion in his utterance that set her own voice throbbing in her throat.

"You've been so perfect to me," he began again. "It's not my fault if you've made me feel that you would understand everything—make allowances for everything—see just how a man may have held out, and fought against a thing—as long as he had the strength. . . . This may be my only chance; and I can't go away without telling you."

He had turned from her now, and was staring at the river, so that his profile was projected against the moonlight in all its beautiful young dejection.

There was a slight pause, as though he waited for her to speak; then she leaned forward and laid her hand on his.

"If I have really been—if I have done for you even the least part of what you say....what you imagine....will you do for me, now, just one thing in return?"

He sat motionless, as if fearing to frighten away the shy touch on his hand, and she left it there, conscious of her gesture only as part of the high ritual of their farewell.

"What do you want me to do?" he asked in a low tone.

"*Not* to tell me!" she breathed on a deep note of entreaty.

"*Not* to tell you—?"

"Anything—*anything*—just to leave our.... our friendship.... as it has been—as—as a painter, if a friend asked him, might leave a picture—not quite finished, perhaps..... but all the more exquisite...."

She felt the hand under hers slip away, recover itself, and seek her own, which had flashed out of reach in the same instant—felt the start that swept him round on her as if he had been caught and turned about by the shoulders.

"You—*you*—?" he stammered, in a strange voice full of fear and tenderness; but she held fast, so centred in her inexorable resolve that she was hardly conscious of the effect her words might be producing.

"Don't you see," she hurried on, "don't you *feel* how much safer it is—yes, I'm willing to put it so!—how much safer to leave everything undisturbed...just as....as it has grown of itself....without trying to say: 'It's this or that'....? It's what we each choose to call it to ourselves, after all, isn't it? Don't let us try to find a name that . . . that we should both agree upon....we probably shouldn't succeed." She laughed abruptly. "And ghosts vanish when one names them!" she ended with a break in her voice.

When she ceased her heart was beating so violently that there was a rush in her ears like the noise of the river after rain, and she did not immediately make out what he was answering. But as she recovered her lucidity she said to herself that, whatever he was saying, she must not hear it; and she began to speak again, half playfully, half appealingly, with an eloquence of entreaty, an ingenuity in argument, of which she had never dreamed herself capable. And then, suddenly, strangling hands seemed to reach up from her heart to her throat, and she had to stop.

Her companion remained motionless. He had not tried to regain her hand, and his eyes were away from her, on the river. But his nearness had become something formidable and exquisite—something she had never before imagined. A flush of guilt swept over her—vague reminiscences of French novels and of opera plots. This was what such women felt, then. . . . this was "shame." . . . .Phrases of the newspaper and the pulpit danced before her. . . .She dared not speak, and his silence began to frighten her. Had ever a heart beat so wildly before in Wentworth?

He turned at last, and taking her two hands, quite simply, kissed them one after the other.

"I shall never forget—" he said in a confused voice, unlike his own.

A return of strength enabled her to rise, and even to let her eyes meet his for a moment.

"Thank you," she said, simply also.

She turned away from the bench, regaining the path that led back to the college buildings, and he walked beside her in silence. When they reached the elm walk it was dotted with dispersing groups. The "speaking" was over, and Hamblin Hall had poured its audience out into the moonlight. Margaret felt a rush of relief, followed by a receding wave of regret. She had the distinct sensation that her hour—her one hour—was over.

One of the groups just ahead broke up as they approached, and projected Ransom's solid bulk against the moonlight.

"My husband," she said, hastening forward; and she never afterward forgot the look of his back—heavy, round-shouldered, yet a little pompous—in a badly fitting overcoat that stood out at the neck and hid his collar. She had never before noticed how he dressed.

4

They met again, inevitably, before Dawnish left; but the thing she feared did not happen—he did not try to see her alone.

It even became clear to her, in looking back, that he had deliberately avoided doing so; and this seemed merely an added proof of his "understanding," of that deep undefinable communion that set them alone in an empty world, as if on a peak above the clouds.

The five days passed in a flash; and when the last one came, it brought to Margaret Ransom an hour of weakness, of profound disorganization, when old barriers fell, old convictions faded—when to be alone with him for a moment became, after all, the one craving of her heart. She knew he was coming that afternoon to say "goodby"—and she knew also that Ransom was to be away at South Wentworth. She waited alone in her pale little drawing-room, with its scant kakemonos, its one or two chilly reproductions from the antique, its slippery Chippendale chairs. At length the bell rang, and her world became a rosy blur—through which she presently discerned the austere form of Mrs. Sperry, wife of the Professor of palaeontology, who had come to talk over with her the next winter's programme for the Higher Thought Club. They debated the question for an hour, and when Mrs. Sperry departed Margaret had a confused impression that the course was to deal with the influence of the First Crusade on the development of European architecture—but the sentient part of her knew only that Dawnish had not come.

He "bobbed in," as he would have put it, after dinner—having, it appeared, run across Ransom early in the day, and learned that the latter would be absent till evening. Margaret was in the study with her husband when the door opened and Dawnish stood there. Ransom—who had not had time to dress—was seated at his desk, a pile of shabby law books at his elbow, the light from a hanging lamp falling on his greyish stubble of hair, his sallow forehead and spectacled eyes. Dawnish, towering higher than usual against the shadows of the room, and refined by his unusual pallor, hung a moment on the threshold, then came in, explaining himself profusely—laughing, accepting a cigar, letting Ransom push an armchair forward—a Dawnish she had never seen, ill at ease, ejaculatory, yet somehow more mature, more obscurely in command of himself.

Margaret drew back, seating herself in the shade, in such a way that she saw her husband's head first, and beyond it their visitor's, relieved against the dusk of the book shelves. Her heart was still—she felt no throbbing in her throat or temples: all her life seemed concentrated in the hand that lay on her knee, the hand he would touch when they said goodbye.

Afterward her heart rang all the changes, and there was a mood in which she reproached herself for cowardice—for having deliberately missed her one moment with him, the moment in which she might have sounded the depths of life, for joy or anguish. But that mood was fleeting and infrequent. In quieter hours she blushed for it—she even trembled to think that he might have guessed such a regret in her. It seemed to convict her of a lack of fineness that he should have had, in his youth and his power, a tenderer, surer sense of the peril of a rash touch—should have handled the case so much more delicately.

At first her days were fire and the nights long solemn vigils. Her thoughts were no longer vulgarized and defaced by any notion of "guilt," of mental disloyalty. She was ashamed now of her shame. What had happened was as much outside the sphere of her marriage as some transaction in a star. It had simply given her a secret life of incommunicable joys, as if all the wasted springs of her youth had been stored in some hidden pool, and she could return there now to bathe in them.

After that there came a phase of loneliness, through which the life about her loomed phantasmal and remote. She thought the dead must feel thus, repeating the vain gestures of the living beside some Stygian shore. She wondered if any other woman had lived to whom *nothing had ever happened?* And then his first letter came. . . . .

It was a charming letter—a perfect letter. The little touch of awkwardness and constraint under its boyish spontaneity told her more than whole pages of eloquence. He spoke of their friendship—of their good days together. . . . Ransom, chancing to come in while she read, noticed the foreign stamps; and she was able to hand him the letter, saying gaily: "There's a message for you," and knowing all the while that *her* message was safe in her heart.

On the days when the letters came the outlines of things grew indistinct, and she could never afterward remember what she had done or how the business of life had been carried on. It was always a surprise when she found dinner on the table as usual, and Ransom seated opposite to her, running over the evening paper.

But though Dawnish continued to write, with all the English loyalty to the outward observances of friendship, his communications came only at intervals of several weeks, and between them she had time to repossess herself, to regain some sort of normal contact with life. And the customary, the recurring, gradually reclaimed her, the net of habit tightened again—her daily life became real, and her one momentary escape from it an exquisite illusion. Not that she ceased to believe in the miracle that had befallen her: she still treasured the reality of her one moment beside the river.

What reason was there for doubting it? She could hear the ring of truth in young Dawnish's voice: "It's not my fault if you've made me feel that you would understand everything. . . ." No! she believed in her miracle, and the belief sweetened and illumined her life; but she came to see that what was for her the transformation of her whole being might well have been, for her companion, a mere passing explosion of gratitude, of boyish good-fellowship touched with the pang of leave-taking. She even reached the point of telling herself that it was "better so": this view of the episode so defended it from the alternating extremes of self-reproach and derision, so enshrined it in a pale immortality to which she could make her secret pilgrimages without reproach.

For a long time, she had not been able to pass by the bench under the willows—she even avoided the elm walk till autumn had stripped its branches. But every day, now, she noted a step toward recovery; and at last a day came when, walking along the river, she said to herself, as she approached the bench: "I used not to be able to pass here without thinking of him; *and now I am not thinking of him at all!*"

This seemed such convincing proof of her recovery that she began, as spring returned, to permit herself, now and then, a quiet session on the bench—a dedicated hour from which she went back fortified to her task.

She had not heard from her friend for six weeks or more—the intervals between his letters were growing longer. But that was "best" too, and she was not anxious, for she knew he had obtained the post he had been preparing for, and that his active life in London had begun. The thought reminded her, one mild March day, that in leaving the house she had thrust in her reticule a letter from a Wentworth friend who was abroad on a holiday. The envelope bore the London post mark, a fact showing that the lady's face was turned toward home. Margaret seated herself on her bench, and drawing out the letter began to read it.

The London described was that of shops and museums—as remote as possible from the setting of Guy Dawnish's existence. But suddenly Margaret's eye fell on his name, and the page began to tremble in her hands.

I heard such a funny thing yesterday about your friend Mr. Dawnish. We went to a tea at Professor Bunce's (I do wish you knew the Bunces—their atmosphere is so *uplifting*), and there I met that Miss Bruce-Pringle who came out last year to take a course in histology at the Annex. Of course she asked about you and Mr. Ransom, and then she told me she had just seen Mr. Dawnish's aunt—the clever one he was always talking about, Lady Caroline something—and that they were all in a dreadful state about him. I wonder if you knew he was engaged when he went to America? He never mentioned it to *us*. She said it was not a positive engagement, but an understanding with a girl he has always been devoted to, who lives near their place in Wiltshire; and both families expected the marriage to take place as soon as he got back.

It seems the girl is an heiress (you know *how low* the English ideals are compared with ours), and Miss Bruce-Pringle said his relations were perfectly delighted at his 'being provided for,' as she called it. Well, when he got back he asked the girl to release him; and she and her family were furious, and so were his people; but he holds out, and won't marry her, and won't give a reason, except that he has 'formed an unfortunate attachment.' Did you ever hear anything so peculiar? His aunt, who is quite wild about it, says it must have happened at Wentworth, because he didn't go anywhere else in America. Do you suppose it *could* have been the Brant girl? But why 'unfortunate' when everybody knows she would have jumped at him?

Margaret folded the letter and looked out across the river. It was not the same river, but a mystic current shot with moonlight. The bare willows wove a leafy veil above her head, and beside her she felt the nearness of youth and tempestuous tenderness. It had all happened just here, on this very seat by the river—it had come to her, and passed her by, and she had not held out a hand to detain it. . . .

Well! Was it not, by that very abstention, made more deeply and ineffaceably hers? She could argue thus while she had thought the episode, on his side, a mere transient effect of propinquity; but now that she knew it had altered the whole course of his life, now that it took on substance and reality, asserted a separate existence outside of her own troubled consciousness—now it seemed almost cowardly to have missed her share in it.

She walked home in a dream. Now and then, when she passed an acquaintance, she wondered if the pain and glory were written on her face. But Mrs. Sperry, who stopped her at the corner of Maverick Street to say a word about the next meeting of the Higher Thought Club, seemed to remark no change in her.

When she reached home Ransom had not yet returned from the office, and she went straight to the library to tidy his writing-table. It was part of her daily duty to bring order out of the chaos of his papers, and of late she had fastened on such small recurring tasks as someone falling over a precipice might snatch at the weak bushes in its clefts.

When she had sorted the letters she took up some pamphlets and newspapers, glancing over them to see if they were to be kept. Among the papers was a page torn from a London *Times* of the previous month. Her eye ran down its columns and suddenly a paragraph flamed out.

We are requested to state that the marriage arranged between Mr. Guy Dawnish, son of the late Colonel the Hon. Roderick Dawnish, of Malby, Wilts, and Gwendolen, daughter of Samuel Matcher, Esq. of Armingham Towers, Wilts, will not take place.

Margaret dropped the paper and sat down, hiding her face against the stained baize of the desk. She remembered the photograph of the tennis-court at Guise—she remembered the handsome girl at whom Guy Dawnish looked up, laughing. A gust of tears shook her, loosening the dry surface of conventional feeling, welling up from unsuspected depths. She was sorry—very sorry, yet so glad—so ineffably, impenitently glad.

5

There came a reaction in which she decided to write to him. She even sketched out a letter of sisterly, almost motherly, remonstrance, in which she reminded him that he "still had all his life before him." But she reflected that so, after all, had she; and that seemed to weaken the argument.

In the end she decided not to send the letter. He had never spoken to her of his engagement to Gwendolen Matcher, and his letters had contained no allusion to any sentimental disturbance in his life. She had only his few broken words, that night by the river, on which to build her theory of the case. But illuminated by the phrase "an unfortunate attachment" the theory towered up, distinct and immovable, like some high landmark by which travellers shape their course. She had been loved—extraordinarily loved. But he had chosen that she should know of it by his silence rather than by his speech. He had understood that only on those terms could their transcendant communion continue—that he must lose her to keep her. To break that silence would be like spilling a cup of water in a waste of sand. There would be nothing left for her thirst.

Her life, thenceforward, was bathed in a tranquil beauty. The days flowed by like a river beneath the moon—each ripple caught the brightness and passed it on. She began to take a renewed interest in her familiar round of duties. The tasks which had once seemed colourless and irksome had now a kind of sacrificial sweetness, a symbolic meaning into which she alone was initiated. She had been restless—had longed to travel; now she felt that she should never again care to leave Wentworth.

But if her desire to wander had ceased, she travelled in spirit, performing invisible pilgrimages in the footsteps of her friend. She regretted that her one short visit to England had taken her so little out of London—that her acquaintance with the landscape had been formed chiefly through the windows of a railway carriage. She threw herself into the architectural studies of the Higher Thought Club, and distinguished herself, at the spring meetings, by her fluency, her competence, her inexhaustible curiosity on the subject of the growth of English Gothic. She ransacked the shelves of the college library, she borrowed photographs of the cathedrals, she pored over the folio pages of *The Seats of Noblemen and Gentlemen*. She was like some banished princess who learns that she has inherited a domain in her own country, who knows that she will never see it, yet feels, wherever she walks, its soil beneath her feet.

May was half over, and the Higher Thought Club was to hold its last meeting, previous to the college festivities which, in early June, agreeably disorganized the social routine of Wentworth. The meeting was to take place in Margaret Ransom's drawing-room, and on the day before she sat upstairs preparing for her dual duties as hostess and orator—for she had been invited to read the final paper of the course. In order to sum up with precision her conclusions on the subject of English Gothic she had been rereading an analysis of the structural features of the principal English cathedrals; and she was murmuring over to herself the phrase: "The longitudinal arches of Lincoln have an approximately elliptical form," when there came a knock on the door, and Maria's voice announced: "There's a lady down in the parlour."

Margaret's soul dropped from the heights of the shadowy vaulting to the dead level of an afternoon call at Wentworth.

"A lady? Did she give no name?"

Maria became confused. "She only said she was a lady—" and in reply to her mistress's look of mild surprise: "Well, ma'am, she told me so three or four times over."

Margaret laid her book down, leaving it open at the description of

Lincoln, and slowly descended the stairs. As she did so, she repeated to herself: "The longitudinal arches are elliptical."

On the threshold below, she had the odd impression that her bare and inanimate drawing-room was brimming with life and noise—an impression produced, as she presently perceived, by the resolute forward dash—it was almost a pounce—of the one small figure restlessly measuring its length.

The dash checked itself within a yard of Margaret, and the lady— a stranger—held back long enough to stamp on her hostess a sharp impression of sallowness, leanness, keenness, before she said, in a voice that might have been addressing an unruly committee meeting: "I am Lady Caroline Duckett—a fact I found it impossible to make clear to the young woman who let me in."

A warm wave rushed up from Margaret's heart to her throat and forehead. She held out both hands impulsively. "Oh, I'm so glad—I'd no idea—"

Her voice sank under her visitor's impartial scrutiny.

"I don't wonder," said the latter drily. "I suppose she didn't mention, either, that my object in calling here was to see Mrs. Ransom?"

"Oh, yes—won't you sit down?" Margaret pushed a chair forward. She seated herself at a little distance, brain and heart humming with a confused interchange of signals. This dark sharp woman was his aunt—the "clever aunt" who had had such a hard life, but had always managed to keep her head above water. Margaret remembered that Guy had spoken of her kindness—perhaps she would seem kinder when they had talked together a little. Meanwhile the first impression she produced was of an amplitude out of all proportion to her somewhat scant exterior. With her small flat figure, her shabby heterogeneous dress, she was as dowdy as any professor's wife at Wentworth; but her dowdiness (Margaret borrowed a literary analogy to define it), her dowdiness was somehow "of the centre." Like the insignificant emissary of a great power, she was to be judged rather by her passports than her person.

While Margaret was receiving these impressions, Lady Caroline, with quick bird-like twists of her head, was gathering others from the pale void spaces of the drawing-room. Her eyes, divided by a sharp nose like a bill, seemed to be set far enough apart to see at separate angles; but suddenly she bent both of them on Margaret.

"This *is* Mrs. Ransom's house?" she asked, with an emphasis on the verb that gave a distinct hint of unfulfilled expectations.

Margaret assented.

"Because your American houses, especially in the provincial towns, all look so remarkably alike, that I thought I might have been mistaken; and as my time is extremely limited—in fact I'm sailing on Wednesday—"

She paused long enough to let Margaret say: "I had no idea you were in this country."

Lady Caroline made no attempt to take this up. "And so much of it," she carried on her sentence, "has been wasted in talking to people I really hadn't the slightest desire to see, that you must excuse me if I go straight to the point."

Margaret felt a sudden tension of the heart. "Of course," she said while a voice within her cried: "He is dead—he has left me a message."

There was another pause; then Lady Caroline went on, with increasing asperity: "So that—in short—if I *could* see Mrs. Ransom at once—"

Margaret looked up in surprise. "I am Mrs. Ransom," she said.

The other stared a moment, with much the same look of cautious incredulity that had marked her inspection of the drawing-room. Then light came to her.

"Oh, I beg your pardon. I should have said that I wished to see Mrs. *Robert* Ransom, not Mrs. Ransom. But I understood that in the States you don't make those distinctions." She paused a moment, and then went on, before Margaret could answer: "Perhaps, after all, it's as well that I should see you instead, since you're evidently one of the household—your son and his wife live with you, I suppose? Yes, on the whole, then, it's better—I shall be able to talk so much more frankly." She spoke as if, as a rule, circumstances prevented her giving rein to this propensity. "And frankness, of course, is the only way out of this—this extremely tiresome complication. You know, I suppose, that my nephew thinks he's in love with your daughter-in-law?"

Margaret made a slight movement, but her visitor pressed on without heeding it. "Oh, don't fancy, please, that I'm pretending to take a high moral ground—though his mother does, poor dear! I can perfectly imagine that in a place like this—I've just been driving about it for two hours—a young man of Guy's age would *have* to provide himself with some sort of distraction, and he's not the kind to go in for anything objectionable. Oh, we quite allow for that—we should allow for the whole affair, if it hadn't so preposterously ended in his throwing over the girl he was engaged to, and upsetting an arrangement that affected a number of people besides himself. I understand that in the States it's different—the young people have only themselves to consider.

"In England—in our class, I mean—a great deal may depend on a young man's making a good match; and in Guy's case I may say that his mother and sisters (I won't include myself, though I might) have been simply stranded—thrown overboard—by his freak. You can understand how serious it is when I tell you that it's that and nothing else that has brought me all the way to America. And my first idea was to go straight to your daughter-in-law, since her influence is the only thing we can count on now, and put it to her fairly, as I'm putting it to you. But, on the whole, I dare say it's better to see you first—you might give me an idea of the line to take with her. I'm prepared to throw myself on her mercy!"

Margaret rose from her chair, outwardly rigid in proportion to her inward tremor.

"You don't understand—" she began.

Lady Caroline brushed the interruption aside. "Oh, but I do—completely! I cast no reflection on your daughter-in-law. Guy has made it quite clear to us that his attachment is—has, in short, not been rewarded. But don't you see that that's the worst part of it? There'd be much more hope of his recovering if Mrs. Robert Ransom had—had—"

Margaret's voice broke from her in a cry. "I am Mrs. Robert Ransom," she said.

If Lady Caroline Duckett had hitherto given her hostess the impression of a person not easily silenced, this fact added sensibly to the effect produced by the intense stillness which now fell on her.

She sat quite motionless, her large bangled hands clasped about the meagre fur boa she had unwound from her neck on entering, her rusty black veil pushed up to the edge of a "fringe" of doubtful authenticity, her thin lips parted on a gasp that seemed to sharpen itself on the edges of her teeth. So overwhelming and helpless was her silence that Margaret began to feel a motion of pity beneath her indignation—a desire at least to facilitate the excuses which must terminate their disastrous colloquy. But when Lady Caroline found voice she did not use it to excuse herself.

"You *can't* be," she said, quite simply.

"Can't be?" Margaret stammered, with a flushing cheek.

"I mean, it's some mistake. Are there *two* Mrs. Robert Ransoms in the same town? Your family arrangements are so extremely puzzling." She had a farther rush of enlightenment. "Oh, I *see!* I ought of course to have asked for Mrs. Robert Ransom 'Junior'!"

The idea sent her to her feet with a haste which showed her impatience to make up for lost time.

"There is no other Mrs. Robert Ransom at Wentworth," said Margaret.

"No other—no 'Junior'? Are you *sure?*" Lady Caroline fell back into her seat again. "Then I simply don't see," she murmured helplessly.

Margaret's blush had fixed itself on her throbbing forehead. She remained standing, while her strange visitor continued to gaze at her with a perturbation in which the consciousness of indiscretion had evidently as yet no part.

"I simply don't see," she repeated.

Suddenly she sprang up, and advancing to Margaret laid an inspired hand on her arm. "But, my dear woman, you can help us out all the same; you can help us to find out *who it is*—and you will, won't you? Because, as it's not you, you can't in the least mind what I've been saying—"

Margaret, freeing her arm from her visitor's hold, drew back a step; but Lady Caroline instantly rejoined her.

"Of course, I can see that if it *had* been, you might have been annoyed: I dare say I put the case stupidly—but I'm so bewildered by this new development—by his using you all this time as a pretext—that I really don't know where to turn for light on the mystery—"

She had Margaret in her imperious grasp again, but the latter broke from her with a more resolute gesture.

"I'm afraid I have no light to give you," she began; but once more Lady Caroline caught her up.

"Oh, but do please understand me! I condemn Guy most strongly for using your name—when we all know you'd been so amazingly kind to him! I haven't a word to say in his defence—but of course the important thing now is: *who is the woman, since you're not?*"

The question rang out loudly, as if all the pale puritan corners of the room flung it back with a shudder at the speaker. In the silence that ensued Margaret felt the blood ebbing back to her heart; then she said, in a distinct and level voice: "I know nothing of the history of Mr. Dawnish."

Lady Caroline gave a stare and a gasp. Her distracted hand groped for her boa and she began to wind it mechanically about her long neck.

"It would really be an enormous help to us—and to poor Gwendolen Matcher," she persisted pleadingly. "And you'd be doing Guy himself a good turn."

Margaret remained silent and motionless while her visitor drew on one of the worn gloves she had pulled off to adjust her veil. Lady Caroline gave the veil a final twitch.

"I've come a tremendously long way," she said, "and, since it isn't you, I can't think why you won't help me....."

When the door had closed on her visitor Margaret Ransom went slowly up the stairs to her room. As she dragged her feet from one step to another, she remembered how she had sprung up the same steep flight after that visit of Guy Dawnish's when she had looked in the glass and seen on her face the blush of youth.

When she reached her room she bolted the door as she had done that day, and again looked at herself in the narrow mirror above her dressing-table. It was just a year since then—the elms were budding again, the willows hanging their green veil above the bench by the river. But there was no trace of youth left in her face—she saw it now as others had doubtless always seen it. If it seemed as it did to Lady Caroline Duckett, what look must it have worn to the fresh gaze of young Guy Dawnish?

A pretext—she had been a pretext. He had used her name to screen someone else—or perhaps merely to escape from a situation of which he was weary. She did not care to conjecture what his motive had been—everything connected with him had grown so remote and alien. She felt no anger—only an unspeakable sadness, a sadness which she knew would never be appeased.

She looked at herself long and steadily; she wished to clear her eyes of all illusions. Then she turned away and took her usual seat beside her work-table. From where she sat she could look down the empty elm-shaded street, up which, at this hour every day, she was sure to see her husband's figure advancing. She would see it presently—she would see it for many years to come. She had a sudden aching sense of the length of the years that stretched before her. Strange that one who was not young should still, in all likelihood, have so long to live!

Nothing was changed in the setting of her life, perhaps nothing would ever change in it. She would certainly live and die in Wentworth. And meanwhile the days would go on as usual, bringing the usual obligations. As the word flitted through her brain she remembered that she had still to put the finishing touches to the paper she was to read the next afternoon at the meeting of the Higher Thought Club.

The book she had been reading lay face downward beside her, where she had left it an hour ago. She took it up, and slowly and painfully, like a child laboriously spelling out the syllables, she went on with the rest of the sentence:

—and they spring from a level not much above that of the springing of the transverse and diagonal ribs, which are so arranged as to give a convex curve to the surface of the vaulting conoid.

LEONAUR

ALSO FROM LEONAUR

AVAILABLE IN SOFTCOVER OR HARDCOVER WITH DUST JACKET

THE COMPLETE FOUR JUST MEN: VOLUME 2 *by Edgar Wallace—The Law of the Four Just Men & The Three Just Men*—disillusioned with a world where the wicked and the abusers of power perpetually go unpunished, the Just Men set about to rectify matters according to their own standards, and retribution is dispensed on swift and deadly wings.

THE COMPLETE RAFFLES: 1 *by E. W. Hornung—The Amateur Cracksman & The Black Mask*—By turns urbane gentleman about town and accomplished cricketer, life is just too ordinary for Raffles and that sets him on a series of adventures that have long been treasured as a real antidote to the 'white knights' who are the usual heroes of the crime fiction of this period.

THE COMPLETE RAFFLES: 2 *by E. W. Hornung—A Thief in the Night & Mr Justice Raffles*—By turns urbane gentleman about town and accomplished cricketer, life is just too ordinary for Raffles and that sets him on a series of adventures that have long been treasured as a real antidote to the 'white knights' who are the usual heroes of the crime fiction of this period.

THE COLLECTED SUPERNATURAL AND WEIRD FICTION OF WILKIE COLLINS: VOLUME 1 *by Wilkie Collins*—Contains one novel 'The Haunted Hotel', one novella 'Mad Monkton', three novelettes 'Mr Percy and the Prophet', 'The Biter Bit' and 'The Dead Alive' and eight short stories to chill the blood.

THE COLLECTED SUPERNATURAL AND WEIRD FICTION OF WILKIE COLLINS: VOLUME 2 *by Wilkie Collins*—Contains one novel 'The Two Destinies', three novellas 'The Frozen deep', 'Sister Rose' and 'The Yellow Mask' and two short stories to chill the blood.

THE COLLECTED SUPERNATURAL AND WEIRD FICTION OF WILKIE COLLINS: VOLUME 3 *by Wilkie Collins*—Contains one novel 'Dead Secret,' two novelettes 'Mrs Zant and the Ghost' and 'The Nun's Story of Gabriel's Marriage' and five short stories to chill the blood.

FUNNY BONES *selected by Dorothy Scarborough*—An Anthology of Humorous Ghost Stories.

MONTEZUMA'S CASTLE AND OTHER WEIRD TALES *by Charles B. Cory*—Cory has written a superb collection of eighteen ghostly and weird stories to chill and thrill the avid enthusiast of supernatural fiction.

SUPERNATURAL BUCHAN *by John Buchan*—Stories of Ancient Spirits, Uncanny Places & Strange Creatures.

LEONAUR

ALSO FROM LEONAUR
AVAILABLE IN SOFTCOVER OR HARDCOVER WITH DUST JACKET

THE COLLECTED SCIENCE FICTION AND FANTASY OF STANLEY G. WEINBAUM 1—INTERPLANETARY ODYSSEYS *by Stanley G. Weinbaum*—Classic Tales of Interplanetary Adventure Including: A Martian Odyssey, its Sequel Valley of Dreams, the Complete 'Ham' Hammond Stories and Others.

THE COLLECTED SCIENCE FICTION AND FANTASY OF STANLEY G. WEINBAUM 2—OTHER EARTHS *by Stanley G. Weinbaum*—Classic Futuristic Tales Including: *Dawn of Flame* & its Sequel The Black Flame, plus The Revolution of 1960 & Others.

THE COLLECTED SCIENCE FICTION AND FANTASY OF STANLEY G. WEINBAUM 3—STRANGE GENIUS *by Stanley G. Weinbaum*—Classic Tales of the Human Mind at Work Including the Complete Novel The New Adam, the 'van Manderpootz' Stories and Others.

THE COLLECTED SCIENCE FICTION AND FANTASY OF STANLEY G. WEINBAUM 4—THE BLACK HEART *by Stanley G. Weinbaum*—Classic Strange Tales Including: the Complete Novel The Dark Other, Plus Proteus Island and Others.

THE COLLECTED SCIENCE FICTION & FANTASY OF JACK LONDON 1—BEFORE ADAM & OTHER STORIES *by Jack London*—included in this Volume Before Adam The Scarlet Plague A Relic of the Pliocene When the World Was Young The Red One Planchette A Thousand Deaths Goliah A Curious Fragment The Rejuvenation of Major Rathbone.

THE COLLECTED SCIENCE FICTION & FANTASY OF JACK LONDON 2—THE IRON HEEL & OTHER STORIES *by Jack London*—included in this Volume The Iron Heel The Enemy of All the World The Shadow and the Flash The Strength of the Strong The Unparalleled Invasion The Dream of Debs.

THE COLLECTED SCIENCE FICTION & FANTASY OF JACK LONDON 3—THE STAR ROVER & OTHER STORIES *by Jack London*—included in this Volume The Star Rover The Minions of Midas The Eternity of Forms The Man With the Gash.

Lightning Source UK Ltd.
Milton Keynes UK
UKHW010639081021
391877UK00001B/179